Praise for the novels of Michelle Sagara

"First-rate fantasy."
—#1 *New York Times* bestselling author Kelley Armstrong

"Enjoyable, entertaining, engaging fantasy."
—*Tor.com* on *The Emperor's Wolves*

"Exciting… Both new readers and Sagara's long-time fans will be delighted to visit the land and people of Elantra."
—*Publishers Weekly* on *The Emperor's Wolves*

"Well-crafted… Readers will appreciate the complex plot and many returning faces in the vast cast of characters. This magical thrill-ride is a treat."
—*Publishers Weekly* on *Cast in Wisdom*

"Full to the brim of magic… Beautiful and intricate…a breathtaking read."
—*Word of the Nerd* on *Cast in Wisdom*

"This is a fast, fun novel, delightfully enjoyable in the best tradition of Sagara's work. While it may be light and entertaining, it's got some serious questions at its core. I'm already looking forward to the next book in the series."
—*Locus Magazine* on *Cast in Oblivion*

"No one provides an emotional payoff like Michelle Sagara. Combine that with a fast-paced police procedural, deadly magics, five very different races and a wickedly dry sense of humor— well, it doesn't get any better than this."
—Bestselling author Tanya Huff on The Chronicles of Elantra series

Also by *New York Times* bestselling author Michelle Sagara

Look for the next story in
The Chronicles of Elantra
coming soon from MIRA.

MICHELLE SAGARA

CAST IN CONFLICT

mira

ISBN-13: 978-0-7783-3203-9

Cast in Conflict

Copyright © 2021 by Michelle Sagara

All rights reserved. No part of this book may be used or reproduced in any manner whatsoever without written permission except in the case of brief quotations embodied in critical articles and reviews.

This is a work of fiction. Names, characters, places and incidents are either the product of the author's imagination or are used fictitiously. Any resemblance to actual persons, living or dead, businesses, companies, events or locales is entirely coincidental.

This edition published by arrangement with Harlequin Books S.A.

For questions and comments about the quality of this book, please contact us at CustomerService@Harlequin.com.

Mira
22 Adelaide St. West, 40th Floor
Toronto, Ontario M5H 4E3, Canada
BookClubbish.com

Printed in U.S.A.

This is for Mark Sano—who showed us all how to fight with grace, good humor and as much tenacity as cancer allowed. You showed us all the value, the preciousness, of one more day, one more week, one more month. You never gave in.

May your memory be a blessing.

CAST IN CONFLICT

01

Corporal Kaylin Neya understood exactly why Bellusdeo, her Dragon roommate, had never really called the Arkon by his title. She had always used his name: Lannagaros. At the time, Kaylin assumed this was because Lannagaros was a name that had sentimental value to Bellusdeo, when so little else did.

Facing Lord Sanabalis—the former Lord Sanabalis—she revised that belief. Sanabalis was now the Arkon. Kaylin was expected to use his title. This had caused some minor embarrassment, and reinforced the notion that Dragons could get away with breaking the social rules when normal people couldn't.

"I've called you Sanabalis—Lord Sanabalis—for the entire time I've known you. I'm sorry. I'll get it right."

Sanabalis's eyes were orange, but his smile was genuine. "As you were, Private."

"I'm a corporal!"

"You've been a private for the entire time I've known you."

Point to the Dragon.

Luckily Kaylin could save a little bit of face because the discussion in progress occurred in the very soundproof west room in which Kaylin had, months ago, taken the magical lessons mandated by the Imperial Court.

Those magic lessons had, in theory, resumed as of today. The bracer meant to restrict the magical power of the marks of the Chosen sat on the desk to one side of the hated candle that once again occupied pride of position on the otherwise empty great table that stood in the center of the room. In theory, she had to wear it All The Time. In practice, its weight had become almost unfamiliar in the past few weeks. If anyone had reported this to the Emperor, he'd decided the lack of bracer was worth the risk. She didn't know and she wasn't about to ask.

The Dragon who was now called the Arkon—this was going to be so confusing—had taken his normal chair. He wore the normal robes. Nothing about his appearance had changed. Even the color of his eyes was the familiar orange, flecked with gold.

"We hear," he said, "that Bellusdeo has been somewhat restless of late."

Kaylin glared at the candle.

"The Emperor is concerned."

She concentrated on fire, on the name of fire, the shape and heat of it. It wasn't hard at the moment.

"Corporal."

She exhaled. She hadn't been looking forward to a resumption of magical classes, but they were mandatory—at Imperial convenience. Imperial convenience meant she hadn't had a lesson in a long time.

She fixed as neutral an expression as she could on her face and turned toward the new Arkon. "If you have something to say to Bellusdeo, you should say it *to* Bellusdeo."

He said nothing.

"I have to live with her. I know you have to live with the

Emperor, but he can't actually kill you when he loses his temper."

"It is my belief that he can," Sanabalis—no, *the Arkon*—replied. "It has not been tested, however."

"Bellusdeo *can* kill me."

"I highly doubt your house would allow it."

This was true. Helen, her house, was sentient, and disliked the idea of her guests murdering either each other or their host.

"When you say 'we,' do you mean 'him'?"

"Him?"

"His Imperial Majesty, the Eternal Emperor."

"No. He is one of the concerned people, yes, but the concern is not entirely his. We would like to know where Bellusdeo has been going in the past two weeks."

"You spy on her. How can you not know?"

"Spy?" Sanabalis snorted. With smoke, because he was a Dragon. "We *monitor* her for reasons of safety, which even you must fully understand."

Even you. Kaylin attempted not to take this personally, or to at least look like she didn't. This involved keeping her hands from becoming fists. "I don't monitor her for reasons of safety. I can't treat her like a child—she's older than me, for one, and she'd turn to me to ash, for two. There's nothing I can face that she can't face, and pretty much nothing that can kill me could kill her."

"This is not true. I assume you are saying this because you believe it, but your observational skills are lacking."

Kaylin revised her opinion of the new Arkon as he exhaled. If he didn't look older, he did look tired.

"Bellusdeo," he said, when he chose to speak again, "was fond of Lannagaros. They shared a history she does not share with the rest of us. But Lannagaros will no longer reside in the palace. I am not certain he will visit it as often as Lord Tiamaris does.

"Her attachment to the former Arkon caused her to be more considerate in her responses to the rest of the Dragon Court. The Emperor is included in that."

"It's only been two weeks," Kaylin began.

"She has been restless and impatient. I am Arkon, but it was not because of his position that she chose to be considerate of Lannagaros, and he was part of the Imperial Court. I cannot gently nudge her across a boundary she's overstepped. She did not respect his title or his position. And I am, frankly, Arkon in a world with very few Dragons.

"Were there more, someone else would have taken the mantle."

"You can't be certain of that."

"I can. I understand what was involved in Lannagaros's promotion." He inhaled, which seemed to go on forever, but still somehow left air in the room for Kaylin to breathe. "Show me what you have been studying and practicing since we last sat in this room."

"Is it even okay for you to be teaching me now, Arkon?"

One brow rose. "That is a deplorably incompetent attempt to get out of magic lessons."

"I take it that's a yes."

It wasn't that Kaylin didn't understand the new Arkon's concerns.

For the past two weeks, Bellusdeo had chosen to stay with Helen instead of accompanying Kaylin to the Halls of Law. This made Marcus happier, but it was clear that the gold Dragon was doing *something* with her day—something that Kaylin couldn't see. Given Bellusdeo, there was zero guarantee that what she was doing was actually safe. Helen said that Maggaron, Bellusdeo's eight-foot-tall Ascendant, had accompanied her. Maggaron was mortal, true, but he'd been trained and raised to both fight for and serve Bellusdeo. Nothing about losing his entire world had changed his core duties.

But Maggaron had been her Ascendant when the position had had actual meaning, and he had served during the war against Shadow—a war that Bellusdeo and her people had lost.

He'd had very little to do in Elantra since their arrival in the city. The rest of his people—the few who could be saved—now lived on the borders of the fief of Tiamaris. The borders that most people did their utmost to avoid. The Norranir watched the Shadows. They watched *Ravellon*. They drummed warnings.

They also killed Ferals; it was like they were a permanent patrol.

Severn caught her elbow and jogged her to the left of a sandwich board sign. It was necessary because the sign practically occupied the entire sidewalk; to avoid it, one had to either get close to the road or too close to the shop the sign advertised.

It was Margot's shop.

"Don't," he said.

"I wasn't going to kick it over. I was going to move it."

"Iron-jaw has three separate complaints from Margot on his desk."

"Can't have been that important if they're still there."

"No. But she has clients who are louder and harder to ignore, and no shortage of people who will step up for her."

"While she fleeces them." Kaylin glared at the window in which she could see her reflection as a shadow. Margot was not immediately visible—and she was very hard to miss.

"She's not holding them up at knifepoint, and that's the only reason for Hawks to interfere with her business."

"Lying should be illegal."

"And when it is, we'll be understaffed, overworked, and fielding complaints about talking pumpkins and man-eating cats."

"We get those anyway."

"We'll get more. Come on." As they continued their patrol beat, Severn added, "What are you worried about now?"

"Sanabalis."

"The Arkon."

"Fine. The *new* Arkon. I hate titles. Why do we need to have fifteen different ways of calling a person?"

Severn shrugged. "I didn't create the rules."

"No. I want to have a few words with the idiots who did, though."

"You won't get to finish the first one—they were all Dragons. Besides, you're Kaylin, Kaylin Neya, Lord Kaylin Neya, Corporal Neya or just Corporal. You've got more than one. You were saying?"

"The Arkon's magic lesson was mostly about Bellusdeo."

"Why?"

"He expects me to know what she's doing when she's not with me."

"Not a good bet."

"He's my superior. He doesn't have to bet."

"No, he doesn't. They should have some sense of her movement, though."

"That's what I said! Sanabalis—sorry, the Arkon—wasn't amused."

"You called him a spy?"

"No! But—I might have used the word *spying*. Look, it's descriptive, okay?"

Severn was smiling as he shook his head. "Are you trying to make sure you never have to talk to anyone above your pay grade?"

Kaylin shrugged.

"You're worried about Bellusdeo."

The shrug was tighter. After a long pause, she said, "Bellusdeo's worse than Teela. I worry at her, she'll probably bite a limb off. One of mine," she added, in case this wasn't clear. "I think they both find it insulting."

"Dragon and Barrani. We're mortal."

"But I have the marks of the Chosen!"

"Which you don't really know how to use, yes."

"Aren't you worried?"

"No. I don't live with Bellusdeo, and the Emperor hasn't tasked me with any part of her safety. She's a better fighter than most of the Dragon Court, though."

"How do you know that?"

"I've watched them. What do you think she's doing?"

"I haven't been thinking. Much. Helen won't tell me," she added.

"Helen does tend to protect privacy, yes."

"Not mine."

"You're unlikely to try to kill people if they know what you're actually thinking. It's never really far beneath the—"

"Thief! Thief! *Help!*"

Both of the Hawks dropped the discussion as they pivoted and turned in the direction of the shouting. At least it was something *normal*.

Kaylin had already come to a decision by the time she reached home. Talking to Bellusdeo was out. Talking to Helen about Bellusdeo—or about what Bellusdeo was thinking or doing—was also a no-go. Kaylin didn't even consider approaching Maggaron, and not just because of his height.

She was, however, living with a host of other people, two of whom were set to move out at any minute. This had caused a bit of a ruckus, but not an unhappy one; more of a frenzied one. Serralyn and Valliant had applied to the new Academia, and they had both been accepted. The chancellor had interviewed them personally. While they had very little experience with Dragons that didn't involve the immediate deaths of all Barrani in sight, they were determined to go through with it.

They were slightly surprised by their encounter. Although they had met the chancellor before—most recently when Sedarias had volunteered the entire cohort as movers between the palace and the Academia—his interaction at that time had been pinched, orange-red-eyed and snappish.

The pinched part, according to Serralyn and Valliant, remained, but his eyes were almost gold when he invited them into his office, and almost the same color when he saw them to the office door. That he didn't then demand to see them to the front doors and shut them in their faces was a bonus.

Because the two had been accepted as students of the Academia, they were expected to live on campus. They were the first of the visiting cohort to actually leave.

Part of their discussion had been negotiations about communication. The Academia interfered with their ability to talk to the other members of the cohort. The chancellor had agreed not to limit the communications, with the clear understanding that visitors—the rest of the cohort—were required to, as he called it, sign in when they visited the campus.

Kaylin was glad; she was half-certain they wouldn't agree to leave without that concession. Well, no. She was certain they'd leave, but equally certain that one of the cohort—likely Terrano—would find some way of communicating regardless. Permission was better. Or at least safer. Probably.

Moving out in the next week was therefore in the cards, and it showed. Had Helen not been sentient, the household would have been in a frenzy of panic and excitement. As it was, panic was never allowed to fully take hold.

But it distracted the cohort and it distracted Helen.

Sedarias would remain based within Helen, but she had begun to make visits to the High Halls as An'Mellarionne. Annarion, Eddorian, Karian and Allaron accompanied her as her personal guards, although they were Lords of the High Court themselves.

From this, Kaylin assumed that Sedarias was the first of the cohort to attempt to establish herself as a more traditional power, and the rest of the cohort had eternity, being immortal, to establish themselves as powers in their own right. It wasn't a surprise that Sedarias was the current priority, though; the resources of Mellarionne were in danger of being subsumed by Mellarionne allies—or former allies who had yet to be swept away in the investigation that had followed the transformation of the High Halls.

Not that it had taken a great amount of investigation. The High Halls was, once again, a fully functional, sentient building. Barrani lords disliked being exposed to sentient buildings; they wanted to keep their thoughts and secrets to themselves. But rooms in the High Halls were a visible sign of rank and power. To abandon them was not as easily done as avoiding the interior of a waking Hallionne.

The cohort had the advantage, there. They had spent almost the entirety of their lives as "guests" of a sentient building. They had no fear of their thoughts being known. Sedarias could move far more freely, far more comfortably, in the reconstituted High Halls than most of the Lords of the High Court.

The cohort had been prisoners, but they had had each other, and the prison had become home. Kaylin was almost certain the Hallionne Alsanis missed them. Their life plans had been interrupted, not ended, although not all of Sedarias's friends planned to take their rightful places among the High Court. They had landed on their feet after a very rocky start.

Watching them, Kaylin finally accepted that Bellusdeo hadn't.

The Dragon was alive, yes. She was a friend. Where permitted by Imperial dictate, she had accompanied Kaylin into unpredictable danger. And thank gods for that.

But everything beneath her feet now, to belabor the metaphor, was not her ground. Helen. Kaylin. The former Arkon, who was the only solid reminder of the home she had lost, had left the Imperial palace for good.

Bellusdeo carried the future of her entire species in both hands. But that wasn't who or what she was, either. Kaylin wondered if—hoped that—Bellusdeo's daily jaunts toward the fiefs were visits to the former Arkon. That would be for the best.

Which is why Kaylin couldn't quite make herself believe it. It was too convenient, and that wasn't how their life worked.

"Helen, where's Mandoran?"

"I believe he and Terrano are in the training room."

Ugh. "Since that's usually not all that safe, can you ask him to come up to the dining room?"

"I can. You'll probably get Terrano as well." The sentence wasn't a question, but the last few words tailed up as if it were.

"That's fine."

Kaylin didn't just get Terrano. She also got Fallessian and Torrisant. There were four members of Teela's cohort of twelve that had remained almost entirely silent for their stay. Two had gone with Sedarias to the High Halls. Two remained with Helen, and had apparently also been in the training room with Mandoran and Terrano. It wasn't likely to kill them.

Teela, of the twelve, had a job she wanted to keep. She had offered to accompany Sedarias to the High Halls—but at hours that didn't conflict with that job. Had she been afraid for Sedarias, she would have taken a leave of absence. She hadn't.

"Karian didn't want to go," Fallessian said, speaking as if he was recovering from a terrible cold. Kaylin couldn't remember hearing him actually speak before, so the cold was unlikely the problem.

"Didn't want to go where?" she asked; she assumed the information had been offered to her because otherwise there was no point in speaking out loud.

"The High Halls," Terrano said.

Kaylin shook her head and waited while Fallessian found exactly the same words Terrano would have used. "Sedarias was in a mood. Frankly, I'd find out where she was going and go in the opposite direction."

This pulled a glimmer of a smile from the still silent Torrisant.

"Why did Karian go?"

"Karian is the direct bloodline heir to Illmarin."

"Illmarin still exists, right?"

"Yes. But it was tightly bound in fortune—and outcome—to the previous head of Mellarionne. Karian can, with Sedarias's backing, take the line; he can become An'Illmarin."

"...and he doesn't want that."

"It's an ongoing discussion," Mandoran said, before the more careful Fallessian could reply.

"That means *no*," Terrano added. "So—why did you call for us?"

"I wanted him." Kaylin pointed at Mandoran.

"Then you got lucky—we come in a set."

"Believe that I've noticed that. You don't have Serralyn or Valliant, though."

"Thank the Lady," Terrano then muttered under his breath. "You have no idea—"

"She does, dear," Helen interjected. Helen didn't bother to bring her Avatar into the dining room; she just used her voice.

"Fine. Why did you want to speak to Mandoran?"

Kaylin wasn't comfortable with either Torrisant or Fallessian, but felt that was unfair. Clearly she tended to privilege noise—speech in this case—over other forms of quiet near-invisibility. Anything she asked Mandoran would be heard by all twelve of the cohort, no matter where they were or what they were doing. There was no such thing as a private discussion.

Exhaling, Kaylin said, "Where has Bellusdeo been going in the past couple of weeks?"

"Why should we know that?" Terrano demanded.

Kaylin folded her arms and met what might have been an annoyed gaze. She didn't answer the question.

Silence ensued, and it was broken by Mandoran. "You know what they say about Dragons, right?"

"Which part?"

"Do not get involved in the business of Dragons."

"Was there a why beyond the obvious?"

"Yes, but it's old Barrani and I didn't study enough of it."

"Did anyone?"

"Serralyn. She can come downstairs and enlighten you, if you want. But—there wasn't a lot *to* study in Alsanis. Helen understands some of the Old Barrani, but—"

"I understand only fragments. Old Barrani, unlike High Barrani, was considered a language for children, for children's stories; High Barrani was the language of power and war."

"Is Serralyn going to the Academia to learn more?"

"You can ask her."

Serralyn appeared in the open doorway. "It's one of the things I want to study, yes. But—" and here, her eyes were a green so bright Kaylin almost couldn't acknowledge the color as belonging to Barrani eyes "—there's not a lot more to the old saying. I mean: Dragons. We're Barrani. They were stories told to children. Dragons don't like people messing with their stuff. Don't mess with their stuff. That kind of thing.

"But the language *wasn't* just used for children's stories. I'm certain that it was an entire functional language at one point."

"But I thought—"

"I know. I think it was, in part, the language of the Ancestors."

"The ones that look like Barrani but cause way more trouble?"

Serralyn grimaced. "Yes, them."

"And...if that's true, it's considered a language for *children* how?"

Serralyn actually laughed. Kaylin had never heard her laugh before. "How do you say it? I know, right?"

"That's what I'd say, yes. You're really looking forward to joining the Academia."

"I *really* am. It—" She shook her head. "I want to say it's the dream of a lifetime, but that's just not strong enough. The chancellor let one of the students—Robin—take us on a tour of the facilities. They had to pick me up and drag me out of the library!" She laughed again and added, "One of the librarians, Starrante, did all the heavy lifting. He's a—"

"Spider," Kaylin supplied.

"I don't think that's the accurate word for his race."

"I'm not sure I could *pronounce* the accurate word. Or that I even heard it."

"It's another language that would be considered lost."

Kaylin's enthusiasm for dead languages was minimal. Her enthusiasm for any learning that wasn't demonstrably practical was equally minimal. She understood that there were people for whom this wasn't the case, but had seldom seen someone as all-out excited as Serralyn.

It almost made her reconsider her own position.

Mandoran cleared his throat. "If you want to talk about dead languages and learning, that's fine—but we're trying to practice and you don't need us here for that."

"Oh, right. Sorry." Kaylin pulled her gaze away from Serralyn's radiantly happy face. "I want to know where Bellusdeo has been going when I'm at work."

"Or at the midwives' guild?"

"She went out then?"

Terrano and Mandoran exchanged a glance. Terrano said, "Why would you think he'd know? You could just ask Helen."

"I have. She cited guest privacy and told me exactly nothing."

Terrano snickered. "Why would you think we'd know?"

"Because you're already bored. It's been two weeks since anything has tried to kill you—or us—and you're fidgeting all the time. There's no way Bellusdeo could sneak out of this house without one of you following her. It's either you or Mandoran, but I'm betting on Mandoran—"

"With real money?"

"With *my own* money. I'm betting that one of you followed her."

"It's not safe to follow a Dragon." This was Fallessian again. She learned he could keep a perfectly straight face, because he did.

Terrano couldn't. His glance slid off Mandoran, who was grinning broadly.

"Don't take that bet," he told Terrano. His eyes were green, his expression verging on smug. Kaylin wanted to kick him.

"Where is she going?"

"Tiamaris."

The fiefs. "Is she staying in Tiamaris?"

"Harder to say."

"By harder you mean?" Kaylin frowned. "You can't follow her without being detected. Tara can see you."

"Pretty much."

"Were you trying to practice moving without being detectable? Is that why you're in the training room?"

Mandoran grinned. "Terrano can sometimes slip by un-detected—but it's work. He has to kind of walk sideways."

Terrano snorted.

"What? I'm trying to explain it to someone who can't do it and has never seen it."

"If she'd seen it, it would mean we failed."

Kaylin exhaled and managed to keep words out of it. "So, as far as you know, she's just heading into the fief of Tiamaris?"

More silence.

"Guys, I'm getting pressure from the new Arkon, and I do not want the follow-up to be 'concerned' Emperor."

"She's a Dragon, in case you forgot. There's precious little that can actually kill her, and anything that can will flatten the rest of us, starting with you. She's not a hatchling. She's got an eight-foot-tall giant as a trained puppy."

Kaylin did kick Mandoran then. He dodged.

"—and she sure as hell doesn't need us."

"And you're following her because you're bored."

The Barrani shrug was almost a fief shrug; clearly Mandoran had spent too much time with Kaylin. "Mostly bored."

"Mostly?"

He now looked distinctly uncomfortable.

Kaylin folded her arms. She couldn't actually hurt Mandoran—or any of the cohort—without Helen's help, and Helen was disinclined to give it.

"Because you don't really want to hurt him, dear," Helen's voice said.

"You wouldn't let me even if I did."

"I feel that you'd regret it, yes."

"Eventually. Spill."

"She's been avoiding you," Mandoran finally said. "She's come down late to breakfast every morning; she won't enter the dining room until you've run out the door. She comes home late for dinner, if at all. She's been in a terrible mood—"

"She hasn't been angry," Helen added, skirting the edge of her rules about privacy. "I would say she's been unsettled since Lannagaros took the chancellorship of the Academia."

"Has she been visiting him?"

No answer.

"Is she doing anything dangerous?"

"I'm sorry," Helen said. Her apologies always sounded genuinely regretful. "If you want to know, you will need to discuss that with Bellusdeo." She hesitated. Kaylin marked the hesitation.

"Bellusdeo's ignoring me."

"She's avoiding you, which is not the same thing."

"What aren't you saying?"

It was Terrano who answered. "I think you might have a visitor. Well, not *exactly* a visitor."

"Make up your mind. And don't think I've forgotten the original question."

"I think the person who's generally supposed to be watching Bellusdeo—for her own safety—is actually standing across the street."

"Across the street isn't part of Helen," Kaylin very reasonably pointed out. "And you, and all the rest of your cohort, are standing inside of Helen's boundaries."

"And?"

"I believe she wishes to know how you could know that, dear."

"Oh. That? That's easy. Sedarias."

"Sedarias."

"She's almost at the door."

Kaylin did not want to run out into the admittedly emptier, upscale streets on which Helen stood. She wanted to hear about Sedarias's day at the High Halls, and wanted to know whether or not any of her cohort companions had actually had reason to, oh, draw their swords in an attempt not to die.

None of the cohort, however, was willing to amble across that street unless they went in their full number, minus Teela, who had returned to her usual living quarters, which weren't part of Helen. Kaylin thought sending twelve people, eleven of whom were Barrani, to address one observer was overkill. It would send the wrong message.

"Sedarias thinks it'll send exactly the right message," Terrano said.

"I do," Sedarias said, joining the conversation that was already in progress.

"I don't," Kaylin replied. She gave the five members of the cohort a brief but intense once-over; none of them appeared to be bleeding and all of their clothing seemed to be in the same state of repair it had left in. "Given the day you've probably had, I want to avoid the *right message* like the plague. If there's an observer stationed outside, he means the cohort no harm. And frankly, Bellusdeo won't appreciate it." The latter was far more relevant, and not even Mandoran could argue that she would.

Kaylin therefore rearranged Hope, who had been snoozing across her shoulders like a shawl made of scales, and headed toward the front door. "Can you see who it is?" she asked her house.

"Yes. I do not believe it will cause you any problems."

Kaylin could see the lone figure on the other side of the road from her open door. This would be because the fence line—and it was a pretty impressively solid fence—*was* part of Helen's domain, and she'd decided to change some of the posts to lamps.

The observer who was now in the glow of radiant and over-done lights—in Kaylin's opinion—didn't seem to be bothered by them. His hands were by his sides, and clearly free of weapons. His clothing was dark, but it was the dark of implied sobriety, not storybook assassins. His eyes were almost gold.

Kaylin exhaled as Hope sat up on her left shoulder and let out a squawk.

"Well met," Lord Emmerian replied.

02

"Bellusdeo isn't home," Kaylin said, after offering Emmerian a passable bow.

"I know."

"You have someone else following her?"

"It is the duty I was tasked with."

"And you're standing outside on the street just waiting?"

Emmerian smiled, the movement of lips brief but genuine. "As you can see."

"How long have you been standing here?"

"Not too long."

"That's not exactly a precise measure."

"No." His smile deepened.

"Fine. She's been avoiding me. I guess it would make sense that she's avoiding you as well. You might as well come in."

Helen's Avatar greeted Lord Emmerian at the door. Emmerian offered her a perfect, deep bow, before he rose. It was Helen who then led him to the parlor. Today, the parlor was small enough that the cohort couldn't all pile in—they wouldn't fit, for one.

They'd fallen entirely silent, for two, which meant they were having strategic discussions about the near future—or near in immortal terms. Helen could, of course, hear them talk, and Helen tended to strongly dissuade them from doing things she felt were unwise.

Unwise from Helen generally meant catastrophic.

"I've been trying to find out where Bellusdeo's been going," Kaylin said. "But the most specific answer I've managed to dig up is: Tiamaris."

"It is where her people—what remains of them—now live," Emmerian replied. "I believe that she has also visited Lannagaros, but he has, as you can imagine, been quite busy of late. He always claimed to be busy, but he was busy with his personal studies; he could be interrupted, if not with any grace."

"He was always happy to see Bellusdeo."

"Ah, yes. He made allowances for Bellusdeo; similar allowances were not made for the rest of the Dragon Court. The Emperor could summon him, and he would obey—but no one else dared. Lannagaros had quite the temper. He does not, at the moment, have leeway to make the same allowances. The Academia is open, but it requires students; it requires teachers and academics. There are several Barrani sages who have petitioned him, and several members of the Arcanum."

"They're not the same?"

"No. There is some overlap, but no."

"I hope he reduces the Arcanists to ash," Kaylin muttered.

"The Arcanum is not beloved by those who work in the Halls of Law."

"It shouldn't be beloved by anyone."

"I believe An'Teela was once a member of the Arcanum; were she not now a Hawk, it would be more socially obvious."

"She quit, though."

Emmerian shook his head. "She was part of the Arcanum for far longer than she has served the Emperor's Law. And it is not of An'Teela or Lannagaros that you wish to speak. You are worried about Bellusdeo."

Kaylin exhaled. "She's been in a funny mood ever since the Arkon became the chancellor. She was happy for him—I'd bet anything on that—but it seemed to..." Kaylin trailed off.

Hope squawked.

"Say that so I can understand it."

Hope snorted. And continued to squawk.

Emmerian's eyes had become orange in the space of what would pass for syllables only among angry birds.

Helen's Avatar offered Lord Emmerian a drink; he took it almost without seeing it. But Helen said nothing. The silence felt significant. Kaylin was almost certain that Helen wouldn't let Bellusdeo do anything that would cause self-harm.

Helen's smile was pained. "That would depend entirely on what you mean by self-harm, dear. I am very fond of Bellusdeo. But she is not a child, and even were she, I am not her mother."

Kaylin poked Hope. "What the hells did you just say to him?"

It was conjecture, Hope replied.

"What was the conjecture?"

It was Helen who answered. "Bellusdeo has been in pain for a very long time. Your intervention saved her from a life of mindless servitude as a sword. It saved Maggaron. But Maggaron is not Bellusdeo. He feels guilt at his failure, but his failures are smaller and less significant than Bellusdeo's.

"She cares for you," Helen added softly. "She understands that you are both mortal and Chosen. She does not wish to involve you in events that could prove fatal."

"To me or to her?"

"Either, dear. You are upsetting our guest."

Emmerian's eyes were fully orange, now. Kaylin thought she could see flecks of red in them.

"Hope."

I told him that I believe it is Bellusdeo's desire to take the Tower that was formally captained by Candallar.

Kaylin broke the silence that followed Hope's words, but it took her some time. Emmerian offered no help, and Helen didn't choose to come to the rescue either. She understood why Emmerian's eyes were the color of Dragon unhappiness, but had learned that *unhappy* had several flavors, mostly because of the Barrani.

Worry. Hurt. Anger. Fear. All of them expressed wordlessly by the color of eyes: orange, blue. She couldn't immediately tell what variation of emotion had caused Emmerian's eyes to shift color so quickly, so she wasn't certain how to address what she didn't know.

She considered what she knew of Emmerian, and came up with almost zero. He wasn't talkative. He wasn't—like Mandoran or Bellusdeo herself—particularly teasing or mischievous. He had spoken about the Arkon's—ugh, the former Arkon's—past, and in so doing had revealed bits and pieces of his own, but not enough.

Had he been Bellusdeo, the Dragon currently at the heart of his response, Kaylin would have known whether or not she was dealing with anger, worry or pain. He wasn't. He was a member of the Dragon Court, and he had been tasked with her security by an Emperor who was trying his best to protect Bellusdeo and the future of his entire race.

Kaylin had once daydreamed about being someone as important as Bellusdeo—a queen, the savior of an entire race. She felt beyond embarrassed about that now. Her only consolation was that she'd never openly resented or envied Bellusdeo for having what she'd dreamed of having.

It was a solid reminder that nightmares were also dreams.

"Would it be bad if Bellusdeo took the Tower?"

Emmerian didn't reply. Kaylin couldn't decide whether that meant yes or no, which made it hard to keep conversation going. She glanced at Helen. Helen failed to notice; she was watching Emmerian, her eyes obsidian rather than the brown she generally adopted. In Helen's case, obsidian was like Dragon orange-red.

Kaylin was usually honest, but didn't consider it a huge moral strength—more a lack of social self-control. But not pissing off a Dragon—although admittedly Emmerian seemed the least likely of the Dragons to slide into fiery, towering rage—was high on her list of priorities.

It was therefore Emmerian who eventually replied. "No. Absent any other considerations, it would not be 'bad,' as you put it." He lowered his chin and inhaled for what seemed a very long time. Lifting his chin, he met Kaylin's gaze with eyes that were orange and a blend of some other color that might have been a trick of the light.

"None of us saw her when she ruled the Norranir. None of us saw her when she took to the field, Maggaron by her side. We can make educated guesses—but the most accurate of those guesses came from Lannagaros and his advice to the Dragon Court.

"She understands that she is the future of the race. It would be impossible for her not to understand this; it is the source of all contention between Bellusdeo and the Emperor. I do not believe that she intends to let the race die out with the passage of time. Will she bear young? Yes. I believe she will.

"But it is not a simple matter for her; her sole focus is not motherhood."

Kaylin nodded, because she agreed.

"The fiefs are not safe. War is not safe. None know this better than Bellusdeo."

"The fiefs are safe as they can be for those who captain the Towers, though."

Emmerian nodded. "But there is no guarantee that she will be allowed to take that Tower."

"Tiamaris—"

"Tiamaris's Tower wanted what Tiamaris wanted."

"And you think Candallar's Tower won't?"

Kaylin's disbelief must have been evident. Emmerian raised one brow—Dragons were good at that—and said, "You have experience with Towers. You understand that the core of each Tower is sentient. You understand as much about sentient buildings as someone who is not a scholar can.

"If Helen were a Tower, perhaps—"

"I could not be a Tower and be Helen," Helen said quietly. Her eyes remained obsidian with flecks of color; it made them look like dark opals. "In order to become the Helen I am now, I destroyed much of myself. Sentient buildings are an existence that is rooted in the words that define their function. I was, but I yearned for a different function.

"Tara almost damaged herself, but it was not through her own volition; she had been deserted by the man who had undertaken the responsibility."

"Tiamaris understood what she wanted; he understood what her core responsibilities were. Of the Dragon Court, Tiamaris was the one who understood the Towers best. Tiamaris," he added, "and Lannagaros." Clearly Emmerian had no difficulty remembering that Arkon was a title, not a name.

"He did not attempt to change Tara," Emmerian continued, his tone shifting as he spoke. "He saw her duties and her needs clearly, and he accepted both. Those things that do not interfere with her duties, she chooses. He accepts her unusual vegetable gardens and her minor obsession about food. He accepts that her guards—decorative guards when she is at home—are not Imperial Guards.

"In turn, she allows him to govern as he sees fit. They are partners in their endeavors; they have balanced the needs of those who live within the fief with the imperatives of defense against Shadow. There are things Tara *cannot* do, even if she might otherwise desire to do so, and Tara does not—I'm sorry, Helen—have the liberty to make the choices you have made."

Helen wasn't offended.

"Bellusdeo's entire life was war," Emmerian continued, his voice much softer.

With a flash of insight, Kaylin said, "You want more for her."

The orange receded briefly; Kaylin had surprised him.

"I cannot want more for her—but I have gone to war. I have seen Dragons who excel at war. Lannagaros was, as I have mentioned, a legend to us. But he forced himself to excel at war because he felt he had no choice." Gold returned to his eyes. "He is happy now. No force but death will move him from the chancellorship he has undertaken." He smiled. "The Academia and its various possibilities, its many paths to the future, are as much his hoard as the Empire is the Emperor's."

"Bellusdeo's nothing like the Arkon. I mean the chancellor."

"No."

"You think she could be?"

"I don't know."

Kaylin exhaled. "You think she might die if she tries to take Candallar's Tower."

"Yes. I have never, however, been in a position to observe such an exchange. You have. Tell me, Corporal. Do you think it is without risk? Was it without risk when Helen adopted you?"

Helen cleared her throat.

"No."

"And when Tiamaris took the Tower, was that without risk?"

Definitely not.

"You can't go with her?" Helen asked of the Dragon.

"I do not feel that she would accept my company." He then looked at Kaylin.

"I am not at all certain that's a good idea," Helen told him. He hadn't spoken. He probably didn't need to.

Clearly, being a corporal changed very little about her relationship with the Imperial Court. "You want me to follow her."

"Not follow. Not precisely," Emmerian replied. "I would, however, like to second you from the Hawks for a small period of time."

"I just became a corporal," Kaylin said, aware that there was more than a hint of whine in her voice. She struggled to squelch it.

"Yes. Congratulations, by the way." Emmerian rose. "I will speak with the Emperor."

"If you try to make me babysit, Bellusdeo's going to be angry." She considered using stronger language, but decided against; Emmerian probably knew exactly what *angry* meant in Bellusdeo's case.

"*Babysit* implies a certain degree of authority and control that would not be applicable in this situation."

Kaylin exhaled. "Look, I've been seconded to the Imperial Court before. There's no *reason* to have me do it now. If you give her any choice, she won't accept me. If you give her no choice, she'll be beyond angry. She's been taking Maggaron everywhere; he's eight feet tall, and while I did well in combat training, he spent most of his life at war."

"She's just going to feel insulted."

Emmerian nodded. Water was wet, after all.

"Why can't you do it?"

"If she feels insulted at your inclusion," he replied, the barest hint of amusement shifting the contours of his face, "she will contain the anger. She might make noise, but there are strict practical limits to how she displays that anger."

"And she can fight with you."

"Yes. In fighting, as you call it, with me—or any other member of the Court—there will be collateral damage. There is a reason that the Emperor created the Halls of Law; you, as Hawk, can safely do what he cannot. When Dragons rage, the damages are far more extensive."

"She knows that she can't go full Dragon in the middle of the city."

"You are certain?"

Kaylin was annoyed. She folded her arms and glared up at Lord Emmerian. "No. You are."

Emmerian closed his eyes and nodded.

That might have been the end of it, but Hope squawked.

"I think that's an excellent idea," Terrano said.

"Why are you even here?" Kaylin demanded. Helen's expression made clear that he hadn't asked for—or received—her permission to enter the room.

"Well, we were talking—"

"You're always talking. About what?"

"Candallar's Tower, actually."

Emmerian's eyes plunged into orange. There was no way Terrano didn't notice.

"It's empty, right? The Arkon killed him."

"Towers can function for some time in the absence of a lord. Tiamaris's Tower did," Helen told him, her voice chillier than usual.

"But it causes problems, even in the short term."

"Terrano."

"Sedarias thinks one of us should take the Tower. Not that we're unhappy with Helen," he added, a rare display of courtesy, if mistimed. "We understand sentient buildings, and we're at home in them."

"Absolutely not," Kaylin snapped. She was thinking of the

beings that had awakened in Castle Nightshade, and the deaths they had caused.

"We need a base of operations we have some control over," Terrano continued. "We can't stay with Helen forever."

Kaylin opened her mouth.

"You're *mortal*, in case it's escaped your notice. And Sedarias has painted a target on her forehead. Helen can keep us all safe in the immediate future—but when you die, there's going to be another tenant. This new mortal, whoever they are, has no reason to let us remain here. We'd have to move, and Sedarias isn't certain she can establish a secure base of operations in the remaining time left.

"She thinks Candallar's Tower could serve as that base."

"The people who captain the Tower have very specific duties and responsibilities. You can't just waltz in and out of the Towers the way you can Helen."

"Yes, we're aware of that. But a couple of us have no home to return to anyway."

Emmerian cleared his throat.

"I don't think he's joking," Helen told the Dragon Lord. "But I must ask a question."

"Sure," Terrano said.

"Of Lord Emmerian, as you well know," Helen said.

Emmerian nodded. His eyes were fully orange, and looked like they were locked into that color.

"I am under the impression from the words you have spoken that the Emperor does not desire that Bellusdeo take the former Tower—if that is even possible."

Emmerian nodded.

"You do not agree."

He exhaled. For the first time Kaylin could remember, there was smoke in the air that left his mouth and nostrils. "She is a Warrior Queen at heart. It is what she knows best, and this is an enemy that she has—"

"Lost against," Terrano chimed in.

Emmerian's eyes darkened.

"Terrano," Kaylin said, through clenched teeth, "go *away*."

"I believe that would be for the best," Helen added, as Terrano dematerialized. "My apologies, Lord Emmerian."

Emmerian returned to his seat. "You understand my dilemma."

"I do. The Emperor's desires are quite clear, and seem entirely logical to me. And there is always a risk when attempting to captain a Tower. Bellusdeo did not kill the former captain, which is a mark in her favor if the Tower was at all attached to Candallar. But it is not a simple matter to take a Tower, and in my opinion, it is not possible at all if the Tower itself does not desire it.

"There *is* a significant risk to Bellusdeo's attempt—if you believe that is what is happening."

"Is that what she is attempting?" Emmerian asked.

Helen's smile was soft, but tinged with regret. "Of all the guests currently beneath my roof, it is Bellusdeo who requires the most privacy. I therefore cannot answer the question. I would, however, consider the cohort more likely to survive an attempt to take a reluctant Tower; they are beings that the Towers or Hallionne, or even buildings such as myself, were not created to withstand. Their existence could not be predicted."

Kaylin cleared her throat. "You know that Alsanis wasn't allowed to harm his guests, right? If Alsanis had wanted to *kill* them, they'd be dead."

"Yes."

"The Towers don't have the whole *don't hurt your guests* thing."

"Probably not, no. You will understand, however, that the Towers, as sentients, are not all of one thing, and no blanket statements you make are guaranteed to be accurate."

Kaylin nodded.

Emmerian ignored the digression. "And you consider the attempt of the cohort to captain such a Tower wise?"

"Pragmatically speaking, they are twelve. Bellusdeo is one. They can travel and interact in ways no other citizen of this Empire can."

"They're twelve, yes. But they're twelve very tightly interconnected people. If they make the attempt and one of them actually perishes—" Kaylin stopped.

Helen's Avatar nodded. "Terrano will be coming back, soon." Her gaze had not moved from Emmerian's face.

"We cannot protect people from themselves," Emmerian replied. "Unless they are children, but even that is entirely temporary."

"I don't know—Terrano seems to have achieved perpetual childhood."

The Dragon coughed. "What Bellusdeo needs," he finally said, "is not necessarily what the Dragon Court—of which she is not part, except in a racial courtesy sense—needs of her. And it has not been her way to seek permission. Were it, I would counsel acceptance." He rose again and turned to face Kaylin. "I want you with her while she examines her options. There is some possibility that the outcome will be a happy one for her."

"But not the Emperor."

"His hoard is by far the most ambitious I have seen," Emmerian replied. "He does not wish Bellusdeo to live in misery. Lannagaros has often offered his counsel, but Lannagaros has been extremely busy these past few weeks, and it is unlikely he will be less busy in the immediate future. He is happy," Emmerian added. "Bellusdeo knows this.

"Lannagaros has found the Academia he thought destroyed by the necessity of the creation of the Towers. He is home. Bellusdeo is not home; her home was destroyed by the Shadows at the heart of *Ravellon*." Emmerian exhaled. His eyes remained orange, but there was an odd shade blended in with that orange that Kaylin didn't recognize. "I have seen her fight," he said, voice soft. "It is when she takes to the skies— or adopts her draconic form—that she seems to burn with a sense of *rightness*."

This made no sense to Kaylin, who had certainly seen more of Bellusdeo in combat than Emmerian had.

The home Bellusdeo had built for herself had been entirely destroyed by Shadow, its people lost, the remnants of the civilization she had ruled abandoned so that some of them might survive. "Do you want her to take the Tower?" Kaylin asked.

Emmerian did not answer.

"Fine. If I get seconded to Bellusdeo, however indirectly, I get paid, right?"

"Is everything money to you?" Terrano asked.

Mandoran kicked him. They had both been waiting for Kaylin in the dining room, which was her usual retreat when she wasn't in her room. Emmerian had been seen to the door.

"Are you guys serious?" she demanded, grateful that they'd waited, because if they hadn't, she'd've had to hunt them down.

"About what?" Terrano asked, while Mandoran replied, "Hardly ever if I can help it." Their words were distinct, but there was a lot of overlap.

"The Tower."

"It's Sedarias," Mandoran said, grimacing. "What do you think?"

"I'm thinking I hope Sedarias spends a lot of time at the High Halls in the very near future. I know that Candallar's Tower liked Candallar. I think it's the reason he wasn't killed until he tried to kill the Academia's students.

"Were any of you guys with us when we talked about what lay at the heart of the Tower?"

"What do you mean?"

"Nightshade's Tower was built around one of the Barrani Ancestors. Tiamaris's Tara wasn't. Castle Nightshade is a murderous, hostile place. Tara is not. It's the same with the Hallionne, except for the murderous and hostile part. I don't know what the base of the Tower—let's call it the heart—was. I think the Arkon said that Candallar's Tower was once named Karriamis."

"Does it matter? Karriamis was attached to Candallar, who was Barrani."

"I'm not sure any of the twelve of you—except Teela—would be considered Barrani by a Tower."

"That's not your problem, is it?"

"Technically none of it's my problem—or it wasn't until Emmerian."

"You don't want to pick a side?"

"I want to know what you two think. This is obviously a Sedarias idea, with a tiny touch of Terrano on the side."

Terrano looked offended. "I spent centuries jailed in a sentient building—you think I want to go back to that?"

"Yes, actually."

He grinned; Mandoran laughed. "If it's any help," the latter added, "I'm totally against it."

"How many of you are totally against it?"

"Does it matter?"

"It does. I'd like for the cohort and the Dragon not to be engaged in mortal fights in the fiefs—where Imperial Law doesn't rule."

Mandoran's grin faded. "I'm totally against it," he repeated. "So I thought, if you were stuck tailing the Dragon, I'd accompany you."

"No thanks."

"And you can stop me, how?"

"Helen can stop you."

"Not permanently, and you know you're just going to piss off Sedarias. Look, I *like* the Dragon. I shouldn't, but I do. She's not unlike us, except for the scales and the fiery breath. I hate to be serious, and if I am, it's entirely on you—but she's not happy here, and if fighting Shadows and constantly risking her life is what makes her happy, who am I to argue? But I don't intend to be one of her targets. If you decide to accept this job—"

"It's not a job. It's a command."

"Fine. If you decide to obey this command, one of us should go with you."

"Sedarias just wants to know what's going on."

"And your point is?"

"Fine."

Mandoran shrugged. "One of us is going. You'd rather it was Annarion?"

"Why are those the only choices?"

"Yeah," Terrano said. "Why only you two?"

Kaylin had a headache, probably because she was clenching her jaw. "You win," she said. "But don't tell me anything else. I'd like at least a smidgen of plausible deniability."

When Kaylin arrived at the office the next morning, she was surprised there was still a working door, because Marcus was glaring at it, fangs exposed, when she stepped over the threshold. To be fair, he said she'd done nothing wrong, but she was clearly at the center of whatever it was he found nearly enraging.

She wasn't terribly surprised when he sent her, without comment, up the tower at the Hawklord's request. Severn joined her before she reached the stairs.

"Did Marcus tell you what the Hawklord wanted?"

"No, but from your expression, you've probably got a decent guess."

She nodded. "I'm being seconded to the Imperial Palace. Sort of."

"Seconded to who?"

"Technically? You know, I'm not sure. Emmerian, probably. He was the one who made the request."

"Lord Emmerian, if we're speaking of technicalities—which we will be, when we enter the Hawklord's tower."

"Fine. Lord Emmerian asked."

"What did he ask of you?"

She shrugged. "He wants me to tail Bellusdeo and Maggaron."

Had they not been climbing stairs, Severn would have stopped to stare at her; as it was, she felt the edge of both surprise and concern, although neither were voiced.

"I don't know what he's said to the Hawklord, but I guess we're about to find out."

03

Severn was kind enough to place his palm over the door ward of the very closed doors. The Hawklord, who knew Kaylin's allergy to wards—or their allergy to *her*—frequently left those doors open when he summoned her to the tower. That they weren't open wasn't a confirmation of his mood, but it was a sign that he was either heavily distracted or displeased.

No one wanted their boss to be pissed off at them, but Kaylin forced all signs of anxiety off her face. Her arms and shoulders were probably stiffer than normal, but...he was the Hawklord. She wasn't, as a corporal, expected to be entirely relaxed in his presence.

The doors rolled open; the Hawklord stood to one side of his large, freestanding oval mirror. It didn't reflect him. In the mirror, she could clearly see Lord Sanabalis. Which was better, she supposed, than Lord Diarmat.

Sanabalis's eyes were a gold-orange as they shifted toward the two new arrivals.

"Corporal, Corporal," he said.

Lord Grammayre nodded. His eyes, unlike Sanabalis's, were a blue-gray, which was the Aerian equivalent of Sanabalis's gold-orange. As she approached, she revised that; the gray was a darker gray, not the ash gray that was the resting almost-happy color.

"I have received an Imperial request, Corporal," the Hawk-lord now said to Kaylin, his expression hooded but mostly neutral.

She waited. When she failed to interrupt, Sanabalis nodded—as if in approval—and Lord Grammayre continued. "I am not entirely pleased with the request."

Closed doors had definitely been a signal. Kaylin continued in silence, although this was harder. She was a corporal now, not a private, which meant she had something to lose.

"Are you aware of the request, Corporal?"

She nodded.

"I would like to hear what was asked of you."

Sanabalis's eyes shaded slightly toward orange, but he wasn't angry. He looked tired.

"The Dragon Court is concerned about Lord Bellusdeo's current excursions. She's not a member of the Court, except as a courtesy."

The Hawklord nodded.

"They want me to accompany her on her various outings."

"To where?"

Kaylin stopped herself from shrugging. "Part of their concern is that they cannot actually answer that question to their own satisfaction."

"And Lord Bellusdeo has chosen not to divulge that information."

Kaylin was almost, but not quite, certain that no one had asked. It was a complicated situation, given Bellusdeo's importance to the Dragons.

"I am not privy," she said, grateful that she'd chosen to speak in Barrani and not the more casual Elantran, "to the discussions that occur between members, or honorary members, of the Dragon Court, sir."

The Hawklord's eyes narrowed. Blue was now predominant. "I would like to hear your thoughts on the matter."

"I've accompanied Bellusdeo before," she replied. *Lord* was not technically correct, and Bellusdeo hated it. "I've always survived it."

"Where do you believe she is going?"

Kaylin exhaled. She absolutely hated it when people asked questions to which they already knew the answers; she understood that this was some test of honesty. Or something. Nevertheless, he was her commander. "The fiefs."

"I have had very little time to peruse your last report. I believe the fiefs figure prominently in that report."

There was a literal hole in the report that Marcus had accidentally put there with extended claws. Kaylin had watched him do it without concern, and regretted that now.

"Yes, sir."

"You believe you will accompany Bellusdeo into the fiefs."

"Yes, sir."

"What do you believe you will achieve there?"

Since Kaylin wanted nothing from the fiefs, she felt this was an unfair question. "I will carry out my orders, sir. If Bellusdeo enters the fiefs, I will enter them with her. If she chooses to visit the new chancellor in the Academia, I will visit with her. If she elects to enter a fief other than Tiamaris or Nightshade, I will accompany her.

"I will," she continued, when he failed to comment, "report."

"That report," Sanabalis said, entering what was only barely a conversation, "will be tendered to the Dragon Court. To me, personally, or Lord Emmerian. The contents will not be a matter for the Halls of Law."

Ah. This is why the Hawklord looked so disgruntled.

"I'm willing to go," she said, when the Hawklord's silence threatened to be almost lethal, it had sucked so much air out of the room. "She lives with me. I understand why the Arkon is concerned. I understand why the Emperor is concerned."

"I believe she has guards. In fact, I believe Lord Emmerian—of the Dragon Court—serves in a security position."

Sanabalis actually winced, but as the mirror was momentarily at the Hawklord's back, he didn't notice. "Lord Grammayre."

"Arkon."

"The requisition of the corporal's services is not done lightly. We are aware that we are—once again—treading on your figurative toes. Were a Dragon deemed suitable company by Lord Bellusdeo, the Dragon would in all ways be preferable. He is not.

"She will accept the corporal's company. She understands that the corporal will report to me, and if this does not please her, Kaylin is of value to her, and she will grudgingly accept it. She will be far less sanguine about Kaylin's safety than she would be about her own, and Kaylin's presence may encourage a caution she does not apparently feel otherwise." He then turned to Kaylin. "The corporal's salary will, of course, be paid by the Dragon Court."

"And her partner's?"

"We do not require Corporal Handred at this time."

The Hawklord smiled. Kaylin often wondered how *smile* could be used to describe such a wide range of expressions, because there was nothing friendly, amused, or otherwise happy about this one. "Corporal Neya is a Hawk."

"We are aware of that."

"Hawks do not patrol without their partners. I believe Imperial Law and custom are quite specific about this."

Sanabalis turned to speak to someone outside of the mirror's frame. He then turned back. "Very well. Far be it for the

Dragon Court to skirt the rigid confines of the Hawks' bureaucracy. Corporal Handred is acceptable, and yes, we will make certain that the loss of his services is not reflected in your budget."

The Hawklord nodded. "When do you intend to start this new assignment?"

"Immediately. It is likely that Corporal Neya will not be able to accompany Lord Bellusdeo today, but she is to leave the Halls of Law and make that attempt."

Severn said a lot of nothing as they headed back down the stairs.

"At least he didn't tell me it was my choice," Kaylin said, her voice bouncing off the rounded stone walls of the stairwell.

"He doesn't usually offer illusory choices. If you said no, the Emperor would have issued a command." Severn exhaled. "The Hawklord doesn't want you in the fiefs."

"I'm better than I used to be," she offered. "Tara helped. I like the idea of the Academia, and you can't reach it without going through one of the fiefs."

"I think we should start in Tiamaris. Head home, check with Helen to see when Bellusdeo left. The Hawklord's right—we're not going to find her today unless she decides to put part of the fiefs to the torch, figuratively speaking. But we can talk to Tara and see what Tara thinks."

"She won't talk about it if she's been told not to."

"Bellusdeo can't command Tara, and Tara's courtesy isn't as strongly rooted as Helen's. Tiamaris is a Dragon, a member of the Dragon Court, and someone who will share Imperial concerns. I don't think he'll tell her not to talk to us."

They both headed to Kaylin's home, and by the time the front door opened, Helen knew why. "She left before you left for the Halls of Law."

"Maggaron was with her."

"Yes, dear." Helen hesitated.

Kaylin cursed in the Leontine she both loved and failed to properly pronounce, given the physical differences in the throats of the two races. "Did Mandoran follow her out?"

When Helen continued to hesitate, Kaylin switched to Aerian. "Did Mandoran *and* Terrano follow her out?"

"Terrano felt that you had accepted Mandoran as a companion, and to be fair, Mandoran frequently accompanies both of you when you patrol. Mandoran is, in my opinion, capable of reining Terrano in. Sedarias and her escorts have returned to the High Halls." She paused. "Valliant and Serralyn have expressed a desire to deliver their more fragile possessions to the Academia now."

Kaylin was not aware that they had any.

"If you would escort them through Tiamaris, they would be grateful."

"Barrani gratitude is not something anyone sane wants."

"Ah, no. Perhaps *grateful* is a poor word choice. They are not quite ready, but if you are willing to eat an early lunch, they will join you."

Kaylin's sour expression, which she felt no need to discard in her own home, softened completely when Serralyn walked into the dining room—if *walked* was the right word. She seemed to be floating, and her eyes were so green it was almost impossible to look away from them.

Valliant, who trailed after, was more traditionally green-eyed; his eyes retained their flecks of blue. Anxious blue, Kaylin thought. Serralyn was looking forward to a future she had never anticipated being a possibility with open, unfettered delight. Kaylin thought Valliant was less trusting of the future—she would have been. She would have been privately certain that something she did would screw everything up. But

Serralyn's unadulterated joy was almost infectious—possibly because Kaylin had seen so little of it in her life. It was fascinating, and outside of her experience enough that she couldn't even envy it—she couldn't imagine feeling it.

Happiness, yes. Of course. But this...wasn't the same. She had no doubt that Serralyn's eyes would once again resume the familiar Barrani shades of emotional color. Life did that. But she wanted to enjoy what she could of this while it lasted.

"I hear we're escorting you guys to the Academia."

Serralyn smiled. "We have a couple of things we want to take there." She lifted a strapped pack. "We don't have enough—we've never had enough—to need an entire caravan's worth of wagons. And we're not the chancellor." Meaning, no one would die if their personal items were somehow scratched or jostled. With the former Arkon, that had never felt like a guarantee.

Kaylin finished eating and stood, lifting Hope from the table where he was playing with what remained of her food. She placed him on her shoulder, where he slumped in a drape of translucent scales. Severn waited until the two Barrani they were to escort were ready. In Serralyn's case, that was instant. In Valliant's case, it was less so, although it was clear that some background conversation between parts of the cohort was in progress by the time he left Helen.

Neither Severn nor Kaylin had chosen to wear tabards, as they weren't officially on roster duties. It was much safer than it had once been to wear the Hawk in the fiefs, especially the one to which they headed: Tiamaris. Tiamaris enforced Imperial Law within the boundaries of his fief, with a few notable exceptions—those governing transformation and flight above the skies of his fief.

Tiamaris did not yet feel like home, but wearing the Hawk's tabard in that fief wasn't an instant invitation to skirmish—at best. Since they weren't certain to remain in Tiamaris, lack of tabards was a simple precaution.

Serralyn had brought her expression of excitement under control. Her feet actually touched the ground and remained there. Valliant, by expression, could have been any garden variety Barrani male. Neither received undue attention from the guards on the Tiamaris side of the bridge; nor did Kaylin or Severn.

It wasn't hard to see why; Tiamaris, the Avatar of his Tower by his side, stood down the road. He was not draconic.

"Can you see what color his eyes are?" Kaylin whispered out of the corner of her mouth.

"Orange," Valliant replied, in a voice only barely audible.

"Bad orange?"

"Is there ever good orange?" This was slightly louder, but it had to be as Kaylin had turned, once again, to face fully forward. Tiamaris didn't move, an indication that he expected his visitors to come to him. Or them.

"You are on the way to the Academia?" Tara asked as they at last reached the rulers of the fief. She meant the question for Serralyn and Valliant. The presence of a Dragon had dimmed the green in Valliant's eyes; it had apparently bounced off the green in Serralyn's. She offered Tiamaris a perfect bow, but did not hold it until given permission to rise. That would have been overkill.

Sometimes the Barrani used manners as a social sword. Sedarias would.

"Valliant and Serralyn are, and they're less familiar with the city, so we're escorting them."

"That is the reason for your outing today?" Tiamaris asked.

Kaylin glanced at Severn. "Not entirely. I mean, it's the entire reason for Serralyn and Valliant."

"I see. Come, let us escort them, then. We have topics to discuss." *In their absence*, his tone heavily implied. Kaylin didn't

bother to tell him that it wouldn't make much of a difference given Valliant and Serralyn were still living with Helen.
Later, they wouldn't be; they'd be the chancellor's problem,
not Helen's.

"I don't think she considers it a problem," Tara said. This
was surprising. They were not near the physical Tower, and
certainly not *in* it, and while the Towers could observe anything that occurred within the boundaries of their responsibilities, they couldn't or didn't generally read thoughts as if
they were.

"It does take effort," Tara replied.

Any other Barrani would have been extremely uncomfortable with this obvious display of such invasive, one-way communication, but Serralyn and Valliant were never going to
be those Barrani. Even had they been, they lived with Helen.
They didn't expect privacy from sentient buildings.

It wasn't wrong to expect privacy when one wasn't inside
said sentient buildings, but they didn't intend to stay in Tiamaris, and Tiamaris had just granted them the only permission
they desired. Serralyn's steps grew bouncy as they traversed
the streets.

"You don't need to take us all the way there," Serralyn told
Kaylin. "We know the way from here."

Kaylin kind of wanted to see the Academia and its Dragon
chancellor, but that wasn't what she'd been ordered to do. She
nodded as Tiamaris came to a stop across an invisible border
that she couldn't see. He could—and had—crossed it before,
but only at need. This was his home, even if it was currently
under construction.

The changes that had occurred in the past few weeks were
obvious to anyone who had either lived on the fief border or
had crossed it; the graying of all visual elements—buildings,
roads—no longer occurred. The streets hadn't completely

shifted and people weren't disgorged into entirely different parts of the fiefs if they simply turned around and walked back.

But the Academia didn't exist on the maps. Something about its existence didn't give it predictable, sensible geography. Kaylin, who had never considered maps to be friends, was fine with this.

"Come to the Tower," Tiamaris said, turning. "We can discuss other possible changes."

The Tower had become characterized by the gardeners who worked in the gardens that now surrounded it. Those gardens had, to Kaylin's eyes, grown, but a stone path cut across the field directly in front of Tara's doors. Tara paused here and there as the people working stopped to greet her or ask her questions, but forward momentum was preserved.

"It is Tiamaris," Tara said, with open affection. "For some reason, they are more anxious when he is present."

"He's a Dragon."

"Yes?"

"He could breathe on them or bite them in two if they anger him."

"She is the greater danger here," Tiamaris pointed out.

This was true. "She just doesn't look all that dangerous when she's in her gardening clothing." Which she was.

"Ah, no, perhaps not."

The doors, untouched, retracted, which was new. The fact that Kaylin didn't have to touch them at all wasn't. Tara led them to the wide, long hall in which Tiamaris could fully go Dragon and still have room; this hall ended at the pool of liquid that served as Tiamaris's mirror.

It was already active when they reached it.

Kaylin exhaled. "We're here to ask a few questions about Bellusdeo. Have you talked to her recently?"

Tiamaris nodded. His eyes remained orange, but no red darkened the shade.

"The Dragon Court is worried. She's been a bit strange since the former Arkon became the chancellor. She liked him," Kaylin added, which was probably unnecessary. "But he's here."

"There," Tara corrected her. "But yes." She paused, glancing at Tiamaris; he nodded.

A bead of light began to glow in the center of the still pool; it split into hundreds of pieces that then began to travel across the surface of the water, or perhaps just beneath it. A map emerged from those lines of light. It traced the boundaries of the fiefs—all of them, including the one in the center the Towers had been created to watch.

"As you are aware," Tara said, "the border zones between the lines drawn on the map were not fixed or solid; they existed between the space defined by the Towers. It was not clear to us why, and it was not our primary concern."

Kaylin nodded.

"Those border zones have disappeared. The streets that could be perceived in them have also disappeared. You are aware that the cohort and Lord Bellusdeo's Ascendant did not perceive what you or Lord Severn did."

"Teela saw what we saw," Severn said quietly.

Tara nodded again.

"Are the streets now as solid as they look?"

The Tower and her lord exchanged a glance. "Not entirely."

"Which is no."

"They are much more solid. Maggaron saw what Bellusdeo saw when they left our fief, and continued to see the same buildings when they approached the Academia. The actual roads from here to the Academia are solid, structural roads. The buildings outside of the Academia are not always in the best repair."

"But?"

"But, as you say. Bellusdeo has confirmed that one or two of the fiefs have borders that are more elastic. They are not what they were, but they are not what Tiamaris and the Academia have become."

"The streets to the Academia from Nightshade are solid?"

Lights brightened. "Yes."

"And the streets from Liatt?"

"Our assumption is that they are—when the Academia existed entirely within the same realm as the fiefs, it occupied geographical space between Liatt and Nightshade. The Academia as it is currently constituted can be reached from any of the fiefs. Or rather," she added, "the Academia can exit into any of those fiefs. The exit is repeatable; the border zone does not prevent it."

"Who investigated?"

Tiamaris exhaled smoke. "Bellusdeo."

"She's been investigating for the past two weeks?"

"I believe Lannagaros requested it."

Kaylin raised a brow. When Tiamaris failed to speak, she folded her arms.

"He is not lying," Tara told her. "And he is not attempting to withhold information. Lannagaros is chancellor, but he is aware that the Academia needs students. In particular, it needs students whose passion for knowledge and learning is genuine. In the past, there were students—or so he told Bellusdeo—who attended because such attendance implied status.

"That will not be the case immediately. I think Lannagaros underestimates the possible attraction of the Academia, but it has only been a few weeks—less than an eye blink in the course of his long and exalted existence."

Kaylin had difficulty imagining the Arkon as exalted. Respected, yes—she'd seen that with her own eyes. Exalted?

"He is exalted by Dragonkind, and many, many of the Barrani elders think of him with respect."

Tiamaris glared at Kaylin, although she hadn't spoken.

"Look—you can't exalt people you actually know."

"The Emperor?"

"I don't actually know him. And as I get to know him—entirely because of Bellusdeo—I don't think I exalt him. Fear him, yes, because anyone who doesn't would be dead. Respect him? Yes, because politics *suck*, and he's dedicated his life to it."

Tara cleared her throat. It sounded like an earthquake.

Hope sat up and squawked loudly.

"I think it best," Tara replied, her voice and expression serene. "You may, however, speak to her later."

Do not make her give me another headache. Hope settled, disgruntled, across her shoulders, fuming slightly—which in his case was literal.

"Next time, stay at home." She wasn't surprised when he bit her ear.

Tiamaris's cleared throat was nowhere near as felt as Tara's. "Lannagaros has an interest in the accessibility of the Academia. He knows that it can be reached from Tiamaris, so the desire for more information is not something on which the fate of the Academia rests. But it is like him to be concerned about the access from the rest of the fiefs.

"I have personal reasons for agreeing that this information should be known. Lord Nightshade has, independently, confirmed that the Academia is easily reached from the fief of Nightshade; Bellusdeo has not been sent to Nightshade."

"But she's been sent everywhere else?"

Tiamaris nodded.

"No wonder the Dragon Court is concerned." *Concerned* hadn't been her first word choice, but she decided to speak in Barrani instead; it was a lot harder to default to inappropriate language in Barrani. On the other hand, there were so many things that could be considered rude or inappropriate by the Barrani.

Culture was complicated.

"Lannagaros understands Bellusdeo better than any of the Dragon Court—and I am no exception. He understands war, and the costs of war; he has found his way through losses that would have driven—that did drive—others of our kind to madness. If Lannagaros did indeed request her aid—"

"He did," Tara said quietly.

"—then I have to trust that in some fashion he feels that this is safe for Bellusdeo."

Kaylin nodded.

Severn, however, so silent he might have been absent, did not. "Not what is safe; what is best," he said quietly. "I believe Lannagaros trusts that this is *best* for Bellusdeo."

Tiamaris couldn't pretend that *safe* and *best* meant the same thing. He didn't try. "I have chosen not to argue with her."

"My lord went to the Academia directly to speak with the chancellor," Tara added. "He wished to confer with the chancellor in person, given the implications for the future."

"The chancellor told him to mind his own business?"

Tara laughed, a surprising, chime-like sound that made her seem vastly younger than even Kaylin—as if joy were something only the young could experience. It was a striking thought.

"He did," she said, as the laugh faded into sober echo. "But very politely. I believe he was annoyed, not at my lord—who, as you are, is accustomed to the chancellor's very curmudgeonly outbursts—but at the Emperor. My lord tells me that Bellusdeo has been the subject of some contention since you first discovered her."

Tiamaris's lips were set in a tight, grim line, and his eyes were orange as he glared at Tara. Kaylin could not remember ever seeing him do so before.

"He does not do so frequently, it's true. But if this were dangerous to you or Bellusdeo—"

"It *is* dangerous," Tiamaris snapped.

Hope squawked.

"Yes. The chancellor, as Tara now calls Lannagaros, considers the dangers inherent in her internal struggle with despair to be far greater. But it will be dangerous to *you*, which is entirely unnecessary."

"You've been talking to Emmerian," Kaylin said, forgetting to speak Barrani.

"There has been much discussion." Tiamaris's eyes calmed. "I find it taxing. Bellusdeo is as old as Lannagaros. She is not a child. Were I Bellusdeo, were I in her position, I would have a clutch or five in order to escape the duties imposed upon me. I am not Bellusdeo.

"But having Tara, and having the fief and the weight of its responsibility, has perhaps influenced my thinking."

"How?"

"It is," Tara said, before Kaylin could continue, "a vast amount of work, and at times, the work can seem overwhelming. Not for me," she added softly. "But for my lord. His decisions—decisions in which his people have little choice—will nonetheless affect the people of the fief. He cannot simply magically transform the fief.

"I can transform large parts of it," she continued. "And I have offered to do so. But in the event of a disaster—in event of a breakdown of the barriers that keep *Ravellon* in check—I will have to withdraw the changes I have made and redirect my power."

"Is the power used consistently? I mean—do you have to always use it?"

Tara nodded. "It is part of me; I will not 'run out' of power. But the consequence of an emergency will be, for the residents, a different emergency. After deliberation, my lord has decided to rebuild the normal way, as he calls it. But even that is fraught. Where? When? Money is not the issue it would be for most of our citizens—but it does remain an issue if we are to do things in the normal fashion.

"Regardless of the work and the stress of making decisions, having the responsibility is what defines him. It's what defines *hoard* for him. I believe that the same could be said of the Emperor or Lannagaros. I do not understand Emmerian, but Emmerian is not easily read."

"You can't read him when he's here?"

"Not always, and not consistently." She frowned. "Yes, Helen can—but that is almost certainly because Lord Emmerian allows it. He has come to speak with Tiamaris three times in the past two weeks; he has passed through the fief to speak with Lannagaros. I believe he returned with a singed cape on the last visit; he has not gone again." She glanced, pointedly, at Tiamaris.

Tiamaris rumbled. "Bellusdeo will accept you as a companion if you desire it."

"I've already been seconded—by Sanabalis—to the Imperial service. So has he," she added, nodding in Severn's direction.

"You do not see your value clearly if you can be so casual."

Kaylin shook her head. "I see my own value clearly. But I'm a *Hawk*. I serve the Imperial Laws. I'm the person who's been trained and taught to interfere when interference is necessary."

"In Elantra, yes. Not in the fiefs."

"I've been sent to the West March," Kaylin countered. "By command, not like last time. I've managed to survive."

"So far," was his dark reply.

"I believe that Bellusdeo is invested in your survival; I am not certain," Tara added, once again glancing at Tiamaris, "that she is nearly as invested in her own. You can keep yourself alive in most circumstances of which we are now aware, but Bellusdeo sees you as a mortal, even if you are Chosen. You are part of her home."

"She's part of *my* home."

"Yes. The home that Bellusdeo has built is fragile because it is not rooted or grounded. She is a warrior who has not been allowed to enter the battle; she is a queen without a country or a throne. She has built a home of hope, but it rests on a foundation of loss and despair. She values you, Kaylin Neya.

"She unwillingly values Mandoran, and this angers her. Favoring a mortal in such a short period of time is essential; a proper reserved approach would waste half your life—if only that. She has no excuse for Mandoran."

"You know that Mandoran insists on coming with me."

Tara smiled. "I do. She is not concerned with Mandoran's safety. She will be concerned with yours."

"Maggaron is mortal."

"Maggaron is Ascendant. There are things she can do to preserve him that she cannot do for you. Regardless, Bellusdeo—as do Tiamaris and the Emperor—desires responsibility. It is the one thing she lacks, and if the burden was almost too great to bear, she has discovered, as no doubt my lord would, that lack of any burden is lack of purpose.

"The Emperor believes, somehow, that continuing the race *is* purpose and responsibility. And my lord agrees."

"But you don't?"

Tara was silent. Given Tiamaris's expression, that silence was probably the right answer.

But she was Tara. "It is not good," she finally said, "for the immortal to have no purpose when they also lack joy. She has done Lannagaros's tasks faithfully and well. This is not, of course, the first time that Bellusdeo has come to Tiamaris—but there is a difference in her, almost a humming, a sense of...rightness. I am sorry," she added softly, to Tiamaris. "She has been idle too long."

Given the events of the past few months, Kaylin thought *idle* entirely the wrong word.

"Tell me, given those events, given the significance of the effects of failure, would you now dedicate your daily life to them?"

"They're one-offs," Kaylin countered.

"Yes. What would make you retire from the Hawks you serve? You offer aid to the guild of midwives, to the foundling hall. Would that not be enough to sustain you?"

No.

04

"I ask only that you think carefully, Kaylin. You are not Bellusdeo; you did not rule—and lose—a world. But as your life as a Hawk has defined you, her life as a queen—a lost queen, far from home—defined far more of her existence. The scattered remnants of her people, the Norranir, are here, but they, too, are not what they were. They are refugees; they cling to our borders, because war with Shadow is what they know.

"What they did before that war became so all-encompassing, you do not know. Some might have been artists or scholars. But here, this is all that is familiar."

Kaylin shrugged uneasily. "I told you—I've been ordered to keep her company. I'll do it."

Tara nodded. "You will not, I think, find her today. But I believe you should also visit the chancellor."

"You've never interrupted him while he's working," was the glum reply.

"Well?" The glumness continued when they left Tara. Tiamaris escorted them out, but added no further words; he was not in agreement with his Tower.

She surprised herself. "You understand that Tara's very existence is about *Ravellon*, right?"

His eyes were orange, and flecks of red could be seen.

"I'm not saying you're stupid," she continued, a rushing press of syllables designed to lessen the red. "But…it makes sense to me that Tara would support Bellusdeo's interests here. Bellusdeo was…not created, not exactly, but—she grew up fighting Shadow. She sacrificed everything to that war. Everything. I don't know what she'd be if the Norranir hadn't arrived. But it's what she knows. The Norranir have ways of influencing and detecting Shadow that even our experts didn't before their arrival.

"For Tara, this job *is* Bellusdeo's job. This fight is Bellusdeo's fight. And it's in the best interests of all of the Towers to allow it."

"You know what Bellusdeo wants."

"I know what she probably wants, yes. But I'm just saying— it makes sense for Tara to privilege Bellusdeo as a warrior, not a mother. If the Towers fall, there won't *be* Dragons because there won't be *anything*."

Tiamaris stared—glared, really—at her for a minute. Or an hour, if one judged by feeling and not actual passage of time. "Speak to Lannagaros. I have as much influence over Bellusdeo as any other member of the Dragon Court, and sadly, that includes the Emperor."

"She's not technically—"

"Out." He breathed a small plume of actual fire as he spoke.

Kaylin didn't need to be told twice. To be fair, she didn't need to be told once, either.

"Is that what you believe?" Severn asked, as they crossed into what had once been the border zone.

"No. I mean, it's true—I think Bellusdeo is the perfect ally for Tara or any of the Towers, but…no. I think she actually cares about Bellusdeo's happiness. And Bellusdeo hasn't been happy for a long, long time."

"War didn't make her happy."

"No."

"War would make her happy now?"

"I'm going to punch you if you keep this up."

Severn grinned.

It was true, though. War hadn't made Bellusdeo happy. Being here, being free, being alive, hadn't exactly made her happy. Knowing that she was the only hope for the continuance of the Dragon race hadn't made her happy. But Kaylin didn't inherently believe that Bellusdeo was doomed to unhappiness.

Maybe all that was left was a choice between different unhappinesses. What was the thing that would make her the *least* unhappy?

She cursed in Leontine. "Fine. I think we *all* want Bellusdeo to be happy, and none of us understand how that would work—but we all have ideas. Except for Tiamaris and the Emperor."

"Let's talk to the chancellor and see what he has to say. We won't be accompanying Bellusdeo anywhere today unless she happens to be at the Academia when we arrive."

Kaylin's shoulders slumped. "I don't expect him to be in a good mood. Not if he singed Emmerian's cape—Emmerian is the least confrontational of the Dragons."

The streets, as Tara had said, didn't become elongated or compressed; they didn't lose color. They seemed solid and as real as any other streets in the fief as Kaylin and Severn walked down them.

They weren't normal streets, however. The border zone as it existed had become absorbed somehow in the resurrection of the Academia, under its new chancellor. All of these newly solid streets somehow formed borders and boundaries that transcribed the Academia. They didn't lead to Nightshade, the next fief over. She could turn heel—and tried—and follow the streets back to Tiamaris; different streets must exist in Nightshade now that led to the Academia.

There seemed to be no streets that connected the actual neighboring fiefs.

This made a kind of sense to Kaylin. If one of the Towers fell, the contamination or corruption could not spread to zones the other Towers occupied. It could, however, spread to Elantra, the city that Kaylin—and many, many others—called home.

"These streets still make no sense."

Severn nodded. "They would be difficult to map, yes." His tone made clear that some intrepid cartographer would be forced to do it anyway.

"The Emperor doesn't rule the fiefs. He can't just order someone to map them."

"And the chancellor doesn't rule Bellusdeo, either."

Fair enough. Kaylin found maps useful—at least Records versions of maps—but not necessary. No doubt their existence in Records implied she was wrong.

"Do you think people could live here?"

"I don't see why not. I imagine that some people will—but that might be at the chancellor's discretion. I'm not sure how or why buildings that aren't related to the Academia nonetheless survive—but clearly they do."

"That's another question to ask the chancellor. Some other day. I figure we'll have our hands full with the Bellusdeo question." It occurred to her that it might be a good idea to stop talking and start thinking, because she had to have an actual question or two to ask if she did manage to get his attention.

The Academia buildings were the buildings that Kaylin had first encountered, but they were, as the rest of the streets that led to it, solid, their colors the natural colors one would expect of stone, wood and glass. The central parkette around which the buildings curved sported trees and incredibly well-tended grass, as it had the first time Kaylin had seen it. But here, the grass was ridiculously emerald, and the trees in such perfect health that none of it looked real.

The buildings themselves were also in perfect repair. To be fair, if she thought about it, so was Helen—and these buildings were the heart of Academia. Killianas—Killian—was the central intelligence that kept the Academia functioning. He was a building with a much more amorphous set of instructions than Helen.

Or so Helen had said. His creation had been the work of not one, but practically all, of the extant Ancients, those beings who had created the various races that now populated both the city and the Empire. And beyond that, as well.

What they had wanted when they created this place was probably what the Arkon—damn it, the *chancellor*—had wanted when he had created his own library. But no, the former Arkon's library had been a private, personal collection of the detritus of the long dead. It wasn't meant to be occupied, touched, interacted with by any save the Arkon himself.

This was different.

The parkette was occupied, but not by mostly Barrani thugs, although Barrani were present. Kaylin recognized two of them: Serralyn and Valliant. They appeared to be eating lunch. She glanced at Severn; he shrugged.

She decided to leave the two to their lunch and their companions, two of whom were mortals Kaylin didn't recognize. Even at this distance, she could see Serralyn's eyes were a brilliant green. Reality would no doubt dim that color, because reality had a way of doing that to hopes and dreams.

But the hopes and dreams that had led Kaylin—eventually—to her life with the Hawks and Helen had still led her to a much better place. Was it perfect? No. And she had certainly daydreamed about perfect, somehow expecting that "better place" would be it. She was almost certain that, reality notwithstanding, Serralyn would be happier here than she had been possibly anywhere else.

"Kaylin!"

It was not the Barrani cohort, or the two members present, who shouted her name. She turned instantly toward the source of that voice; Robin was running across the edge of the grass toward her, narrowly avoiding collision with one tree.

"It *is* you!"

She smiled. "Robin. Have you met Serralyn and Valliant?"

He nodded, grinning. "Things have been *so much better* since you guys came. Like, the classes are actually different. They don't just repeat over and over. And Serralyn and Valliant *want* to be here. Everyone who's here wants to be here—no one is a prisoner."

"Not anymore, no."

"Have you seen Calarnenne?"

"Please tell me he's not a student here."

"Sort of? I mean, he's not one of us—but he's welcome here. I think the chancellor likes him. I take it that means no."

"No, we haven't seen him."

"Are you coming to apply?"

"Gods, no. I was a terrible student in the Halls of Law, and I'd be a terrible student now. I get that Serralyn *wants* to be here—she's been walking on air for days—and I don't think she's stupid for it. But she thinks it'll be fun and I think I'll just get expelled. But you want to be here, too."

"I like it here. I get fed—for free—and I have a safe place to stay, and there's just so much that's so *interesting*. I can leave now, if I want. I couldn't before." He lowered his voice. "The chancellor wants students *like me*." He beamed. "He said it's important."

There probably weren't a lot of kids like Robin around.

Kaylin had thought maybe—just maybe—this could be a home for the children of the fiefs, a safe place for them to learn, if they wanted to learn. A place where starvation and fear of Ferals were irrelevant. Listening to Robin, watching Serralyn, she was less certain.

Robin had, in some fashion that she didn't understand, been the lynchpin of the Academia's revival. Something about the way he approached information and knowledge—knowledge that would be impractical and useless for Kaylin's chosen life—had affected Killian.

"I have a friend," he said, his voice still low. "She would *love* it here. I think. The chancellor said I could find her, but—he doesn't want me to find her on my own."

"Where does she live?"

"The east warrens. Same as me. Or same as I used to." His expression fell. "I want her to come here if she's still alive." A world of words about life in the warrens—which was not dissimilar to Kaylin's life in the fiefs, except for the absence of Ferals—was implied by those words.

"When are you going to look for her?"

"I'm not sure."

"No?"

"I have classes," he said, as if classes were the job that Kaylin so prized. "And I have to wait until the chancellor has time."

"You want to wait?"

"Well, he's a Dragon," Robin replied, as if that explained everything. It did. No one in the east warrens would be stupid enough to attack a Dragon, if they recognized a Dragon. No one in the east warrens would survive attacking a Dragon if they didn't. Regardless, Kaylin had a job, and that job probably didn't include heading into the east warrens to find a friend of Robin's.

"How long were you in the Academia as a prisoner?"

"I think a year, maybe a bit more or a bit less. Time here—

at least when none of us could leave—was a bit strange. It's normal now."

So it might have been longer. She didn't ask if he was certain his friend had survived in the interim. No profit to that question.

"Did you come to talk to the chancellor?"

"If he's available, yes."

"You're supposed to make an appointment."

"We didn't know we were coming. Tell me, have you seen Bellusdeo? She was the gold Dragon."

Robin nodded. "She's helping the chancellor. Somehow."

"I live with her. Well, she lives with me."

"She's not supposed to be helping the chancellor?"

"Robin, you are *way* too observant. There's some disagreement about what Bellusdeo should be doing—but take it from me: it's never safe to tell a Dragon what to do. Or what not to do. Can you take us to the chancellor's office?"

"It's the same place it was before."

"Yes, but I'm not familiar enough with the building to remember it."

He nodded and led the way. "We'll have to hurry," he added, half apologetically. "Lunch is almost over."

There was no door ward on the very closed door. Kaylin hesitated. Robin didn't. He knocked. He was not yet full-grown, and his hands were lighter than Kaylin's, although the length of his fingers implied they wouldn't, in the fullness of time, remain that way. He was clearly not afraid to knock on this door or face this particular Dragon in his personal den.

The door rolled open.

The chancellor was in his office, which Robin had said wasn't guaranteed. He was even seated behind his desk, but didn't appear to be attending to paperwork. A mirror—long and oval—was situated beside that desk; it was active.

There was a lot of roaring from the mirror, and a few words of similar volume from the chancellor, who appeared to be wreathed in smoke. Kaylin covered both of Robin's ears with her hands.

In mortals, this volume would have been an indication of dangerous fury.

The Arkon's eyes, however, as he turned toward the door and the people foolish enough to interrupt him, were orange. Not red-orange; he was annoyed or concerned, but not yet angry.

Kaylin hoped that her presence here wouldn't change that.

The Arkon turned to the mirror—Kaylin could see its shape, but couldn't see what the Arkon saw; she knew he spoke to a Dragon, but not which one. When they spoke in their native tongue, there was often too much sound distortion for her to distinguish between their voices. "We will continue this later," he said, in Barrani.

He then turned fully to face her. "Corporal."

"Chancellor."

"What brings you to my office? In general, one is required to have an appointment."

"Yes, sir. But…I needed appointments to see you in the palace, as well."

"And never had the courtesy to make them."

"I mostly came with Bellusdeo, and—"

He lifted a hand. "Yes. I understand. You are not, however, with Bellusdeo today, and you still lack an appointment." He glanced at Robin. "If you hurry, you will make your class on time. And Robin? The matters that bring the corporal here are not matters that involve the Academia; they are the sad detritus of my previous duties. Understood?"

"Yes, sir." Robin bobbed a bow that would have had Diarmat raging at Kaylin for weeks, grinned at Kaylin as he rose, and was gone.

"Do not run in the halls!" The chancellor's raised voice followed him, bouncing off the walls of the office. But his eyes were a shade of gold that strongly implied he was fond of Robin, that he knew Robin knew this, but was content to let it be.

His eyes were less gold when they turned, once again, to Kaylin. Of course they were. He gestured and the doors once again closed, a politer word for slammed shut.

"You understand," the chancellor said, "that I am an *honorary* member of the Dragon Court?"

She nodded. She'd guessed as much.

"Perhaps you don't understand what honorary means."

Now that was uncalled for. Kaylin opened her mouth, but the chancellor had not yet finished.

"Lord Tiamaris is an *active* member of the Dragon Court." He steepled his hands above the fall of his beard, drawing it closer to his chest. "What have you come to discuss? You have fifteen minutes, unless I feel the discussion is personally relevant to someone who is not an active member of the Court."

Fine. "We've come to ask a couple of questions about Bellusdeo. Tiamaris said she's been running errands for you."

The chancellor's eyes grew orange, and Kaylin decided that Barrani should have been the go-to language. It would have been, had she not been irritated.

"She has undertaken the responsibility of examining the access to the Academia from each of the fiefs."

"The Emperor—the Dragon Emperor—has asked that I accompany her."

"I believe some diplomacy, at least in the fief of Farlonne, is involved. That has not been traditionally where your... talents...have been put to use."

"I will refrain from speaking. I'm meant to be a guard."

"You are meant to be a babysitter," he replied. "And Bellusdeo is not in need of one."

"Imperial command," Kaylin replied. "I don't have to like it. I just have to obey."

The chancellor exhaled. It was a small wonder that he hadn't managed to reduce his desk to ash.

"It is not," a familiar voice said. Killian—Killianas—walked through the closed door, without bothering to open it first. "Within the buildings that comprise the Academia, I have some control over the physical state of the furniture."

The first thing Kaylin noticed was that Killian was no longer missing an eye. The second was that he looked fully Barrani; he might have been a Barrani student were it not for the way he'd entered the chancellor's office.

The former Arkon didn't seem to resent his presence the way he resented Kaylin's, which was fair. In some fashion Killianas *was* the Academia.

"Bellusdeo has, as you are aware, been meeting with the chancellor. He has offered what little advice he feels competent to offer."

"Have you talked with her?"

"I have. I have spoken with her more frequently than the chancellor, who is extremely busy at the moment. We have much to do in order to rebuild what was almost lost. She has also visited the librarians and spoken at length with at least one of them."

"Why did she want to talk to you?"

"I am not at all certain that she did. She is not natural student material, but she is absolutely willing to do the research necessary when she feels it is germane to her duties."

Kaylin frowned. "Was it Starrante she talked to?"

"Yes. Before you ask, I was not privy to their discussion. The library is a space that is accessed through the Academia, but I have no control over, or command of, the librarians, and no ability to influence what occurs within their space."

Kaylin nodded.

"You are concerned for Bellusdeo?"

"Always. My life depends on it."

"I see. Lannagaros?"

"Speak with the corporal, by all means."

Killian nodded.

Kaylin then turned to Killian and said, "Tell me everything you know about Karriamis."

"Everything? That might take longer than you have."

"The Arkon—I mean the chancellor—said that Karriamis was, before he became the heart of a Tower, a Dragon."

Killian nodded.

"Candallar was the captain of the Tower Karriamis became."

Killian nodded again.

"Karriamis was interested in finding the Academia, if it still existed."

"Yes. He was not the only Tower who had that interest. And his was not the only Tower that anchored the very little that remained of the Academia after the Towers rose. Even Towers that were not personally interested in the Academia provided an anchor; I am not certain all of the Towers were aware of this, but I do not see how they could not be."

"Nightshade's Tower never talked to Nightshade about the Academia," Kaylin pointed out. "I mean, if it had, Nightshade would have sought the Academia out himself."

"I believe this is materially true. You have enough experience to understand two things: that the Towers were built, just as the Academia was, from living people, and that those people were not the same; they had different underlying likes and dislikes, hopes and dreams, over which the responsibility of guarding against *Ravellon* had primacy.

"You wish to know what Towers look for in a lord. I cannot answer. I know what I look for in a chancellor. You know what Helen looks for in a tenant. You understand some part of what Tara wanted from Tiamaris. These three things are not the same. No more were the lords the same.

"Towers have some attachment to their captains. Karriamis did not wish Candallar to be destroyed—and the chancellor would not have destroyed him, in the end, had Candallar not decided that he could wrest control of the Academia from the chancellor by destroying the handful of students upon whom the heart of the Academia—me—depends.

"Candallar overstepped; he is dead. His Tower is uncaptained."

"From personal experience, I can tell you that the Towers without captains can protect their territories for a few years."

Killian nodded. "The power of the Tower within its own confines is absolute. But within the confines of its territory, less so. There is a reason the Towers have captains, but I am not at all certain that the reasons are the same for each of the Towers."

"Did you know them?"

"No. Their responsibilities were not my responsibilities. I could not become a Tower, even were I to somehow be extracted from the Academia; I would never have been chosen."

"You were aware of Karriamis."

Killian nodded again. "I am aware of Karriamis now. He is called Candallar by the people of his fief. I do not understand this."

"Most people don't willingly walk into a Tower. They know who the fieflord is; they call the fief—and its Tower—by that name. When the fieflord dies, or when the fieflord abandons his or her Tower, the person who replaces the fieflord becomes the name associated with the fief."

"Why?"

"Because the fieflords rule? I don't honestly know. Maybe in other fiefs the custom isn't the same. I didn't know that

Castle Nightshade was sentient. I believed that the fieflord in his own Tower was omnipotent."

"That is not the case."

"No, I've since learned more about it. But—"

"You want to know what Karriamis wants."

She nodded.

"You are not the only interested party who does."

"Bellusdeo asked you."

"She did."

"Who else?"

Killian glanced at the chancellor, who nodded.

"Terrano. I am somewhat fond of him, but grateful that he has not applied to become a student."

"No Tower would accept Terrano!"

"In that, we agree. But it is not Terrano who would become the lord, as you must suspect."

Kaylin nodded. "Has Bellusdeo visited Candallar?"

Silence.

Kaylin understood this one, and turned once again to the chancellor. Before he could speak—if he intended to speak— she said, "I want Bellusdeo to be happy and safe. I think she'd be *good* at being a captain, and frankly, if Tiamaris could rule every single fief, I think the citizens of all the fiefs would be better off."

"He cannot, as you well know."

She nodded. "But...I think Bellusdeo would be more like Tiamaris than Nightshade."

"Karriamis accepted Candallar."

Kaylin nodded.

"You are wondering why."

"I don't think Candallar wanted to *be* captain of a Tower."

"No. In that I agree. A series of events led him to the Tower, and he had the will and the power to take it. But it was not his primary desire. Discovering the Academia after all this time was not his primary desire, either; it was—I was—a tool. A way to return to the power he *did* desire. Lord Nightshade is different in every aspect; they shared a race, and a status within that race, but they are not the same men. Lord Nightshade is fully capable of defending himself against those who would use his status as an excuse to murder him. He would be capable were he not a fieflord. Candallar did not have that confidence."

With reason. Candallar was not Nightshade's equal.

"No." Killian's smile was soft; his eyes were obsidian, but he corrected that color as she noticed. "I cannot tell you what you want to know—I do not have the answer. I am uncertain that Karriamis will accept any of your friends; it appeared to me that he was fond of Candallar, and your friends in aggregate were responsible for his death."

"That was the chancellor!"

"In the end, yes—but the opportunity to do so was provided by your various associates."

"Is there a reason you feel that way?"

"Bellusdeo is expected to make a report to the chancellor before the end of day. If you wish, you may retrace her conversational steps while you wait."

"We don't need to wait—"

We want to talk to Starrante, Severn surprised her by saying.

"…could we get dinner with the rest of the students?"

The chancellor graciously gave permission to the two Hawks. It was, Killian explained, his permission to either give or withhold.

"You may join the students in the dining hall if you exit my office immediately and fail to return."

"Ever, or today?"

"I would like to say *ever*, but Killianas is fond of you and I do not feel he would enforce it."

Kaylin and Severn left the office as if he were the Hawk-lord and they were his Hawks.

"I would be unlikely to enforce it," Killian agreed—after the door had all but slammed shut on their backs. "He is un-likely to mean it."

"If he forbade anyone else the Academia?"

"If he forbids anyone the Academia in a serious fashion, yes, I am capable of that, just as your Helen is; I am perhaps *more* capable of it than your Helen currently is. He finds you frustrating, but you are less frustrating at the moment than much of the work he must do, and he understands that your unique properties often provide an early warning that might otherwise be lacking."

"Unique properties?"

"You are Chosen. But come. The library is not generally open to random visitors; I believe Starrante will be pleased to see you."

"Did Bellusdeo visit him?"

"Yes."

Starrante was, as Killian had suggested, pleased to speak with Kaylin and Severn. What she hadn't expected, upon entering a library that looked very much like the library she had first entered, was that Kavallac and Androsse would also be present. Kavallac was, or had been, a Dragon before she became a librarian; Androsse had been a Barrani Ancestor.

If the three weren't sentient buildings in the way Killian was, they were confined in a similar fashion. Within the con-fines of the library, they were more powerful than they had probably been when they had walked the city streets—or the forests that preceded them—but they were bound here. They couldn't leave.

If they could, Kavallac would have been a second living female Dragon. It would have taken the heat off Bellusdeo, although Kavallac seemed no more likely to want to become the mother of her race than Bellusdeo.

Kavallac, however, couldn't make the choice to do so, even if she desired the continuation of the race.

"Corporal," Starrante said, his forelegs weaving a complicated web directly between them. She understood that this was meant as an honor or an acknowledgment, but still found it unsettling. She wondered if Starrante found her as unsettling, but doubted it. He'd been the librarian for a long damn time, and he'd no doubt encountered the many student races who didn't possess the legs, body, and web-spitting abilities his own race considered normal.

"Arbiter." She offered him a bow that Diarmat wouldn't have held in contempt had he been present. She then bowed to both Kavallac and Androsse in turn, as did Severn.

"Corporal Handred wished to speak with you."

Severn nodded.

"What do you wish to speak about?"

"The Towers," he replied.

The three arbiters glanced at each other. "The creation of the Towers almost doomed the Academia." It was Kavallac who replied.

Severn nodded. "Did you know Karriamis, or know of him?"

Silence again, as if the air had been sucked out of the room. It was Kavallac who replied. "Yes."

05

"You knew him before he agreed to become the heart of a Tower?"

Kavallac nodded. "Why do you ask?" Her voice was cool, her eyes orange—but it was a silver-orange; all of the eyes of the Arbiters had a silver cast to their base color.

"Candallar attempted to revive the Academia."

This time, when Starrante spit, he did not make a web of the results.

Kavallac nodded, the nod controlled.

"Killian implied heavily that he was aware of Karriamis—the Tower we call Candallar—and that Karriamis's instructions were instrumental in the revival of the Academia."

"I do not concur," Androsse said. As he was not a Dragon and had not yet made claims of familiarity, this was surprising. One brow rose as he glanced at Kaylin. "You are very expressive, Corporal. What Candallar desired was not the Academia; I am not certain that he understood it at all. He understood the trappings. He understood that there was knowledge here for the taking if it could be found.

"He understood that knowledge is power. It is a phrase that

has retained its use over the ages. But the desire for knowledge was predicated on the desire for power, and at that, a narrow definition of power.

"What Karriamis wanted was not what Candallar wanted."

"So he used Candallar to get what he wanted?"

"Do you somehow believe that the Towers must love their captains?"

"It's just—someone said he held Candallar in some affection."

"It is not outside the realm of possibility, but—and I mean no disrespect to the person who issued that opinion—this is not something that can be relied on as fact, as truth. Killian's decision was not Karriamis's decision, and if Killian is aware of Karriamis, he is just as aware of the rest of the Towers on the periphery of his responsibility."

Kaylin immediately raised a hand.

If the librarians didn't teach classes in the various classrooms or lecture halls, they had nonetheless dealt with groups of students before.

"Can you repeat that last bit? I mean the part where Killian's aware of the Towers on the periphery?"

"As you appear to have heard it, I do not believe *repeat* is the word you meant."

"I don't understand but—can Killian deliberately communicate with the Towers?"

Another glance bounced between the Arbiters.

It was Starrante who chose to answer. "We believe that *communicate* is the wrong word. He is aware of the Towers; they are—on some peripheral level—aware of Killian. Karriamis wished to find the Academia he was certain still existed in some form.

"It is our belief that the sleeping Academia was anchored in a space similar to the outlands, which we are informed you have traversed."

"The outlands are—"

"Similar to, not the same. The Tower imperatives did not allow such a preservation where Shadow might intrude; we stand in a space created by the power of the Towers themselves."

"You don't think they're aware of this?"

"There has been much lively debate about that very question. For my part, no."

"And if no," Kavallac snapped, "you imply an error on the part of the Ancients. How could power be drained from the Towers who were meant to be our last—our best—line of defense, if the Towers themselves were not aware of the source of that drain? That implies a dangerously lax and foolish architecture on the part of the Ancients who also created *us*."

Kaylin took all of this as a maybe.

"Did Karriamis teach Candallar how to find this place?"

"I doubt it. Had Karriamis been able to clearly delineate the steps to do so, Candallar would likely be chancellor. I believe that magical strides have been made in the past several decades—perhaps the past century. You will have seen the results of some of them personally. Two of those who we believe would have had a far greater chance at accomplishing what Candallar hoped to accomplish are now students within the Academia."

Serralyn and Valliant.

She could guess where some of the "magical strides" had originated—but nothing remained static. Terrano had once traded his hard-won knowledge with some of the Barrani in an attempt to buy freedom for the cohort. Terrano's knowledge was practical. His lessons had been changed, studied, improved, and used in ways Terrano hadn't bothered to predict.

She wondered if Serralyn's knowledge would become more esoteric, and shook her head to clear it. What Serralyn would do was irrelevant in the immediate future, and the far future was unlikely to be Kaylin's problem.

"It is to Killian you wish to speak."

"And Karriamis," Kaylin replied.

"I would not advise that," Kavallac said. "I understand the stakes. I understand what is at play here. But one cannot take a Tower that does not, in the end, consent. Towers will test. The tests are dependent on the Towers; they were not and are not meant to be predictable. Fail that test, and you will be lucky to survive. Most were not meant to.

"Bellusdeo has asked questions very similar to yours."

Severn cleared his throat. "Did she ask Arbiter Starrante if his ability to weave portals could be used to access areas that are not within the Academia?"

It was hard to determine whether or not Starrante smiled in response. Kaylin felt guilty. She understood that Starrante was fond of Robin, and that Starrante's intervention had saved both the child and the library, but her visceral dislike of large, hairy insects made it difficult to relax. His spoken Barrani, while precise and perfect, was encased in something that sounded like insectoid *clicking*, which caused the hair on the back of her neck to rise.

She was grateful to Diarmat, though—a thought that she'd've bet she'd never have. His etiquette lessons meant she could interact with Starrante as Starrante deserved, in spite of her visceral response. Her fears were her problem; they shouldn't be made his.

Manners are choices, Diarmat had said. *Yours are appalling. In this class we will attempt to teach you to make better choices.*

She made better choices today, and hoped a day would come when giant talking spiders with multiple eyes seemed like just more people. It wasn't going to be this one.

"Yes, Corporal. Bellusdeo has asked."

"And your answer?"

"I can create portals easily between one part of the Academia and another; I have not yet attempted to create a portal that leads outside of these grounds."

Severn didn't ask why; he simply waited. Clearly, Starrante approved.

"There are risks inherent in the creation of such doors. You were not alive when *Ravellon* fell, and your history is perhaps incomplete."

"It is *deplorable*," Androsse interjected. People with power seldom had to learn good manners, or at least seldom felt the need to practice them.

"As I said, it is incomplete. We were architects of some of the doors that lead on to other worlds, other planes of existence. And it is through our architecture, in the end, that the Shadow spread to those worlds. Bellusdeo has spoken to us at length of the fate of her own world and her people.

"Were I to begin to recreate what was lost, the door itself would be vulnerable in the same way. It is a risk that we— the Arbiters—are not comfortable taking. Yes, it would provide knowledge and information, but it is incumbent upon teachers—and librarians—to assess when that knowledge is profoundly dangerous. We cannot put our students, or the Academia, at risk.

"Before you ask," he continued, when Kaylin opened her mouth, "it is also the will of the chancellor. He has mentioned the Arcanum, an august body of people who have, for their own purposes, taken risks that might well have destroyed this world. I believe you are familiar with the Arcanum."

Kaylin's newly acquired manners prevented her from spitting. That, and the certain sense that spitting in the library would probably be a capital crime. "Yes."

"Even were I to be familiar with Karriamis in the fashion that Candallar was before his death, I would not attempt to create a door between Karriamis and the Academia. I doubt that Karriamis would accept the attempted research. What we do in desperation and for survival is not what we should do when we have the time to reflect."

Severn nodded.

It was Kaylin who said, "Bellusdeo isn't the only person who wants to captain the Tower."

"No."

Killian was waiting for them when they left the library; it was almost dinnertime in the great hall, and having been given permission to eat there, Kaylin intended to do so.

"I will take you to the hall," Killian said, his Avatar materializing out of thin air. "I have always found that phrase interesting. Why is air described as thin?"

"You've asked other students this question before."

"I have asked very few; thin air is, when used in Barrani, an adopted concept. Answers to questions of this nature are very individual, and interesting in and of themselves, both for the similarity to other answers, and the differences. This way, please."

"Will the chancellor be at dinner?"

"Yes. So will the teachers. It is only at dinner that attendance is mandatory."

"For the chancellor?"

"Yes. It is otherwise considered mandatory for the students. Larrantin, in particular, feels that hungry students are artificially stupid students."

"Are there classes after dinner?"

"No; after dinner there are study periods, in which students attempt to work with and better understand the lessons of the day. We have a much smaller student body at the moment than we had the last time you visited—but the student body is now active and interested. The Academia is a type of freedom, rather than an inescapable cage—as it should be."

★ ★ ★

Kaylin was not surprised to see that the chancellor was not the only Dragon in attendance in the dining hall. Bellusdeo was also present. She sat beside the former Arkon at a long table that was elevated on a dais. Kaylin grimaced when she caught sight of the gold Dragon; it would have been impossible to miss her. Instead of the Imperial clothing she generally disdained, she was wearing Dragon armor, which apparently magically folded in the middle to allow her to sit.

Maggaron was beside her; he towered over the rest of the table, although his shoulders were slumped in a way that implied he was trying to minimize the difference in height.

Kaylin and Severn weren't offered a seat at the high table. If, in a distant childhood, she might have resented this as an obvious slight, no resentment followed. She'd learned that being important in specific ways often came with burdens that she was certain she couldn't carry. She couldn't captain a Tower. She couldn't be chancellor. She certainly couldn't carry the weight of an Empire; the thought that her decisions could cause the deaths of hundreds left her feeling queasy.

She gratefully avoided the scrutiny that Bellusdeo now endured.

"Hey!" Glancing in the direction of the voice, she saw Robin frantically waving an arm. He was seated between two Barrani, and as they turned, she saw Serralyn and Valliant. Serralyn's eyes were still unnaturally green; Valliant's were the usual green-blue that meant Barrani happiness.

"I have permission to eat dinner here," Kaylin said, as she made a place for herself on the long student bench.

"You're not dressed for it."

"No—but I wasn't told there was a dress code. I'm not a student; I think the chancellor would cut off both his hands— or both of mine—before he accepted me into the Academia."

Serralyn laughed. Valliant smiled.

"How's the first day been?"

"Perfect," Serralyn replied. She wasn't—or hadn't been—the most voluble of speakers when she had been a guest in Kaylin's home. "The only bad thing so far is that I haven't been allowed to visit the library."

"No?"

She shook her head. "There's a period of three months in which we have to do well enough to prove that we deserve the privilege. You were in the library today."

"We came from there."

"And Bellusdeo visits it."

Kaylin nodded again. "Neither of us are ever going to be students, though. We're visitors. If we have anything to prove, we proved it on our last visit."

"I'm not allowed to visit the library," Robin said cheerfully.

"But you've already seen it," Serralyn pointed out.

He had. But *visit* wasn't the word Kaylin would have used to describe it.

"I don't have any of the books," he told her. "I don't think I could read most of them."

"Me either," Valliant said, speaking the Elantran that Robin and Kaylin spoke. "There are so. Many. Languages."

"Are there language classes?"

Robin nodded. "But the best person to teach them is Arbiter Androsse, and he doesn't technically leave the library—so we have to reach a point where we can take classes in the library. Like, next year."

The idea that Robin was willing to work his butt off for the privilege of attending classes was a strange one for Kaylin, who had done her level best to avoid ever having to take another one. Some, like the surprisingly and bitterly useful etiquette lessons, had been mandatory, and she'd hated every minute she spent cooling her heels in a class where condescending men and women looked down their noses at her.

And maybe, she thought, she'd deserved some of that. It was not a comfortable thought.

The food was good. She expected that Robin would find almost anything acceptable as long as it was edible—they'd had similar childhoods, and anything was preferable to starvation. But it was simple food, not the fancier Barrani fare that Kaylin could eat but didn't enjoy. Barrani were often stuck up and arrogant, and even their *food* could make her feel self-conscious.

She found herself relaxing. This dining hall reminded her of the mess hall in the Halls of Law—except without the carvings and small burn marks on the surfaces of the tables and benches. It was large, and it was—as Starrante had implied—mostly empty. The student body present on the last visit had been largely imprisoned here. They were gone, now.

Only those students like Robin, and there were perhaps five in total, had chosen to remain; Robin had been almost terrified that he, like the rest of the people imprisoned here, would be unwanted. Kaylin understood his fear—she'd felt it herself. He was from the warrens, and she was from the fiefs. They both knew that they didn't belong, that there were better people.

And what they knew was wrong.

Didn't stop the doubts, but if a person couldn't live with a few doubts about themselves, they probably wouldn't survive long.

Serralyn and Valliant were new; they weren't the first new admissions, but they were the first to arrive. Packing up the almost nothing they owned had taken no time, and Serralyn was bouncing down the halls in her excitement and anticipation; nothing could have delayed her.

Kaylin thought there was a small chance that Sedarias had tried.

She listened to the three students—Robin, Valliant and Serralyn—as they chattered. To be fair, she mostly listened to Robin and Serralyn; Valliant didn't talk much. But she believed that his interest in the Academia was genuine; she was certain the Arkon—damn it! the *chancellor*—wouldn't have accepted his application if he wasn't.

She wondered what the dining hall would look like when all of the benches and tables were full. Decided it didn't matter. Ate while thinking.

Eventually, she swallowed and turned to Severn. "Bellusdeo is helping the Arkon."

Serralyn cleared her throat.

"The chancellor, sorry. Arkon was like his name for me, and I forget when I'm thinking."

"That's not what we generally call thinking," she said, her grin very reminiscent of Mandoran's.

"Can you hear the others while you're here?"

She nodded. That was a second change. She wondered if that was Killian's choice. Killian, not being Helen, did not immediately answer the question she hadn't asked aloud.

"Was that Mandoran?"

Serralyn laughed. "It was. He's bored."

"Luckily, that's not my problem." She turned once again to her partner. "Bellusdeo is helping the chancellor. Do you think the chancellor is concerned that the Shadows will somehow enter the Academia now that it's more corporeal?"

"If he isn't, she will be. I'm sure that's part of the reason she volunteered."

The other being Candallar's Tower. Kaylin kept this to herself, not because she wished to withhold information from the cohort—they already knew, now—but because she didn't wish to have an argument about the Tower with Sedarias, who was no doubt busy fighting for their survival in the High Halls in a very Barrani way.

"Look." Serralyn leaned across the table. "That's *Larrantin*."

He was the one Barrani man who was unmistakable, even

at this distance: his hair was gray, the white strands very white, the dark, very black. The only other Barrani Kaylin knew that had nonblack hair was the Consort. She had never asked if the hair had started out the normal color and changed.

"You've heard of him?" It was Severn who asked.

Serralyn nodded emphatically. "He was—even when we were sent to the green—almost a legend. He was offered one of The Three, did you know?"

Kaylin shook her head.

"He wouldn't take it. Or so the story goes."

"Sedarias doesn't believe it?"

Serralyn grimaced. "Of course not. It would have been an emblem of power and significance—what Barrani wouldn't want that?"

"I'm tempted to say a rational one, but I'm not sure I've met many."

To Kaylin's surprise, Valliant chuckled—but she couldn't be certain it was at anything she'd just said.

"You've met at least three," Serralyn replied. "But we probably have the luxury of being your version of rational because Sedarias is on our side."

"Can you ask Terrano if the Academia is barred to him?"

"Technically it's not barred to anyone at the moment. People can visit if they're willing to risk the fiefs. The chancellor can leave."

"No wonder Bellusdeo is now aiding the chancellor." Kaylin hadn't considered Shadow encroachment as a threat. No doubt the chancellor had, and Bellusdeo never, ever forgot about Shadow. She knew that Helen could detect and protect against most incursions—but not all. Even some of the Hallionne had been compromised in Kaylin's immediate experience.

The High Halls had also suffered from the influence and effect of Shadow. Of the heart of *Ravellon*. Kaylin had begun to distinguish between the two, but it was difficult. *Ravellon* had been home to Starrante's entire race; she wondered if there was something about either his abilities or his physical form that required whatever *Ravellon* had been before its fall.

Kaylin shook her head. "This place was completely free of any taint of Shadow except what Candallar and associates brought with them. The Academia had been here, undetected, for a long damn time—and the Shadows couldn't gain a foothold here while it was unoccupied."

Serralyn's eyes darkened for the first time in two days, but she nodded. "It's an interesting question. The people in the Academia—trapped almost in stasis—were free from the danger of Shadow. If Bellusdeo—or anyone in the Academia— could figure out why, they might be able to suspend whole worlds in the same way."

"You think that's possible?"

Serralyn said, "I hope it's possible. I don't know. It's one of the questions of import."

"I don't think the few lecturers the Academia retained will know, either."

"No. But they know more about sentient buildings than we do. They know more about the library we're not technically allowed to enter than we do. They know about Starrante. I really wanted to meet him."

Robin perked up. "You can."

"I'm not allowed in the library. Technically, neither are you."

"Starrante's the only librarian who can easily leave the library. I'm pretty sure he can't leave the Academia, though. He does this really cool thing with webs; he can build portals out of them. But he can stabilize spaces with them as well. It's not a magic that exists—or existed—among either Dragons or Barrani. He's a bit scary to look at, and sometimes when he's talking really close to my ear, it makes my spine tingle, because the clacking is terrible.

"But of the three Arbiters, I think he's the least dangerous." He paused, and then corrected himself. "He's the least likely to kill someone because he's angry."

"I'm surprised this place isn't crawling with Arcanists."

Serralyn grinned. "If it were up to the Arcanum, it would be."

"Arcanists aren't allowed as students?"

"They're already students—of the Arcanum. Given the difficulty Arcanists caused the past couple of weeks, when they worked to destabilize the Academia, I don't think anyone wants members of the Arcanum here *as* students."

Kaylin certainly didn't, but the choice wasn't hers.

"You've heard of at least one of them—I think you've met him a number of times, according to Teela."

Ugh. "Evarrim."

Serralyn nodded. "Teela doesn't hate him."

"He's saved my life, so I shouldn't."

"There's a chance he'll come here."

"He's very much part of the High Lord's inner court. The Consort trusts him. I can't imagine either of them would willingly cede him to student life."

Serralyn nodded. "It's the one advantage to having no power to speak of—no one cares what I do."

"Sedarias very definitely cares. So do the other ten."

"You know what I meant. I'm not useful in the same way. If Sedarias's attempts to rein in her family required my presence, I couldn't be here. Anyway, you should finish eating. You've been staring into space too much. If you're worried about the Dragon, you'll be seeing what she's doing firsthand from tomorrow."

"So will you."

In a much more serious tone, Serralyn said, "Mandoran

really *likes* Bellusdeo. For most of us, she's a Dragon. I mean, so's the chancellor, so it's not all bad, but…we were sent to the green because of the Dragon wars. Personal history doesn't immediately make Dragons objects of affection."

"Unless you're Mandoran."

"Unless you're Mandoran. To be fair, Annarion and Teela like her as well, just not in the same way."

"Oh?"

"Mandoran would happily have her join the cohort. I mean, he wanted to give you his name as well."

"So…he's more trusting."

"Not trusting, not exactly."

Valliant cleared his throat. "Mandoran tends to trust humor and affection. But he's always had good instincts. I think he could give you his name safely. Sedarias doesn't agree. And no one joins us without consensus."

In Kaylin's admittedly brief experience, consensus was not something the cohort could expect to achieve. But not even Sedarias attempted to use True Names the way the Barrani feared they would always be used.

"So if one of you wanted to share your True Name with someone else, they couldn't?"

"They could," Valliant said. "But you understand why none of us want that."

She did. She finished eating and rose. "I'll leave you guys to talk about the Academia and its local legends. Try not to get in trouble."

"You're not going to talk to the Dragon?"

Bellusdeo was engaged in conversation with the chancellor. "No thanks. I just ate."

Helen opened the front door before Kaylin reached it, and stood in its frame watching her as she made her way up the walk.

"You've eaten dinner, I assume," Helen said.

Kaylin nodded. "Has everyone else?"

"Sedarias has not returned yet, nor have her companions. Mandoran and Terrano are in the dining room with Fallessian and Torrisant." Kaylin had spent little time with the latter two; even in the larger group gatherings, they, like Valliant and Serralyn, tended to be silent. They were content to communicate with the cohort. And probably Helen. Kaylin was neither.

"Well?" Mandoran asked as she trudged into the dining room.

"I've eaten."

Hope squawked, but the sound was muted; he seemed tired. Or lazy. *I dislike the sound of Starrante's voice; it is very poorly modulated.*

Kaylin couldn't exactly criticize him for this. "Did you two visit Candallar?"

Terrano nodded.

"Did you visit the Tower?"

Silence.

"Why are you glaring at me?" Terrano demanded.

"I want an answer."

More silence. To Kaylin's surprise, it was Torrisant, the definition of strong and silent, who answered. "They tried." She had no idea whether or not this was true, but Terrano's eyes were blue now.

"Together or separately?"

"Together. Separate wouldn't usually matter, but Hallionne—and Helen—can usually separate us," Fallessian replied, picking up the conversation from where Torrisant had entered it.

"He means I can prevent them from speaking through their name bond, dear."

"It didn't seem safe for either of them to enter the Tower alone. Terrano didn't expect that it would be impossible to enter the Tower at all, and he's sulking."

These were more words than Kaylin had heard from Fallessian in the entire time she'd known him. Terrano had turned to physically glare in Fallessian's direction, which was unnecessary; if Terrano was actually annoyed, Fallessian couldn't avoid knowing.

Fallessian folded his arms.

Kaylin didn't want to be in the middle of this argument. She'd seen the cohort's arguments before; it usually ended up with some—or all—of them being sent to the training room in which all dangerous research was performed, and frequently ended with some of them disincorporating into splashes of livid color against the walls of that room.

But no, that wasn't it. If the lack of corporeal cohesion was disturbing—and it was—that wasn't what she wanted to avoid. She wanted to avoid a serious conflict between Bellusdeo and the cohort.

In the end, the cohort resolved their difficulties without murdering each other.

Bellusdeo wasn't one of them.

Helen could only keep Bellusdeo—or the cohort—safe if they were under this roof; she had no control when they left home.

This was why the Emperor hadn't wanted Bellusdeo living here. Kaylin had thought it stupid, and repented. In theory, the Dragon could handle the cohort; had they been twelve normal Barrani, it would have been a concern, but not enough to cause panic.

Only one of the twelve was normal Barrani. No, that wasn't true. The one who was normal wielded one of The Three—blades created to kill Dragons—and was a lord of the High Court, a former Arcanist, *and* an Imperial Hawk.

Kaylin was certain Teela wouldn't attempt to kill Bellusdeo. Not unless Bellusdeo attacked or attempted to kill one of the cohort. But if hostilities began between the two—Bellusdeo and cohort—that was bound to happen sooner or later.

She needed the conflict to be resolved *now*.

Fallessian rose from the dining table. He faced Kaylin fully. "We were created for war. We were created to fight—and kill—Dragons."

Kaylin nodded uneasily.

"In pursuit of the end of war, our people did things they should never have done."

"I'm sure the Dragons did things they should never have done, either."

Fallessian nodded. "None of the things the Dragons did prevented us from continuing as a species. Nothing they did stopped our children—few in number compared to mortals—from being born. But our Lords were willing to sacrifice us, and if we are angry, the anger is personal. We would feel far less anger had we not been *personally* abandoned. Except for Sedarias; in Mellarionne, they fought a tournament; the winner was selected."

"We almost committed genocide." His eyes were unblinking as they met Kaylin's. "That was the intent. And no, we don't know how it was accomplished. We know only that Bellusdeo is the last of the female Dragons, and the only one who can lay a clutch." He hesitated as Terrano turned to him; so did Torrisant. "She's like our only chance at redemption."

Kaylin's mouth was half-open; she closed it, staring at Fallessian. "Redemption? It's not like you personally had anything to do with near genocide; you almost died yourselves."

"That's what we've been telling him," Terrano said.

Fallessian shook his head.

"So you can accept that you were thrown away, but you can't accept that an act of war killed all the female Dragons?"

"We survived," he replied. "And if she survives, if she has children..." He trailed off, his skin slightly flushed. "I don't care," he snapped. "It's what I believe." He turned on his heel, as if he could not stand to remain in the physical presence of his friends.

The silence left in his wake was awkward verging on lethal.

"Don't look at me," Terrano said. "I think he's being an idiot."

Torrisant was one of the anti-Dragon faction among the cohort. It was probably why he spoke so little and avoided any chance of encountering Bellusdeo in person.

Mandoran, however, was not. "It's not that I like Dragons," he snapped. "But I like Bellusdeo, and we owe her. We'd've lost most of you if it weren't for that Dragon. We're important enough—to me—that I feel like the debt is huge. We should pay it."

"We can pay it when we're more established."

Mandoran snorted. "And when exactly is that going to be?"

"She's not our problem. In case you missed it, we've got problems of our own!" Torrisant's eyes were now indigo.

Fair enough. So were Mandoran's. Kaylin made her way—quickly—to the dining room door and headed to the safety of her room.

Kaylin knew Sedarias and the rest of the cohort were now at home. She was certain that the entire neighborhood—possibly half the city—could hear it. The cohort didn't need to actually speak when they were arguing, because they could read each other's thoughts with the ease of both comfort and long practice.

When their tempers frayed, they resorted to more physical interactions, many of which did not always involve having a properly corporeal body. If they couldn't be bothered to use unnecessary speech, they sometimes descended into what Kaylin could only describe as roaring.

And for people who claimed to dislike Dragons, there wasn't

a lot of difference in the volume and sound of the cohort's roars and the Dragons'—but there were more cohort.

She rolled over onto her stomach and pulled her pillow over her head, which dislodged small and squawky and caused his version of roar—angry bird noises.

"Kaylin," Helen's voice woke her fully as light flooded what had been a dark room.

"There's nothing I can do about the cohort and their arguments."

"It is not only the cohort involved in this argument."

Kaylin cursed in the foulest Leontine she knew.

06

Years of emergency work with the midwives' guild had their uses; Kaylin was fully dressed and ready to run in minutes. Helen opened the bedroom door as Kaylin approached it and stepped into the hall.

The hall was no longer the familiar hall composed mostly of doors that bore silhouettes related to their occupants. The warm wood tones of the floor had been stained or replaced by ebony, and the doors themselves were missing.

"Helen?"

"My apologies," Helen replied. "There is some destabilization."

"Caused by you or by the cohort?"

"A combination of both, I suspect. There has been—" the words were lost to roars of fury "—very little physical combat. I believe Maggaron was injured."

Kaylin, who intended to run to wherever the shouting originated, froze in place.

"The injury is minor, and it was not caused by the cohort."

"You're telling me Bellusdeo injured Maggaron? I don't believe it."

"Ah, no. It is slightly more complicated than that."

Hope squawked.

"Did you remove all the stairs?" Kaylin asked, having run to the end of the hall. Without reaching it.

"No, dear, but I'm not certain it's entirely safe."

"Then why did you wake me up?"

"I was not responsible for waking you, if you recall."

"You turned the lights on."

"True."

"Can you remake the stairs? No, belay that. Can you make a path that'll take me to wherever—" The rest of the words were drowned out. The roaring appeared to have lessened. "Now?"

"I am attempting to do so. I do not wish to have you open a door into a face full of fire."

"What *happened*?"

"Sedarias returned from the High Halls. There was some difficulty in those halls, but no deaths of significance to Sedarias." Meaning, none of the cohort had died. "Indeed. This was not the preference of a few of the Barrani in the High Halls, some of whom did. She was, however, not in the best of moods upon arrival."

"Yes and?"

"Bellusdeo arrived perhaps half an hour later—" Helen paused for the interruption of roaring and waited until most of it had passed. "She had a somewhat difficult day. She has not made direct contact with Candallar's Tower, but she has been patrolling the Candallar border, and she noticed anomalies there that she is not absolutely certain existed before Candallar's unfortunate fall. She has been working in concert with Tiamaris; such anomalies are of concern to Tiamaris and Tara.

"She is therefore somewhat sensitive."

"And she started shouting?" Or the Dragon equivalent thereof.

"Not immediately, no. But Terrano decided that tonight

was the night in which to sit down and discuss, civilly, the growing concerns the cohort has about the Tower of Candallar."

"And Sedarias didn't shut him up?"

"She did make the attempt. It was not appreciated. Her failure was...annoying. To her."

"So...most of the argument was between the cohort?"

"Ah, no. Terrano wanted to make clear *why* the cohort wanted to take the Tower."

Kaylin closed her eyes and her shoulders briefly slumped.

"Yes, dear. Their reasoning, while it makes sound sense to you in some fashion, offended Bellusdeo."

It would. A safe base of operations, while it might be provided by a fief Tower, was *not* the reason the Towers existed. And if Bellusdeo was already concerned about the state of the Candallar border, this was not a discussion she could be sanguine about.

"No. The argument started at that point, and rapidly grew heated. It was Fallessian who pointed out that the Tower might be the safest environment into which a Dragon clutch could be born; the Aeries of old are no longer in use—nor have they been reclaimed enough to be put to the use for which they were originally intended.

"Towers, like Hallionne, can create internal environments that would be largely safe to the young."

"Let me guess. Sedarias wasn't impressed."

"Ah, no. She has heard this before, I believe, but not spoken out loud."

"So Bellusdeo was also angry about that."

"Yes, dear."

"Can I strangle Terrano?"

"I would be tempted at this point to allow it, but unfortunately he is not entirely corporeal at the moment, and I don't think—"

"There's no way you could get your hands around my throat, is what she means," Terrano's disembodied voice said.

"I'm sure with Helen's help, we could manage. Why in the hells did you think that discussion was a good idea *tonight*?"

"If we wait for the right time, we'll never have it. I thought it'd be safer to have it here, with Helen, than in the open streets or the fief of Candallar—you're always so concerned about the fate of the civilians.

"And it was only loud, which I expected. I know we're not singly a match for the Dragon. It's like she's stepped out of every bedtime story—"

"You don't need to sleep."

"Fine. Every nursery story, better? She's what we were warned we'd be facing. But we're not what we were when we first heard those stories. There are ten of us here."

"Nine."

"Teela's here."

"She said she was moving out!"

"Yes, and that would have been useful for us, because she intended to occupy her rooms in the High Halls. But—she's here, too. If it helps, Tain's not."

"Look—the High Halls are not what they've been for most of Teela's life."

"No. They're sentient, now. The Tower of Test has become the heart of the High Halls."

"And the Tower doesn't frown on Barrani attempts to murder each other?"

"It's Barrani politics." She couldn't see Terrano, but she could almost hear his shrug.

"The Hallionne don't allow it. Helen, please, *stairs*." She could feel the ground tremble beneath her feet.

"That wouldn't be smart," Terrano said.

"If smart were your concern, you would have waited to have this stupid discussion!"

"Until when? This is going to be a problem, and you know it. You already know there are arguments brewing. And you know what the Dragon is like."

"That Dragon saved your lives."

"Some of them, yes. Look—it's not personal. We don't want the Tower to spite her or injure her. We're not trying to take something that's hers, okay?"

"You *don't get it*. The *reason* Candallar did whatever he did was because he *didn't care* about *Ravellon*. He didn't care about Shadow as more than an irrelevant passing concern. He *certainly* didn't care about the citizens of his fief."

"For Bellusdeo, someone with your needs captaining that Tower is—what's the word, Helen?"

"Anathema, I believe."

"Right. It's that. If she wasn't angry, if she expected competition, this is exactly the worst thing for her to hear if there are already problems with the Candallar border."

"We think she's wrong."

"Kaylin," Helen said. "I have created a bubble. Is it visible to you?"

"It's visible to me," Terrano said.

"Is your name Kaylin?" Kaylin snapped. Hope squawked.

"That has nothing to do with us—that's Helen's fault!" Terrano told Kaylin's familiar.

"Helen, is there more?"

The silence was heavy with hesitance. If buildings could exhale on an embarrassed sigh, this one now did. "There is one other factor. Teela is attempting—was attempting—to draw the debate to a close; Bellusdeo's eyes were a very disturbing shade of red. She roared—the roaring started with Bellusdeo—and it is possible that the person monitoring her from outside heard that roar."

"You're not talking about Emmerian, are you?"

"Yes, dear. I'm sorry."

"So...you let Emmerian in."

"I had hoped that he would have a calming effect on Bellusdeo, or at least on the debate itself."

Terrano had found the bubble that Helen had created. Kaylin knew this because he cohered within the space, becoming the annoying Barrani cohort member she knew. Kaylin couldn't see the bubble itself, but understood that it was where Terrano currently stood. She moved quickly to join him.

"We'd probably lose at least a person or two to Bellusdeo if we were fighting at all fair. And if Helen allowed us *to* fight."

Since neither of these things—fair fighting or Helen's approval—were likely to happen, Kaylin snorted.

"But we're not really keen on fighting two Dragons. Teela called *Kariannos* only after Emmerian burned down half the dining room."

"*Emmerian* did?"

"Yes, dear."

Kaylin reached the ground floor. If Emmerian had, as Helen said, burned down half the building, it was the back half.

"No. But I elected to move everyone, given the unfortunate heat of the argument."

In anyone else, this would have been an attempt at black humor. In Helen's case, the description was likely literal.

"Are they in the training rooms?"

"They are in a variant of the training room that I have not had cause to use for a *very* long time."

"You do remember that Emmerian is part of the Dragon Court, right?"

"Yes, dear."

"And that shutting him in a windowless dungeon is likely to be frowned on by the Emperor?"

"Burning down half a building is also frowned on by the Emperor."

"So, wait—the roaring is coming from the training room?"

Since the answer was now obvious to Helen, she failed to reply.

Kaylin glanced at Terrano. "Just what in the hells did you guys do?"

"Us? In case it's escaped your attention, none of us are fire-breathers. We tend to, what is that phrase, Helen? Use our words."

"So does Emmerian. I don't think I've ever seen him truly Dragon-angry. Not like this. You're *sure* it was Emmerian?"

"She's sure," Terrano replied, before Helen could. "It's not like the rest of us don't recognize him. He might not stand out compared to the Emperor or the Arkon, but he's a *Dragon*. We're not likely to miss him."

The basement stairs, usually an unstable spiral around a central column, were not the stairs Kaylin recognized. This was good; Terrano had been walking almost in lockstep with Kaylin, and they wouldn't both fit, otherwise.

There was no central pillar here. The kitchen closet door opened out onto a large, flat platform. Across from the door, steps that wouldn't look out of place in the High Halls appeared; they led down. Solid walls formed boundaries on either side, and torches—well, sort-of torches in that the light didn't flicker at all—followed the incline into the darkness.

All things equal, Kaylin vastly preferred these stairs, but had a suspicion that the previous iteration existed to underscore the dangers the various rooms here contained.

The stone beneath her feet shook; here, the roaring was more felt than seen—a destructive act of nature, not an act of communication.

"Terrano, move *faster*!"

"I'm trying," he snapped.

Kaylin reached out, caught his hand, felt a small, sharp

shock as their palms made contact. "I really, *really* think we don't have time to meander." She picked up the pace; Helen's bubble was almost certainly centered around Kaylin, not one of the most difficult members of the cohort. Dragging him by the hand as if he were an errant foundling, she began to run.

The training room was only a room if one called enormous, grand halls rooms. Kaylin, not an architect of any kind, didn't quibble. There were large, closed doors at the far end—one suited for very fancy carriages and wagons; were it not for the intricate details carved into the wood of those doors, Kaylin might have confused it for the doors that fronted loading docks on account of their size.

Hope was now standing on her shoulder, his body upright and canted slightly forward. He squawked. Since she couldn't understand the words, she assumed they weren't meant for her.

The doors rolled open. She forgot about the doors as they rolled to either side, as if pushed by invisible hands.

The hall they opened into wasn't composed of the bare walls of the previous training room. The ceilings here were high, the halls wide, and the walls for as far as the eye could see—and admittedly Kaylin's vision had nothing on Barrani or Dragon sight—were decorated with statues, engravings, small alcoves. Every decorative detail was rendered in stone.

Some of that stone had melted, but even as Kaylin's gaze swept across the mess, form reasserted itself.

"How far away from your core is this?" Kaylin asked.

Helen didn't answer.

Kaylin and Terrano entered the hall. At this distance, she couldn't see people.

"They are there," Helen said, although Kaylin hadn't spoken aloud. "Most of the cohort is—or was—less corporeal."

A flash of blue lightning changed the color of the hall. "Is that Teela?"

"Yes, dear. I did say most."

"Are both of the Dragons draconic?"

Helen didn't answer.

The hall was longer than most city blocks. Kaylin, who had to patrol, was familiar with the length of those blocks. She'd traveled three before she could see the Dragons. She could also see Maggaron.

Teela was not actively attempting to harm either the gold Dragon or the blue one. Maggaron stood by the gold Dragon's side, not in front; he was wielding a great sword in one hand. Teela appeared, at this distance, to be talking. The Dragons were speaking as well, but Kaylin didn't understand a word of it, which was probably for the best.

Hope squawked; he was a storm of squawking as Kaylin picked up the pace.

I am going to ask Helen, Severn unexpectedly said, *if I might remain under her roof for a while.*

Stay where you are, Kaylin told him. *We don't need any more combatants.* She exhaled.

"Teela!"

Teela's gaze remained fixed on the two Dragons; her sword continued to glow and crackle, as if it were the barely controlled heart of a storm. She spoke two words, or what might have been two words; her voice carried as if it were draconic.

"Yes," Helen said quietly. "Teela does understand rudimentary Dragon. She is making herself heard, here, in a multitude of ways."

"She's impressive," Terrano whispered. "I mean—we all knew she had one of The Three, and we all knew she'd distinguished herself on the battlefield. But it's different to see it with our own eyes."

"The eyes most of you don't possess right now on account of having no physical form?"

"Those ones, yes."

Teela wasn't trying to hurt Emmerian. She was trying to survive him. Bellusdeo's roars, which, at a distance, Kaylin assumed were aimed at the Barrani cohort, were now apparently aimed at Emmerian. The blue Dragon had stepped between Bellusdeo and Teela, and his claws had cracked stone; he didn't intend to be dislodged.

"Helen, what *happened*?"

"A discussion became heated. It broke down. People lost their tempers."

"How did Emmerian join this so-called discussion?"

"The beginning took place in the dining room, and the dining room windows were actual windows at the time. Lord Emmerian doesn't approve of this; he considers the windows a weakness assassins might exploit. As of this evening, I am almost willing to concede his point."

If Kaylin had been closer to an actual wall, she would have banged it with her forehead. "Where is the rest of the cohort?"

"They are with Teela, but phased."

"Do you consider Emmerian and Bellusdeo more of a threat than the cohort?"

"To whom?"

"Teela!"

Teela did look away from Emmerian as Kaylin's voice penetrated her concentration. Even from this distance, Kaylin could see the color of her eyes; they were indigo. They were almost black. "Go back to your room," the Barrani Hawk told Kaylin.

This caught Bellusdeo's attention. And Emmerian's. Kaylin almost let go of Terrano's hand, but decided against it given what remained of the conflict.

Hope squawked up a storm, and as he did, Bellusdeo's draconic form dwindled, the scales becoming the armor that

Dragons wore in their human forms. There was, in theory, magical clothing that could withstand the transformation between the two forms, but Kaylin had never personally seen it happen. Maggaron now towered over Bellusdeo. As did Emmerian. Although Emmerian did shift his enormous head in Kaylin's direction, his eyes were a blood red that implied death.

Kaylin noted the position he had taken—or at least the part where he'd inserted himself between Bellusdeo and Teela, and winced.

Hope squawked again, and Emmerian blinked.

Blinked and then turned to look over his shoulder.

Kaylin couldn't see Bellusdeo's expression; she could only see her profile. Emmerian, however, was closer, and Dragons had better vision regardless. He swiveled his head toward Teela again. Toward Teela and the phased cohort.

Teela grimaced.

"She's going to put up the sword," Terrano whispered.

"She probably wants to keep her job," Kaylin replied, just as quietly.

The sword vanished. Only when it was gone did Emmerian dwindle in size and shape; he wore indigo armor, streaked in a black that gleamed.

"She is going to be so pissed off at him," Kaylin told Terrano.

"Maybe I can hide with Emmerian," Terrano replied. "Sedarias is *furious*."

"With you?"

"Maybe?"

The sleep that had been interrupted by the conflict had fled to another continent.

"Are they done now?"

They had better be, Hope said. He wasn't sleeping—or slumping, which was probably more accurate—either. He was alert, and if small, transparent lizards could look furious, he did. She had rarely seen Hope angry. Annoyed, yes. Irritated, yes. Possibly outraged or shocked. This was different.

Helen was more worried than angry, but Helen felt responsible for the safety of her guests.

Kaylin was neutral. She wanted what Helen wanted: everyone to get along like civilized people. Or a variant of civilized that included far less Barrani etiquette.

"We will not repair to the dining room," Helen said, in a voice that could be heard by anyone standing in the long, wide hall, "until we are certain we are all calm enough to speak."

Squawk.

"Especially you."

Calm enough to speak took surprisingly little time, given the presence of Teela's sword and a livid member of the Dragon Court.

Helen's Avatar had joined them all; she was wearing obsidian armor, and it matched the color of her eyes. This seemed to suggest to the cohort that silence was golden.

"They are not being silent in the traditional sense," Helen said. "This is not the first time that there has been conflict among my guests. You are *all* aware of the danger inherent in losing your tempers. All of you. Were you to have had this discussion anywhere else—in the fiefs, in the streets—any part of *Ravellon* that had been sleeping would be wide awake.

"Annarion."

Annarion was corporeal; the entire cohort now was, although it had taken far longer than the transformations of the Dragons.

He nodded, less grim than chagrined. "Please accept my apologies," he said, bowing deeply to Helen.

Terrano, true to his word, remained with Kaylin. Mandoran detached himself from the general group and joined them.

"Serralyn and Valliant are still in the Academia, right?"

It was Mandoran who nodded. Barrani didn't require sleep, but on occasion, looked like they should revisit that concept. This was one of those occasions. "Serralyn wasn't really worried. Valliant was, but she managed to talk him out of storming Helen."

"Serralyn wasn't worried?"

Mandoran shrugged. "Helen wasn't about to let any of us kill each other."

"What started this?" Kaylin kept her voice low out of habit; it wasn't going to stop the cohort from hearing her or being aware of her. It wasn't going to stop the Dragons, either.

"Terrano wanted to discuss—"

"I meant, what started the actual fighting?"

"Terrano's discussion was the top of a very steep incline." He grimaced.

"And that led to this?"

"Indirectly. Look—you weren't here, and you were lucky to miss it. Take my word for this."

Helen cleared her throat. "I believe we are clear to move to the dining room. We will have a very early breakfast."

No one wanted to claim credit for the eventual outcome of the first attempt at discussion. Kaylin didn't blame them. Maybe she was being unfair, but the two people who had shocked her the most were Teela and Emmerian. She would have understood if the cohort had drawn swords, either singly or collectively, but none of the cohort were armed with Teela's sword. Teela knew what it meant; she knew why it had been created.

She understood what had set Bellusdeo's teeth on edge; Shadow—to Sedarias—was pragmatically irrelevant to her concerns. It was not, and would never be, irrelevant to Bellusdeo. Bellusdeo losing her temper, given the loss of her *entire world* to Shadow, also made sense.

Kaylin wanted to speak with Emmerian.

"I think that would be wise, dear," Helen said. She had ditched the armor, but her eyes remained the color-flecked obsidian that Kaylin disliked.

Emmerian, in indigo armor, turned at the sound of Helen's voice. No doubt he heard what Kaylin didn't; Helen was capable of speaking to individuals in a way no eavesdroppers could hear. He turned to Kaylin. His eyes were red. No surprise there.

"Can you keep things more or less civil until we're done?" Kaylin whispered to Mandoran.

"Why me? You have no idea what kind of mood Sedarias is in."

"I can guess. Bellusdeo's only marginally better. I'm not sure this is an agree-to-disagree discussion—but it *has to be.*"

Mandoran nodded.

Bellusdeo, for her part, glanced once at Emmerian; her eyes were flecked with hints of orange in a sea of red. Of the two, it was Emmerian who was angriest. Or most worried. The colors indicated good moods and bad moods, but the underlying reasons for either were left as an exercise for the observer.

"I will commit," the golden Dragon said, "to not burning any part of Helen down."

Helen ushered people into the dining room, leaving Kaylin and Emmerian in the hall. Kaylin then headed toward the parlor, wondering how large it would be this time.

She waited until the door closed before she faced the red-eyed Dragon head-on. "What were you thinking, exactly? Helen says you burned down a third of the house. Or tried."

To her surprise, Emmerian shrugged. "It was not my intent

to harm Helen; I did not believe—and do not believe—that I could. Not with a cursory breath."

"I don't think she let you in so you could set things on fire." Kaylin waited until Emmerian took a seat; the parlor itself was a small, cozy room, the table between them both high and small.

"No, dear, I did not."

"Why did you, as the corporal put it, let me in?"

"You are generally rational, objective, and pragmatic. I had hoped that your presence might calm Bellusdeo."

Emmerian bowed his head. He left it in the bent position, hands in his lap palm-down, as if he were studying them.

"She's going to be angry," Kaylin said, her tone softening.

"I am aware of that. She is angry now."

"So you thought it would be better if she were angry at you?"

He raised his head; his eyes had shifted, finally, from blood red to a red with orange bits that was the usual indicator of Dragon anger. Or at least Dragon anger when it was under control and not the driver.

"No. Thinking was not part of my actions. I am familiar with the cohort on paper; I have never seen them in action."

"Bellusdeo *has*."

He nodded. "I have no other explanation to offer. For what it's worth, you have my genuine apology. I did not intend—" He stopped. "You are correct. Bellusdeo has lived in the same environs as the cohort. I should not have interfered."

"Did you think they were going to kill her?"

"I told you, Corporal: I did not think. Yes, on some visceral level, I believed she was in danger. I will tender my apologies to Bellusdeo, and perhaps I will assign less…draconic observers in future."

Kaylin wasn't certain the Emperor would agree.

"Can you maybe not mention this entire thing to the Emperor?"

Emmerian's smile was almost rueful. His eyes were now orange. "It is never wise to attempt to hide things from the Emperor." His lids fell shut, obscuring the color of his eyes. "I will apologize directly to Bellusdeo, and with Helen's permission, will take my leave."

Kaylin wasn't quite finished yet.

"Why did Teela draw her sword?"

"I believe she hoped it would shock me into sensibility. She did not attempt to injure me; she did not draw it—at all—when Bellusdeo chose to make a point by transforming."

A knock sounded at the closed door. Emmerian tensed, but said nothing.

"Come in."

The door rolled open on Bellusdeo. Maggaron was not with her. Emmerian rose instantly. She met his gaze; he broke what might have become a staring contest by offering her a complete, graceful bow. "My apologies," he said.

"For what?"

"I should not have interfered in the fight you had chosen."

"No. You shouldn't. It implies you think I can't take care of myself. Or worse, that I am somehow your responsibility."

Technically, given the Imperial command, she kind of was. Kaylin kept that firmly to herself. If Bellusdeo had not been blocking the door, she'd've been out it so fast she'd have caused her own windstorm.

Hope squawked.

"I should not have transformed," Bellusdeo said, looking in Kaylin's direction. "I was...angry."

Emmerian said nothing.

Squawk.

"Yes, I know." She then stepped into the parlor, where a chair waited for her. Her eyes were orange, now, but a hint of something metallic, maybe copper, had changed the natural color. "I will not ask you," she told Emmerian, "not to mention the events of this evening. I understand the oaths you have sworn to your lord, and I know enough about you by now to know that it is an impossible request."

He nodded. Kaylin expected a certain wariness; it was absent.

"Did you think that you would be able to withstand what I could not?"

"No. I was not thinking at all. They were Barrani; you were a lone Dragon. It has been centuries since I have been victim to instinct and instinctive acts of violence."

"Instincts kept me alive," she replied, the line of her shoulders softening. She took the empty chair. "Helen?"

"Yes, dear."

"Might we both get a drink?"

Kaylin had no illusions about who *both* meant. She left the room. Hope hesitated—notable by the tightening of his claws—but said nothing; he left with his portable chair.

07

Kaylin wasn't privy to the discussion between the two dragons, as she'd fled the room, but no roaring followed her departure, which she took—given the events of the very early morning so far—as a good sign.

"I'm sorry," Helen's voice said. "I did try to warn him—but he was, as he said, reacting entirely instinctively. I don't believe he'll mention Teela's sword."

"Unless asked."

"Unless asked," Helen agreed. "He is really quite ashamed of his part in the difficulty."

Kaylin understood it.

"Yes, dear. Because you would have done the same thing—but with far poorer results, in my opinion."

"He burned down part of the house!"

"He caused damage that was, in the end, trivial to repair. I am not sure you would have survived—and I consider that far worse."

Fair enough. Emmerian might not have spent all of his adult life fighting a war—a losing war—but he was still a Dragon.

"Teela isn't angry with him. She understands the reaction."

"And the rest of the cohort?"

"Are in the dining room." Meaning, Kaylin could find out for herself. As there was no point in going back to bed—she wouldn't sleep anyway, and if she did, she'd mess up her first day of new duties—she headed toward the open dining room door.

All of the cohort, with the exception of Serralyn and Valliant, had taken up chairs in the dining room. The cohort often just occupied a large corner of the floor, their arms, legs, and bodies overlapping like a puppy pile; they were all seated at the table, as if this were a council of war.

They were silent until Kaylin entered, but that certainly didn't mean they weren't talking. Or arguing, given the thunderous expressions and deeply blue eyes of half of them.

Mandoran was not among that half, and Terrano was at the foot of the table—as far from Sedarias as it was physically possible to be. He was emotionally close to Sedarias—Kaylin privately believed she was one of the people he'd missed the most when he'd chosen total freedom—but that didn't mean he enjoyed her anger.

A chair appeared for her at the table. Given the color of the sky, it was an hour before breakfast, and breakfast had never been a full-house affair. Plates began to appear on the table.

Everyone turned to look past the food at Kaylin.

"I didn't say anything!"

"It's Helen," Terrano said. "You don't have to say anything. Why are you always hungry, anyway?"

"It's not that I'm always hungry, it's just that I learned to eat when food was available." Because mostly, it hadn't been.

Sedarias looked at the plate set in front of her as if it was a cockroach. She didn't complain that it was there. In true Sedarias fashion she accepted its presence as Helen's prerogative. She didn't eat, though.

Teela, blue-eyed, did. Although she was no longer in residence officially—she'd moved in for the duration of the preparation for the Test of Name—she'd been spending time in the rooms Helen had created for her use. In theory, she'd moved out after the cohort had, as a collective, passed the Test of Name. Given Emmerian's presence tonight, Kaylin was grateful for the difference between theory and practice.

Kaylin also ate. Among other things, it gave her something to do with her hands. It also gave her an excuse not to talk, as she'd finally mastered the art of chewing and swallowing before she opened her mouth. This had been surprisingly difficult.

The sound of only Kaylin chewing and swallowing filled the silent room. Kaylin put down her fork. "What exactly happened earlier?" She spoke to Teela.

"You pretty much saw it yourself," Terrano began.

"Fine. Don't talk about the parts I saw." She was still looking at Teela.

Teela was silent.

"Teela."

"Yes?"

"You drew your damn sword."

"I considered it wise, but it was purely precautionary. I made no attempt to injure either Lord Emmerian or Bellusdeo." Teela also set her fork down, swiveling in her chair to face Kaylin.

"Emmerian didn't go full Dragon for no reason." Kaylin folded her arms. She had never liked it when Teela's eyes were this color, but she wasn't thirteen anymore.

"He is unaccustomed to the cohort. I don't believe Bellusdeo felt threatened by the turn the argument took." She exhaled. "Lord Emmerian is generally levelheaded, but Bellusdeo is important to the Dragons. I believe he overreacted. I had no desire to harm him. I merely wished to show him—"

"That you could?"

"That it would be costly were he to attempt to kill us—any of us—yes."

Fair enough. Even Emmerian had said he'd lost his temper. "Why, exactly, did Bellusdeo go full Dragon?"

"That is not a question to ask of us."

"Fine. Why did you—or most of you—disincorporate?"

"Face full of angry Dragon," Terrano muttered. He then winced.

"No, please do continue," Sedarias said sweetly. Sweet, it was clear, was a poison, and possibly a deadly one. "Since this was entirely started by you."

"I just wanted to settle the question of the Tower and the fiefs. And it was better to do it here than do it on the actual site."

Kaylin had no argument with that. Her guess as to how things unfolded was probably right: the cohort's reason for wanting the Tower would offend the hells out of Bellusdeo, the only person present who had firsthand experience with what Shadow could and would do to an entire world if given its freedom.

"I don't suppose you've decided to step back?" she asked Sedarias.

Sedarias said a cold, loud nothing.

Severn's arrival saved them all from a conversation that was going to be entirely pointless.

Bellusdeo did not leave the house early; she remained in the parlor with Emmerian while Helen escorted Severn back to the questionable safety of the dining hall. Helen had a chair waiting for him by the time he entered the room, and breakfast as well.

"Didn't you already eat?" Terrano asked, as Kaylin joined him.

"When we head out for the day, we're often forced to skip lunch," Kaylin replied. "This is lunch."

Terrano rolled his eyes. "I can't sit here and watch you do nothing but eat." He rose.

"You're not coming with us."

"You can't stop me."

"Helen can."

"Not easily."

"*I* can," Sedarias said.

No one was stupid enough to argue with that.

"Mandoran is coming with us." Kaylin offered this as a concession.

"Given the Dragon's mood?" Mandoran said; he'd been almost entirely silent, which was unlike him.

"I'm going out with her, and she's probably taking her mood with her."

"You're getting paid."

She had better be. And even if the current special assignment tripled her pay, Kaylin wasn't certain it was worth it. Since Imperial Command meant do it or be out of the job you otherwise loved, it wasn't about the money. Well, not *entirely* about the money; here, pay was the consolation prize. She would also be much, much happier to have none of the cohort with them, given the events that had pretty much thrown her out of bed in a panic.

Mandoran groused, but when Kaylin and Severn rose to leave—at Helen's less than subtle prompting—he rose as well. His eyes were very blue, but that wasn't necessarily because of Bellusdeo.

Bellusdeo started the rest of her day—which involved the expected incursion into the fiefs—in Dragon armor. Kaylin stared at it. She opened her mouth once, but words failed to emerge.

"I have already destroyed another dress," Bellusdeo said, answering the words Kaylin hadn't said. "And there's no guarantee I won't be forced to fight. I see no reason my possible emergencies should deplete the Imperial coffers further."

"Did Emmerian—Lord Emmerian—leave?"

"He is currently speaking with Helen. And no, I do not believe they require interruption. If, however, you don't intend to accompany me, please feel free to join them." Her smile was very toothy.

She was going to attract a lot of attention on her way to the fiefs. She was going to attract even more when she was in them. Kaylin exhaled; Severn offered a brief grin, but no words.

Maggaron accompanied Bellusdeo, looking far taller than he normally looked on the rare occasions he chose to leave his own rooms. Mandoran kept to one side of Kaylin, which was the side Bellusdeo wasn't occupying. Severn fell in beside Maggaron. This wasn't as hard as it might have been otherwise, given the differing lengths of their respective strides; Maggaron was used to walking far more slowly when he accompanied his Dragon.

"Look," Mandoran said, breaking an unusual silence. "I'm personally sorry about what happened last night."

Bellusdeo glanced at him.

Whatever Emmerian and Bellusdeo had discussed had caused her eyes to ramp down into a more normal, cautious orange.

Mandoran's remained blue. When Bellusdeo failed to answer his peace offering, he changed the subject. "So...where are we going today?"

"That will have to be a surprise," the Dragon replied, and this time she did smile.

"I think I'm done with surprises for now."

"Optimist."

Kaylin wanted the answer to Mandoran's question as well,

but left it alone. It's not like they weren't going to find out anyway. It would just take longer.

And she really didn't want to set off either Mandoran or Bellusdeo in the city streets. Maggaron was already enough of a visual draw that people were staring, moving, or on the edge of panic.

Bellusdeo chose to cross the bridge over the Ablayne into the fief of Tiamaris. There were other bridges—and other gates—but Tiamaris had two advantages. One, its fieflord was currently still a member of the Dragon Court, and therefore beholden to the Emperor in a way no other fieflords were, and two, even if it was constantly under construction in one way or another, the construction spoke of hope, not despair.

There was more foot traffic into Tiamaris than Kaylin thought normal—but normal for the fiefs, or at least Tiamaris's fief, had been steadily increasing ever since he made the Tower his own.

Kaylin mulled. Tiamaris hadn't taken the Tower because it was a necessary bastion against the incursion of Shadow. She'd never actually asked why he'd done so; at the time, it was perfectly clear that he had made his choice, and only death would change it—no, that was wrong. Death would render it irrelevant.

Sedarias's desire to have a Tower of their own made sense to Kaylin. In the early days of her childhood and youth, she would have wanted the same thing.

It was entirely possible that the person who the Tower accepted would be like Tiamaris or Sedarias, not like Bellusdeo. The decision, given Kaylin's limited experience, seemed to be in the hands of the *Tower*, not the Dragon or the Barrani. And that made sense because it was the Tower who was going to have to live with the captain. If the Towers weren't sentient, it wouldn't matter.

But Tara with Tiamaris was happy.

Tara without had been on the point of breakdown.

"You're thinking," Bellusdeo said, once they'd crossed the bridge.

"I've been told it's helpful."

"To who?"

"Me, according to every pissed-off teacher I've ever had."

"How did that work out for them?"

"Well, I told them what I was thinking and apparently that didn't qualify as thought. So, probably not as well as it should have."

Bellusdeo grinned. Tiamaris was a comfortable place for the gold Dragon. For one, draconic form was not illegal here, and for two, Bellusdeo could therefore fly. The airspace was smaller than it would have been over the city proper, but she'd break no laws if she chose to do so. Mostly, she didn't, but she chafed at Imperial expectations, and here there were fewer of them.

In general, she respected—possibly even admired—Imperial Law. But forbidding Dragons their draconic forms was like forbidding them half of their selves. Kaylin understood the reasoning for it, and the Swords, if asked, would trumpet the importance of that denial for as long as it took to be heard. But their job was crowd control when citizens were panicking; Kaylin's wasn't. People were people everywhere—they strongly disliked anything that added more work to their desks.

Because Kaylin knew a lot of the Swords—as lunch companions if not beat partners—she had some sympathy for their position. Their position was guided by Imperial Law, nothing else. And people *would* panic.

Bellusdeo believed that if Dragons were allowed to *be* Dragons everywhere, panic would go away; it would become a mundane event, much like wagons in the streets.

Kaylin, as a non-Dragon, couldn't agree. She understood

why Bellusdeo hated it; she understood that, in Bellusdeo's world, Dragons had been better than Shadow; they'd become a sign of comfort, rather than a sign of impending death. But Elantra wasn't that world. Not yet, and hopefully not ever.

Kaylin had no idea what the laws that governed the Academia were; it hadn't occurred to her to ask. "We're not going to visit the Arkon?"

"Lannagaros, or, in your case, the chancellor, and no, not immediately. I have nothing to report yet."

"Yet?"

Bellusdeo turned down the street that led from Tiamaris to the Academia, where she said she wasn't going. "I have one potential meeting today, possibly two if the first meeting is brief."

"When you say potential, do you mean you have an appointment?"

The Dragon snorted. With smoke. "You were curious about one of the fiefs when we did our brief pass through it. We are going to that fief in an attempt to speak with the man who owns the Tower with the…happy face adornment that can be seen from the air."

Durant. Durant was the name of the fief, and therefore the name of the current fieflord. That was the sum total of what Kaylin knew about the fief, that and the fact that the buildings on the *Ravellon* border were in decent repair. In Nightshade, decent repair would have meant occupied; she was less certain about Durant.

Durant bordered the Ablayne for a small fraction of its Elantra-facing border length; most of Durant was walled off on the Elantra-facing border. Bellusdeo hadn't been all that concerned about the Elantra border; Kaylin, a Hawk, paid more attention. The wrong activities near the borders of the city fell squarely into the Hawks' domain.

But if things went to hell, it would be a far larger problem than the Hawks were created to handle. The Towers weren't the Halls of Law, but they were absolutely necessary. On this, both Kaylin and Bellusdeo could agree.

"You use the Academia as a pass-through now?"

"It seems safest. I am highly concerned with the possible effects of Shadow on its current, solid form; Lannagaros is aware that it might become an issue. The Academia is not under the remit of the Towers, but is somehow engaged with them or linked to them. It is the reason that I have agreed to undertake these...scouting missions for Lannagaros."

"What does Killian think?"

"He agrees that it could be a possible concern. As a sentient building, he accrues knowledge from my visits, and he has also been encouraging. My discussions with Arbiter Starrante have been inconclusive. His racial ability—the creation of portals—is, we all believe, a possible danger or weakness, but he would not do anything to endanger the Academia now. In the future, there may be more experimentation, but Starrante is not necessarily eager to do so."

"So the Academia is nothing like the Arcanum."

"Nothing at all like the Arcanum. Even were it once, Lannagaros is chancellor. Here," she added, for no reason that Kaylin could see. "This is the Durant boundary."

As they'd been walking through streets that looked entirely normal—if in very solid repair—Kaylin was a bit surprised. "So the streets never change anymore?"

"They don't. It's been suggested that it would be of use if the prior border zone effects could—in a much smaller area—be deliberately deployed. Lannagaros is against this," she added. "His current drive is to open the Academia to students. The border zone made this all but impossible, and until the Academia is much more established..." Bellusdeo shrugged. It was clearly not the choice she would have made, but she understood and grudgingly accepted it.

Kaylin felt no difference in the streets—or no immediate difference—when she crossed what Bellusdeo had labeled a border. Like borders in the city proper, it was a thing of paper and theory for most of the people who traversed the city streets. Not that the paper wasn't important, because laws cropped up around such papers, but it didn't materially affect most of the citizens.

As they entered Durant, conversation stopped. Severn was far more alert, as was Maggaron. Bellusdeo wasn't, but she didn't really have to be—nothing that the streets naturally produced was likely to harm a Dragon.

Hope, draped across Kaylin's shoulders, shifted position, moving slowly. He, too, was alert in a fashion, but he wasn't alarmed. Not yet.

Kaylin resented Nightshade as she looked through these streets. Although none of the buildings here were new, and none as solid as the newly revealed buildings that surrounded the Academia, they were in decent repair.

"Repairs," Bellusdeo said, intuiting Kaylin's reaction from her expression, "cost money. You are employed as a Hawk. What similar employ exists in Nightshade?"

Kaylin had no answer.

No, Nightshade said. *The answers are not simple.*

You didn't care.

I accepted the responsibility of stewarding the borders; I did not accept responsible for the citizens.

Is this how you would have ruled your own family?

She felt his amusement. Hated it. Wondered how Annarion would have felt.

He would feel as you feel, Nightshade replied, *as you well know. Where are you?*

I am, oddly enough, in the Academia. I have an appointment with the chancellor in less than an hour.

Have you ever met Durant?

No. I have encountered Liatt once.

"Have you talked to Liatt?" Kaylin asked Bellusdeo.

"No, not yet. I have spoken with Farlonne at length; she is the only fieflord to make herself instantly and readily available."

She would, Kaylin thought. Bellusdeo was a Dragon. But that was unfair. Farlonne clearly took the reason for the Tower's existence seriously—as seriously as Bellusdeo herself did. If Bellusdeo's first war with Shadow had ended in failure, there were still lessons to take from that failure. Farlonne was probably willing to learn them.

What was Liatt like?

Surprising. I feel I should offer a warning, however.

What warning?

You expect that Liatt and Durant—both human—are mortal as you are. Ah, no, as most of the Hawks are. You will find that this is not necessarily the case. Go back to Records, and look at the fief demarcations. In at least one case, were Durant to be like your Hawks, he would be well over eighty years old. Liatt would be…older.

What? Wait.

I am not, at the moment, going anywhere. I like the Academia. It is surprising to me. It reminds me of my youth. The better parts of it, he added. *And I confess that I am very pleased with the chancellor. Killian, however, keeps his distance. Yes,* he said, before Kaylin could even think the words, *he is not so distant with you. He has reason to trust you, just as Helen or the Hallionne did.*

He doesn't trust you? This shouldn't have come as a surprise to Kaylin.

We use the word trust *in different fashions. Killian is Barrani, or close; I am Barrani. The cohort is not, in Killian's eyes. We do not insult each other by open trust. Trust is given to those who cannot harm us—although it is still a risk. It is far simpler for the cohort to trust you than it would be for them to trust me. Or any Lord of the High Court. Regardless, what you are is not what I am; Killian interacts with me as if I am Barrani. And as if he still is.*

Killian doesn't think I'm harmless, Kaylin pointed out.

It is entirely possible you are correct, Nightshade replied, which was like agreement on the surface.

"Kaylin." Bellusdeo's voice was a quiet snap of syllables.

She left Nightshade wherever it was one waited for an appointment to speak with the chancellor and gave the Dragon her full attention. Bellusdeo indicated a group of people walking down the street in a loose pack. One glance at Hope indicated that he was ready for trouble, but not anticipating it yet; he was standing on two legs, but he wasn't rigid with tension.

"This looks promising," Bellusdeo said.

Kaylin said nothing. She wasn't wearing her tabard, and briefly regretted it.

"I am deputized to speak on behalf of the Academia," the Dragon added. "I am certain that Durant has some questions."

"He may—but there's no guarantee that he's one of the group walking to head us off."

"No."

Kaylin thought it highly likely that he wasn't. If Bellusdeo was deputized to speak with Durant on behalf of the chancellor, these people were likely to be deputized to speak with intruders on behalf of Durant. Fieflords didn't generally join patrols like these. At least not in Nightshade or Tiamaris.

Maggaron drew the eye from a distance, but it wasn't Maggaron who attracted most of the attention; it was, as expected, the Dragon wearing gold plate armor. Lack of visible weapons in her hands didn't really change the attention she received. Maggaron didn't *help*, but Kaylin and Severn were practically invisible.

Maggaron had weapons, but hadn't drawn any of them,

and he stood behind his Dragon, waiting; Bellusdeo had come to a stop in the open streets. The windows above street level seemed mostly unoccupied, and as Bellusdeo wasn't patrolling, Kaylin ignored the exceptions. Had she lived in a building with an actual window that wasn't on the verge of collapse, she'd've been peeping out the windows in Nightshade as well.

Severn was slightly more cautious, but agreed.

A woman was at the head of a loose, triangular formation, and she detached herself from the group as the Durant people also came to a halt. She crossed the distance between the Dragon and what Kaylin assumed were her guards.

To Kaylin's surprise, she offered Bellusdeo a crisp—if brief—bow. Bellusdeo returned a nod, but no one expected people wearing plate to be able to bow with any competence. That Dragons were exceptions to this practical expectation was perhaps less well known, given how often Dragons were forced to bow to anyone but each other.

"We've been expecting you. I am Marshalle. You are Lord Bellusdeo?"

"Bellusdeo. I am a Dragon, but I am not an official member of the Dragon Court."

"Ah."

Kaylin, beside Bellusdeo, glanced at the Dragon; she was smiling, and her eyes were orange, but shading now away from red. "I have not made an appointment to speak with Lord Durant."

"Durant," the woman then said, her own smile evident. "No. But we've received reports that a Dragon—a gold Dragon—has been seen in the air above the fief in the past week, and we're aware that a Dragon has been landing in Farlonne. If you will take the risk, Durant is more than willing to meet with you."

Kaylin watched the guards; they seemed relaxed. They, like Maggaron, were armed, but hadn't drawn weapons either.

"I would be both honored and delighted."

"And your companions?"

"Maggaron is my Ascendant—my personal guard. He has been with me since childhood. His," she added, in case this wasn't obvious. "To my left is Corporal Kaylin Neya. To her left is Lord Mandoran of Casarre, and behind, Corporal Severn Handred. Kaylin and Severn are Imperial Hawks—and they are well aware that Imperial Law is neither enforced nor observed in the fiefs. They have been ordered by the Emperor to accompany me."

"And you accept this?"

At this, Bellusdeo's smile deepened. "One of the corporals is my—what is the Elantran word?—roommate. Lord Mandoran also shares that distinction."

"Clearly things are more interesting across the wall than we realized. Please follow me."

Durant's streets were in decent repair; the roads themselves had some ruts, but nothing that would cripple a wagon if the wagon was unlucky. The buildings were a mix of wood and stone, and if the stone was aged, cracked or chipped, it wasn't in danger of crumbling. Windows were a mix of shutters and glass—and it was the glass, which was definitely not new and probably in need of some serious cleaning—that was most surprising. To be fair, there were glass windows and elements of finery in parts of Nightshade as well, but they were parts of Nightshade that everyone who lived there knew to avoid like the plague.

She had assumed—until Tiamaris—that all fiefs were the same.

But Farlonne was not. And clearly, neither was Durant.

Durant wasn't Tara—his Tower wasn't girded by vegetable gardens. There was a gate and a gatehouse similar in form to Helen's, and probably just as practical. But Marshalle walked up to the gatehouse, a man left it, and the gates opened.

Kaylin turned to face Bellusdeo. Bellusdeo's eyes were a more martial orange; she didn't need to be told that entry was a risk.

"What do you counsel?" the Dragon asked the Hawk.

Kaylin exhaled. Flight—of the turn around and retreat variety, *not* the draconic one—was the smart choice here. She glanced at Marshalle; the woman's attention was shifting between Kaylin and Bellusdeo, as if assessing both Kaylin's role and the Dragon's intent.

"I would prefer our first meeting to be somewhere more neutral," Bellusdeo finally said.

Marshalle's easy smile faded.

"Gestures of trust are acts of confidence when any two strangers first meet," the Dragon continued, voice soft. "And only a fool displays such confidence when the place of meeting is inside the territory of a building such as a Tower. There, all martial prowess and experience are reduced by the building, should the building desire it, to utter irrelevance.

"For reasons that I trust are obvious, some minor caution is desirable on my part. I am willing to speak with Durant in any other building of his choosing in the fief of Durant. The fief of Durant is still a place of power for him, but the power is less absolute; should I desire it, I can escape."

"Or kill him?"

Bellusdeo did not smile. She did not respond at all.

Kaylin did. "Bellusdeo, more than anyone except the Norranir, has reason to respect the Towers and their function. The last thing she would do, given any other choice, is attack the fieflord."

"Rumors indicate that Candallar may be without its captain," Marshalle replied.

Kaylin offered a fief shrug. "Bellusdeo had nothing to do with that death."

"You are so certain?"

"I am. I was there."

Marshalle's brows rose. "Who, then, was responsible for Candallar's death?"

"In my opinion? Candallar himself. He attempted to destroy the foundation of the Academia. His death occurred because only his death would prevent it." She'd fallen into High Barrani.

To her surprise, High Barrani didn't come naturally to Marshalle; she seemed to be concentrating on Kaylin's actual words.

She therefore slid into Elantran again. "The new chancellor of the Academia had to kill him or he'd have murdered all the remaining students. And us," she added. "I'm not sure he was all that worried about us, either."

"Durant has questions about the…Academia."

"Neither of us," Kaylin said, indicating Bellusdeo as well, "can really answer them. I mean, we can try, but there's probably going to be a lot of hand-waving. Have any of you actually tried to visit the Academia?"

"We're not, frankly, certain what it *is*," Marshalle replied. "Anyone living in the fief has noticed the lack of the border zone by now. Is that because of the Academia's rise?"

"It's complicated. I really think you should talk to the chancellor."

"Very well," the gates said.

Since gates couldn't normally converse, Kaylin assumed the Tower had an Avatar somewhere else—but no. The gates rolled open, as if they were normal gates, and a man stood between them.

"I am Durant," he said. He offered Bellusdeo a nod, not a bow. Human eyes didn't shift color; they had to use the rest of their face to express emotion, if they wanted to take that risk. Durant hadn't, but as he met Kaylin's eyes, he did smile.

"You appear to know more about this Academia, this lack of a border zone, than we have currently discovered.

"If you are willing to accept my escort—and my guards, of course—I would like to visit it, or at least see it with my own eyes. We might talk while we walk," he added, addressing Bellusdeo.

Bellusdeo's eyes were once again orange with flecks of gold, not red. "I believe I would enjoy that."

08

Kaylin wasn't certain what she had expected of Durant, given the fact that his Tower looked as if it could have been built by perfectly normal architects, with its brick and stone face, its shorter, squatter size, and its unusual wall adornment. Her expectations, given the shape and size of his Tower and her prior experience with fieflords, had been mixed.

He wasn't Tara; he wasn't dressed in gardening clothing, and his front yard hadn't become a large vegetable-and-food garden. But Tara was the Tower; it was Tiamaris who was lord.

Durant was not particularly tall—Severn was visibly taller—and not particularly striking; his face was round in shape, lacking the Barrani length and angularity. His beard was not the impressive beards of the Dragons who chose to grow them—if *grow* was even the right word. Had she met him on patrol, he might have blended in well with most of the citizens on her beat.

But she would have given him a second look, or even a third. If he lacked Barrani slenderness, he also lacked the coldness, the reserve, the innate arrogance, with which the Barrani girded themselves. Even thinking this, her eyes flicked to Mandoran, whose eyes were a steady Barrani blue.

She couldn't pinpoint Durant's age, but thought him a man in his midthirties, perhaps early forties; his hair had not yet grayed, but lines had worn themselves into the corners of his eyes. He wasn't a small man, even given his average height, his hands square and solid, his eyes a pale brown. His eyelashes seemed absurdly full as they framed those eyes.

"Do I pass muster?" he asked, as he held out a hand.

She took it. Some people tightened their grip, as if handshakes were a gesture of dominance. Durant didn't. Nor did he simply brush palms as if Kaylin were a possibly contagious disease or petty criminal.

"Sorry," she said, half meaning it. "You're the first mortal fieflord I've met."

"You've met others?"

She nodded. "Tiamaris, Nightshade, Candallar. I've seen Farlonne but haven't really spoken to her."

"You're taking a tour of the fiefs? You left the best for last?" He grinned.

She matched it. Had she been on her own, she'd've been willing to risk his Tower.

Hope squawked, with words in it. *Too impulsive.*

Since she couldn't speak to Hope without speaking, she ignored the comment. Durant, however, didn't. His gaze moved off her face to the left of it, where Hope was standing. If Hope was being critical, he didn't sense any immediate danger.

"What is that?" Durant asked.

"Her familiar." It was Bellusdeo who replied. She placed a slight emphasis on the first word of the two-word sentence.

This caused Durant's grin to deepen. Marshalle, on the other hand, looked unamused. If Durant was at ease, Marshalle was not. Marshalle's reaction made more sense: there was a gold Dragon, a giant, and a Barrani at the front gates. Durant didn't seem to care.

That, Kaylin thought, was why she would have noticed him on any street in the city: there was an ease in the way he occupied this street that spoke of confidence. He had no need to be thought of as a danger, as an important man, as a power. He might have been at home in *any* of the Hawk beats. She half thought the people in those beats would adapt to him, even if they were in the warrens.

"You've met Tiamaris?" Durant asked, as he began to walk.

Bellusdeo fell in on his left, Kaylin on his right. Mandoran, however, lagged slightly behind as he stared at the Durant Tower. Hope's imperious squawk caused him to blink, shake himself, and follow.

"This is where the border zone was." It was Marshalle who spoke. Durant had come to a halt. His eyes were slightly narrowed as he studied the street—a street that continued, unbroken and unobscured by the mist or fog that had previously characterized that zone.

Bellusdeo nodded. "The fog has cleared from all of the areas known, in the fiefs, as the border zones."

"You've visited them all?"

"Yes. Both before—shortly before—and after. The fog wasn't visible in the same way from the air before the zone vanished."

"We discovered that the border zone affected individuals—or individual races—in different ways," Kaylin added.

This was news to Durant, or appeared to be.

"Maggaron didn't see the buildings we saw once we entered it; much of what he saw were buildings that conform to his size and his people."

"His people?"

Clearly news traveled poorly between fiefs. "The Norranir. They arrived here from the ruins of another world—and it was a long walk. They make their home on the *Ravellon* border in Tiamaris."

"Are they all as tall as he is?"

"More or less. Not the children," she added.

"Some of the children are taller than the corporal." Bellusdeo's nod indicated which corporal. "You haven't heard about them?"

Durant shook his head.

"And you knew about Candallar because you share a border with him?"

He nodded again. "I would know if either Candallar or Farlonne fell."

"Had you met Candallar or Farlonne?"

"Not directly, no." He grinned again. "The fieflords tend to remain in their own territories. Acquisition of land means nothing in the fiefs; the borders are fixed and solid. Or they were." His gaze once again returned to the nonexistent border zone.

"Have you spoken to your Tower about the border zone—or its lack?"

"Some." It was a noncommittal answer. Fair enough.

"How long have you held Durant?" Bellusdeo asked, the question casual.

The lack of answer implied that the answer wasn't. "Long enough," the fieflord eventually said, when it was clear that the Dragon was waiting for an answer anyway. "The Academia is this way?"

The Dragon nodded.

Marshalle cleared her throat; Durant shook his head, a short no.

"If it helps," Kaylin said to the woman who seemed to be second in command here, "Nightshade has visited the Academia multiple times in the past week."

"Interesting. Do you know why?"

Kaylin shrugged. "I think, at heart, he wants what the Academia offers. If he'd had a less Barrani life, he'd probably have made a good student."

"Student of what?"

"The Academia," Mandoran said, the word almost brusque for Mandoran.

"I am now deeply curious. Please lead the way."

He is concerned for me, Nightshade said as they walked. Durant was far quieter for the first two blocks; he observed the streets, the repair of the buildings, the state of the road. There was some calculation in the observation, but Kaylin expected that.

"There have been no Shadow incursions?" he asked, his tone neutral, shorn of the almost avuncular warmth that seemed to otherwise characterize it.

He couldn't have asked a better question of Bellusdeo, and she answered.

You mean Mandoran?

Yes. You consider his trust easily given.

For a Barrani, it was.

The cohort desires some information about the Towers. They do not desire that information to be immediately offered to Bellusdeo.

And you don't care.

It is, I admit, less of a concern to me—but the Towers do not overlap. Their territories do not overlap. And there is no way to captain two of the Towers. In the world beyond the fiefs, territory both expands and contracts frequently, given the relative power of those who desire that expansion. Durant understands the hard limits of the Towers and their mission.

Kaylin nodded, and then grimaced; Nightshade couldn't see it.

Amused, he continued. *Durant and his Tower would be aware*

of the lack of Candallar; we can hear the names of the fiefs to either side of us, and we are aware when those names fall silent. The Towers, he added, *speak the names of their captains; it is my suspicion that is how the names of the original Towers were lost to history. Either way, it would not be of concern to Durant, unless he is worried about the incursion of Shadow.*

You knew that Tiamaris—that Barren—wasn't captained.

That is more difficult, but yes. The fieflord prior to Tiamaris was not dead. Yes, we did not hear Barren's name. Tell me, Kaylin, what do you think Bellusdeo is attempting?

I think she wants Candallar's former Tower.

And that is the reason she has agreed to take Durant on a tour of the Academia? He was amused. *I believe I will join that tour. It should prove interesting.*

Kaylin had zero desire to experience any more *interesting* in her life.

True to his word, Nightshade was waiting as they entered the mouth of the large circular road on which the main buildings stood. He was dressed casually, and as the students didn't appear to have mandated uniforms, might have been one of them. The small park in the middle of this campus was almost, but not quite, empty; a handful of people occupied benches.

Mandoran sucked in air. "Annarion's not happy," he said, voice low.

"Are any of you?" Kaylin's voice was just as low.

"Serralyn and Valliant."

"They're coming out to play?"

He shook his head. "They're in a class."

"So, small mercies still exist."

Bellusdeo's eyes were the normal color—orange with gold bits—as Nightshade approached. She halted what was already a slow walk, threw Kaylin a look, and exhaled.

Nightshade stopped two yards in front of Bellusdeo and

the fieflord. "Lord Bellusdeo, Lord Durant," he said, granting Bellusdeo a title she didn't generally claim.

The Dragon turned to Durant. "This is Lord Nightshade."

"You're away from home," Durant said, extending a hand.

Nightshade didn't pause; he extended his own. "As are you. I have grown somewhat fond of the Academia and its new chancellor."

"This would be my first experience with both. Your border zone has also largely vanished?"

"It has. I consider it, at a local level, a vast improvement."

"I am uncertain; the consequences have yet to be felt. But I'm curious about the buildings on the streets that lead here. Bellusdeo tells me that such streets now extend to the edge of every fief."

Nightshade nodded.

"The Academia would seem, if geography is to be believed, to now exist between the fiefs of Nightshade and Liatt."

"Yes. It would. My fief—I cannot speak for Liatt's except in the usual way—has not been altered in any way. If I do not take the streets that turn towards the Academia, I will now end up in Liatt."

"So, a pocket space?"

"Again, I hesitate to answer questions when my ignorance is so profound. It is my belief that it is a pocket space, a pocket dimension—but it is now reachable in a purely quotidian way. If there is a portal—or portals—from our fiefs to the Academia, they are extremely subtle."

Durant, frowning, nodded. "I noticed none on our walk here. But the buildings are in good repair. They are empty?"

"They will not remain empty, according to the chancellor, but they are considered part of the larger campus property."

Durant shrugged.

"You hoped to have some put to use?"

"They're in good repair," the mortal fieflord repeated. "And that cost none of Durant's resources. Yes, I would have attempted to have them used. Prior to this, no one wanted to live in the border zone, even if the buildings were in decent repair. I don't blame them—I wouldn't, either."

"There is only one place you might live. It is the same with me."

Durant nodded. "We had no problems with Shadow or its incursions from the border zones. We did watch, but admittedly in a desultory fashion; we've no history of any difficulties that weren't caused by idiots."

Kaylin pointedly did not look at Mandoran.

Bellusdeo had said nothing during this time, but seemed to reach a decision. "I am early for my appointment to meet with the chancellor, but my appointment consists of a report on the accessibility of Durant."

"Accessible to the Academia?" Durant's eyes couldn't change color, but in this case, his tone remained friendly.

"Yes. It is a school on a grand scale, and it has only recently opened to students."

Kaylin didn't hear the rest of the explanation; she caught sight of Killian. Surprised to see him outside the large building in which she'd first met him, she broke away from the group and headed in his direction. Mandoran followed; Severn chose to remain with Bellusdeo. This wasn't a situation in which a partner was either mandated or needed.

Killian smiled as she approached.

"Lord Kaylin."

"Please don't."

The smile deepened. "Kaylin, then. The chancellor informed me that the correct use of titles for our visitors was necessary."

"Corporal Neya would work. But I prefer plain Kaylin."

"I believe he feels that the greater title is the one that is used as a gesture of respect."

"Well, I believe that the preferred title is the better way to go."

Killian was almost green-eyed; he lost the obsidian eyes of an Avatar. "In general, so do I. But the chancellor believes any gesture of respect for outsiders is necessary. You are to speak with him."

"I think so?"

"Ah, apologies, Kaylin. That was not a question. He has time, and I believe he is now expecting Bellusdeo."

"She has two fieflords with her."

"Yes. He feels this will save time and the gray area of reporting."

"Should we go?"

Killian was silent for a moment. "He expects your presence but asks that you keep disruptions to a minimum."

"And Mandoran?"

"He will accept all of your companions." Killian grimaced. "I am, however, to keep Lord Mandoran's disruption to a minimum."

Mandoran had the same reaction to the word *Lord* in front of his name as Kaylin had, which was ironic, given how he felt about hers.

"He won't cause trouble."

"He intends no trouble at all—but I have had some experience with your friends, and their good intentions are not always relevant."

"Serralyn and Valliant can't be causing problems. Serralyn was so excited to come here."

"Valliant causes very little difficulty. Serralyn's excitement, however, is very loud."

"She was always pretty quiet at home."

"Perhaps. But the type of loud is not one you would necessarily notice. Helen would, and I do. I do not think it will cause problems, but it requires a certain amount of vigilance on my part."

Kaylin wondered if Serralyn was like Annarion.

"Come. Introduce me to your friends and inform them that the chancellor is waiting."

The chancellor was waiting in his office. If Kaylin had questioned Killian's abilities as a sentient building, she repented; the office was much, much larger on the interior than it had ever been, in part to accommodate chairs, and in part to accommodate what appeared to be a buffet table. Smaller tables, usually to one side of larger chairs not meant for dining halls, had also appeared.

Killian took over introductions as if they were pronouncements, but no one else seemed to find this strange.

The chancellor wasn't seated behind his desk; he was seated in one of the chairs. The desk remained in the room, but it was nowhere near the current furniture meant for this casual first meeting. He rose when the doors were fully open, and offered Bellusdeo and the fieflord of Durant a bow. He nodded at Nightshade, and Nightshade returned the nod.

"Bellusdeo offered to show me the Academia," Durant said. "I hope you'll forgive the intrusion."

"It is no intrusion. I am not in competition with the fiefs or their lords, and I am well aware of the very necessary function the Towers serve. Perhaps more aware of it now that I am situated in the fiefs."

"In some fashion. I find the question of geography very interesting. The Academia is similar to the Towers?" Durant took the chair offered him by the chancellor.

"It is not," Killian answered. "The Academia is meant to house scholars, researchers, and the library; its function is both preservation and discovery. These have never been limited to race or gender. The Towers are meant to preserve lives in the face of *Ravellon*. If, however, you refer to sentience or central intelligence, then yes, the Academia is similar to the Towers, but the concerns of the Academia and the concerns of the Towers are not the same."

"I, of course—ah, forgive me. I am Killianas."

"Killianas," the chancellor said, "is the heart of the Academia; he frequently chooses to appear in person."

Durant nodded.

"Does your Tower have an Avatar?" Kaylin received a frown particular to the chancellor; it was familiar and almost comfortable.

"It does. But she is not often moved to meet strangers, and when she is, it usually means trouble." He spoke with respect, but without any particular fear. Kaylin, however, understood that the heart of Nightshade's Tower was possibly the most dangerous thing about it, and said nothing.

Durant then returned his attention to the chancellor. "I am told you desire open access to the Academia through Durant, should there be those who wish to apply as students here."

"I do. Such access exists through the fief of Tiamaris, and that access will not be revoked."

"Such permission as the chancellor desires has already been granted through the fief of Nightshade as well," Nightshade said.

Durant's grin widened in what appeared to be genuine amusement to Kaylin. "You're warning me that I have no leg to stand on if I want to negotiate some price for open access?"

"I am informing you of facts that might be relevant should you consider it, yes." It was the chancellor who replied. If his tone was stiff, his eyes remained the orange-gold mix that was Dragon neutral.

"You house the students, you feed them, and you teach them what they want to learn?"

"That is succinct, and I am certain some of the students

might quibble with the last part, but yes, that is the intent. We are not a prison. What we want, here, are those who are committed to learning. There are currently few who are qualified to teach, but many experts, many scholars, have professed an interest in doing so, and we are interviewing them and sorting them out."

"How will you pay them?"

This wasn't the question the chancellor had been expecting, but Kaylin liked Durant the better for asking it.

"That is surely a concern of the scholars themselves."

"In Durant, money doesn't grow on trees. Some food does, but not much. The Tower can produce wood and stone—and as long as neither wood nor stone is to leave the fief, it will last."

"It will last," Killian said, "as long as the Tower does—and as long as the captain desires that outlay of the Tower's power."

Durant nodded. He radiated a warmth that Nightshade in particular didn't possess.

He has been fieflord for many years, given his apparent age. You cannot imagine that a fieflord could be avuncular in any substantial fashion.

She thought of Tara. *It probably depends on the Tower's core.*

Nightshade's Tower would probably commit suicide—if that was possible for Towers—before it became like Tara in any way. The thought amused him briefly.

Kaylin was thinking about wood and stone and the area in which the Tower might effect permanent changes to the buildings the fief's residents inhabited. She had no doubt that his comment about wood and stone had been tested. And buildings seldom moved themselves out of the fiefs in which they'd been built.

"The question of remuneration is an exercise left to the Academia and the scholars. It is not through the fiefs, or the citizens of the fiefs, that such scholars are likely to come;

those that have the capability but choose to dwell in the fiefs often have legal difficulties that would render them unsuitable." The chancellor glanced at Bellusdeo, whose eyes were a touch more orange than his.

"I don't intend to set up a blockade to prevent people from entering the Academia," Durant said. "How strict are your admission standards?"

"Define strict."

"I admit I don't understand enough to offer a reasonable definition. How many students have applied for entry, and how many have you accepted?"

The chancellor didn't reply with actual numbers; Kaylin had no doubt that he had them. The Arkon—ugh, the *former* Arkon—held on to facts and knowledge as if they were the air that sustained his breathing.

"I am aware that some students will seek entrance simply because it guarantees both food and shelter," he offered instead. "But a majority of those who are driven by desperation will not provide the Academia what it needs. Knowledge is not the sole province of the rich and powerful; the desire for knowledge can be found in any corner of this city—or this Empire.

"We will have Barrani students; we will have human students. Some interest has been expressed by the Aerians, but that is in its infancy. A delegate has been sent to the Leontine quarter, as well."

"Ah. The Tha'alani?" This was asked more sharply.

"We have not yet had a Tha'alani applicant. I would, however, accept Tha'alani students who displayed the correct attitude."

"Not aptitude?"

The chancellor declined to accept the possible correction. Kaylin half understood why. She had the wrong attitude for the Academia, and knew it. Sitting in a class and listening to someone drone on and on when she could be out in the streets *doing her job* would have been almost unbearable.

Perhaps, had you found the Academia when you chose to flee Nightshade, you might feel differently.

Kaylin shook her head. *I needed—I still need—to be doing something that I personally consider useful. Being a Hawk is useful.*

Being knowledgeable is useful, Nightshade countered; he was still amused. *It is less predictable, certainly. Esoteric studies about historical use of portals would have no bearing on your former life. In theory, it has no bearing on your present life—but you have experienced the ways in which that knowledge is profoundly important.*

Kaylin had heard this before.

The existence of the Academia is not somehow a personal slight; it is not an act of condescension.

This was less common. And she knew this already. But sometimes she confused feeling vaguely stupid with being treated as if she were, as if her feelings were the responsibility of external forces and opinions. She exhaled slowly. Sitting in the chancellor's office with two fieflords had not been on her to-do list for the day. Following Bellusdeo was.

Durant turned to Nightshade. "If possible, in the neutral territory of the Academia, I would like to have a small discussion with you, as a fellow fieflord. There are some issues with *Ravellon* and the border that have long provoked questions in me."

"If there is anywhere to find answers," Nightshade replied, "it is here. I alone may not have the information you desire—but all past research and all historical knowledge exist within the Academia's library."

He had not expected that Durant would know much about the library. The fieflord's expression, however, made it clear that he had heard about it from somewhere.

Maybe his Tower. Kaylin desperately wanted to know who

or what the core of Durant's Tower had been on the day the Towers rose.

And it occurred to her, as she sat in this office, that Nightshade was right. Information and knowledge were here. But the library was often off-limits to even junior students.

"There is much," Bellusdeo said, finally entering the discussion in her own right, "to discuss. The fieflords handle their responsibilities as captains to the Towers in ways that best suit them—but some have allowed people to pass through the *Ravellon* border. And return."

Durant's eyes rounded slightly in what Kaylin assumed was genuine surprise. "I hesitate to call you a liar," he said, "but your source must be misinformed. I am not entirely certain it is even possible."

"Your Tower was not his Tower. Candallar, for reasons of his own, allowed this. Something was brought from *Ravellon* into Elantra in the hands of a Barrani Lord of the High Court."

Durant glanced at Nightshade; Nightshade nodded. "I believe it."

"How was this even accomplished? The Towers themselves are built to prevent exactly that—among other things." The ease and friendly aura of welcome vanished as Durant leaned forward in his chair.

"My Tower would not allow it," Nightshade replied. "I cannot therefore answer with any accuracy. There are other matters we might, as fieflords who shoulder very similar responsibilities, discuss. I believe, if Tiamaris considered the risk necessary, his Tower *would* allow it. The Towers are not, and were never, all of one thing."

"They were *built* to prevent exactly that!" Durant snapped.

"I highly doubt Farlonne's Tower would allow what Candallar's Tower did," Bellusdeo told the fieflord. "But perhaps it would be best to allow Farlonne to speak for herself."

Durant's expression once again offered a genial, even

amused, smile. Kaylin no longer believed it. "Lord Nightshade, how often have you spoken with either Tiamaris or Liatt?"

"Very, very seldom, as you are aware."

"And if you wanted to 'discuss' a difficulty with Liatt, how would you go about that?"

"In the worst case, I would send a messenger with the message I desired to convey. There are mirrors within the Towers, but they do not function in the same fashion as mirrors in the rest of Elantra do. I would wait on her reply."

"And Tiamaris?"

"I would visit Tiamaris in person."

Durant's smile faltered before it resumed. "I would not."

"No. I have some experience with Tiamaris, and the corporal—" here he nodded in Kaylin's direction "—is very, very familiar with Tiamaris's Tower. She was present when the Tower chose Tiamaris as her lord."

"You would trust yourself to another Tower?"

"I would trust my safety in this case to Tiamaris's Tower. I would, however, insist the corporal accompany me."

"Why?"

"Because the Tower of Tiamaris is extremely fond of the corporal. And the Tower has allowed things that my own Tower would forbid utterly unless I wished to…argue with its imperatives. For our part, we get along because I understand that the Tower *has* imperatives that are not mine, and I do not interfere in them. Is your Tower different?"

This time, Durant grimaced. "My Tower is…my Tower. She's incredibly pretentious, and that pretension has been a source of conflict from time to time."

"Is that why your Tower looks like that?" Kaylin cut in.

"Like what?"

"Like something we—normal people—could actually build?"

He grinned, and this felt genuine. "You liked that, did you?"

"Actually, yes."

"My Tower has imperatives that, as Lord Nightshade has said, are immutable. We don't disagree about those; we don't disagree about the threat that *Ravellon* poses. We've had experience with it." He hesitated and then said, "It's been worse in the past decade than any of the decades prior to this one."

Bellusdeo was leaning forward, her eyes orange-red, her expression almost peaceful, which was a striking contradiction. "I would like to hear about the changes. In return, I can speak to you about the difficulties my people encountered. We lost our war, and only a handful of people survived. The others were subsumed by *Ravellon* and the spread of Shadow. They might even be trapped there now." As Bellusdeo had been.

Durant nodded. "I would hear it. I would hear it all. I would share it with my own Tower, with your permission."

"And likely, without it," the Dragon said, smiling. "I have had the privilege of sharing a roof with the corporal. I understand how sentient buildings function. But I am not entirely willing to visit your Tower at this time."

"Is there anything stopping us from speaking here?"

The chancellor cleared his throat. "Bellusdeo and I have been discussing this very problem in the past few days," he said, as all eyes turned toward him. His eyes, unlike Bellusdeo's, were an orange-gold; nothing he had heard so far had alarmed him. He had always considered Shadow a threat; he had never argued against the importance of the Towers.

The Emperor, who claimed Elantra—and the Empire—as his hoard nonetheless allowed the fiefs to evade his laws and his rule *because of* the Towers. In some fashion, he understood that they were necessary for the good of the people he *did* rule.

"And what was the thrust of the discussion?" It was Durant who asked. Nightshade believed he already knew.

"The Academia can be accessed by roads that lead from any of the fiefs. It exists in a space that is slightly displaced. It has been—to date—immune to the incursion of Shadow, but that immunity might be compromised now."

"Because it can be reached."

The chancellor nodded gravely. "It is absolutely in the interest of the Academia that the Towers stand, that they continue to contain *Ravellon*. We understand the importance of the Towers; we understand the importance of the information the captains might have, individually.

"And we believe—"

"We?"

"Ah, apologies. Killianas and I. The Arbiters also agree; I believe one might have some reservations, but as the library will stand in the face of the destruction of the universe, it is a more academic concern."

Killian said, "I am, to the chancellor, what your Towers are to you. The Academia is me, and of me."

"But not the library?"

"No. We are connected, but no. The library is its Arbiters, but we have always relied on their advice and their accumulated knowledge when we feel that knowledge relevant." He turned. "My apologies for the interruption, chancellor."

"A necessary interruption, unlike so many." He glanced at Kaylin as he spoke, and Kaylin reddened. She was used to this from the Arkon—the chancellor—and let it pass without comment, which took more effort than it should have.

Squawk. Squawk.

"Indeed. Some of the interruptions were, in the end, necessary when one reviews them; it is why Lord Kaylin is present."

"Lord?" Durant said.

Kaylin did flush, then. "It's a joke."

Mandoran, silent until that moment, cleared his throat. Loudly.

"It's a joke to anyone who isn't Barrani."

"There is clearly much that I have not heard in recent times."

"Tell your Tower to look to the High Halls," Kaylin told him. "A place I suggest you never visit for idle curiosity."

"Oh?"

"Barrani nobles make our street gangs look civilized and reasonable by comparison."

"She's exaggerating," Mandoran said.

"You are more aware, one assumes, of the Barrani customs?"

"I didn't say she was entirely wrong, just that she was exaggerating. She's called Lord Kaylin because she accidentally took the Barrani Test of Name and survived it. It's what defined a Lord of the High Court. We think that's changing," he added. "But we're not sure when." He spoke Elantran.

"Clearly there are advantages and disadvantages to remaining in my own fief. However, we have interrupted the chancellor."

"Good of you to notice," the chancellor replied. "What we have been discussing is the Academia as a safe and neutral ground on which the fieflords might meet and discuss the current situation."

"The Academia is considered neutral?"

"The Academia—in this case, Killianas—may choose to eject those he feels mean harm to the Academia or its students. He does not, however, kill. Candallar attempted to murder important students—and almost succeeded. His death, however, is on my hands. Killianas asked me to spare him—it was a request, I believe, from Candallar's Tower—but attempts to do so failed.

"If, on the other hand, you are uncomfortable in the company of Dragons, so be it. I offer the Academia as a place where you might, fieflords all, meet to discuss individual success and possible failures. What you make of it is entirely up to you."

Durant looked across the room at Nightshade. "You are comfortable here?"

"I am demonstrably comfortable here."

"Tiamaris?"

"I cannot speak for Tiamaris, and would not be so presumptuous as to try."

"Tiamaris," the chancellor said, "is in agreement."

This caused Durant to grin again. Clearly the chancellor wasn't worried about presumption.

"He is, on the other hand, a Dragon. Killianas, you can prevent the fieflords from killing or injuring each other, correct?" the chancellor then asked.

"Indeed."

"I will need to discuss this with my own Tower."

"Do you talk to your Tower's Avatar?" Kaylin asked.

He blinked. "You are going to give me whiplash," he said. "And yes, I do."

"I," Nightshade said, "almost never do."

This surprised Durant. "Never?"

"Almost never."

"How do you communicate with the Tower, then?"

"Clearly the form of communication suits the Tower. My Tower in general considers beings who must breathe and eat to be little better than animals. Except for the occasions when he considers animals far superior."

Silence. Nightshade was amused. Highly amused. And nothing he had said was a lie.

It is not necessary to lie, here. Perhaps later.

"If I attempted to cut my Tower out of crucial decisions, it would be me who was ejected—if I survived her ire." Durant chuckled. Kaylin had heard similar words before—mostly from married men in the office. He clearly held the Tower's Avatar in some affection. And she clearly did have a temper.

"It is good, then, that we are with Towers who suit our disparate temperaments. However: my Tower has no say in this decision, and I believe it to be a sound one. If the chancellor is gracious enough to offer safe quarters in which we might meet and discuss our various issues, I will accept with gratitude."

"Then let me say I provisionally accept the offer, contingent upon discussion and negotiation with my own Tower. I believe that I would consider placement in the Academia to be a boon to my own people, and I will not block you. I do have a few questions, however."

Killian bowed to the assembled gathering. "I believe Lord Kaylin wishes to speak with the librarians. I will leave you to your negotiations and discussions."

09

"I'm working," she told Killian once the door was firmly closed at her back. "And I don't remember thinking that I wanted to speak with the librarians. Or did you get that confused?"

Killian inclined his head. "Perhaps. Words are sometimes taxing."

"What you meant to say was: the librarians want to speak with me, right?"

"The result would be the same in either version. And I believe you have questions for them."

She did have a few questions. She had had no intention of actually asking any of them today. "By Imperial dictate, I can't just stop and chat with the librarians while Bellusdeo is free to wander around."

"Bellusdeo does not intend to leave the Academia without you."

"Did she tell you—or did I—about her trip to the West March?"

"No. Ah," he added. "I see. I highly doubt that will happen here. Not now. And you have left Lord Severn with Bellusdeo; you are certain to be informed if she feels the need to leave in haste."

"I'd ask the chancellor to make sure of that, but he's busy, and he hates to be interrupted."

"He is concerned for the immediate future, and the discussion between the chancellor, Bellusdeo, and the two fieflords is by no means complete," Killian replied. "It is possible you could speak with Larrantin."

"Why don't we do that instead?" she asked hopefully. While she liked Starrante, he was still a giant spider, and seeing him pushed childish fear buttons she had to work to suppress. She wasn't proud of them.

"No, that will not do. Starrante may not have the answers you seek immediately at his fingers, but Androsse will." More gently he said, "The fear doesn't suit the tabard you wear."

"Not wearing it today," Kaylin said, but she reddened. Killian was right. Of course he was right. And maybe if she'd grown up in the presence of giant spiders, policing and protecting them as necessary, those childhood fears wouldn't exist.

Starrante had clearly been informed of her arrival; he was waiting when Killian opened the door. Killian didn't enter the library, or at least his Avatar didn't.

"The library is not my domain," he told her. "It is the domain of the Arbiters. The Arbiters have some influence beyond the boundaries of the library, but they have no control of the Academia. The chancellor accepts—and even seeks—their guidance, but it is his decision that is law. They have power equivalent to Helen's or mine within the library itself. I remember the classes taught here." He smiled. The smile faded.

"You are welcome, as always, to visit," Starrante said, the Barrani words underscored by the clicking that characterized Starrante's speech. "Kaylin." His forelegs—or arms—did a complicated dance in the air. Kaylin was pretty sure it was a greeting.

"It is a greeting," Killian agreed. "And one that shows great respect. You will note it was not offered to me."

"Well," Kaylin replied, "you're family. I don't greet Helen that way, either."

Killian smiled. When he smiled he looked less Barrani.

"You want information about the rise of the Towers?" Starrante asked. He began to amble into the library beneath ceilings that would have made the arches of cathedrals look short and squat.

She nodded. Starrante moved slowly out of consideration for her legs—two in total, and shorter by far than any of his. "May I ask why?"

"Isn't curiosity for its own sake supposed to be a necessary feature of the Academia?"

"In students, yes—although that reply would be worth several demerits were it uttered by a student."

"Not respectful enough?"

"Absolutely not." A man who looked very like the Barrani stepped into view. If he'd come around a corner, Kaylin could have pretended that he'd simply been obscured by the presence of bookshelves; as it was, he stepped out of midair on the path Starrante was now walking.

"Arbiter Androsse," she said, offering him a bow. It was a Diarmat-taught bow, and given Androsse's nod, one of which the Dragon might have approved.

"Starrante feels that I might have a better understanding of the composition of the Towers, but I feel that the answer to the question he asked is necessary before we proceed. Understand that we have been the library for as long as the Academia has existed. We will be the library if it falls. We were not asked for input or opinions about the people who stepped up to take on the responsibility of becoming a Tower."

"That is not true," Starrante said. "The decision was not ours, but input was encouraged, and if I recall, we did have opinions."

"We always have opinions. We're Arbiters."

"I thought Arbiters were supposed to be neutral," Kaylin said.

"Ah. That would be a different definition of a word that is used here as a title. And regardless, answers are necessary."

Kaylin exhaled words. "We want to know because we want to know what we're dealing with in regards to the Towers themselves. The captains don't define the Towers, as was once previously thought; I have some experience with the Avatar of one of them, so I understand possible dangerous instability."

"All Towers save one are currently captained; the Towers have accepted their lords, and that is unlikely to change in the near future. I perceive that the reason you desire the information involves the Tower that Candallar captained."

"It's empty, yes."

"You have no desire to captain it yourself."

"Gods, no." She exhaled. "We were told that the Tower was once called Karriamis."

"The chancellor said this?"

"I don't remember who said it."

Androsse snorted. "I curse the Ancients for the creation of races with so little memory. It is a wonder that you retain the use of language at all. Karriamis was, indeed, the individual chosen to become the heart of that Tower."

"And he was a Dragon?"

"He was. He was both a Dragon and a scholar; he understood the dangers of *Ravellon* well, and he considered the position—the becoming—necessary. Many people did, and many people volunteered to become the base or the core of the Towers that now stand around *Ravellon*; only six could be chosen.

"We were not present to question the choices; nor were we present to demand a better understanding of what the Towers' imperatives and contingencies were. Karriamis once taught at the Academia."

She nodded. "Do you think that's why he sent Candallar to look for it?"

"I could not say."

"But..." She trailed off, uncertain if her next question would be insulting.

"We are not like the Towers." It was Starrante who spoke, perhaps sensitive to the reasons for her hesitance. "We are not sentient buildings. Killianas is, and was; we are slightly different."

"You can't leave the library."

"We can of course leave the library. I encountered you outside of the library, if you recall."

She did. "You weren't in the best frame of mind."

"No. I was somewhat controlled at the time. And I am being a pedant. Leaving the library is possible with the permission of Killian; there is never a time when all of the Arbiters will leave the library at once." He coughed. Or he made a series of sounds that would have been coughing had he been any of the other races Kaylin knew. "You might recall—"

"They had your book."

"Yes. I am uncertain how. It is of some small concern to us, but at the moment it is of academic interest. We are not as Karriamis became. We are tied to the library and its vast space, and within the library, we exert control in a way that might seem reminiscent of the Towers or your Helen, but the library itself is a found space."

At Kaylin's expression, he exhaled. "Never mind. I perceive

that this is not the correct time for this discussion. All of the Arbiters were familiar with Karriamis."

"I knew him well," the third Arbiter said, as she appeared beside her two companions. Kavallac, the Dragon librarian, had arrived. "I considered his ascension a loss to Dragonkind, but understood his decision."

"How did Candallar come to be captain of the Tower?"

Kavallac shrugged. "How did any of the captains come to be captains?"

"I only know of one—and at the time, the Tower had been all but abandoned by the Barrani chosen to captain it."

"It is not impossible—as you have seen—to dispatch the captains if they are not in residence. Had you attacked Candallar within his Tower, the outcome would have been different. But captains die. This was understood before the Towers were created; it is the reason they were designed and built as they were. The Towers can assimilate new information, but it is difficult if that new information remains outside of their boundaries. The captains are mobile." The Dragon librarian exhaled.

"You have your Helen; Killian has talked a bit about your current status. You are her tenant, I believe?"

Kaylin nodded.

"It is a different word for lord. I understand that she made attempts to change her core so that she might have choice of the lord who gave her commands?"

Kaylin nodded again.

"This flexibility was built into the Towers. Helen's creation was not the same, and her role, intentionally different. She was not meant to house tenants or guests, and her name was known; it was the key to enforcing her obedience.

"Arbiters are not obedient," Kavallac added, in case this wasn't obvious. "That was never required of us. I don't recall what was."

Living in the library for the rest of their immortal existence,

Kaylin thought. But she also thought that more than three had queued up for the privilege of doing so.

"Helen has chosen you. She can, however, function without a tenant. The Towers will function for some time without a captain. In the case of your Tara, this was suboptimal. I do not think Karriamis will have that difficulty. He was never entirely comfortable in the presence of too many people and disliked noise and fuss.

"If your concern is the state of the defense of the area over which he presides, worry will be unlikely to be essential for the entirety of your life. Possibly for a century beyond that. If we had to lose a captain, Karriamis's would be the least inconvenient.

"But that is not what you're really asking, is it?"

"I don't understand how a Dragon could or would choose a Barrani as its captain."

"In my opinion, it is likely that Candallar was both desperate and strong enough to unseat—that's kill, in any reasonable tongue—the previous captain. I don't know that for a fact. Candallar himself was outcaste." She glanced at Androsse.

"We did not make our kin outcaste," he replied. "Not in our time."

"Which has passed," Starrante added. "Durandel became the Tower you call Nightshade; he and Androsse were distant kin."

Durandel was an Ancestor. Durandel's brothers, sleeping in the basement of the Tower Durandel became, had attempted to destroy the Barrani High Halls. They had almost succeeded.

"None of your kin became Towers?"

She couldn't tell if Arbiter Starrante was frowning or not.

"That is untrue," he replied. "Aggarok did."

She made a mental note of the name. "You wouldn't happen to know—"

"Liatt is his current captain."

"And Durant's Tower?"

"Endoralle. She was of the next generation—what you now refer to as Barrani. Farlonne's Tower was Beyanne; it was not their original name."

"And their race?"

"Morphosys."

Kaylin hadn't heard of them. Then again, she'd never heard of Starrante's people before now, either. She frowned. "What characterized the Morphosys' original race?"

"Physical flexibility. They could choose their appearances and alter every element of them; they could see multiple planes at once."

Her frown shifting into one of frustration and concentration, she said, "I...think I might have met some of them when we went to the West March."

"Very likely. They were never numerous, but they were considered an excellent choice as a building's core. I believe some of the buildings in the Western reach may have been constructed with Morphosys at their core."

She was certain this was true, but less certain it was relevant.

"But I confess I fail to understand why any of this information is of relevance to you," Androsse continued. "Understand that the act of becoming—as it was called—changed those who became. They are not, and could not remain, what they were."

Kaylin understood this, but partially disagreed. "They couldn't be entirely changed or the choice of the Tower core wouldn't matter; the Ancients could have chosen six random people—it would certainly have saved them time, and a lot of conflict.

"Some essential part of their former identity remains. Nightshade's Tower even had brothers of Durandel sleeping in its basement—I assume they decided to do it when the Towers rose." Nor were they the only kin to do so. "If we're dealing with fieflords we don't know, we're dealing indirectly with Towers we don't know. We can infer the imperatives at the core of *all* Towers, but there's clearly a lot of leeway in things not related to their...job.

"Candallar heavily implied that Karriamis sent him here. The chancellor believes that Karriamis, possibly with the co-operation of other Towers, managed to preserve the Academia in a kind of broken stasis, until Candallar could somehow make his way in. Candallar wouldn't have looked because he wouldn't have known to look, were it not for his Tower.

"And yes, it's Candallar's empty Tower we're mostly concerned with—but the information about the other Towers could prove helpful."

"How?"

She exhaled. "We think it's a really good idea for the captains of the Towers to meet and discuss the situation with *Ravellon*. In person."

Starrante, Androsse and Kavallac shared a wordless glance. Silence was a prod to continue, and Kaylin did.

"If the captains are necessary because they're more flexible and because our knowledge of Shadow—and the abilities of that Shadow—change with time, more captains means more knowledge, right? The captains—the fieflords—can exchange knowledge vital to their Tower's defense."

Starrante clicked. If there were syllables contained in that clicking, Kaylin couldn't hear enough of them to transform them into words on the inside of her head.

They are words, Nightshade said. *But yes, the language is extremely difficult for even me.*

"I fail to see how that is relevant to the discussion of the original Tower cores." Androsse glanced at Kavallac.

"We'll need to talk to the current fieflords—men and women who didn't exist at the time of the Towers' rise. We'll need to negotiate with them, if we want them on board. Negotiations—I'm told—rely on knowledge of context. So, the more we know about the Towers' peculiarities, the better we'll be at presenting the idea.

"We're not Shadow; we're not seeking openings into the Towers themselves. Frankly, I never want to enter Nightshade's Tower again while I'm still breathing."

"You wish to be buried there?" Starrante asked, his tone almost implying confusion.

"No—but I'll be a corpse, so I won't care."

"This is not the usual view of death among your—"

"Starrante, now is *not* the time. You encountered Durandel?" Androsse's brow was folded into what was almost a single line.

"Nightshade's Tower has never been entirely friendly," Kaylin replied. "And two of the people sleeping in his basement decided to take a walk and ended up trying to torch the High Halls to the ground. I don't need to know more about Durandel—I mean, we don't. Nightshade is willing to talk."

I would be highly interested in speaking with Androsse about Durandel. Perhaps I will gain permission to visit the library.

"And the others?"

"We intend—no, sorry. Lord Bellusdeo intends to approach all of the fieflords in an attempt to somehow arrange a meeting of the fieflords."

She does indeed. Lannagaros has allowed such meetings going forward to take place within specified buildings on the Academia campus. He, too, desires some access to the fieflords, if for entirely different reasons. Durant is willing to take the risk of a full meeting; he has also agreed to keep his borders open for those who might apply to become students here.

That was the heart of the chancellor's concern. But...he and Bellusdeo were friends. He understood her in a way no one else did—and this, this meeting of fieflords, was probably a concession to her experience with Shadow. *Ravellon* was personal to Bellusdeo.

"You've given us some information to work with. I know the Towers' base personalities do change—I mean, they're like gods in their own domain, but like prisoners outside of them, so that's going to have an effect.

"But...I'm a little bit surprised that Durant is...Durant, given the core of his Tower was a Barrani woman."

"How so?" Androsse asked.

"You'd kind of have to see his Tower. It's...a building that we could make. I mean, mortals, humans, us. Most Barrani architecture is..." She struggled to find a polite word for pretentious, and failed.

Majestic.

It's not majestic. It's—it's all overdone. It's like it was designed to make visitors feel grubby and unworthy.

That is entirely your impression. Architecture is meant to create a mood, a tone, within a dwelling. It is not meant for visitors, but for occupants.

"Anyway, it's very simple, very plain—I mean, creating a Tower like that would cost a lot of money, so it's not like we could just randomly build it ourselves, but—it looks like it could, without magic, be built by us."

"I see."

"I don't know what it looked like before Durant took the captaincy, but."

"Yes?"

"You said he took the Tower eighty years ago?"

"It is information that we've been given, not information we've experienced, but we have reason to trust that information, yes."

Does he look like he's a century old to you?

No.

"Can the Towers grant immortality?"

"An interesting question, and one to which we do not have answers. And while answers might eventually be forthcoming, may I suggest that mortality's desperate desire for longer life makes sharing this question unwise?"

Kaylin nodded. They had an empty Tower, and she personally knew of two people who wanted it. No one needed grubby powerful humans joining the queue—not when their desire had nothing to do with why the Tower was built. She could well imagine that people wouldn't *care* if they were tied to the Tower—fieflords did leave them, after all.

Do you know how long Liatt has held her Tower?

For some time.

Longer than Durant?

I cannot confirm with regards to Durant; our fiefs do not border each other. But Liatt is fieflord in a way Barren wasn't. The Tower has not fallen; she is the fieflord.

Have you met her?

I believe you've asked this question before, but mortal memories being what they are, no. We are not playing polite neighbors; we do not show up at the doorsteps of other fieflords with welcome baskets.

Kaylin laughed out loud, which caused all three Arbiters to stare at her. She glanced at Mandoran. He had not spoken a word since his entry to the library; he said nothing now. His eyes were blue, his lips pursed; clearly Kaylin wasn't the only person in the room who was talking to someone at a distance.

"Sorry. Nightshade is irritated."

"And this is amusing?"

"Sometimes. I'm sorry to have bothered you, and I'd like to know a bit about Liatt's Tower."

"The core of the Tower was Aggarok, a kinsman," Starrante replied. "If you dislike Lord Nightshade's Tower, I am not certain you will find Liatt's Tower hospitable; Aggarok was always responsible, but he was very *aggressive* about it. I suggest avoiding him if that is at all possible."

"It should be."

"And if," Kavallac interjected, "you manage to meet with Liatt and she offers you the hospitality of her home, will you then baldly refuse it?"

"I think she'd understand why."

"That is not an answer, Lord Kaylin."

"I'd refuse, yes." Kaylin exhaled. "I can't speak for Bellusdeo. Even if I were empowered to do it, she wouldn't listen. If she assesses the risk as acceptable, she's going to do what she thinks is best."

"Does she understand that she is critical to the future survival of our race?"

Ah. "Believe that there's no way she could not understand that."

"Good. I am not in a position to relieve her of that burden; I am tied to the library."

"Could you be untied?"

Kavallac's eyes were orange, and they moved toward red. Kaylin held her ground but couldn't prevent her shoulders from stiffening. Hope, however, seemed unconcerned.

"No, Corporal Neya. Upon death, perhaps—but as you've seen, it's hard to kill a Dragon when they fight from the seat of their power. If I die, I believe contingencies might exist that would allow a new Arbiter, but we were chosen with that in mind.

"We understand that Bellusdeo is interested in the Tower Candallar once occupied. Her concern is *Ravellon*. I'm certain that others would like her to have different concerns—but the chancellor has made clear why she considers all other factors almost irrelevant. I," Kavallac added, her eyes narrowing as something about Mandoran caught her attention, "would prefer that she attended to the duties incumbent upon her by race and circumstance—but I have been told that I am not the only Dragon who desires this."

"The chancellor doesn't?"

"The chancellor is somewhat sentimental when it comes to your friend. Does he desire it? Yes, but only if that shift is natural. He will not press her, and has asked that we refrain from making the attempt."

Kaylin was almost certain this was a royal *we*, but failed to put this into words.

"I am uncertain that Karriamis will not agree with me." This was not what Kaylin had hoped to hear. "He is a Dragon."

"He *was* a Dragon, and for a couple of centuries, he's had a Barrani captain. I'd say he's more flexible than he seems."

"Having not met him, you might indeed say that. But he would never have volunteered for the position he was literally built to fulfill had he not had an extremely strong sense of duty and responsibility. I believe he will see children and babies as Bellusdeo's responsibility, and he is unlikely to be swayed by any other concern."

"But Candallar didn't *go to the Tower* in order to become a steward in the fight against Shadow."

"No. I believe he fled to the fiefs in order to preserve his own life. But Lord Nightshade is also outcaste, is he not?"

"According to Candallar, their circumstances were different."

"How so?"

"Nightshade could probably walk into the High Halls and leave alive. Candallar couldn't. Also, the Consort actually likes Nightshade. If it were up to her, he'd be part of the Barrani High Court tomorrow. And unlike Dragons, outcaste Barrani have been—I'm told—repatriated in the past. It's not impossible for Nightshade to return home.

"I think Candallar believed that if *he* possessed the power Nightshade possesses, he'd be allowed to return home. Well, that and if an ally became the new High Lord. Regardless, Nightshade accepts being outcaste."

"He possesses one of The Three," Kavallac said.

"Yes. And he'll continue to possess it. I don't think the Consort has issues with that, either—and the sword was very useful half a month ago, where the High Halls are concerned. I think he's been asked to return it, but, well. He invited them to retrieve it."

In almost those exact words, yes. You are worried.

I'm worried that Kavallac is right. That Barrani captaincy would be preferable to Karriamis if Bellusdeo is the only Dragon alive who can bear young.

Mandoran looks concerned.

He probably is. Look, he likes *Bellusdeo. He knows she's not happy. He has eleven other inescapable people in his head; she has no one. He thinks her obsession with Shadow would be a perfect fit for a Tower. Not all of the cohort agree.*

No. I understand that Sedarias would like a base of operations, a safe base, in the future. You think of them as like you; they are not. You will die; you are mortal. They will die only if they are foolish or unlucky. Outlasting you would increase the danger they will find themselves in, and the Tower would be the ideal solution.

It wouldn't.

It is not me you must convince of that, but Sedarias. Were I Sedarias, I would make the choices she is making.

And if you were you?

I know what Towers demand, he replied. *And I do not think she is capable, in the end, of meeting those demands. For her cohort, she would. But a Tower is not part of that cohort; I believe she expects obedience—just as prior owners of Helen did.*

In theory, isn't that what a captain is for, though?

Theory is a pleasant conceit when it is built upon a lack of solid information. I accept what I cannot change—but you have seen some of the cost of that, and it is a cost I would not have anticipated.

"Very well. We have told you what we know," Kavallac said, into the growing silence.

"I want Starrante to explain what *aggressive* means in relation to Liatt's Tower."

Starrante clicked. "It means I would advise against entering Liatt's Tower if you have the choice. Yes, becoming changes the person at the heart of the Tower, but never completely. He was always a kill first, and apologize as appropriate later, person."

When they left the library, Bellusdeo was waiting. Maggaron was beside her. The chancellor was not. The gold Dragon declined to enter the library at the invitation of Starrante. Kaylin was surprised.

Then again, given Kavallac's reaction, maybe she shouldn't have been. Kavallac definitely didn't think Bellusdeo should attempt to captain a Tower when the future of the entire race was in the balance, and she was likely to make this clear.

Since Bellusdeo had more than enough of that particular clarity in her life, she was probably wise to avoid it. Kaylin could just imagine the reverberations of two angry Dragons shouting in their native tongue, and was grateful.

"I've been waiting," the Dragon said—once the library doors were closed.

"Sorry—I wanted to find out a bit about the original people who were chosen to become the heart of, the core of, the Towers."

"Did you glean any useful information?"

"I'm not sure how useful it's going to be. You already know that the one empty Tower was built on a Dragon. Karriamis. Kavallac seemed to know him, or know of him; apparently he used to lecture here. It was Karriamis who chose Candallar—but no one understands how the mechanism of that choice works.

"I mean, in Tara's case, it was clear she was angry and lonely and afraid—and I can't imagine a Dragon being lonely or afraid."

"Angry?"

"That doesn't take imagination."

Bellusdeo chuckled. "No, I don't imagine it does. Lannagaros seems happy, to me."

"He hasn't exhaled fire the few times I've spoken with him here, no."

Squawk.

"I realize that," Bellusdeo said, voice soft, as she glanced at Kaylin's shoulder ornament. "But at the moment, the Academia's existence is fragile. Had Candallar managed to kill Robin, I'm not sure the Academia would be reachable the way it is now. Lannagaros's search for students—and for the scholars who might be suitable to teach them—is urgent. Accepting the fieflords here is part of that search.

"Should there be hostilities on the campus, Killian can deal with them as effectively as Helen deals with the cohort. But I would say the cohort is far more challenging." She then turned to Mandoran. "Well?"

He looked uncomfortable; he was blue-eyed. "I don't suppose you're tired after a long afternoon of negotiation?"

"I wasn't doing the negotiating. The chancellor was. And the fieflords. I am now restless, and I intend to continue on to the fief of Liatt. Are you coming?"

Mandoran grimaced. "Yes, unless I'm dead. I don't suppose you'd like to kill me now and put me out of my misery?"

Her chuckle deepened. "I don't think Killianas would allow it."

"Why not? I'm not a student."

"You are a visitor," Killian said. "And the chancellor would be upset if you were killed anywhere on the campus."

"Fine. I don't suppose Liatt will care."

"Why don't we find out?"

10

The Academia resided in a pocket space between Liatt and Nightshade. Killian was certain that Karriamis, Candallar's Tower, had been instrumental in the revival of the Academia; he was also certain that he had been instrumental in its preservation, even if that preservation had been in stasis.

The absence of the border zone implied that the link between the Towers and the Academia had been lifted. Or maybe transformed. Kaylin wasn't certain because Killian wasn't certain. She didn't understand the lack of certainty on his part, and hoped that Helen might have information, or at least a solid opinion.

But it wasn't to Helen they were going, right now; it was to Liatt. Bellusdeo knew which roads would lead to that fief; she knew which roads would lead to all of the fiefs, including Candallar.

Mandoran seemed mostly relieved that Candallar wasn't the Dragon's destination, but if Kaylin were being honest, so was she. She didn't want to choose sides. She didn't want her housemates to become enemies or bitter rivals while they were still living under the same roof.

But…maybe it would be better, because at least Helen could contain the damage from the fallout of hostilities. And avoiding Candallar put off the day of reckoning.

The streets that led to Liatt were in good repair, as were the roads. The buildings beyond those streets made a stark contrast.

Liatt's native streets were very like the more run-down sections of Nightshade, to Kaylin's eye; the buildings were in need of repair, the windows—where shutters weren't so warped they couldn't be properly closed—were shuttered. Most of the buildings were two stories; some were three, and some were flat, single-story dwellings. Weeds, not grass, fronted them, and the road was pocked enough it would have given wagon wheels a hard time.

She looked above street level to see the Tower.

It was a tall, elegant spire of silver and gold, although the metallic hues didn't reflect the sunlight the way natural metals might have. There was just enough glow inherent in their visual presentation that the Tower itself didn't seem to be flat gray and yellow. Even had those been the primary colors, there was nothing workmanlike about this Tower. Tara's Tower was an ivory white, and it stood out anywhere in Tiamaris.

This Tower stood out more—but it looked down upon run-down streets. Or at least run-down streets near what had been the border zone. Perhaps as they approached the Tower, the streets would improve.

Kaylin had never considered the run-down streets to be an affront before she'd managed to escape the fiefs. She might not have considered them worse than, say, the warrens, had she not known Tiamaris.

But she did know the Dragon, and she'd seen what he and his Tower, in concert, were attempting to make of the fief, and now? She was resentful for the child she had been. For the children that were still trapped as she'd been trapped. She wanted change.

You might ask, Nightshade said, his tone far more neutral than usual.

Who? You? Your Tower? She snorted. *You made clear, the first time we met, that the citizens of the fiefs weren't your concern—except when they displeased you.*

Durandel would never consent to the sweeping changes Tara has made in Tiamaris. Can you imagine the front of my castle becoming vegetable gardens? Can you imagine that an Ancestor would care what the weak and the helpless do?

She couldn't.

But there are things that might be done. Durant's use of his Tower, to make wood and stone that lasts throughout all weather and its difficulties, is not one that I would have considered.

Your Tower would never allow it.

My Tower requires a certain amount of finessing, yes. But I do not think it entirely impossible. Understand that you are correct. The heart of the Tower is an echo of the person who became it, and our people change slowly. But they can change; you have seen that with your own eyes. And Kaylin, while you bear that mark, you have the right to ask.

The mark was so much a part of her face now, she forgot it existed unless she was introduced to a Barrani stranger. She wanted to keep it that way, and fell silent, prickling with discomfort.

It amused—and annoyed—Nightshade. It had been almost eight years since she had lived in his fief, but some of the reflexes persisted. Annoyed fieflord: bad.

Tell me what you know of Liatt.

You've asked this already. And I can see her Tower clearly, now. It is impressive.

It looks Barrani.

His silence was one of studied disgust.

It doesn't look Barrani to you?

It looks nothing like our architecture to me. Nothing at all. You identify silver and gold as the colors of wealth—and therefore power. You consider the Barrani to be powerful. Therefore you believe somehow this looks like our architecture. And our architecture is not all of one thing. The residences in the West March do not resemble the High Halls.

"What are you thinking?" Mandoran asked.

"I'm not thinking. I'm being thought at." She turned to him. "Does Liatt's Tower look like a Barrani building to you?"

He looked at the Tower. He looked back to Kaylin. One brow was crooked. "Is this a trick question?"

Nightshade was smug. Silent, but smug.

"Fine. Bellusdeo?"

"It looks like it could be, to my eye—but our homes, even our great Aeries, did not resemble Towers."

"It doesn't look Barrani to me," Severn said quietly, before she could demand his opinion.

"Seriously?"

"It's disproportionate. The height of the Tower on its own, you could make an argument for—but the base, no."

"Maggaron?"

Maggaron had stopped walking. He had practically stopped breathing. He shook his head, wordless.

Bellusdeo was instantly almost red-eyed as she turned to her Ascendant. "What?" she demanded. "What do you see?"

"I've seen buildings like this before," he whispered, the softness of his words belying his size.

Bellusdeo didn't ask where. She knew.

Kaylin suspected, because she now remembered the first time she had seen Maggaron. He had been on the wrong side of the *Ravellon* border, wielding a sword that had once been a person: Bellusdeo herself.

They had been lost to Shadow with the fall of their world,

and Kaylin had, with the marks of the Chosen on her skin, somehow managed to draw them *back*.

It was Kaylin who said, "In *Ravellon*?"

Maggaron nodded. "They were not...exactly like this. But close, except for the color."

"Starrante said his people—talking, sentient, giant spiders—lived in *Ravellon*. I think they might have been responsible for the portals that lead to other worlds, and that lead other worlds here."

Maggaron was almost green. "Spiders?"

She nodded. "The main body is probably my size; the legs make it all look larger. And eyes. There are lots of eyes. They can spin webs, but their webs aren't the usual envelop-your-prey kind of webs." She thought they could be, but tried, hard, to keep this to herself. "Did you see spiders like that in *Ravellon*? Do you remember?"

He was silent. The green tinge to his skin didn't improve.

"He did," Bellusdeo replied. Her eyes remained almost crimson as she stared up at the Tower's height. Her lips were compressed in a thin line, as if to stop a draconic roar from emerging. "I have very little memory of my time in that place. Maggaron has more."

"Starrante's people were likely enslaved, just as he was," Kaylin said. "And Starrante saved our lives. We owe him."

"He did not save mine," the Dragon snapped. She closed her eyes, the inner membrane rising first, the lids falling second. She then exhaled slowly. Kaylin was surprised to see the lack of smoke.

"Starrante's kinsman was chosen to be the heart of this Tower. Liatt's Tower."

Bellusdeo nodded.

"No one chosen to be the heart of the Tower could be associated with *Ravellon*. Perhaps Aggarok—I think that was his name—was chosen because he understood what his people could do. They needed someone who understood the nature of the portals woven by Starrante's people in order to block their access to the rest of *this* world."

"You're thinking out loud," the Dragon observed.

"It's relevant, though." Kaylin watched as the Dragon opened her eyelids; the lower membrane stayed in place, muting the orange her eyes had become. There were still flecks of red in the iris, but it was a distinct improvement.

"It is." Bellusdeo inhaled. "Thank you."

Maggaron was less grateful, but not less green. Clearly, he had the same spider buttons Kaylin had. Or maybe worse; he had seen more.

"They spin together," he whispered. "They create gates and portals that can move hundreds of those in the Shadow's command."

"Is there a central command?"

"What does central mean? Are you asking if Shadow has a king?"

"Maybe?"

He shook his head. "It is not the way Shadows think of themselves. They are part of a whole, not separate individuals."

"Were you?"

He nodded.

Bellusdeo stepped on Kaylin's foot. "Enough. That is not why we are here."

"No?" a new voice said. As there were no new people—no visible people—on the streets, Kaylin's hand fell to her dagger. "I would be delighted to know why you *are* here." The voice came from the left.

Bellusdeo had already turned toward it when Hope sat up, digging claws into Kaylin's left collarbone. He roared, which came out as the usual very loud squawk. If Liatt was mortal, he probably sounded like an angry bird to her.

She appeared, as if stepping through mist, or rather, she seemed to be a thing of mist, of silver mist, as she solidified in the streets of her fief.

Kaylin wasn't certain what she expected. She knew that Durant and Liatt were the two mortal captains of the six Towers. Durant had seemed entirely relatable and friendly; his architectural choices matched Kaylin's. She knew he was a fieflord, but...she liked him.

She was certain she would never feel the same way about Liatt. Nightshade had said she'd been the Tower's lord for longer than Durant; that meant longer than eighty years.

She wasn't young. She looked double Kaylin's age—possibly closer to triple. Her hair was a silver-gray, and her eyes a striking blue—a gray-blue that implied ice, not clear sky. Her face was long, the lines of it etched there by facial expressions like this one: grim.

Bellusdeo recovered quickly. She offered the fieflord a bow. "Lord Liatt. I am Bellusdeo. This is Maggaron, my Ascendant."

"I am not familiar with the concept of Ascendant," Liatt replied. "And your other companions?" Her gaze lingered longest on Mandoran, her eyes narrowing.

"This is Lord Mandoran. He is newly come to his title in the High Court of the Barrani. This is Corporal Neya and Corporal Handred. They serve the Hawks in the Halls of Law."

"Which has, as I'm sure you are aware, no jurisdiction here."

Bellusdeo nodded.

"You have been speaking for some time about the nature of my Tower." This was directed to Kaylin.

Kaylin felt underdressed and poorly mannered; there was something about Liatt's age that implied wisdom and regality. She was clearly the most significant power present. How she achieved the impression wasn't clear; she wasn't extravagantly dressed, she wore no emblems of office, and there was nothing about her appearance that implied her position here.

Maybe it was the confidence with which she faced a Dragon, a Norranir and a Barrani in the open streets.

"I spoke with Arbiter Starrante, in the newly reopened Academia. He's a librarian."

"Starrante, is it?"

"It's what he's chosen to be called by people who don't have the same vocal cords as his people do. He's a giant spider, by look."

She was silent for a much longer beat—as if she were an Avatar, not a person.

"The library is now accessible?" she finally asked.

"The Academia is accessible." Although it hadn't been Kaylin's intent to take over the conversation, she did because Liatt was speaking to her. "The library and its Arbiters can be reached through the Academia—and that's mostly why we're here. Bellusdeo, speaking on behalf of the chancellor, wishes to discuss the Academia and the possibility of students from Liatt.

"You'll note that the border zone has now disappeared. The border zone was, in some fashion we don't understand, the Academia. Or the Academia's stasis. Before the Towers rose, the Academia occupied a large chunk of land between Nightshade and Liatt. After the Towers rose, the border zones rose as well—and I think we all assumed—"

"We?"

"I grew up in Nightshade."

Her brows rose. After a pause she said, "You don't live there now."

"No. I live in Elantra. I couldn't be a Hawk, otherwise."

"I interrupted you. Apologies. Continue."

Kaylin exhaled. "We thought the border zones were there

because of the Towers. But they're not there now, and the Academia is."

"I have lost no land, and surrendered no responsibility," Liatt replied. "Liatt is mine. Its people and the barriers that protect us from *Ravellon*, my responsibility. If this Academia exists in its previous location, it does not exist on this plane."

"I don't understand it, either. But there are streets—solid streets—that lead from the Academia into Liatt, and from Liatt into the Academia and the buildings that surround it. There are streets that lead from the Academia to each of the six fiefs; we walked one to reach this fief today. We didn't cross a border zone. I'm very sensitive to portals and portal transitions, and I believe that I'd notice if we'd crossed one."

"Interesting." Liatt's expression implied the opposite. She fell silent again; it was the silence of winter. "Does the Academia accept visitors?"

"The chancellor accepts visitors, yes."

"And is the library open to visitors?"

Ah. "You want to speak with Arbiter Starrante?"

"I wish to ascertain the veracity of your statements, yes."

This was what they wanted, if sideways; Kaylin took a moment to untangle her offense at the implication she was lying. She glanced once at Bellusdeo, whose eyes remained a martial orange. But…Aggarok was a Tower. Even if Maggaron's memories were entirely accurate—and Kaylin suspected they were—she *knew* what it was like to be enslaved by Shadow.

And she wasn't enslaved, now. Shadow made everything complicated. It had been way easier to dismiss all of the Shadows as evil, as if anyone of any race could be counted on to be monolithic—a new word for Kaylin—in their behavior. Kaylin could even understand part of Bellusdeo's concern: Candallar was a fieflord, and Candallar had allowed a Barrani lord to walk into—and out of—*Ravellon*, carrying a Shadow with him.

Where before, the fieflords would be above suspicion, now they were all...people. People with their own goals and their own desires, some of which conflicted with the duties the Towers were created to fulfill.

"If you are comfortable doing so, we can take you to the Academia."

"I require a few moments," Liatt replied. She vanished, leaving a sparkling afterimage in the air in her wake.

"She's gone," Mandoran said. "She hasn't turned invisible." He was staring, brow furrowed in concentration, at the space she'd occupied. "There's something here, though—something sticky."

Kaylin passed a hand through the space she'd occupied. "I can't feel anything."

"It's not that kind of sticky. I think... I think she doesn't bother to walk to a destination if she wants to get there."

"Well, Aggarok—the heart of Liatt's Tower—is like Starrante; they're the same race. And Starrante weaves portals out of..."

"Stuff he spits out of his mouth, yes." He frowned. "We really don't understand how Towers work. The Hallionne are sentient buildings, but their internal architecture is very similar."

"They had a different purpose; they were built to stop you all from killing each other when you checked in."

"Which is why so many of our people won't, as you call it, check in. But that's beside the point. I think Liatt is making use of the portals Aggarok could once spin."

"I wonder if he talks to her. Durandel doesn't talk to Nightshade much."

"And according to you, Tara never stops. It's fifty-fifty. We don't know. But I'd guess there's more communication because she wants to visit the library."

"Maybe because she doesn't believe me."

Mandoran shrugged. "You are so accustomed to people believing you, it must be frustrating to be you."

"You aren't?"

"We can't lie to each other," he replied, indirectly referencing the cohort. "But we certainly don't expect anyone else to tell us the truth. A version of the truth, yes—but people are different. They want different things. They might consider us rivals or enemies in the far future. Or," he added, with far more guilt, "the near future."

"I do not consider you an enemy," Bellusdeo said softly.

"A rival?"

She snorted, with smoke. "Hardly."

Mandoran laughed. His eyes were green-blue, which was a distinct improvement; Bellusdeo's also showed flecks of gold. Kaylin wanted them to remain friends, but she understood, better than many, the rules of scarcity. They could not both get what they wanted—or even needed—here. There was only one Tower.

"I think...she's coming back." Mandoran's face lost even the hint of amusement.

Seconds later, Liatt once again emerged from thin air—or at least thin air in the vision of anyone who wasn't part of Mandoran's cohort.

"I would like to take a few of my own people with me. Will this cause difficulties?"

"Depends on what you mean by few."

"Two."

Kaylin shook her head. "That shouldn't be a problem. Would you like us to give the chancellor advance notice?"

"Is that possible, for you?"

Kaylin didn't grind her teeth.

Bellusdeo, however, was amused. "It is possible for *me*, and as I am the chancellor's representative here, I can certainly give early notice." Her grin deepened.

Kaylin reached up to cover both of her ears; the hells with constabulary dignity.

"Don't be ridiculous," Bellusdeo said. "There is no guarantee that Lannagaros would hear me, given the unusual nature of the Academia's geography. No, I have a better method."

Kaylin lowered her hands.

"Give me space," the Dragon said sweetly to the fieflord.

Liatt stepped back but seemed entirely unimpressed. She might have seemed unamused, but Kaylin would have bet money that she didn't have amusement in her.

Bellusdeo transformed, golden armor becoming golden scales, neck elongating, face stretching—without tearing—into a much larger shape. A tail emerged to balance it.

"Impressive," Liatt said quietly. "I have never seen a proper Dragon transformation before. How large are your wings?"

"Watch," the Dragon said, in a much deeper voice. The aforementioned wings, curled across her back, tightened. She *roared*.

Kaylin grimaced, certain she'd done it on purpose. Bellusdeo then pushed off the ground, the leap of draconic muscles carrying her up as if she was lunging at the sky. Her wings then snapped open.

"Impressive," Liatt said, her voice even softer, her neck craned up, exposing her throat to watch as the gold Dragon headed toward the Academia.

They did not follow immediately, because Liatt was waiting for her attendants, who emerged from thin air, as Liatt had done. To Kaylin's eye, they emerged in the same place their lord had, and they moved—naturally and casually—out of the way for the next person.

The first person through was a woman half Liatt's age. "This is Liannor. She is my daughter, and when I reach an age at which I can no longer carry out my duties, my heir."

Kaylin said nothing, but her expression must have been less than neutral.

"How other Towers and other fiefs guarantee that they will always have a lord is not my concern. She will be the lord of the Tower; the Tower has agreed."

"He would," said a voice that was too familiar. There was clicking and hissing in it, an undertone that implied either deeper meanings or a swarm of insects. Kaylin wasn't surprised when two hairy, insect-like legs emerged, and she backed up to give the second guard room. "I will have to have a word with him. This portal was clearly not designed for normal people to use." He spoke Elantran.

Liannor barely moved as this second guard emerged. "You're certain you're not eating too much?"

Liatt said nothing. Only when the last bit of the creature exited the invisible portal did she introduce him. "This is Riaknon. He is kin to the Tower."

"Does he live in the basement?"

"I imagine he lives wherever he chooses," was the cool reply. It invited no further questions. She did watch Kaylin carefully. Even so, she couldn't help but notice Severn.

Severn had lifted both of his arms in greeting, his elbows and fingers bending.

Liatt's expression shifted. She glanced at Riaknon. "Well?"

"It is clear he has met *something* that at least apes our customs. That," he added, "was perhaps meant as a greeting?"

Severn nodded. "I apologize. It's crude; Arbiter Starrante did not offer to teach me the appropriate moves with arms that naturally bend in the opposite direction."

Riaknon clicked. "Our limbs bend in *both* directions; we merely favor this one for movement." He hissed at Liannor.

Liannor grimaced and mounted Riaknon's back.

"We are ready, Liatt," Riaknon said.

"And excited to be so, I see. Very well." She turned to Kaylin. "These are my guards; I require no others."

"No, I imagine you don't. Starrante was involved in some of the fighting; I can well imagine that one of his kin would be more than enough to guarantee safety."

"Starrante was fighting?" Riaknon asked.

"It's a long story."

"I would hear it." Riaknon lifted his front arms, briefly. He then paused. "That is 'please' in our tongue."

"We will walk on foot," Liatt said. "The story of how you met Starrante will be much more pleasant than idle chatter." Implying, heavily, that otherwise they'd be walking in stiff silence.

Kaylin exhaled. She glanced at Mandoran, who very determinedly refused to meet her eyes. When she stepped on his foot, he said, "What? He didn't ask me. He asked you."

Kaylin told the story. She attempted to start at the beginning, but felt obliged to answer Riaknon's questions, and Mandoran threw an oar in, usually to correct her, which didn't help. Riaknon took the correction, but didn't expect mortals to have infallible or perfect memory. He also understood that with only two eyes, most races had difficulty accessing all available visual information.

Still, he told Liatt, he was now convinced that the corporals and their Barrani companion were telling as much of the truth as they were capable of processing.

Liatt nodded as if this was expected. Nothing about her posture, even while walking, implied that she had relaxed. Or that she could. She walked slowly; she might have been taking a leisurely stroll alongside visitors she didn't trust to wander about her property at will. But she followed where Kaylin led, noting, as they crossed the border of her fief, the repair of the buildings that had been removed by the creation of the Towers themselves.

The roads hadn't changed; they remained the roads that led out of the Academia. When they reached the circular road upon which the building that housed both students and library stood, Bellusdeo came to greet them.

"I should warn you," Kaylin told Riaknon as they approached, "that the chancellor is also a Dragon."

"Dragons are ferocious in their protection of the things they value and prize," Riaknon replied. "And it is likely a Dragon that is needed now. I can hear my hearts beating; I feel almost young again."

"Did you attend the Academia?"

"No. Aggarok did; I am not sure he loved it as much as was expected."

Bellusdeo had been watching them come, and if the presence of one of Starrante's people had come as a surprise, none of it showed. Her eyes were orange, but with the exception of a single interaction, that was the best they'd been all day.

"The chancellor would be pleased to meet with you," she told the fieflord. "Here, you will be styled as Lord Liatt, unless you express a different preference. Appropriate titles of respect are to be offered in the absence of stated preference." She glanced at Kaylin. "The woman who led you here is known as Lord Kaylin or Corporal Neya, when titles are to be used."

"I prefer Kaylin."

"Indeed? And I prefer Liatt." This was the first thing the fieflord had said that came as a surprise to Kaylin.

Kaylin saw Liatt to the chancellor's office; it was, and remained, large. The chancellor rose when Riaknon entered the room; Liannor, who had remained mounted for the entire journey, now dismounted.

Liatt introduced them all, and Liannor immediately availed

herself of a chair. There were no chairs available for Riaknon. Or rather, no regular chairs. The chancellor, however, said, "Those two sections of wall, and a portion of the ceiling, have been modified for your use, if you wish to take weight off your feet."

"I had best not. Liatt doesn't like the webbing."

"I do not dislike it, but it is not meant to be passable for my kin."

Liannor said, "And if you didn't forget it was there, it wouldn't be a problem."

Riaknon clicked.

Kaylin found herself relaxing. Liannor had spent much of her life around Riaknon and didn't find him terrifying at all. Which meant, in time, Kaylin wouldn't either.

Her reactions were her reactions, yes. They were visceral and instinctive. But her *behavior* was a choice—and if she had to struggle to make the right one, that was part of her job, wasn't it? She did look forward to the day when those instincts replaced raw primal terror with the comfort Liannor clearly felt.

"Before we begin," Liatt said, "I have a request."

"You wish to meet with Arbiter Starrante."

"I do, yes. Or perhaps it would be more accurate to say Riaknon does. I am not certain that a man trapped in a library for a large part of eternity will have much of relevance to say to me, but for Riaknon he is one of a handful of kin, no matter how distant."

"We understand sparsity of kin," the chancellor replied, voice grave and slightly rumbly although he wasn't in draconic form. On the other hand, he could probably transition into full draconic form in a room this size, without damaging himself—or the room—too badly.

"We might have the discussion your adjutant requested—"

here, she nodded to Bellusdeo "—while Riaknon visits the library, if you will grant your permission that he do so."

"He has my permission to request a visit, but the Arbiters and the interior of the library are not entirely under the jurisdiction of the chancellor."

"Interesting. The library is housed in this building, but you are not the final authority?"

"No. The library space is its own space. The Arbiters rule there, as certainly as if they were Towers. They are not," he added. "Something about the space itself allows this. I believe the Arbiters can leave the library, but there are some risks associated with it; to my knowledge, only Starrante has done so in the brief period the Academia has been open to visitors."

"Very well. How would I petition the Arbiters?"

"Killianas?"

"I will convey the request," the disembodied Avatar replied.

To Liatt's credit, she saw nothing unusual about this.

11

Riaknon followed Kaylin—and Mandoran—out of the conference room the chancellor's office had become; Liatt and Liannor remained behind. He was muttering to himself, which involved a lot of clicking and a very few dissonant syllables. At any other time, this would have worried Kaylin, but she felt the anxiety, the possibility of meeting distant kin for the first time in centuries, was nonetheless a familiar one; it mapped onto her understanding of people.

She herself had no such ties—but if she'd discovered that she had sisters or brothers somewhere in the world, she would have both wanted and dreaded the meeting. What if they didn't want to meet her? What if they weren't happy to discover her? What if she hated them on sight?

So many what-ifs. Riaknon's clicking probably expressed a lot of them, in a language she couldn't otherwise understand. She exhaled.

You're right. She was surprised to hear Severn's voice. Unless things were on fire—sometimes literally—he tended to avoid the communication given by a True Name she shouldn't have had. *I liked Starrante. I would trust him, if trust were a relevant issue.*

So would I. I just… Spiders.

She felt both amusement and chagrin; they might have been her own feelings, they were so much in keeping with hers.

You should ask Starrante what we—or Barrani—called their people. I'm almost certain we couldn't pronounce the native word.

She frowned. *Robin called him* Wevaran. *I think Robin had read about his race, somewhere in the library.*

Try to use that instead of "spider" when you're thinking.

He can't hear the words, anyway. It's not like I've insulted him.

Not for his sake, for your own.

Fair enough. Wevaran. Starrante and Riaknon were members of the Wevaran race.

Kaylin led and Riaknon followed, although he seemed to have difficulty walking in a straight line; for half of the walk through the halls he ended up skittering sideways on the walls, returning to the floor when he approached a door.

Students were in the hall. They watched with a mix of dread, fascination, and curiosity—much like Kaylin herself. She didn't blame them.

A very familiar voice caught her attention. "Are you going to see Starrante?" Robin was standing in the door frame of a wall that Riaknon had just deserted.

"*Arbiter* Starrante," came the immediate correction from an unseen teacher in the room behind Robin.

"Yes."

Robin lifted both arms in Riaknon's direction; his elbows implied he was trying to take flight.

Riaknon lifted his forelegs and repeated the gestures. "Starrante taught you?"

"I asked him. He says I have a good eye. Do you also weave portals?"

"Robin," the distant voice said.

"Tell your teacher we need you to lead a visitor—at the chancellor's command—to the library."

Robin grimaced. "I can't lie."

Fine. "Robin is being seconded to help a visitor reach the library. The visitor is a relative of Arbiter Starrante."

Silence, followed by the scraping—or the clattering—of a chair.

A Barrani man with gray hair—white and black strands that were otherwise perfect and long—appeared immediately in the doorway. It was Larrantin; his eyes were narrowed with either concern or anger. They were very, very blue.

Riaknon came to an immediate halt, repositioning his bulk without altering the orientation of his legs. "You!"

Larrantin spoke in a series of extended clicks, lifting his arms just as Robin had done, but—because he was Barrani—with infinitely more grace. "Riaknon."

The Wevaran clicked and spoke, the syllables clearly a language that *could* be learned.

"And your brother?"

"Zabarrok remained at home. If Starrante is truly present, I doubt we will be able to keep him there. You know how they were."

Larrantin's eyes had lightened; they were almost green.

"Were you concerned that I was infected?"

"You know what your kin were capable of when enslaved and set to work," Larrantin replied softly. "Yes. The students here are from a much benighted era; they are familiar with so few of the great races, they feel that true understanding of history is a waste of their precious time."

"They are mortal?"

"Not all of them have that excuse, no. But yes, many—like Robin—are mortal."

Riaknon clicked. "But mortals burn so brightly in their need to make use of the few decades they are given; much of what we learned we learned because of their curiosity and their odd interventions."

"Then if it will comfort you, I will tell you this: Starrante is indeed Starrante, he is whole, and he is still purely We-varan. We had some excitement in our attempt to once again reach reality."

"And you?"

"Do I look much changed?"

"Somewhat, although perhaps I should not say that—forgive me. Some of your customs—the clothing for one, and the importance of hair—have always eluded my understanding."

"But you have the tattoos and the markings that serve as identifiers; most of us would be unlikely to survive the process to lay them down. Certainly it would kill mortals."

"And it would look ridiculous. But come, come—I am to visit this library space in which Starrante lives and weaves, and I do not want to miss it. I will have to leave with Lord Liatt, and she is not a woman for many words when a single word will do."

"But she speaks with the chancellor now," Larrantin pointed out, leaving the class—and whatever students it had contained. "And the chancellor can, at need, be a Dragon of many, many words where one would suffice." He glanced at Robin, glared briefly at Kaylin, and then exhaled. "If you wouldn't mind my company, I will join you."

Robin didn't attempt to chatter at Riaknon; Larrantin was doing that just fine on his own. He did, however, talk quietly to Kaylin, theoretically still in the lead. He also chattered at Mandoran with none of the fear that children his age from the warrens would have shown so instinctively.

"I met your friends," Robin told him. "They say hi. I really like them. Serralyn especially."

"They like it here," Mandoran replied, at ease with Robin in a way that implied Serralyn at least returned Robin's regard.

"You don't think you would?"

"I have Sedarias constantly lecturing me. Why would I want to sit captive in a chair while anyone else does?"

Kaylin did her level best not to break out laughing, and only in part because she was at the head of the procession and Riaknon and Larrantin were certain to notice. In Larrantin's mind, Kaylin wasn't an officer of the law—she was like a student, but worse. A *lazy* student with no intention of applying herself to her studies.

But Robin and Mandoran started to talk about magical theory—and at greater and greater speed; Kaylin suspected that the person who really wanted the answers was Terrano, who wasn't present, as these weren't the normal questions the laid-back Mandoran usually asked.

Robin is, as Starrante suspected, promising indeed, Nightshade said softly. If the conversation was not one Kaylin was interested in, the same couldn't be said of Nightshade; he was listening, largely to Robin. Kaylin listened only because the kid was so excited and so enthusiastic, she could *almost* see what he saw.

And frankly, if he'd been talking about playing ball, she would probably have listened just as attentively. Happiness in the fiefs had been brief, and to be grasped whenever one could. Unhappy moments were bound to follow, one after the other.

Robin was from the warrens, not the fiefs; there were no Ferals to deal with. The streets might be unsafe at night, but for entirely human reasons. But his life hadn't been easy, either. To Robin, the Academia was heaven. And the library was like the highest perch in that heaven. He was practically bouncing on the pads of his feet, even through shoes, when the doors finally opened: the Arbiters had agreed to entertain visitors.

There was *noise*, a cacophony of clicks and crackles that had syllables of a kind in them. Riaknon entered the library vibrating in place; had Liannor been mounted, Kaylin thought there was a good chance she would have fallen off, he was shaking so much.

Starrante appeared at the sound of Riaknon's voice—and then there were two Wevaran clicking up a storm of sound that reminded Kaylin of...rattles, maybe? It was a strangely comforting analogy. She didn't step through the doors, but the library emerged around her anyway. The doors were part of library space.

Arbiter Kavallac chose to join them, as did Arbiter Androsse. Androsse, however, had eyes for Mandoran, and only Mandoran; two extremely delighted and loud Wevaran might have been an everyday occurrence, given his reaction.

Mandoran was watching the Wevaran, his eyes narrowed, his brow furrowed.

"What do you observe so carefully?" Androsse asked him.

"The boy," Mandoran replied, without otherwise turning to offer the expected, polite greeting.

Robin stood between the Wevaran, or rather, between and to one side, as if he were the apex of a triangle. His head bounced back and forth between the two, the way it might if he were following a normal conversation between two fascinating people.

"Why?" Mandoran's lack of manners were returned.

"The floor at his feet—and only at his feet—appears to be different. Or different from the floor beneath either of the other two."

"Interesting. And the floor upon which we are standing?"

Mandoran shook his head as if to clear it. He then turned to fully face Androsse and tendered him a perfect bow. "Apologies, Arbiter Androsse. I find the Wevaran fascinating."

"Dangerously so," Androsse replied. "And you have not answered my question."

"He is not your student." It was Larrantin, who had chosen to stand back from the meeting of the two Wevaran, who replied.

"Have I made the mistake of somehow inviting your opinion?"

Kaylin coughed.

Larrantin glanced in her direction, but it was brief; he was eyeing Androsse. "What is your concern?"

"You have functional eyes, ears, and magical sensitivity. My concern should be clear to you."

Ah. Old argument. It hadn't occurred to her that Larrantin could dislike the Arbiter, or vice versa. People tended to be less hostile to each other in the face of a pressing emergency. She was very glad that it was the chancellor's problem.

Mandoran, for his part, had ceased to stare at Robin and the two spiders; he was now completely blue-eyed and neutral.

"My question?"

"The ground beneath your feet—and mine—is remarkably similar. The ground beneath the corporal's feet, and Robin's, seems solid and mundane in comparison. The ground beneath the feet of the Wevaran is different again."

To Kaylin, it all looked like wood. Or stone.

Larrantin snorted. "You should take classes, boy," he told Mandoran. "You are lacking the proper vocabulary to discuss what you see."

"And you can see it?"

"Yes, although it was not something I was searching for upon arrival. But perhaps the Arbiter cares to explain. This is, in essence, his classroom."

"It is a vast repository of knowledge available for those who have the desire to better themselves; I have little use for people who must be led and cozened." His expression soured. "Perhaps you would care to describe it."

Kaylin, however, was confused. "It's your building. You don't know?"

"This was a found space," Arbiter Kavallac said. She did not seem to consider Mandoran the threat Androsse did, but that might have been because to her eyes Mandoran was a lone Barrani, and she was a Dragon.

"Found space?" Robin perked up instantly. Given he was standing beside the two loud Wevaran, Kaylin was certain she wouldn't have heard the comment had she been standing in his shoes.

Robin's sudden interest caused a distinct decline in clicking. The two Wevaran didn't move to face Kavallac—but given the smattering of eyes all over their central bodies, didn't need to.

"What have you been taught about found spaces?"

"Not a lot, and Garravus is *grouchy* when you ask him a question and the answer is: nobody knows."

"Ah. I do not think I have met Garravus. Barrani?"

"Yes. He's new."

"You don't care for him?"

"Well, he's not Larrantin."

"Some," Androsse cut in, "would consider that a good thing."

Robin clearly didn't. But Kavallac had asked a question, and if he looked hesitant, she *was* a Dragon. "The answer really seems to be: nobody knows. I didn't know the library was built in a found space, either. I mean—who found it?"

It was clearly a question of import to Mandoran, who had been off his stride all day.

"The Ancients found it."

"Did they build the library?"

"The library was built in the found space. When we speak of found spaces, we are not talking about geography; we aren't talking about space as might exist in the largest of your lecture halls. That space is, without Killianas's direct intervention, fixed. It is created by walls and architecture.

"This space is not that space; it is, in a physical sense, extensible in the way the Academia, or the Towers, are. I think we could expand the collection without pause for eternity, and the library would grow to accommodate the entirety of it. There are shelves in places that I have once or twice accidentally encountered; they are," she added, glaring at Robin, "entirely off-limits to students."

Robin flushed.

"Have you ever found living beings in your basement?"

The two Arbiters with obvious eyes shared a glance; Kaylin had no doubt Starrante had been part of it as well. "That is a question for another day," the Wevaran told her. "As is the question of this space. We call it library space, but if our library is to contain all knowledge, some of it is not considered safe."

"By who?"

"By the library space itself."

Kaylin felt her jaw drop. "Are you saying the library is *sentient*?"

"It is not sentient in the way we are, no. And that is what has concerned Arbiter Androsse, even if he is too curmudgeonly to own concern as a general concept. The library is reacting to your Mandoran."

Why did people insist on saying "your" in that tone of voice? She knew enough Dragons that she didn't bother to ask.

"I'm not doing anything," Mandoran said quickly, lifting both of his hands in the universal gesture that meant either surrender or *I'm harmless, look, no weapons.*

"If we believed you were deliberately doing...whatever it is you're doing, you would be ejected unceremoniously, regardless of your external status. But Androsse is perceptive. Starrante, if we might interrupt your reunion for a moment?"

Starrante did rearrange his body posture then—he pointed the bulk of his form, or at least his forelegs, in Mandoran's direction. He said, speaking in Barrani rather than his native tongue, "Riaknon, perhaps you have not gone entirely blind in your life outside of our home?"

"I have not gone, as you put it, blind at all. You will see that I still have all of my eyes. Unlike some people." He too angled his body in Mandoran's direction. Mandoran looked about as comfortable with this attention as Kaylin would have felt.

"Larrantin," Starrante then said, "you said you have friends of this boy in your class?"

"Yes. Two. I consider them gifted but unusual."

"Unusual?"

"Unusual for Barrani."

"How so?"

"They are...quite young for their professed age, and their attitudes have a surprising flexibility. This flexibility would not be met with approval among most of our kin. I find it interesting. They have spoken about their unusual childhood," he added.

Mandoran grimaced and Kaylin winced. She imagined that a few of the cohort had words to say about that and hoped that those words didn't spill out into another middle of the night emergency.

"Very little study has been done to determine how the green in the West March influences our kin, but it has been the suspicion of some experts that the green is also a found space."

"Might we speak with those students as well?"

"If they are amenable, and as my class has already been interrupted." Here he gave Robin a reproving glance that had too much approval in it to become a glare. To Starrante, he offered an apology.

"I am not certain I can accept an apology that is offered without reasons."

"They are new, and they are excitable. Although they have of course asked, they have yet to be granted permission to visit the library."

"Ah. Then perhaps I will accept what is graciously offered."

★ ★ ★

They must have run down the halls at breakneck speed, because at least one of them was slightly winded. Serralyn was glowing. Her eyes—unlike the eyes of every other Barrani present, including Mandoran—were emerald green. She was practically quivering in place. She did remember her manners, and she expressed such a profound sense of awe at her first sight of walls and walls of shelving that the Arbiters could not—or at least didn't—find it in their hearts to be quelling.

"Androsse?" Kavallac asked, as Serralyn, dragging Valliant and Mandoran by their arms, headed toward the nearest shelves as if she had finally reached the destination of a religious pilgrimage and meant to share.

Androsse, frowning, watched them. While green was the happy Barrani color and no one present could deny that Serralyn, at least, was radiant with happiness, suspicion existed regardless. Kaylin was impressed.

"They are," he finally said, "like Mandoran. Can you not sense the small disturbances their feet create when they walk?"

"She is hardly walking," Kavallac added, amused despite genuine worry. "Do you not remember the first time you encountered the library? Has so much time passed that even your memory has become fallible?"

"I believe I had a great deal more dignity."

"Ah, well. That is no doubt true. But I cannot find it in my heart to be suspicious of her intentions."

"I am not suspicious of her *intentions*. But there are disturbances now, where the three walk." He turned to Starrante, being possessed of only two eyes.

Starrante, his kinsman beside him, had turned in the direction of the three as the distance between them grew. "Yes," he finally said. "I can see what you see. It is...fascinating. I do not think the three are in control of the effects they are having; they have them simply by existing in this space at all. If we were prudent, we would deny them entry until we better understand those effects."

"If?"

"I feel that her joy is perhaps the heart of what this knowledge should represent, and it would pain me to forbid her the library."

"They have no Wevaran in their history, do they?" Riaknon asked, watching as Starrante watched. Multiple eyes were now open across their bodies, aimed in all directions. Kaylin couldn't make out distinct colors in the light but suspected that the emotional state of the Wevaran was not announced by a simple shift of eye color. But then she remembered Starrante's eyes when they were red.

"None whatsoever that I know of."

Since Kaylin's response would have been *that's impossible, look at them*, she was slightly discomfited by Starrante's reply; it implied somehow that the question hadn't been rhetorical.

"Do you know, Starrante, I've had an idea?"

Clicking became a storm of sound—one of those summer storms that dumps all the water in the sky in five minutes.

Starrante looked highly doubtful, and how Kaylin recognized this, she didn't know.

"It is possible that these new students of yours—"

"Not a student," Mandoran said quickly.

"—could actually be taught."

"And me?" Robin asked.

"No, child. It is not just about spinning webs—" or spitting them, Kaylin thought "—it's about walking the lines. Webs are spun but the lines they draw together are specific. It is not an accident; it is a deliberate choice on the part of the spinner.

"We—Starrante and I, and the rest of our kin—walked those lines from birth. We had favorites, and we were territorial; many did not survive their youth." He spoke without apparent grief. So, too, the Dragons. "We could not, of course, be what we were with one simple line, but we were capable of learning, and as we did, we were able to combine what we'd learned in new and different ways.

"And no, before you ask, we do not believe it was our experimentation that destroyed *Ravellon*—our home, and home to many. It is an art that is all but lost. Starrante was a master.

"And we have no young—not here, and perhaps not even in *Ravellon*. Those of our kin who were not destroyed have become a terrible danger to the worlds." Kaylin did not want Bellusdeo to hear this.

She is not a fool, and she is not a child, Nightshade said, chiding Kaylin as if she were both. *Do not think she does not know.*

"It is possible that these students might be capable of learning some small part of the art of walking."

"Perhaps," Starrante replied. "But they are new here, and they have not proven themselves in the most basic of subjects. I am willing to revisit this discussion should it become something of true relevance to their interests."

"It won't," a direly familiar voice said. Kaylin didn't bang her head against the wall because she wasn't standing near one. She did send a very pointed glare at Mandoran.

"Ah, young man," Starrante said.

"I'm Terrano."

"I believe I have seen the traces you have left here in your previous passage." To Riaknon he said, "I do consider this one promising."

"He isn't even a student," Larrantin pointed out. "And I do not believe he has received permission to enter the library."

"Clearly he has," Starrante said, "because he is demonstrably here."

"I couldn't get in very far the first time," Terrano added.

"Did your friends call you?" Starrante asked.

"No," Serralyn said promptly. "And Mandoran was begging him to stay at home." She seemed amused by both things.

"I was bored and Sedarias is in a mood, and Helen told me it was okay for me to leave." He then turned to the Arbiters and offered them a perfect bow. "What did you mean, walk a line?"

Starrante clicked.

Terrano clicked *back*.

Riaknon froze in place, but all of Starrante's eyes opened at once; it seemed to be the equivalent of hair rising.

Serralyn said, "Show off." In Elantran, of course.

Mandoran snorted. Valliant, however, said nothing; of the three he was most likely to pass for Barrani normal.

"In a fashion, it's impressive," Larrantin said. "I could not make the alterations that would allow me to speak to Starrante on the fly, and there are risks should I choose to make the attempt otherwise. You are not, however, a student here."

"I could apply?"

"You could, yes. I am not entirely certain that I would support your acceptance, but," he added quickly as Serralyn opened her mouth, "I believe you would have supporters among the student body."

"I would be interested," Starrante said. "I am not sure what I have to teach can be learned by most of the races, but you and your kin are different. It might work."

"Are some of the books here yours?"

"No. That is not the way we teach."

"But…you became a librarian?"

"I did not say I did not revere the knowledge contained herein—but it was not a form of teaching that could be condensed into words. Or perhaps not by us; words were perhaps a third of our lessons, if even that much."

"But…how did you teach without words?"

"Demonstration, of course. We are a practical people. Or were."

"Can I at least watch?" Robin asked.

"If it does not interfere with your classes, yes," Starrante replied, before anyone else could.

"I am against this," Androsse then said. "No, not you, Robin," he added, to the crestfallen boy, "but the teaching of Terrano. I do not feel it is either safe or wise, and I would forbid the library to all of those who are...slightly displaced." He turned to Kavallac, because her vote would be the tiebreaker.

"The boy almost reached the library when it was disconnected from any other world," she finally said, glancing once at Terrano, her eyes narrowed. "What Starrante sees, I do not see. But you are right—there is a perturbation that was less clear, given the excitement from which we have only just recovered.

"I would agree with you," she added, "but I do not think the decision is entirely ours. This is a found space. I believe on some level it desired to be found."

Riaknon was trembling in place. And clicking a lot.

Starrante was still, but it was an unusual stillness; he was silent as well, although he broke the silence eventually. "Remember the first line," he said quietly to his compatriot. "I am overjoyed to see you well after all this time. You have clearly made adjustments to living in what remains of the world."

"I live with mortals, yes," Riaknon replied. "And I will, with your permission and the permission of Lord Liatt, send Zabarrok to visit."

"If it is only my permission you require, you have it. I believe that the chancellor will also have some say. Zabarrok is living with...mortals. I think I almost have to see him in person to believe it."

"He does not leave the Tower much, it is true. Aggarok's presence is strongest there. But I am certain he will make an exception for you. Can you leave this place?"

"Experiments have long been held in abeyance. I can walk the halls of the Academia, and I imagine I could leave this particular building, but I am not at all certain I could now survive once I cross the boundaries. It is not captivity. It is choice, and I chose the library long, long ago."

"Just as Aggarok chose the Tower?"

"For different reasons, but yes. I believe that mine were innately more selfish, but I cannot imagine being trapped in one place and unable to weave at all for a week, let alone eternity." He then reoriented his body in Kaylin's direction. "You have my gratitude, Chosen. I had not thought to see any of my own kin in person again, and memories, even ours, lack substance and warmth; the facts remain but the emotions become extenuated."

"I had nothing to do with it," Kaylin said quickly. She'd inferred that Starrante and his kin—like the Dragons and Barrani—were immortal. She wondered if they had True Names, as the two immortal races she knew did. "Bellusdeo contacted Liatt, and Liatt insisted on bringing a guard—Riaknon. Probably because she wanted to be able to escape if she walked into a trap. You *can* do that, right?"

"I am not confined to this place, yes," Riaknon replied. "But surely you do not discuss security precautions with strangers?"

"Ah, no. Sorry. I was thinking out loud."

Mandoran snorted. "The chancellor's permission was required; make sure to thank him. Do you think the meeting is over now?"

"It is not," Riaknon replied. "But it's possible that Lord Liatt has extended the meeting to give me time to greet my kinsman. She wished me to come," he added, "to ascertain whether or not you had truly survived. She was inclined to believe it, but she is lord, and caution is necessary. Have you tried to weave the external into this place?"

"If you mean can I open a tunnel for Zabarrok, the answer at the moment is a very qualified yes."

This meant something to Riaknon. It didn't clearly have the same meaning for anyone else in the room, although Androsse grimaced.

"Qualified how?" Kaylin was left to ask. She'd waited a bit hoping Robin would do it, but he was silent—probably waiting for Riaknon, who had nothing to lose by asking.

"I can open portals and pathways back to the library from anywhere I happen to be standing. I believe Riaknon believes he can do the same—but I would not advise that you try while you are inside the library itself."

"Understood."

"Opening pathways from the library to other places is more challenging. The texture of the threads, the spinning itself, is often pulled by a gravity that affects very little else; the shape cannot always be guaranteed to maintain structural stability. The portal itself, yes; you no doubt think of our similarities to spiders, and our webs are similar in some fashion—they resist the equivalent of breeze and wind. They will not survive a gale.

"But they are persistent, and while we weave, there is some probability that the tunnel itself will become attached to the wrong place. It is not a risk, given the current precarious position of the Academia, I would be willing to take; I imagine the chancellor would be strongly against it."

"Bellusdeo would breathe fire," Kaylin pointed out.

"Yes? She is a Dragon."

"On you."

"Ah. You mean she would disapprove."

"Strongly. We don't yet know—" Kaylin exhaled. "We know that there were no Shadows in the border zones. We didn't know why. If the border zones were somehow attached to the Towers, it would make sense—but the Academia is no longer a border zone and we don't want to attract the attention of Shadow if we're not certain this is secure. It doesn't exist in normal space, but it can be reached by crossing it."

"If there were an infestation, as you fear, it is only the Academia that is likely to suffer; the Towers are aware of their strict boundaries, and that awareness has not changed," Riaknon informed them. "But I believe Lord Liatt would also be against the risk—not that she has final say." He clicked a bit but seemed to be thinking out loud. "I will tell Zabarrok that he will have to visit the mortal way."

"He doesn't like it?"

"No. He dislikes it intensely. In that, he has only grown more cantankerous with age. I will take my leave for today, but with the permission of the Arbiters and the chancellor, I will visit again."

"For my part, you have permission," Starrante replied.

"And for mine as well," Kavallac said. "Androsse?"

"I am fine with Zabarrok's visit. I am very concerned, however, with the presence of a possible visitor who is not even a student."

"I'll apply," Terrano said promptly. He offered Androsse a perfect bow.

Androsse was not comforted. "This is not a good idea."

"No, but most of the best ones aren't," Terrano replied. He couldn't keep the grin off his face; he was green-eyed and almost as excited as Serralyn.

This soured Androsse's mood, which hadn't been good to begin with, but Kavallac chuckled. "Does he not remind you of someone, Arbiter?"

"He does not."

"He does remind me of someone," Larrantin said. He had been so silent, Kaylin had almost forgotten he existed. "But that is my problem, not his."

"He is one of those unintentional dangers. He does not

think through the possible consequences of his actions," Androsse snapped.

"Some of those consequences are new, as the actions themselves must be; he has done and seen things that none of our kin have done or seen. I am certain there is information to share—and things to learn—that we would not have considered, given the limitations of our forms and our current existences. You are Arbiter, but your kin could see farther, and for longer, than ours. Are you not even slightly curious?"

"Please escort yourselves out of my library. Now."

12

Liatt's meeting concluded almost the instant Kaylin returned with Riaknon. Humans had eyes that didn't change color with emotion, but she seemed, if not pleased, cautiously optimistic. "Riaknon, you have arrived at a good time. We have just finished our discussion, and I have much to consider. Are you ready to leave?"

"I am. Starrante was well. There was a curious young man who entered the library; Starrante was distracted."

"And you appear to be distracted as well." She spoke fondly, and with obvious affection. Wevaran didn't appear to blush, but he lifted his forearms in motions Kaylin was pretty certain she hadn't seen before, clicking as he did.

"He has not changed very much."

"You are certain?"

"I am. I do not understand the Academia's location; the geography seems impossible given the existence of the fiefs. But he is Arbiter, in his library space. With the chancellor's permission—and yours, of course—I would like Zabarrok to visit. I think it would do him some good."

"If you can pry him out of the Tower, I would be grateful," Liatt replied. "I worry."

This was as much human warmth as Kaylin had yet seen Liatt show, and she was almost shocked by it.

"As do we all. Liannor?"

"I'm ready."

Riaknon then headed out of the office doors; Liannor walked—slowly—to join him. Once there, he flattened his body against the stone floors, and she climbed up his back. He then resumed his regular height, with passenger, but the ceilings here were more than tall enough for their joint passage.

Bellusdeo left the chancellor's office as well. She looked tired to Kaylin's eye, but not angry or irritated. "The chancellor invites you to remain for lunch," she told Kaylin. The emphasis on the word *invite* made it a command, but…it was lunch, and it was free.

"Corporal Handred as well?"

"Of course. He understands the practical importance of partners within the Halls of Law."

"And me?" Mandoran asked.

"I am certain he will tolerate it, although he will not be pleased if either you or Terrano causes difficulties in the dining hall. Remember that Serralyn and Valliant are new students here, and the reputation they establish will serve as their grounding when dealing with the various scholars who are willing—at the moment—to teach them."

Mandoran rolled his eyes. "Lunch sounds better than lecture," he said.

Bellusdeo snorted smoke.

"You're not staying?"

"I am to join the chancellor at the head table," she replied, which was yes. "Lannagaros seemed to feel that if I did not remain for lunch, Kaylin wouldn't, and I'm not spending the rest of the afternoon listening to her stomach."

★ ★ ★

The cohort, Robin and the two Hawks shared a table together. Terrano was sparkling at Serralyn, who was radiant in return. Valliant was much quieter, but his eyes were mostly green. Mandoran's, however, had descended into blue and from his expression, looked likely to remain there. He wasn't speaking out loud; no doubt Sedarias had advice. Or orders.

But it was interesting to observe. The other three heard the same things that Mandoran did; he seemed to take them far more seriously.

Robin, excited as well, was a burble of words and questions, and Serralyn appeared to be happy to answer them. Terrano might have, but she got there first, a dynamic that had never existed while she'd lived under Helen's roof.

"So, after lunch, what are you two doing?" she asked Kaylin.

"Not sure—mostly following Bellusdeo. At Imperial command."

"Meaning you're getting paid for this."

"I'd better be."

Serralyn laughed. "She's been in a bit of a mood, since…"

"I'm sure Sedarias has as well."

"No. Sedarias has been in a *lot* of a mood. I'm surprised Terrano escaped it."

"Oh?"

"They talk a lot. Even in person. He really shouldn't be here. But he heard the Arbiters, and he wanted to talk to Starrante, so he came anyway. I don't think he could have walked into the library if Mandoran hadn't been there as well." She glanced at Mandoran, who ate very little, and chewed as if his food was made of leather.

Her expression dimmed, and she reached out and put an arm around Mandoran's shoulders. Instead of stiffening, which is what Kaylin would have done, he relaxed. "I like being able to do different things," he said quietly.

"But he doesn't like being seen as different or abnormal," Terrano finished.

"And you don't care."

"Not even the tiniest bit. We *are* different. But it's not a bad thing."

"The High Halls?"

"It's not bad for most of us. Annarion still has difficulty if he doesn't concentrate. And *we* didn't attack the High Halls. We might be different, but we're still Barrani."

Serralyn frowned. "You're going to follow Bellusdeo?"

Kaylin nodded.

"And Mandoran is going to follow you. Maybe you could take Terrano instead?"

Mandoran shook his head. "He's too distracted right now. And I want to know where you learned to speak like that."

"Like what?" Terrano asked, around a mouthful of food.

"Like a spider."

"Wevaran," Robin said, correcting him.

"Fine. Like a Wevaran."

"I've heard the speech before," Terrano replied.

"You've met Wevaran before?" This time it was Kaylin who asked.

"Not exactly met, no. But I've heard them before. I listened for a long time."

"I've listened—"

"No, I mean, I did nothing *but* listen. To the clicking. There's a tone to it, and a beat to it, and if you listen long enough you can distinguish individual speakers."

"*Where?*"

He shrugged. "Nowhere dangerous, I promise."

All three of the cohort turned their eyes on him.

"No, really. I'm not an idiot. I can listen from a safe distance."

"Please do not tell me you were listening on the edge of *Ravellon*."

"Okay."

"I am so grateful Bellusdeo is sitting up there and not here. She would strangle you."

"I'm considering it myself," Mandoran muttered. "Sedarias is now screaming in *my* ear because you're ignoring her."

"I'm not ignoring her—I can hear every word she says." He grinned. "She's worried. You know what she's like when she worries."

Mandoran grimaced—but so did the other two. Only Terrano seemed to find any amusement in it. "Anyway, I listened. I listened for a long time."

"How long is long?" Kaylin asked.

"Long enough. I couldn't make the noises myself, not initially—and I wasn't stupid enough to try to get their attention. But some phrases were used here and there. It's strange," he added, his voice becoming momentarily more serious. "If I wasn't certain they were in *Ravellon*, I wouldn't necessarily have known. I think they might be, in the end, like the creature in the High Halls after their enslavement; they're talking as themselves, but they don't have full control of what they do."

"If what Starrante has said is true—and I believe it," Kaylin said quickly, because she did, "they were fundamental in the finding of the many worlds, in the doors that led to and from them. At the height of *Ravellon's* golden age, before its fall, they were the heart of the movements between those worlds."

"They can't spin like that now, at least not in the fiefs." It was Robin who supplied this information. "The Towers prevent it. I think the Towers will always prevent it—it's too dangerous. To allow the webbing—I mean, it's not webbing, but that's the word we've got—to take hold anywhere in the fiefs is to allow one of the greatest threats purchase in our lands."

Kaylin's frown deepened. "That's not true, though."

"Oh?"

"Aggarok is—or was—Wevaran. Liatt's his captain, now. And I'd bet any money you want that Liatt travels her own fief with the use of those portals, those webs."

"Maybe she can trust Aggarok because he *is* a Tower?"

"Or maybe she can trust him to tell the difference—I don't know. But at a guess, I'd say he volunteered *because* he could. Starrante was an Arbiter before the Towers rose. You'd probably have to ask him."

Robin brightened. "I will. He likes it when I ask interesting questions," he added, as everyone swiveled to look in his direction. "And this would be an interesting question—I'm sure of it."

"We'll leave that to you, then," Kaylin told the boy. She'd been eating throughout. "I think Bellusdeo is getting ready to leave, and we have to follow her." She turned to Terrano. "Please don't do anything stupid."

"Killianas is like Helen," Serralyn said, when Terrano failed to answer. "I'm pretty sure he can protect the Academia from any of Terrano's acts of stupidity."

Kaylin had been certain, but Androsse's reaction had unsettled her more than she wanted to admit. She nodded anyway.

"We have Liatt on board," Bellusdeo said, when they met up outside of the dining hall. "Durant. Tiamaris and Nightshade."

"Farlonne?"

"Farlonne was not only on board, but happy to be so. The little details—timing, number of meetings, forms of communication—are still being worked out. Most of the Towers have very, very little mirror capability. Even Tara confines all such communications to one room. If Tiamaris was not in part dependent on mirror use, I highly doubt she would have that capability at all."

"Helen's the same."

"There are enough incidents on record of disasters with the mirror network that I consider them both to be wise."

Kaylin nodded. The Dragon was orange-eyed; Mandoran, silent, was blue-eyed. Severn was himself.

"Candallar," Kaylin said.

Bellusdeo exhaled. "The fief that was formerly Candallar, yes."

"The Tower's core was provided by Karriamis." It was Mandoran who said this, which surprised Kaylin, although he'd been present for the whole of the conversation.

"You think that gives me an advantage?"

"Not really," he surprised them both by saying. "I'm sorry to say this, but—if you were Emmerian, I think it would."

"I do not believe Lord Emmerian has any interest in captaining a Tower," she replied, her lips crooked in the left corner in something that was midway between a grimace and an actual smile. "You refer to my gender?"

He nodded. "I didn't think it would be as much of a problem, but..."

"Arbiter Kavallac did not approve."

He failed to answer, and Bellusdeo turned to Kaylin. Kaylin hesitated. "She didn't approve, no. But—she can't leave the library, and I think she'd be happier to have children than you'd be."

"And you think she would hate it."

"I think what she wanted was the library. I don't think it's her hoard—I mean, she has to share it with Androsse and Starrante—but it was the thing she was willing to devote the rest of her life to. But...she's also a Dragon. Being a librarian didn't change that. I also think she'd have children if she could."

"And I can."

"I think that's what she believes, yes."

"And you?"

Kaylin clamped her teeth together. The silence lasted for at least fifteen seconds. "I don't get why it's such a big deal right now. I mean, I get it with us—with mortals—because we're going to age and die. We've got decades. You've got forever. Does it matter right now?"

"She could die," Mandoran said quietly. "Immortal doesn't mean invulnerable. And Dragon families—well, Aeries—are not like mortal families. They're more like Barrani families."

"Even that is inaccurate," Bellusdeo said, but softly.

Barrani often considered their closest relatives their most dangerous enemies. Kaylin cringed because in her limited experience with Barrani families, this had proven true.

"Given that there are no others who can bear clutches, the lack of a clutch, even now, is a threat to the race."

"But they did just fine when Bellusdeo wasn't here."

Mandoran and Bellusdeo exchanged a single glance.

"I just... I don't get it. They've been where they are for a long time now. Centuries, right? And they've been fine. But now that she's here she's supposed to drop her entire life and have babies—"

"Eggs," Mandoran said.

"Whatever. Babies. Eggs. She's supposed to just have them all right now when she doesn't even have a father in mind? She's got time."

Mandoran glanced at Kaylin. "Coward."

"What?"

"You just want this entire fight and its decision to happen sixty years from now, when it won't be your problem. You think like a mortal."

"I *am* one. How do immortals think?"

Mandoran shrugged. "I think it's up to Bellusdeo."

"But you just argued against it!"

"No, I didn't. I'm pointing out what Dragons are probably thinking. I figure Bellusdeo can speak for herself. And you'll note she hasn't argued with my interpretation. Kavallac's feelings are immaterial because she can't affect what happens.

"But Karriamis? He can. If it's Bellusdeo who wants the Tower and he understands the position his former race—or present race—is in, it's going to affect his decision."

"And there's no way he doesn't know."

"No."

"Candallar probably supported their attempts to kill or smear her."

"Yes. That is the only possible sliver of light presented. It's possible Karriamis is far enough removed from the Dragons that it won't matter."

"And there's only one way to find that out, isn't there?" Bellusdeo said. Her eyes were orange, but flecked with neither red nor gold. The inner eye membrane was up, muting the color. She started to walk away, stopped, and looked over her shoulder at Mandoran. "Thanks."

The road that led to the fief of Candallar—as it was currently named on official documents—was in the same state of repair as the road that had led to Liatt. Kaylin thought it a pity that these buildings weren't occupied, and then pulled back; she had no idea if they were occupied or not. They would have been, when she had lived in Nightshade, wouldn't they? By people as desperate as she had been when she'd been younger.

But she saw no faces in the windows, and knew that the warnings about the border zones had, and would have, lingering effects. She wondered if Ferals crossed over here, in a way they wouldn't when she'd been a citizen of Nightshade—if *citizen* had any meaning in that fief.

That is unkind.

You never cared.

No. He was both amused and very slightly chagrined. *Do not look for sympathy or empathy from the Barrani; you are bound to be disappointed.*

That's just an excuse, she shot back. *Teela. The Consort. Even members of the cohort. None of them would be like you.*

Sedarias would, in all likelihood.

That was, Kaylin thought, the core of her problem. She liked individual members of the cohort; she could even truthfully say she liked Sedarias. But Sedarias would, in her view, be like Nightshade and not like Tiamaris or Durant. Maybe he was right. Maybe the Barrani who took power assumed that power itself was the defining social trait, the only one that needed to be respected.

She didn't know the people of Candallar, but felt she still had more in common with them than she did many of the citizens of Elantra, whose laws she was sworn to uphold.

You are a Hawk. What you might have had in common with the people of my fief has long since been lost.

"Do you think people could live here?" It was Mandoran who asked.

"I don't see why not. Do you think the Ferals could come here now?"

"I don't see why not," he replied, mimicking her tone. "But the buildings of the fiefs provided some protection against them?"

"Some. You didn't want to be in the streets. But if parts of a wall were missing, you didn't want to be in the building either—they'd enter through them. They'd scratch doors as well—but they couldn't bring them down. Or not easily." She shook her head to clear it. She still had nightmares about Ferals. Even knowing that she walked the streets beside a Barrani and a Dragon didn't change those.

She could mark the point of transition between the streets

that led to the Academia and the streets that had been part of
Candallar for much longer. The Candallar buildings, like the
Nightshade buildings, hadn't been preserved in the odd stasis
of the border zone; they looked worn and run-down.

Kaylin became less concerned about the buildings and her
own history in dwellings that were practically falling down.
They'd been empty because they were almost as unsafe as the
Ferals themselves to the people who'd abandoned them. They
were infinitely safer to people who would otherwise be in the
streets when the Ferals roamed.

She looked up as Bellusdeo paused.

"Is…that what the Tower looked like when you did your
flyover?"

"No."

"Do you think someone else got here before either of us
could?" Mandoran asked.

"I know as much about the Towers as either of you do. Why
would you expect me to have the answers?"

"Tara changed," Kaylin said. "When Tiamaris claimed the
Tower, she changed."

"Tara and Karriamis were alike only in their determina-
tion to protect the rest of the world from *Ravellon*." But Bellusdeo looked at this new edifice, frowning.

It didn't look like a Tower, to Kaylin's eye; it looked like a
cliff face. This was only disturbing because it lacked the bulk
of the rest of the cliff; it might have been a standing stone,
worn by the passage of many rivers, all of which had long
since dried up.

It was as broad at the base as the entirety of Castle Nightshade's visible grounds, and it seemed to lack something as
architecturally practical as a door.

The streets were, predictably, almost entirely empty in all
directions—but someone wearing golden plate mail and attended by at least one Barrani was someone to go out of one's

way to avoid. Kaylin would have looked only if she'd been safe above the ground and there were shutters to peer through.

As they stared at the Tower, Bellusdeo frowned.

Kaylin understood why almost immediately; a shadow, moving in the opposite direction of the wind, passed overhead.

If they had had any hope of enticing the fief's citizens into the streets where they might ask questions, Bellusdeo dashed them. She lifted her face, exposing her throat as she looked in the direction of, yes, the Dragon flying overhead. She *roared*.

Kaylin was not a native Dragon speaker or interpreter. The roar meant one of two things: *land* or *go away*.

As the Dragon that had cast the familiar shadow landed, Kaylin assumed Bellusdeo had said the former, because she recognized the Dragon: it was Emmerian. He immediately transformed into the person-with-plate-armor form, and dropped to one knee before the gold Dragon. Kaylin then revised her assumption.

Bellusdeo glared at him, but her eyes, although still orange, revealed flecks of gold. "Have you been circling the fiefs since we left home this morning?"

"No."

"Have you been circling Candallar?"

He grimaced, lifting his head. "It is in Candallar that the greatest threat to your safety would be. Lannagaros has the Academia well in hand, and I doubt occupied Towers would seek to antagonize a Dragon of your stature and abilities."

"Get up. I dislike the entire bent knee paradigm. It implies that I can't see respect when it's offered otherwise."

Emmerian rose, a single fluid unbending of knee and head and shoulders. His armor, blue to Bellusdeo's gold, was a statement. If he did not expect that she would encounter difficulty she could not handle, he intended to be her backup.

Just as Severn had been Kaylin's. Or maybe she'd been his;

in the thick of things it was harder to separate. Oddly, watching Bellusdeo's orange eyes, she thought there was very little chance that the gold Dragon would send the blue one away. But little chance wasn't zero chance. They all waited, except for Hope, who was once again draped limply across her shoulders.

Bellusdeo finally snorted smoke and turned, once again, toward the Tower of Candallar, such as it was. "Do you imagine that the Tower looked like this before Candallar's death?" she asked.

"It did not," Emmerian replied. "Young Tiamaris—ah, apologies, Lord Tiamaris—entered the fiefs. He kept a safe distance from the Towers, but this is not what his report described. I would say the Tower is announcing the lack of a lord."

Mandoran nodded. "What do you want to bet that the door is on the top of the cliff?" he asked Kaylin.

"Wouldn't touch it."

"But you bet about everything!"

"I don't bet to lose."

"But you lose a lot."

"Not on purpose. And yes, this means I think the entrance is at the top."

"So…made for Dragons?"

"Or Aerians." She grimaced, turned, and met his blue gaze. "Or the cohort, because I know damn well you can fly."

"We don't call it flying."

"I don't care what you call it—you would reach the top of that cliff if you wanted, and you wouldn't be climbing."

"And you?"

Kaylin glanced at Severn. He shook his head. "I don't think flight is necessary."

"You see a door or a portal?" Her expression made clear which of the two was worse.

Severn then turned to Bellusdeo. "We are your escort. Do you wish to fly up to the Tower height?"

"Without you?" Bellusdeo grinned.

"Lord Emmerian is here, and Lord Emmerian can—demonstrably—fly."

We can't just let her fly off!

Severn said nothing, waiting.

Emmerian, however, said, "There did not seem to be an entrance at the top of the cliff, at least not in the aerial view. I did not think it wise to land."

Mandoran, however, began to rise, his feet leaving the cobbled stone that looked so incongruous at the foot of a cliff. "I'll look."

The two Dragons exchanged a longer glance. Bellusdeo, however, shook her head. "Lead on, Corporal."

It was clear that the corporal in question was Severn. He bowed briefly, a bob of acknowledgment, and turned toward the cliff base. Kaylin followed him as he approached. It looked to be mostly dirt and stone, although weeds also figured into the mess.

A door of the regular kind would stand out like a sore thumb; a door that was a cleft in the cliff face, or possibly a cave entrance, wouldn't. They therefore looked for gaps of that kind. Although approaching from one side gave the appearance of a solid wall of cliff face, that cliff face was almost circular. What rose, rose in the same space Kaylin suspected the Tower occupied, stretching toward the sky.

Two full circuits failed to reveal an entrance. Bellusdeo was surprisingly patient; Kaylin was not.

"My skin is prickling," she finally said.

Severn didn't miss a step. "Magic?"

"Like magic. It's not painful, yet—more ticklish."

Severn's expression made clear this wasn't good. Kaylin's

skin didn't react this way to Helen's magic, or the magic of the Hallionne. Then again, she'd never stood outside of one, desperately seeking entrance.

"Do you think Mandoran will find a way in?" she asked.

"Probably."

"Could Teela?"

"If she listens to the rest of the cohort, yes."

"Let me try something."

He stiffened for the first time. "What?"

She turned to face the patch of cliff in which the remnants of roots seemed to be exposed. Reaching out with her left hand, she touched a gnarled, desiccated root. She cursed.

"What is it?"

"It's bloody *cold*. I think my hand might be stuck to it."

"Good thing you didn't lick it, then."

"I was seven years old!"

Bellusdeo snickered. Emmerian didn't.

Severn reached out to touch the root as well. He nodded. He then touched the dirt in which the root was lodged and shook his head.

Kaylin exhaled. Hand on ice, she said, "Hello. My name is Kaylin Neya. I'm here with friends, and I hope you're accepting visitors."

She felt movement in the ice beneath her hand; the side of the cliff seemed to absorb the root whole, changing, as it did, into something infinitely more rocky. She stepped back; the transformation didn't seem to require contact.

"I think that's a qualified yes," Bellusdeo said, joining Kaylin although she kept her hands to herself. "There," she added. A cave mouth emerged from the rock face.

"You brought light?" Kaylin asked Severn.

The gold Dragon snorted. "I can light the way. You can, as well, and it's good practice."

"I can't consistently—"

"The marks of the Chosen. But that shouldn't be necessary while either I or Emmerian is here." She stepped past Kaylin.

Emmerian cleared his throat, a rumble of sound. Nothing Dragons verbalized was ever subtle.

"You are not here as my guard," Bellusdeo said stiffly, without looking back.

"No. I believe the two Hawks are. The Emperor's Imperial Guard is, with a single exception, comprised entirely of mortals. Allow Lords Kaylin and Severn to scout. It is the duty they've been given."

"We are not at war. Scouts are not required."

"We are always at war," was the very soft reply.

Her exhalation was smokeless. Kaylin felt her shoulders inch down her back. "Yes," the gold Dragon said. "You are right. Hope, I will eat you if anything bad happens to her."

Hope sat up—slowly and somewhat reluctantly—and squawked a reply.

"You know how it goes," Kaylin whispered. "The only person who's not allowed to worry about her friends is me."

"I heard that. And you are allowed to worry as you please—you're just not allowed to make it our problem."

The mouth of the cave was one and a half people wide—if you were Kaylin-sized, and most of the people present weren't. Mandoran hadn't drifted down from the heights, either—but he didn't care if she worried about him.

"We're going to need light." She glanced over her shoulder—the one Hope wasn't snickering on. Having received Emmerian's support for scouting, she didn't want to go back to Bellusdeo and ask her to create magical light. Not when—as the Dragon had pointed out—she could provide illumination on her own. Grimacing, she rolled up one sleeve and stared at her arm.

The marks that adorned it began to glow. The glow was

gold, but the edges of each runic mark were blue, and this time, they didn't all emerge from her skin to rotate in a pattern around the forearm. She touched the one that looked the most familiar, and it rose, shedding light. She felt its weight as if she were carrying actual gold.

The mark's light illuminated curved, roughened cave walls. As it did, the walls transformed, bumps and cracks flattening as if in response to the word Kaylin carried, until they were standing in a regular stone hall, with a taller than necessary ceiling, no obvious windows, and no doors. She couldn't see the end of the hall and hoped that a door might exist once they reached it.

Ten yards into the cave that had become hall, she felt a wave of dizziness; it was met in the other direction by a wave of nausea.

"Are you all right?"

"This…is a portal passage," she told him. "I apologize in advance."

"I'll try to stand back if you feel the need to lose lunch."

She shook her head, and instantly regretted the motion. "Go get the Dragons and Mandoran if he's joined them. This is the portal. If they can see and enter the cave, we're in."

Kaylin was green and queasy by the time she managed to drag herself to the expected door at the end of the hall. She had managed not to lose her lunch and would have considered that a win if her stomach wasn't trying hard to even the score in round two.

"Next time," Bellusdeo said, looking in Kaylin's direction, "we are flying to the top of the cliff."

Mandoran had not returned.

"I'm not sure that would make much difference."

"You don't have this problem with Tara."

"No. But I have it every single time I've ever visited Nightshade's castle. Tara is taking a risk by skipping the portal part of entry. She's leaving herself open just to accommodate my stupid magic allergy. Clearly the Tower formerly captained by Candallar isn't as kind."

"*Foolish* is the word you want," Bellusdeo replied.

"I don't consider it foolish."

"You should—she is taking a risk that no Tower should willingly take, except at the command of its captain, and I am absolutely certain that this was not done at Tiamaris's command."

So was Kaylin. "There are a lot of ways to be more secure. Most of them are illegal."

"Tiamaris—as are all fiefs—is considered a sovereign state. He gets to make the rules."

"If he were the type of lord to be neglectful, like Nightshade or Candallar, I don't think Tara would have accepted him."

"Why not? You've said she was desperate. And lonely."

"Because she'd *already* suffered the loss of a lord who just lost interest and wandered away? I don't think she was looking to repeat the same mistake. And Tiamaris..."

"Yes?"

"She's his hoard, as you well know."

"You think that's what she needed?"

"I think she knows how Dragons feel about their hoard—but he didn't seem insane and destructive about it. She didn't have a lot of time to make the decision. What he wanted, she wanted to give. Or to be given."

"She wasn't a Dragon."

"No, and Karriamis was. Or is. You want me to open the door?" she asked of Severn.

"No. It's warded."

"I don't see a ward."

Silence.

"Bellusdeo? Emmerian?"

"I see a door ward," Bellusdeo said. Emmerian nodded.

Great. This was not the ideal start to their first visit to a Tower. She turned to Severn, who nodded; she then borrowed his eyes, or at least his vision, through the True Name bond. The True Name that Kaylin shouldn't have had, because she was mortal and mortals could live perfectly fine without them.

There was a ward on the door, at the height of Kaylin's head. Or rather, there was a mark on the door that would— on normal but more expensive Elantran doors—have been a door ward. It was strangely shaped; it didn't bear the usual structural form of the marks that adorned over half her skin.

"I don't think the ward is a word," she finally said.

"It is," Emmerian replied. He glanced at Bellusdeo, who was frowning. After a pause, she nodded. Kaylin hadn't known that Dragons even had a written language; none of the official documents were written in it. Imperial documents were Barrani all the tedious, long-winded way down.

"Writing was not something actively pursued except by the dedicated or the obsessed," Bellusdeo added. "It is not necessary for a race with almost perfect memory, and it would not hone our ability to fight. But...I recognize it."

"Do you know what it means?" Kaylin asked.

Bellusdeo shook her head slowly, as if reluctant to expose ignorance in this place. Emmerian said, "It means flight."

"Like—flying, flight?"

"Yes."

"But weren't your military units called flights?"

"Yes, in Barrani."

"Was it used on doors?"

"The Aerie had very few doors," he replied. "But some arches had been constructed, and this was the keystone to one."

"And if there was no written language, how did the Arkon—the chancellor—ever come to be what he was?"

"There was a written language. My greatest pity at the moment is reserved for Sanabalis, who must now learn the parts of it he did not learn in his youth. And no, Lord Kaylin, I did not learn it, either. I was young, strong, healthy, and there was a war. But this particular word was used in the presence of those of us who could both fly and walk as you normally walk. It was above arches that were meant for people our current size to pass through."

"Did they have a different word for those who couldn't?"

"Children. If it helps," he added, at her expression, "Bellusdeo would not have been allowed through that particular arch."

"I was."

"Passing through it doesn't imply permission. Your test was different."

"It wasn't a test."

"No? Perhaps not in your Aerie. In ours it was a declaration of adulthood: we found, for ourselves, the duality of name that defines us as adults, and we did not lose that knowledge. The one side did not overwhelm the other. Only those who could transform could fit beneath the arch."

Meaning males. Females could have walked beneath the arch from birth. "So...you think this is meant for you two? For Dragons?"

Emmerian nodded.

"Then why can Severn see it?"

"That is a reasonable question; I cannot answer it. The ward, such as it is, is meant for us."

"For you," Bellusdeo replied.

"Us. I have no intention of becoming the Tower's lord; I have sworn my oaths of allegiance, and I will not break them for anything less than the hoard I have not yet found."

"The Tower could not expect that all Dragons seeing this would understand it."

"The former Arkon couldn't expect that either. You will note it never stopped him."

Bellusdeo's grin was brief, but genuine. "I don't think that's what he expected from me." She spoke Elantran.

"No, and not for the reasons that occupy others," he continued in Barrani.

"If I had to guess," Kaylin said, almost sorry to interrupt them, because what Emmerian had said was important with regards to Bellusdeo, "I'd say *if* this is a door ward, it's meant for Emmerian to open."

13

Emmerian considered this, and nodded. He stepped forward, an odd shadow of a smile on his lips, and placed his left palm across the ward, the gesture almost possessive, as if he were claiming it for himself.

The door didn't open; it vanished, fading from sight beneath Emmerian's palm.

It was therefore Emmerian who led the way in. If Bellusdeo resented this, it didn't show. Hope squawked loudly, his screechy, almost birdlike tone filling the room beyond the door. It was a very, very tall, very wide hall, and it reminded Kaylin of the High Halls in its construction, except for one thing: while the floors, ceilings, and pillars were stone, they appeared to be made from a single piece; there were no seams, nothing that implied this had been built by people who had to rely on experience and tools.

The superficial resemblance to the High Halls ended; although pillars supported the vaulted ceilings above, there were no statues, no paintings, no tapestries, on any of the walls. There was an arch, not a door, at the far end—which she had to squint to see, the room was so vast. She had walked beats smaller in her time as a Hawk.

"One could fly in this room," Bellusdeo said softly.

Emmerian nodded. "The door ward implies it."

"And simultaneously implies the inverse: one can, but should not."

Hope's squawking had taken figurative wing, and now rebounded off uncarpeted stone, from floor to ceiling. If the Tower could hear and understand Kaylin's familiar, it gave no sign.

"Hello?" she said, joining what she hoped was her familiar's attempt to greet or otherwise converse with the core of the Tower.

Emmerian added Barrani words of greeting.

Bellusdeo, however, added draconic. Her voice was loud enough to cause tremors in the floor on which they all stood.

None of these attempts reached the Tower. Kaylin didn't think the Tower was like Killianas; it wasn't so shuttered or injured that it couldn't, or didn't, hear. The door ward had been placed; the cave and the tunnel leading to it had been created as unspoken permission to enter.

Or to risk entering.

Tiamaris had, long ago, said something about visiting the Towers; he didn't consider survival—in the absence of a neutral lord—to be guaranteed.

Tiamaris's Tower had had no lord. And...Tara was *not* the Tower's name. She had had a name. She had forgotten it. And she had offered Kaylin the opportunity to give her a name that real people would use. Not that Tiamaris wasn't a real person—but he was lord, not citizen. He was not what Kaylin had once been.

The Tower had reminded Kaylin of every wrong she had ever committed in the fief of Barren. Every wrong, every mistake she couldn't fix, every death she couldn't atone for. She bowed her head.

Bowed her head and lifted it.

It was true. It was all true, just as it had been when Tara had pushed her. But there were *other* truths, and she had chosen to live by them, no matter how difficult it became. She hated to be judged, it was true—but the judgment that mattered here, if one didn't include fire-breathing Emperors or Leontine sergeants, was hers. And the only thing she had offered it, and could offer it now, was *never again*.

She wondered if either Emmerian or Bellusdeo were now experiencing what she had experienced her first time in Tara.

Bellusdeo roared; Kaylin wasn't given enough time to cover her ears, given proximity and the silence the Dragon broke. She roared again, and this time, she began to transform in a hall that was large enough she could.

Emmerian, however, did not. He was grim, his eyes a steady, darkening orange. Whatever Bellusdeo had heard, he had heard, but he let her take the lead. Kaylin thought he might let her take the lead for the rest of eternity, his involvement in the household argument an error he was determined never to repeat.

She couldn't tell if Bellusdeo had been threatened; she could tell the Dragon was angry; her eyes were red.

Red, Kaylin realized, with growing horror, and weeping.

It was the answer to the question she'd been way too smart to ask out loud. Yes. At least one person present was being tested and prodded. She liked it no more than Kaylin had. But Kaylin's anger wasn't a Dragon's anger, or rather, the outcome of the two angers differed. Dragons could cause a lot of damage when they went on the rampage. Maybe that's the reason there was no art in this room. Just the pillars themselves, standing between floor and ceiling.

Kaylin looked to Emmerian; he hadn't taken his eyes off Bellusdeo, but his lips were a compressed, white line.

Severn kept his distance as well.

Kaylin poked her familiar, who squawked softly. *It is her choice*, he said. *She will endure.*

"I don't want her to have to face this alone."

You did.

"I wasn't alone."

She is not alone in the same way you were not. I do not understand. The Towers test. As did I.

"You didn't."

He squawked in frustration. *I did. The Tower will do the same.*

"Tara did this to me, and she didn't want me as lord. And not because I failed her tests; I didn't. There was *no point* to it, in the end." Lifting her face, she glared at the ceiling. "Are you *listening*, Karriamis? This is pointless—it's just proof you can *cause* pain. You're a Tower; you're a sentient building. We already know."

Emmerian placed a gentle hand on Kaylin's shoulder.

"You can't think this is right?"

"It is not a matter of right or wrong," was his soft reply. "You know the generalities of the war she fought—and lost. If you pause to think, you will understand many of the probable events and consequences. You know that that war and its loss affect her daily.

"But the choice you made in the High Halls, Bellusdeo could not have made, not then. You believe that she is right for the Tower because of her dedication to fighting this war—continuing this war—with *Ravellon*. But think: Candallar's Tower allowed a shadow to be removed from *Ravellon*. Candallar's Tower, if I understand the chancellor's view correctly, preserved the Academia—and there were risks in that. It was an outlay of power that was not turned toward, devoted to, its reason for creation.

"Were I Karriamis, I would need to know what I believe he is attempting to learn."

"And what would you do with what you think he's learning?"

Emmerian shook his head. "You cannot hear him. You can't help but hear her, but you can't understand what she is saying." His eyes were a dark, dark orange, but he had lifted his inner eye membrane to mute the color. To Kaylin's lasting surprise, he turned to Severn. "It is not as easy as you make it look."

Severn's lips tightened in a grimace.

"What? What's not as easy?"

"Staying at a distance," Emmerian replied. "Allowing the pain to infect and influence someone that you care about."

She blinked. "That you care about? Is that what you just said?"

He failed to reply.

You heard him. This is a good time to pretend you didn't, Severn said.

Kaylin shook Emmerian's hand off. "We can't just let her—" The words, the rest of the words, were lost to the sound of Bellusdeo's voice as it cracked. The Dragon screamed.

Maybe, Kaylin thought, as she practically knocked the much heavier Emmerian off his feet in her haste to cross the room, they were right. Severn. Emmerian. Maybe this was a test that Bellusdeo had to pass on her own.

But she couldn't just ignore her. Not when the pain in the strained, loud cry was so obvious. Kaylin was certain that nothing physical could cause the Dragon to scream like this.

And what are you going to say? Hope squawked, in clear agreement with Severn and Emmerian.

Something is better than nothing, she replied, and shoved him off her shoulder. He held on by virtue of claws now digging through cloth into her collarbone.

"Bellusdeo!"

Her arms—or the marks across them—began to glow a blue that implied lightning in an otherwise clear sky. She raced across the shaking stone and saw, as she drew closer and closer to the Dragon's side, that a glimmering of red, like cracks, had started between the scale's plates, running down Bellusdeo's side like bright blood.

She had healed a resentful Dragon before.

Her hands, palm out, reached for Bellusdeo's side, and she was instantly lifted off the ground before she could make contact.

"What do you think you're doing?" a familiar voice shrieked in her ear.

Mandoran had arrived.

She couldn't see him. She could feel his hands, hear his voice; he was undeniably solid, just...invisible.

"Listen to her!" she shouted, as Bellusdeo continued to roar. "We have to do something!"

"Yes, we do—but *not* you."

"I'm Chosen, damn it—my marks are glowing! I can survive it!"

"Personally I'd be willing to drop you, but Teela would murder me. And possibly the rest of the cohort."

"She can't. Helen would never allow it."

"And as long as we can stay inside Helen for eternity, we'd be safe. But if we could do that, we wouldn't have sent *me* here, and frankly, I resent the hell out of it." He dropped Kaylin almost directly on top of Severn, who caught and braced her rather than getting out of the way.

She still couldn't see Mandoran.

She could hear him, though. Because he roared. He roared at the top of his lungs, but his roar had syllables in it.

"Was that native dragon?" she shouted at Emmerian.

He nodded. His hands, which had been resting by his side, were now firmly clasped behind his back.

"Can you see him?"

He shook his head. "I can hear him," he said softly. "If I did not know who—or what—he was, I would have mistaken him for a kinsman."

Bellusdeo, however, didn't. She turned instantly in the direction the voice came from, her eyes blood red, her inner membranes down. Fire filled the empty air; a Mandoran shape didn't emerge from the heat.

"Seriously," he shouted, from beneath a different part of the vaulted ceiling, "that's the best you can do? Gust of hot air?"

The next breath was hotter; Kaylin felt as if it should have singed her hair, and it was now pointing in a direction that didn't include her.

Bellusdeo crouched low; she reminded Kaylin, oddly, of a cat that had decided it had a solid chance of taking a bird out of the air from the ground. Mostly, this failed.

Emmerian finally broke down, the stiff neutrality of his posture instantly realigning itself with the blurry mess of transformation; blue plates became blue scales. He didn't immediately take to the air.

"He's not trying to hurt her!" Kaylin shouted.

"I know." His voice was lower, a rumble of sensation over words that Kaylin understood. "But she *is* trying to hurt him, and she'll regret it forever if she manages to succeed." He, too, bent into his knees, stretched his wings, or at least did something with them, and leaped into the air.

The blue dragon hit the gold dragon. The gold dragon was close enough to the ground to be thrown off course; she landed on all four feet and roared in rage. Emmerian roared back.

So did Mandoran.

Kaylin looked to Severn, breath held. He wasn't worried.

He's right. She'll regret it if she manages to hurt him in her frenzy.

So it's fine if she hurts Emmerian? Because that's what's going to happen.

And we can prevent it how?

They couldn't. She poked Hope.

I can interfere, Hope said, his voice eerily free of screech. *But you will pay the price for the intervention. This is not something you could naturally do with greater effort or more time. It is something I could do—but not for free.*

Kaylin exhaled. She hadn't been willing to make the sacrifices Hope would ask for—not even when it would have saved the lives of fellow Hawks. Hope understood this. She wondered if there would ever be a time when she would be so desperate, the sacrifices would seem a reasonable cost.

She hoped not.

And she understood, watching the Dragons she could see, and inferring the presence of Mandoran, who she couldn't, that this was something Bellusdeo had to deal with. Somehow.

You need to have more faith in the friends you have chosen.

They don't.

Yes. It is much harder for some to have faith in themselves than it is to have faith in others. But that faith can be of critical import.

Emmerian was driven back, into a pillar. The pillar cracked.

Mandoran proved he hadn't been injured. "Come *on*! You came all the way to the Tower to lose your temper and destroy it? What is *wrong* with you?" His words didn't come from a single fixed location; parts of the sentence—the first parts—came from far too close to angry dragon, but the rest, from behind. Kaylin wished she could *see* him.

Hope obligingly lifted one translucent wing. He didn't even smack her across the face with it.

Mandoran didn't have wings. He looked, at this distance, like himself. But he appeared to be walking—to be leaping—on air, his feet touching nothing, his legs bunched to aid his momentum. She couldn't see the color of his eyes at this distance, but could see his expression; he was concentrating, his brows slanting inward, his gaze bouncing around the room as if seeking the right spots on which to land—and instantly leap away.

Emmerian couldn't see him; he could see Emmerian. He didn't consider Emmerian a threat.

She wondered if this magic, this almost-flight, had been used by the Barrani in their wars with the Dragons; if it had, she had never heard of it. Maybe she'd just never listened.

"Breathe," Severn said, far more loudly than he usually did.

She nodded. She knew the cohort had abilities that the normal Barrani—even Arcanists—didn't. In this gigantic room, it was Mandoran she watched.

Emmerian didn't attack Bellusdeo. He shouted at her, just as Mandoran had, but made no attempt to hurt her; Kaylin wished Bellusdeo was half as aware of the harm her own actions might cause. The gold Dragon landed sideways against a different pillar. This one cracked as well. The ground was shaking with the reverberations of angry Dragon words. Kaylin looked down the hall, and then up, to the heights; she wasn't certain the pillars would remain standing, and she didn't know enough about architectural structure to accurately guess how many pillars the hall could lose before the ceiling came down on their heads.

The three who were in an odd dance of not-quite-combat would survive. She and Severn might not.

He nodded, although she hadn't spoken a word, and began to head toward the arch that implied exit on the far side of a room that was three city blocks in length.

But when the third column cracked, Mandoran shouted, "You'll kill Kaylin if you keep this up!"

Bellusdeo turned, then, her gaze finding the ground that Kaylin and Severn had only just deserted.

Blood red eyes snapped shut as the largest person in the room came fully, and finally, to a halt.

Emmerian landed immediately, and shed the draconic form just as quickly; Mandoran, however, remained in the air, looking down. He met Kaylin's gaze and nodded, but his expression remained strained; the cheeky grin that was so at home on his face it seemed permanent was nowhere in sight. He looked exhausted, to her eye—and no wonder. His eyes returned to Bellusdeo.

The mortal form failed to emerge from the draconic one, but Bellusdeo's eyes remained closed. "Lord Emmerian?" she said in Barrani, the words a rumble of sound that didn't threaten to deafen people with normal ears. Or Kaylin's ears, at any rate.

"I am uninjured," Emmerian replied. "You?"

Bellusdeo inhaled, a long, loud rasp of sound. Kaylin tensed—anyone who had seen a Dragon breathe fire would have—but the tension was unnecessary. What Bellusdeo exhaled was air and a small amount of smoke, normal when she was irritated.

"I believe the room has been structurally impaired," Emmerian continued, when she failed to speak. "If you feel it is safe to do so, we should leave this hall."

She nodded. She did not, however, resume her usual form.

The hall was easily wide enough and tall enough to support a Dragon walking down it. Emmerian chose to walk by Bellusdeo's side; Kaylin and Severn were shunted to the rear. Bellusdeo clearly now felt that the Tower itself, or the intelligence behind it, was a threat; allowing the Hawks to serve as scouts was off the table. Kaylin's attempt to put it back on the table was dismissed without a single word.

She accepted it. She understood. Protecting people—no,

protecting weaker people, which currently meant Kaylin—was something Bellusdeo could cling to; it was normal. It was the type of normal that often frustrated Kaylin, but not today. Today, she was almost willing to go full pathetic, just to help the gold Dragon cling to sanity.

I would not suggest it. It was Nightshade.

Did you see everything?

No. But the area you are now in allows communication. I would guess it is entirely the prerogative of the Tower. Bellusdeo will know that you are acting, and she will find it insulting. Insulting a Dragon has never been wise.

No kidding.

She will take it very poorly if you express your current worry.

I know that.

He chuckled. *You know it, yes. But you know other things as well, and they vie for dominance until one becomes expressed in action. I merely wish to add weight to what I believe the wise course of action to be.*

She wasn't sure she wanted to follow the Barrani idea of wisdom. Hope smacked her face before she could reply. Mandoran had finally landed. Not only had he landed, but when Hope lowered his wing, Kaylin could still see him.

"You're a reckless idiot," Bellusdeo said, as she slowly pried her eyes open. They were orange with deep flecks of red in them. But...they were orange, which was as good a sign as could be hoped for.

Mandoran shrugged. "How long have you known me?"

"It feels like centuries."

Mandoran's eyes were a midnight blue; they lightened slightly as he chuckled. "Right back at you. I'm *always* reckless, at least according to anyone who isn't Terrano."

"Terrano doesn't think you're reckless?"

"Mostly he thinks I'm timid; sometimes he thinks I'm a coward."

"Terrano *is* reckless," Kaylin said.

"He's disagreeing. Sedarias still won't give me permission to give you my True Name," he added. "And it would have been hugely helpful, here."

Kaylin both agreed and disagreed. But Sedarias—and in this case probably a good number of the rest of the cohort—held far more influence than she did.

She glanced at Bellusdeo. Mandoran had been part of the cohort for, realistically, all of his life. He'd known Bellusdeo for months. But…he understood her, and in the end, he'd risked his life to save her from herself.

Bellusdeo knew it, as well. She made no further attempt to harm Mandoran, and Kaylin doubted she would. Whatever she needed to bring herself under control, she'd managed to find it. She was rigid and draconic; she was probably still struggling.

But Kaylin had had days—even weeks—with that struggle. She'd once, when much younger, believed that people who didn't lose their tempers just…didn't have a temper. They didn't *get* angry, because if they did, they'd be breaking things, too. She'd come to understand—probably because she spent so much time around people whose eye colors shifted with mood—that this was wrong.

People did get angry.

And they did lose their tempers—by which she meant, lose control of their own actions when rage was too intense. Sometimes it wasn't a choice. But…most of the people she now knew understood that it should be. Bellusdeo understood it. And although it had been really, really hard when Kaylin had first encountered the Hawks, it was easier now. Not easy, but…easier.

What hadn't become any easier was the guilt. Kaylin's terrible choices had destroyed lives—literally destroyed them—when her fear and her own desperate attempt to survive had been the only driving forces in her life. Bellusdeo's mistakes had allowed a world to be destroyed.

She was queen, or had been. The responsibility was therefore hers.

Tara's testing had invoked the worst of Kaylin's guilt and self-loathing; she had no doubt at all that Karriamis's testing—aimed at Bellusdeo—had done the same. And Kaylin could only barely accept her own dark past, her own guilt, her own responsibility. She could not imagine living under the weight of Bellusdeo's.

And yet, the Dragon shouldered it constantly.

"Yes," a disembodied—and unfamiliar—voice said. "That is the weight of rulership."

Kaylin turned; there was no physical accompaniment to the voice.

"I should not have let you in," the voice continued. "You are Chosen; your duties are already marked. You cannot captain a Tower, and in the past, the Towers would have been ridiculed for choosing to allow you to do so."

Kaylin was afraid, for one moment, that she would be ejected; she had no doubt that the Tower could do it.

Hope, however, relaxed on her shoulder, which meant he either thought it unlikely, or thought it would be harmless. Physically, if one discounted extreme nausea, it probably would be. But Bellusdeo would still be here, and Kaylin didn't want to desert her.

"No," the voice agreed. "But we can understand much of a person by the friends they choose. I will not force you to leave."

Bellusdeo's eyes had darkened to a more normal red—and even thinking that caused Kaylin to cringe. If the gold Dragon had heard the voice that had spoken to Kaylin, there was no other sign.

Mandoran's eyes widened.

"Is the Tower speaking to you?" Kaylin asked.

He nodded.

"Can you see something that serves as an Avatar?"

"The whole damn Tower is an Avatar," Mandoran replied. "Imagine what Helen would be like if Helen were a Dragon."

Imagination failed.

"Come," the voice said again. "I have seen enough that I am slightly curious. If you will forgive the manner of greeting, I would take tea with you."

Tea. With a Dragon. Kaylin swallowed and said, "We'd love to."

The Tower's Avatar did not emerge, but the voice had reminded her that she was in a sentient building, which meant her thoughts were being read and processed before she could properly hide them. Not that she had ever truly tried; she wondered how Nightshade or Teela managed it.

"They can separate themselves from the immediacy of their thoughts," the helpful voice replied. "It is not something that comes easily to one of your race, although your companion— ah, no, partner?—partner is more adept than his age would imply. He is, however, the only one trying at the moment."

"Lord Emmerian?"

"No. He understands what I was, and what I am. He is not interested in putting out effort when he believes that effort to be, at best, futile, and at worst counter to his reasons for being here. And I believe your young Barrani friend feels the same."

Kaylin shook her head. "He's not young, and he's always like that."

"I see. He is Barrani, by appearance. And he has much in common with the race of his birth."

She nodded more carefully, suddenly remembering Castle Nightshade's reaction to Annarion. Remembering it and wishing, viscerally, that they had somehow managed to leave Mandoran at home.

"I am not Durandel of old," the Tower replied. "It was always his way to kill first and investigate later—if he could be bothered to investigate at all. But he was both cunning and perceptive, especially with regards to *Ravellon*. If he considered your friend a danger, it is likely that he was."

"Danger to who? He wasn't *doing* anything!"

Severn coughed.

"Danger to all who might be killed or corrupted by *Ravellon*. We are not as you are. Nor is Mandoran."

She stiffened further, but Mandoran shook his head.

"I prefer to investigate first; it stops me from making the occasional mistake."

"And Durandel doesn't care?"

"If you destroy enough," the Tower replied, "no one will ever know."

That didn't make her feel any better. Mandoran, however, grinned. His skin color was off, and his eyes were too blue, but other than that he was normal. For Mandoran.

They walked down the large hall, passed beneath an arch, and were suddenly outside.

Kaylin had experience with these shifts of reality when confined in a sentient building, but it was still jarring. What she'd seen while walking toward the arch was another hall, a continuation of stone and austerity. The moment her foot crossed over an invisible line that somehow signaled the end of the first hall, it came down on grass.

Very short, very well-kept grass. There was a path of laid stones that wound its way through that grass, and Kaylin made haste to step on it instead. Only here did Bellusdeo finally surrender the draconic form, shrinking in place until she looked like a Warrior Queen of old, not the Dragon that the queen was tasked with defeating.

They followed the path; the Tower offered no further words. At the end of the path was a large pavilion, and seated at a long table was an old man, with a beard that seemed to drape from chin to lap, folding a bit to cover his knees. He wore a crimson robe, but no tiara.

If it weren't for his eyes—obsidian, as Tara's and Helen's were when things were tense—he would have reminded her strongly of the Arkon. The Arkon had never been friendly to Kaylin, but there were degrees of unfriendliness; this would have been a good Arkon day, not a bad one.

And she *had* to stop calling him that.

"You really do," the old man said, rising as they approached, his voice enclosed by an actual throat and mouth. "Arkon is a title; it is a function. I believe the former Arkon has chosen to undertake an entirely different responsibility."

"Did you know him?" she asked softly.

The old man smiled. It was the whole of his answer. "Come," he said. "Be seated wherever you feel comfortable. Ah, no," he added, swiveling his head to look at Mandoran. "Be seated wherever I can comfortably speak with you."

"You can speak with me anywhere, clearly," Mandoran replied.

"Yes, but your companions can't."

"For my part, I speak with him more than enough in daily life, so you needn't be bothered on my account," Bellusdeo said.

The Dragon—the Tower—smiled. "It is entirely, as you all suspect, on my own account. I apologize," he added, his voice grave, "for the manner of my first greeting. But I had to know."

He gestured. Kaylin, not Mandoran and not a Dragon, took a seat, as did Severn. Hope hopped down off her shoulder to sit beside her plate. Apparently he recognized some of the foods that had been laid out for them, and expected to be able to pick at some of them. As far as she knew, he didn't really need to eat, so it was a waste.

On the other hand, a cranky, loud familiar complaining in her ear was its own misery, so maybe it wasn't.

"What did you have to know?" Bellusdeo asked, voice pleasant, eyes the color of blood. She'd raised her inner membranes to mute the color, but it wasn't going well. "That I failed? That all but a bare handful of my people were lost to Shadow and death? You might have asked. I would have told you."

"It is not a question one asks in polite company."

This caused Bellusdeo's lips to quirk up in what might have been a smile, if smiles were dark and edged. "Were you perhaps under the impression that you were in polite company?"

"At the moment, that is my hope. You must forgive me; I am very seldom host to guests who arrive here. Usually that is both the prerogative and the responsibility of my captain, or lord if you prefer." His eyes didn't darken, but they were obsidian.

"Who is dead," Bellusdeo replied, not giving a conversational inch, although she did take a seat. Emmerian, as Severn and Kaylin, had taken a seat immediately. Mandoran grimaced and pulled up a chair—scraping it across stones—beside the gold Dragon. It was where he often sat at breakfast.

"Yes. You did not kill him."

"No. And I resent it."

The older Dragon nodded almost sagely. "You have questions."

"I do."

"I may not tender answers you like, or answers at all, but I will make the attempt."

"Why did you choose Candallar as lord?"

"What you saw of him at his end was not all that he was," the Tower replied, after a long pause. "What he was when he first arrived is not what he became. We—or perhaps, you and Lord Emmerian—are creatures of solitude except in the crèche and in times of war. It is effort to live with too many in one space, and it does not always bring out the best in us. I am amazed that you have managed."

Kaylin knew why.

And Kaylin knew Karriamis knew it as well. She almost rose.

"It is difficult to have contested hoards; I am certain you will have been taught these lessons."

She nodded.

"Barrani are not driven by the same imperative, the same biological frenzy. They are social creatures by nature. Candallar was. He was driven out of his home, and he came in desperation to my Tower at a time when it was convenient for me."

"Is it true," Kaylin asked, before Bellusdeo could, "that you allowed a guest of Candallar's to pass through the *Ravellon* barrier and bring a Shadow back with him?"

14

The very clear, blue skies above this artificial garden darkened.

"You are correct," Karriamis said, to Bellusdeo. "My assumption about polite company was clearly an overabundance of optimism."

Bellusdeo's face would have cracked had she smiled; the question Kaylin had asked was the heart of her concern. Kaylin realized, watching her, that although the gold Dragon had seriously considered captaining a Tower—this one—the reason she'd come here was to ascertain that the Tower itself hadn't been dangerously corrupted.

This world wasn't the world she'd ruled at the end, but she'd been born here, and if she had a home—if she could make herself a home—it was here. What had happened to her people on their world must *never* happen here.

The Avatar of the Tower met and held Bellusdeo's gaze. "I did allow it."

"*Why?*" It was Kaylin who spoke; Bellusdeo said nothing.

"Candallar had done, for me, a great favor, and my thoughts were turned towards that favor, and the possible outcomes of it."

"You were willing to risk *Shadow infiltration* for those out-comes? Why did you volunteer for these responsibilities in the first place?"

"I understood the danger Shadow presents."

"And yet you allowed *this*? We don't know enough to—" Kaylin stopped, snapping her mouth shut over words she might be unable to easily retract.

"I would tell you not to interrupt me, but you are deliberately choosing to keep the words to yourself. You think, however, very loudly.

"We do not know enough, yes. But in our ignorance, in the risks we take, we have changed the constitution of the High Halls, and returned to that building the capacity for defense that was thought to be lost at the dawn of the long wars between our people and yours." This last, he directed to Mandoran.

"It is often considered crucial in times of war not to see one's enemies as people. But I will note that, according to Kaylin, those who were combatants in time of war greet former enemies as if they are comrades. Your Teela, your Night-shade, your former Arkon. Death lies between them all, but those deaths no longer define them. Causing death is no longer their reason for interaction.

"You are at war," he continued, watching Bellusdeo. "And I understand, now, the reason for its continuation. But Spike—that is the name you gave them, yes?" When Kaylin nodded, he once again turned his focus to Bellusdeo. "Spike, in the end, was freed. I believe it was through the efforts of your Terrano," he added, obviously to Mandoran, although he didn't look away from Bellusdeo. "But it may well have been through the combination of Terrano's effort and the effort of your Chosen.

"Regardless, the outcome was positive."

"That wasn't your intent." Kaylin's eyes narrowed.

"My intent, as you must suspect, was to save the Academia. And Candallar's work to bring students to the Academia gave Killianas just enough power that the Academia could, finally, leave the stasis in which it's been trapped. Much of my power, and much of my thought, has turned to the Academia of late."

"Candallar's effort was to kidnap people and toss them into what was basically a prison," Kaylin snapped.

"And yet there are students there who considered it a blessing. As you yourself thought you once might."

Leave, Nightshade said quietly. *This Tower is far more of a danger than your Helen. What Helen wanted was the patina of domesticity—*

That is not *what Helen wanted. It's not what she wants now.*

—but Karriamis is not Helen. He knows far, far too much; you have not consciously been thinking of all of these things during your visit. What he has read is deeper than even what the Hallionne would read. He is dangerous, Kaylin. Do not remain.

Kaylin didn't reply. No answer she could give wouldn't cause a deepening of the argument; she wasn't leaving without Bellusdeo, and Bellusdeo wasn't leaving.

"The Academia is awake, and it grows stronger as the chancellor finds those students from whom the very institution draws life and power. And no, Corporal, the Academia is not *feeding* on them. As the Academia grows stronger, much less of my power is required to stabilize it. I am content."

"Is that your way of saying that you're not going to let the *next* fieflord fish Shadows out of *Ravellon*?"

His eyes were now orange-red, rather than the obsidian they had originally been; it was a Dragon warning.

But...Kaylin felt she had to ask, because Bellusdeo couldn't. And in the end, Bellusdeo lived with her. They were friends.

"In a fashion, yes. But consider this, and consider it carefully. Spike did not choose his captivity or his enslavement. No more did Bellusdeo, hers."

Silence.

Bellusdeo had come *out* of *Ravellon*. Just as Spike had.

"They are both free, and I cannot imagine that their freedom is not more preferable—for all of us—than their enslavement was. You think of all Shadow as one will. Even if experience has now taught you more, you are still wed to that mode of considering a war. You will take no risks, or rather, would counsel that none of us do."

Kaylin hesitated. She was now in territory that Bellusdeo herself would barely acknowledge and would not consider; she couldn't speak for the Dragon here, couldn't speak in her stead. "The cost of a mistake…"

"Yes. That is fear speaking. Fear is, with the correct mix of experience and knowledge, the foundation of caution, and caution is admirable. But tell me, Chosen, did you not have this very argument with the Consort of the Barrani?"

"No?"

"Ah, perhaps the term *Shadow* is confusing you. Let me say, instead, the Devourer."

Kaylin looked down at her food as all appetite deserted her. "Oh. That."

Karriamis's eyes had shaded toward gold as he chuckled. "I see them as fundamentally the same. Bellusdeo does not. It was the remnants of her people that you saved. But the risk was as large as the risk of unknown Shadow: the loss of an entire world."

He then turned to Bellusdeo. "Or is it different for you because you have, and have had, a vested interest in the outcome?"

"I wasn't aware of the struggle at the time."

"Ah, no, forgive me. Bellusdeo does not and would not fault the Consort for her decision or her anger. Had you been mistaken, this world would be gone. I personally believe the Consort was correct; the risk was too high. And yet, again, the outcome is desirable. It is certainly desirable for my people. It is not a risk I would have taken. It is not a risk the Consort could take. And I believe that it is not a risk Bellusdeo herself would condone.

"Would you change what you did?"

Kaylin shook her head.

"It is a combination of risk and belief that allows such changes to happen. When they do not work well, it's considered an act of dangerous idealism, dangerous naivete after the fact. But without it, I feel that too little would change, and whole new avenues of existence would never be explored or brought to light."

"That's not why you let him leave the border zone with a Shadow in his hands."

"They were not in his hands. Perhaps, however, you do not understand the function of your Spike prior to the fall of worlds. Spike would have been at home as an Arbiter in the Academia. They would have been at home—more than at home—as one of the experts and scholars who dwelled there. In the fullness of time, I believe they may apply to do just that. I believe your Robin would be delighted."

Nightshade was right. This Tower was dangerous in a way the other sentient buildings were not. His advice—to leave immediately—was going to be difficult to follow without the building's permission.

Karriamis chose not to comment on that. "Spike was a historian. A recorder of truths and events."

"Wait—how do you know this?"

Karriamis said nothing.

Bellusdeo, however, said, "Did you know Spike?"

"I knew of Spike's people—they were, like Starrante's, few."

But the gold Dragon shook her head. "You thought you recognized him."

"Enslaved as he was? How would that be possible?"

"You tell us. I will concede your points: Spike was enslaved. When freed from that enslavement, that control, he was helpful." She exhaled. "He was more than helpful. And I, too, was enslaved for years beyond count. But I was not of the Shadow, and I believe Spike was."

"Both Spike and Starrante's people require certain environments in which to thrive, yes. But you speak of Shadow as if it is one thing." He held up a hand before she could breathe flame. "And those who are enslaved by it become part of it. It drives their thoughts, their desires, their intent. Do you understand, you who spent so much time in its thrall, what Shadow is?"

"No."

"A pity. And a further pity that I cannot visit the High Halls in person to ask the question of those who might have a broader perspective. But Spike—honestly, I am trying not to find the name offensively dismissive—was, if I am not mistaken, instrumental in your escape from the West March. You have seen what Spike is capable of, and you have seen it put to a use of which you must approve."

"The most dangerous incursions are always the subtle ones."

"Indeed. But if, as a people, we assume that nothing changes—"

"The very nature of Shadow is change."

"—then we make assumptions that can be harmful to both our own development and our defenses. If you demand, of a Tower, that rigidity, you have failed to understand the nature of Towers."

"She has not," Kaylin snapped.

"Oh?"

"Tara would never, ever take that risk. And Tiamaris wouldn't ask it."

"Ah. Perhaps you think all sentient buildings are somehow the same? That the beings who agreed to become their heart or part of their core become so uniform you cannot tell one apart from the other?" He snorted smoke, exactly the way the former Arkon would have.

"Candallar did not command me." He rose and turned to Bellusdeo. "Had he tried, he would have been reduced to less than ash. I understand my own duties, my own responsibilities. But it has long been my belief that knowledge is essential, that new knowledge sheds light on the incomplete knowledge it replaces.

"It is the reason I wished to preserve the Academia in whatever small fashion I could. It is in the Academia that the library can be reached."

"Candallar was your captain, but he did not command you."

"Yes. Does Kaylin command Helen?"

"Yes, in her own particular fashion." Bellusdeo exhaled. "And no, as it is clear you must know. Kaylin is her tenant. If Kaylin commanded Helen, I believe Helen would be forced to obey—but that is inferred. It is not a proven or known fact."

"I don't think she would be forced to obey," Mandoran said.

"Helen has implied that she would."

"She's just being polite. Look—she damaged herself enough that she doesn't even have all of her memories. She did this because she *wanted* the freedom of choice. And apparently the freedom of choice means she chooses mortals as lords, and offers them a home until age kills them. But she doesn't *need* a tenant; there was a long gap, in mortal time, between her prior tenant and Kaylin.

"She wouldn't take a tenant who would command her to do things against her will. And Kaylin's garbage at hiding her thoughts, so she'd absolutely know."

"You are not much better, young man," Karriamis said, voice stern, eyes far less orange.

Mandoran shrugged. "I don't care. You can't keep me trapped here if I want to leave. You can possibly kill me—" He winced, no doubt at something Sedarias was saying. Or shouting.

"Let us not talk of killing. You are not interested in becoming a Tower's partner."

"So you only attempt to kill or injure those who are?"

"Any injuries you have suffered since you entered my domain were not caused by me."

Mandoran's eyes went indigo. Kaylin opened her mouth, but Bellusdeo reached out and placed a hand very gently on Mandoran's arm. "My biggest regret is not that I didn't injure you," she said, head tilted slightly, "but that I will never be allowed to forget or live it down."

Mandoran's eyes lightened almost instantly as he laughed. So did Bellusdeo's.

"I'll let you take this from here," Mandoran told her.

She raised one brow.

"I'll do my best to let you take this from here?"

"More accurate, unfortunately."

Karriamis gestured at the food on the table—food that Kaylin and Severn had been eating. "While I will not say that the food will be wasted when the starving might appreciate it, it would be a pity if you failed to avail yourself of my hospitality."

Kaylin was severely underimpressed by the Tower's hospitality, but struggled not to put it into words. Yes, the Tower would know—but Mandoran and Bellusdeo wouldn't.

Karriamis snorted in her direction before turning, once again, to Bellusdeo. "Your rage and pain are dangerous. Were that rage and pain aimed only at Shadow, this would be a survivable flaw, at least among our kin. But strands of that anger threaten to overwhelm what would otherwise be pragmatism or common sense."

"That's not true," Kaylin snapped. Mandoran got his arm patted; Kaylin got a warning glare. Sometimes life sucked. "No, I'm not going to stop talking."

"Talking isn't a requirement."

"It is if he's making statements like that."

"My rage and pain *are* dangerous."

"You can control it—you've done it before. You did it with Gilbert. You did it with Spike. You weren't *happy* about it, but you didn't blast the rest of us into ash and you didn't try to hurt either of them." Her eyes narrowed as she turned to Karriamis, who was watching with interest. And amusement.

It was the amusement she hated. "You know so much about my life and about things that haven't even been brought up in conversation here, there's *no way* you didn't already know that."

"I fail to see your point."

"You're being unfair to her, and you know it. Why?"

Bellusdeo coughed. Mandoran nudged her foot under the table, as if Karriamis wouldn't notice.

"Would you care to field that question?" Karriamis asked Bellusdeo.

"Not particularly. Not here. We'll talk about it later."

"Later being?"

"When we get home."

"Ah, home." Karriamis smiled. "Is that what you call Helen?"

"It's what Kaylin calls Helen in a fundamental sense, and I live with her."

Karriamis rose. "Is that how you see it, then?"

Bellusdeo's face was utterly neutral. "Yes."

"Very well. I will ask no further questions, but will say one thing: you have made excellent choices in your friends. Even this one," he added, glancing at Mandoran, "who would be considered at best an acquaintance by most of our kin—or his own—given the scant time you have known him.

"And you, boy, are a friend worth keeping and preserving. You were willing to risk your own life to preserve hers."

"It wasn't her life I was worried about. She's a big, scary Dragon."

"It wasn't her existence, but her life as I understand it." He then turned to Kaylin. "How much has Helen discussed her previous tenants with you?"

Kaylin frowned. "She's talked a bit about the very first tenant, but other than that, she's said nothing."

"And you have failed to ask."

"No, I...I did ask."

"And she refused to answer?"

"She cares about them, even if they're dead. She's protecting their privacy."

"It is not practical. It is not pragmatic. In my experience, the dead care very little about their privacy; the dying frequently care about their legacy: they wish to be remembered."

Kaylin thought about this. "I don't care if I'm remembered. It won't do me any good."

"Ah, yes. Yes, that is true. But I will talk just as much as Helen does about my previous partner." He then turned again. "And so we come at last to Lord Emmerian."

Bellusdeo rose.

"You should take notes from this one," he said, although he did not look away from Emmerian. "He is adept at layering his thoughts to protect his motivation. Were it not so obvious to these old eyes, I would not know most of what he is thinking."

"He is not generally discussed in the third person when he is present," Emmerian said.

"Not generally, no. Pardon my manners. You are angry."

Emmerian inclined his head. He looked alert and cautious to Kaylin's eye, not angry.

"I understand. But surely your ability to stand by while Bellusdeo is in danger makes you ineligible to be guardian of your race?"

Emmerian said nothing for five seconds. Kaylin counted, almost holding her breath. On the sixth second, Bellusdeo breathed fire directly at the Avatar.

The flame of her breath was red, not the white-gold that could melt stone. Among Dragons, it was very much like swearing. Kaylin could still feel the heat of the flames.

Karriamis's clothing did not turn to flame and its resultant ash. "I see," he said, "that the time for temperate conversation has passed. It might be difficult to believe this, but I am pleased to have made your acquaintance. I am uncertain that you are right for the Tower, but there is one major mitigating factor in any judgment I might render."

Bellusdeo's very red eyes indicated that she didn't give a crap about either his judgment or his so-called mitigating factors.

Emmerian, however, remained orange-eyed.

"I will note you have not answered my question," Karriamis said to Emmerian.

"No."

"And will not."

"No. It is, in the parlance of the young corporal—" and here he nodded in Kaylin's direction "—none of your business."

Silence. It was broken by Karriamis's unexpected and booming laughter.

"I have no desire to captain a Tower, even this one. The question is therefore irrelevant."

"And neither you nor Bellusdeo has any interest in my mitigating factors?"

"I have none; they are irrelevant to me. But I cannot and will not speak for Bellusdeo."

Bellusdeo was silent.

Mandoran, however, said, "I'd like to know, if it's all the same to you."

"You are in the same position. You have no desire to captain this Tower, and even had you, I would not consider you a possibility. You are young and foolhardy. You are immortal, but not—as I often told the hatchlings—invulnerable." At Mandoran's expression, he added, "She could have killed you."

"She wasn't trying."

"She was."

He snorted. "I've seen her fight. Trust me, she wasn't trying."

"Your loyalties are entirely too personal."

"You've clearly met Sedarias." He winced. "But, regardless, I'm not here as a candidate, if this is what this lunch is for. I'm here as an emissary."

"You have an interesting idea of diplomacy."

Mandoran shrugged, as if he'd heard it all before. He had, of course. While Kaylin had sometimes wished she could join the cohort group mind, she was distinctly glad at this moment that she wasn't part of it.

"Very well. I will not accuse you of failing to understand the import. I see that this is not strictly speaking the truth. The mitigating factor in any decision I might make does not reside directly with Bellusdeo or your Sedarias.

"It is with you. With Lord Emmerian. With Lord Kaylin. Bellusdeo has chosen her allies wisely."

"She didn't have much choice, and *allies* isn't quite the right word."

"It is exactly the wrong word," Karriamis said, smiling. "You are her friends. She has chosen her friends wisely. Necessity makes some choices mandatory, of course—but the friendship she has offered you has clearly been returned. She values you. You value her. This is a striking point in her favor.

"But you are aware of this, surely? It is what Sedarias herself has done. If she formed bonds for reasons of necessity, she would die for any of you."

Mandoran grimaced. "I really wish you hadn't said that."

"Oh?"

"Among our kin, it's not considered a compliment."

"I am not responsible for your reaction to my words; that lies with you. Or in this case, with your Sedarias. Regardless, for today, we are done. You may see yourselves out; I have much to think about." He rose. "And you may tell Sedarias— or whoever feels they have the merit to captain a Tower, to captain *me*—that they may take the risk that Bellusdeo has taken. They may visit in person."

The walk back from the Tower of Candallar was not as quiet as the walk there had been. Bellusdeo was silent until she passed through the portal that led to the fief; she offered Kaylin an arm and a shoulder as Kaylin also passed through the portal. The passage was rough.

There was no way, in Kaylin's admittedly minor experience, that Karriamis would do what Tara had done: take the risk of opening up the Tower to unwanted guests in order to allow Kaylin a single entrance that didn't rely on portal magic.

But when they had left Candallar and entered Tiamaris, the woman in gold plate armor turned to the man in blue plate armor, her eyes once again orange-red.

"Why didn't you say anything? Why did you let him talk to you like that?"

"Because he is not wrong," Emmerian replied.

"He is wrong in every particular!"

"I did stand back. When he tested you, when you were... in distress, I waited."

"And that somehow makes you unfit?"

"I intruded on Helen's sanctuary. I...lost my temper. It has been a long, long time since I've experienced such a loss. If I cannot remain in your presence and allow you to be who, and what, you are, I have no business being in your presence. You are not, Lannagaros's opinion aside, a child. It has been some years since you have been one."

"And?"

"Adults make their own decisions, weighing the possible consequences. Mandoran," he added, glancing at the silent member of the cohort, "understood the nature of the consequences to you before I did or could. My concern was your health, your well-being; I did not think that the Tower was intent on causing you physical injury.

"Mandoran understood where the true danger lay. Had Kaylin been killed as collateral damage, it would have harmed you in ways that mere physical injury would not. You would, if you survived, heal from physical damage. The…other damage would have been profound."

"What did he mean by guardian of your race?" Kaylin asked.

Both Dragons swiveled toward her, their eyes the distinctly unfriendly color.

"Forget I asked."

"Karriamis was not wrong," Emmerian said again. "What would you have said were you in my position?"

"I said it," was the curt reply. Bellusdeo stared at Emmerian for one long moment, and then pulled ahead, picking up the pace in a way that would have been punishing for any mortals not used to spending an entire day on their feet.

Helen was waiting at the door when they arrived, her eyes obsidian, which was never a good sign. "Dear," she said, to Mandoran, not Kaylin, "what exactly did you do?"

He shrugged. "I tagged along with a Dragon and a person who can't stay out of trouble to save her own life?"

Helen frowned. "Things have been a bit...uncomfortable here. I believe your friends are arguing."

He groaned. "Look, I'm just going to go for a walk."

"I believe they're expecting you."

"That's *why* I'm going to go for a walk. Somewhere safer and quieter. Like, say, *Ravellon*."

Bellusdeo smacked the back of his head. "Not even as a joke," she said. She didn't look angry.

"Lord Emmerian, I am not certain this is the best time for a visit. I am sorry."

Emmerian nodded.

Bellusdeo, however, said, "It's not a good time, no. It is a necessary one. If Emmerian enters, can you keep him relatively safe?"

Helen closed her eyes. When she opened them, they were brown. "I'm sorry, dear," she said, opening her arms to enfold Kaylin in the "welcome home" hug. "Yes, of course I can keep him relatively safe. I have not sent the cohort to the training room, but I am seriously considering it."

"*Definitely* going for a walk."

"Oh no you're not," a familiar voice boomed from the top of the foyer stairs. Since it was Sedarias, Mandoran sighed.

"Or not."

"Come upstairs. We've got a lot to discuss."

"I've already heard most of it."

"You can listen again, but this time, you can *pay attention*."

"I was kind of busy," he said, as he dragged his feet toward the stairs.

"Yes, we know." She glanced, once, at Bellusdeo and her guest, and turned heel without comment.

"Has she been like that all day?"

"Yes. I believe she is arguing with Terrano, as well."

"Terrano came back?"

"No, dear. That's why she's arguing." Helen frowned.
"Would you like to tell me about your day?"

"Not the long, normal way, no. But you can see it, right?"
Helen nodded.

"Good. I've got questions about Towers and captains and
tenants."

"Let me see Lord Emmerian and Bellusdeo properly settled," Helen said, her expression almost sorrowful. "And then
I will meet you on the patio."

The patio, such as it was, was not actually a normal version
of a patio—not that Kaylin had a lot of experience with normal patios, given her life to date. This one was reached from
a door at the end of the hall that otherwise contained the private rooms of Helen's guests. And Kaylin.

Severn had chosen to remain for dinner, but dinner wasn't
going to be served in the dining room; there were too many
discussions happening, and some of them required Helen's
focused attention.

Kaylin was therefore down the list. Nothing she could do
constituted a possibly dangerous emergency.

"That is not true, dear," Helen's voice said. Her Avatar was
serving tea—or drinks—to the two Dragons who were now
ensconced in the parlor.

"Compared to the cohort?"

"You would, admittedly, have to put in some effort, especially these days. But I have confidence in you."

The patio no longer contained a dining table suitable for
several people; there was a single, round table suitable for four,
but only two chairs; Helen didn't need one. "I may take a bit
longer to answer your questions than I otherwise would. What
do you wish to ask?"

"Well, Karriamis told me to talk to you about tenants."

"Yes, I see that. He was perhaps overly impressed with my abilities."

"We want to know—"

"Bellusdeo wants to know."

"Fine. Bellusdeo wants to know why Karriamis accepted Candallar as a captain."

"Ah. What he told you is materially true: people change. Life changes them. Fearful people become more fearful—or less—as they gain experience. Candallar fled the High Halls when he was declared outcaste."

"We don't know why he was declared outcaste."

"With your friends at Court? You should be able to find out."

"Do you know?"

"No. I believe the cohort might, but their information sources are not as good as yours, given their long absence, and the information they've received has been conflicting."

She wondered what Bellusdeo and Emmerian were doing.

"Talking."

"About what?"

Helen tsked, and Kaylin fell silent. "I'm worried about Bellusdeo."

"I know. So am I. Mandoran is more concerned about her welfare than he is about the cohort, which is why Sedarias is incensed."

Kaylin could understand that, as well. She didn't approve, but it wasn't her job to approve or disapprove.

"I find it odd that here, Barrani and Dragon can become friends in a fashion familiar to you. Odd, but gratifying."

"Fine. You can't tell me about Candallar, and Karriamis won't. Your previous tenant died before I arrived to apply for a room."

"Yes."

"How long had he been dead?"

Silence. Kaylin thought Helen wasn't going to answer.
"Years. I'm afraid a more accurate measure would take—
Excuse me."

"Helen?"

"I have either a fire—or worse. I'm sorry, dear. I'll be back."

15

"I have no idea why I *ever* thought this was a good idea," Kaylin said as she left the patio table, Severn in her wake.

"Which part?"

"Any of it!"

"They had nowhere else to safely go."

"You mean the cohort?"

"Any of them. The danger to Bellusdeo wasn't physical—or not purely physical. But she had nowhere to go, either."

"I just—"

"Wish everyone could get along?"

She nodded.

He shrugged. "We'd both be out of jobs if that was a realistic possibility. And on most days you love your job."

"I want to leave my job *outside* of my home."

Severn shrugged. "Training room?"

"Parlor first." She was reasonably certain the cohort wouldn't actually kill each other, and she was absolutely certain Emmerian wouldn't injure Bellusdeo, possibly even in self-defense. No.

She understood why Mandoran had risked his life to interfere with Bellusdeo in the Tower; she understood what the danger he'd faced then was. She wanted to make certain that it wasn't happening again.

The door to the parlor was closed; no smoke trailed out from the space between door and jamb. If Bellusdeo and Emmerian were fighting, no evidence of that was clear.

Until Bellusdeo roared.

Kaylin reached for the door. Severn caught her arm and shook his head. "She's angry, she's not enraged. They're having a discussion. It's the cohort we need to see."

Helen's voice didn't tell them to stay put, which confirmed Severn's opinion. She did, however, caution them about the avenues of safe approach.

"What does that even mean?" Kaylin demanded, as she jogged towards the closet door that led to the expansive training rooms.

Helen didn't answer. Then again, she didn't need to. Kaylin opened the door into a field. A battlefield, apparently, given the broken standards that awkwardly adorned it. There were as yet no bodies, but grass had been stripped from the earth by the passage of many feet—some of them hoofed, by the look of the damage. "Wrong room."

Severn was looking at the banners. He turned back toward the door and exhaled, shoulders slumping.

There was no door. Of course there was no door.

Kaylin let out a stream of Leontine invective.

"She did warn us."

"I want more information in my warnings. Damn it." Kaylin listened for the sound of clashing armies, clashing forces, that these banners implied. Severn, however, walked to the nearest. Kaylin had missed it; the pole had been sheared in half at an angle, and the cloth lay across the ground. He lifted it.

It was, to Kaylin's eye, Barrani.

"It's Carmanne's standard. Serralyn's family."

"She's not here."

"I don't think this is an entirely physical fight." He carefully flattened the standard and then rolled it up, as if it were a carpet. "Helen?"

A small wagon appeared to the left of where Kaylin was standing. Helen herself didn't speak.

They picked their way across this field of standards; some listed; some were slashed or torn. At each, Severn paused to retrieve the cloth, or what remained of it, and at each, he named the Barrani family that it signified, adding the names of the cohort as necessary.

Each name added to the weight of Kaylin's worry, enlarging it. She liked the cohort. As a group. As individuals. Even Sedarias. She liked what they had built; that they had chosen to trust each other, that they were willing to kill and die for each other.

This was the downside of that. The air fairly thrummed with enraged betrayal.

She stopped.

Air *did not* thrum with enraged betrayal. But she felt it, simmering in the earth beneath both of their feet. This was a battlefield, yes—but Kaylin was almost certain it was a battlefield of one.

Kaylin spoke a single name out loud. "Sedarias."

A hand reached out and clamped itself over her mouth. She drove her elbow backward. Connected with nothing. The hand was disembodied. One of the cohort, then. She didn't know which one; she'd never taken the time to memorize what their hands looked like. She nodded.

The hand fell instantly away from her mouth.

Speaking far more quietly, Kaylin said, "This is Sedarias's battlefield."

"It is." It was Terrano.

"I thought you were at the Academia."

"I was—and I'd much rather be there. But Mandoran said it was serious."

Severn stood, and put another banner in the wagon. He glanced back, but there was no visible sign of Terrano; even the hand had vanished.

"Are we going to find your family's banner here?"

"Probably. Farther in."

"Farther in?"

"This is a large, flat field, like a circle. The edges are all cliff."

"She's down the cliff."

"Yes."

"Which direction?"

"Damned if I know."

"Where is everyone else?"

Silence.

"Helen?" No answer. Kaylin wondered if they were even contained in Helen anymore. It was a thought that made her very uneasy.

"She's here," Terrano's voice said. "But it's harder for her to communicate with you."

"Why?"

"Because you brought him with you."

"What?"

"You—you're not normal, you know that, right? You're as human as the rest of us are Barrani."

"But you *are* Barrani."

"Sure," he said. It sounded like a no. "I'd tell you to send him back, but you can't; Helen's entire focus is on protecting Severn. I think you could do it, but she's not certain, and she *is* certain Severn's death will cause severe fractures in this current iteration of reality."

Kaylin wasn't stupid. "Because of me."

"Because you'll be upset, yes."

"Will Sedarias try to kill us?"

"No." It sounded like a yes. "Come on, we need to find Mandoran."

"He's here?"

"Yes."

"In Sedarias's head, for want of a better word?"

"Yes—but that's normal for us."

"This battlefield is not normal."

"Actually, it is. Some of us are better at words than others. Some of us are excellent at words—but only as weapons. Guess who's the latter?"

"This is what it always looks like?"

"To me, yes." Terrano exhaled. "You need to remember something—both of you need to remember it. I don't see what you see. But I see what Severn is doing. It's complicated. We're looking at the same things, but...we're not interpreting them the same way."

"If vision were interpretative, the law would be in serious trouble when it came to witnesses," Kaylin said.

"Most people don't have the flexibility to even see what you're looking at now. We're seeing what Sedarias sees. There's no way to tell you how to interpret if you...can't already do some of that on your own."

"So, can we fly here? Because jumping down the side of a cliff isn't likely to be healthy."

"Tell me about it," Terrano said, a note of resignation in an otherwise tense voice. "You don't have to jump. I'm sure there are stairs somewhere."

"In a cliff?"

"Somewhere. I'm taking the fast way down."

"We're going to look for safe."

He snorted. "It's *Sedarias*. You'll be looking for a long damn time."

When Terrano was gone and the rest of the banners had been collected and carefully placed in the small wagon, Kaylin poked Hope. He was seated, not draped across her shoulders, but didn't look particularly alert.

"We need to get down to wherever Sedarias is."

He nodded.

"Can you help?"

I can.

"Will I have to sacrifice something for it?"

No. This is something you could do yourself.

Without stairs or wings, Kaylin didn't see how.

Hope snorted. He pushed himself off her shoulder, hovering in the air for a moment in front of her face. *Here, those marks have a greater weight and meaning. Remember that.*

"Hope—I don't even understand where *here* is. If Helen is somehow stabilizing things so that Severn survives here, we're obviously still in Helen somehow. But Terrano seemed to think that this was all Sedarias. Those two things don't line up to my pathetic, tiny, mortal mind."

Severn glanced at Hope, who seemed to be waiting for something. "Helen creates the rooms for her tenants and guests; those rooms are a merging of what Helen is, at base, with what they need. There's already a lack of distinct separation in our interactions. This is…more difficult."

"Sedarias has taken control of some part of Helen?"

"Or Helen has, for reasons of her own, ceded that control to Sedarias in this space. It's probably a containment measure."

Hope squawked. He then landed.

"Can we take that control back from her?"

"I wouldn't try it unless we had no other options." He watched Hope as Hope began to transform.

Hope's adoption of the draconic form—that's the way Kaylin thought of it—was not similar to watching either Bellusdeo or Emmerian. Hope seemed to expand, rather than transform. His body was already translucent, glass-like in appearance; it was far less disturbing to watch a familiar face warp and extend—almost as if it were stretched to a breaking point that never quite arrived.

Hope's transition seemed far less painful, far more natural.

Climb, Hope told them both. *I will carry your wagon.*

Kaylin scrambled up on his back; Severn took a seat behind her. True to his word, he carefully grasped the wagon in much, much larger feet, and lifted his bulk into the air with the movement of enormous, translucent wings.

"Can you see Sedarias?"

"Not yet."

"Terrano?"

"We couldn't see him when he spoke to us."

It was a fair point. She couldn't ask Hope to place a wing across her face; he'd flatten her. Terrano had said the rise of the plain that looked very much like a battlefield after a war had been fought was at the height of a flat peak; that it was cliff all the way down. Seen from the air, he was right. What she didn't see, as Hope circled this edifice of rising stone, was anything at all that resembled stairs.

Terrano—and Mandoran—had ways of reaching the ground; the landscape itself wouldn't otherwise try to kill them. But it was going to be work, regardless.

"Can you see Mandoran?" She couldn't. "He's likely to be where Sedarias is."

"No sign of Mandoran. I'd wait on Terrano's signal."

"You think he'll remember to signal us?"

She could feel Severn's nod from the inside; she couldn't see it because she didn't have eyes in the back of her head.

Hope felt no need to land quickly, possibly because the peak was so high. Rock was the landscape, all the way down; Kaylin couldn't see an end to the drop. There was no distant patch of greenery, nothing that visually implied that life existed anywhere but the flat plain they'd left. There, at least, evidence of plant life remained, even if much of it had been destroyed.

Severn's eyes had always been better than hers; she wasn't surprised when Severn said, "There. Start there."

"What's there?"

"A river."

Hope turned, slowly, to the right, still intent on descent.

The river was much wider than it had looked from above, which wasn't hard; from above, Kaylin hadn't seen it. As they approached, it seemed to widen and lengthen, rushing in a way that made swimming or rafting guaranteed suicide. Rocks and wood had been carried in the current, and rocks had worn away at the stone that served as its partial tunnel; there was no shore here.

Hope flew in the direction of the current, following the water so closely the spray dampened his passengers.

Kaylin glanced once over her shoulder; the peak could no longer be seen.

She thought of the portal paths, their natural gray emptiness, the nothing that was somehow the potential out of which the Towers could create everything. Sedarias had done that here. But Terrano's reaction implied it wasn't deliberate; it was a state of mind.

Why had the battlefield been placed at the top of a peak? It was the highest standing peak in this bleak landscape. She understood the symbolism of the fallen banners: Sedarias felt betrayed by those who had been, and who were, the only family she had ever known.

Family, in the sense that Kaylin defined it. Kaylin had tried to build a family in the absence of the one she was born to; she'd been drawn to people who would, or could, provide her with some of what she had desperately missed.

Sedarias hadn't had any of that; her upbringing—given her sister and brother—had been a deadly version of every man for themselves. She had killed both of them in the end, not for reasons of politics or power, but survival. But she was now An'Mellarionne, and power came with the title, if she could survive long enough to hold it.

She'd been taught not to trust; most of them had. Annarion, however, had never stopped trusting his brother, which is why his anger at his brother's behavior cut him so deeply. Teela had killed her father *because* she loved her mother, who had died at his hands.

Family, Barrani family, was complicated.

Maybe there was no other way to express it than the way Sedarias had chosen to express it: as a war, a battlefield, a place of conflict and only conflict.

She realized then that she didn't know what Severn's childhood had been like; that it had never truly occurred to her to ask.

"You did," he said, proof that her thoughts were heard, even if they weren't voiced. "But you were young, when we first met. In your memories I was always there. I was part of your family."

And now was not the time to ask. She therefore dutifully bit back a flood of questions and turned her thoughts, once again, to Sedarias. What did Sedarias want? What had she wanted when she had first offered eleven strangers the power of her True Name?

What had she tried to do with the power of theirs?

Ah. Yes. That was the question.

"Family is difficult," she said aloud.

"All the best," Severn said quietly, "and all the worst. Sedarias's birth family offered nothing but the worst by our standards. To the Barrani, it might have been considered best."

It was not. Kaylin was surprised to hear Nightshade's voice. She couldn't tell if this was because Helen let him in—which she sometimes did—or if Helen was so distracted the basic securities had been loosened.

I believe it is the former. She is aware that she is not Barrani, and her experience of Barrani was not...what yours is. Sedarias's family would be considered extreme by many of our kin. All comments of weakness aside, your own understanding of her in the context of her cohort might prove more valuable than the opinion of her people. This is impressive, he added, the texture of the interior voice changing.

Impressive?

It is a wilderness as harsh as any we have had to endure. I have never attempted to create something of this scope within Castle Nightshade. I admit I am tempted to try. But you are now speaking to the wrong person.

Who should I be speaking to?

Terrano, but I perceive he is not present. He was not, however, the person I meant to suggest.

Please don't say Ynpharion.

Silence.

He only ever talks to me when the Consort insists on conveying information, or when he thinks I'm an idiot. He's not going to want to talk to me about Barrani happy families.

No. I doubt very much he will desire to talk about unhappy families, either. But I believe he may have information that would be of use.

And not you.

And not me, no. I had very little conflict with either my mother or my father, while they lived. With my cousins, with my aunts, yes—but they were not considered family unless we were at war.

Kaylin sagged in place. *Ynpharion won't want to talk to me about this.*

No. But you might infer some of it from his general attitude.

Which is judgmental.

Yes. It is, however, similar to Sedarias's—or to what Sedarias would be had she had neither true power nor the cohort. She took a risk. But Kaylin, Ynpharion took a risk, in the end, as well. As the one who has knowledge of True Names you have never been a threat. But the Consort? She is Barrani.

She loved her brothers. They loved each other.

And still does, yes. But Ynpharion is not her brother. Perhaps, in time, the risk will—as you say in Elantran—pay out. Regardless, he took that risk. And in my estimation, there is some pride for him in that.

He didn't do that for me.

Nightshade said nothing for long enough, Kaylin thought he had withdrawn. *No. But you needed to be in contact with the Consort; it was a matter of importance to the High Halls, and he knew it. He could talk to you, but he could not make decisions, and admitting that a mortal held his True Name would have been a public humiliation beyond his fragile endurance.*

And you don't care.

And I do not care. There was amusement in those words. *Unlike those who wish they did not, it is of little relevance to me. I am outcaste. I have nothing at all to lose.*

But Nightshade was a power.

Was? a familiar voice snapped. *Calarnenne is a power. He wields one of The Three. He was known for his prowess in war, and none who rose to challenge him survived it. In his fashion, he shares renown with An'Teela.*

How long have you been listening?

Subjectively? Decades. Ynpharion was frustrated. This was

almost a comfort, because Ynpharion appeared to have only one state: frustration.

That is not true.

Fine. Anger and resentment, too.

You have never understood.

I've always *understood,* she snapped back. *You're not a power. Fine. I spent all of my life until I arrived in the city being even less of a power than you. Maybe it's a shorter period of time—but my whole life is a short period of time compared to yours. I* know *what it's like to be terrified that I won't even survive. But I also know what it's like to fear starving to death—to be so damn hungry there's almost nothing I wouldn't do for food. Do you?*

Silence.

You don't.

You're Chosen, he finally said, the words a grudging acknowledgment of the truth.

Now, yes. And that cost me. It cost fourteen children their lives.

More silence. It occurred to Kaylin, as the waves of anger began to abate, that this was not what Nightshade had had in mind.

Anger, Ynpharion said, *is better than fear. If you have nothing, you have nothing to lose. I had my life. I wanted to keep it.*

Kaylin was silent. *I didn't,* she finally said. *I didn't want to keep mine.*

Ynpharion added a new emotion: surprise.

I wouldn't throw it away, now. I like the life I have, the life *I've found. But I didn't build it—I tripped over it. And kept tripping. I didn't know Helen. I didn't know the cohort. I didn't know Bellusdeo—or Nightshade, if it comes to that. I didn't have Teela or the Hawks.*

Is that what you believe?

Yes, because it's the truth.

If the cohort has taught you nothing, it should have taught you this: truth is mutable, flexible, dependent on context. I was never Sedarias. Never.

Because you see her as a power.

Because she is a power. She always was. You think that her centuries-long fate somehow negates that truth. We know better.

Who is "we"?

Her people. The Barrani. She lived the life I lived, but she—

You survived it. So did she.

Silence, this one larger and louder. *So did you,* Ynpharion finally said.

I'm not Barrani.

Neither is Sedarias.

And you?

I am Barrani. I do not have the freedom that Sedarias gained for herself. I did not kill my brother or my sister; I did not kill my parents.

She didn't kill her parents.

No. An'Teela killed her only living parent—and she is free.

And that's what you want? The question itself was harsh, but the tone was not. It wasn't meant as an accusation. For a moment, on Hope's back, the wind howling in her ears and pulling strands of loose hair toward Severn's face, she simply wanted to know more about him.

It's not what Sedarias wants, he finally said.

What do you think she wants?

What you wanted. I think she started out wanting what you wanted. Your mother died when you were young—you didn't want that. Neither did An'Teela. But An'Teela could build a life on vengeance. You didn't have that. Sedarias did. But...Sedarias is not An'Teela.

Teela took the same risk the rest of the cohort did.

Yes, and she was abandoned. And she survived.

She wasn't abandoned. They couldn't escape, at the start. When they could, Teela was the first person they looked for. Kaylin shook herself.

I want what she built, Ynpharion said.

Have you killed your brother and sister?

I believe she would far rather have Annarion's troubled relationship with his brother than the one she had with hers.

If you were Sedarias—I know you're not—how would you reach her?

The battlefield was the loftiest point of this barren place. You thought of it as a place where a war had been fought—and possibly lost. I think...

She waited. It was hard.

I think that it is a place that is precious to her; the battle is always fought. What waits beneath it is what you now fly over: a barren, rocky landscape where even water causes damage. Her life, like my life, was a battle. And if I did not have her power, neither did my siblings. It is the battlefield that you must protect, and to which you must return her.

But I don't want her to fight.

His chuckle was quiet enough that she might have mistaken his voice for another's if it weren't for the fact of the True Name that bound them.

She will always fight. And the person she fights now is herself. You are afraid that she attempted to use names she knows against those who hold them.

She was.

That she has not done it before—or often—is a symbol of the battlefield; it is herself she fights, because that fight was the whole of her childhood until she met the cohort.

Kaylin said nothing, willing him to continue.

But the risk taken was the hope. We are ridiculed for hope, and often it fails us and causes us to fail ourselves. She does not believe it. And she does believe it. Terrano did not seem surprised to be here. What he said is true: this is what Sedarias is like. He cannot know her name, she cannot know theirs, without this knowledge.

I don't know anything about you, though.

No. But we did not begin as they began; it could never have happened. I could not have allowed it. Were I they, I might have. He doubted it. She heard the doubt clearly.

I want the war to end.

Yes. I imagine Sedarias does as well. But we are also products of the lives we have been born and bred to live. This is the best she can do, for now. Perhaps, in the Hallionne it was different; there, there was no family, no Barrani enemy, nothing that could disturb the peace they built. But she is An'Mellarionne, as she desired. Everything old is new and visceral again.

And Mandoran had betrayed her.

That is the nature of our lives. What she expects—what I expected—is betrayal. To separate her from that expectation would almost be to separate her from herself.

She's had centuries of no betrayal. She wasn't that old when she was sent to the green. More of her life has been defined by the cohort than her family.

Yes. He spoke no other words, but they weren't really needed. *Hope is pain.*

Kaylin knew this. She knew it better than anyone. Ynpharion disagreed, but silently. *Hope is necessary.*

For how long? For how long must hope burden us when it causes nothing but pain?

I don't know. Don't ask me. I just know that I tried to die—by Hawk, because I couldn't bring myself to end my own life. This was not where she had thought this literal descent into the mind of Sedarias would lead. And because she was talking to Ynpharion, emotions she would have bet had finally died reared their heads. *The Hawklord gave me hope. And I've carried it since then.*

He said nothing as she continued. *And I'm glad I carried it.*

Perhaps in time Sedarias will be—but what you see now is a direct consequence of that hope.

Mandoran hasn't—

No. But if you truly understood her fear, you would know that it is the lens through which she views her world. She has been waiting for this.

Kaylin didn't argue. Didn't feel she could. But Terrano had seemed resigned, not surprised. Worried, not terrified. Perhaps they could do this.

But do what, exactly? Get her attention? Return her to normal? Force the cohort to hug and make up? She rolled her eyes hard enough she should have sprained them.

She didn't understand the cohort. Knowing True Names hadn't given her much insight, either. Every person whose True Name she knew was separate from her; they lived their own lives, they had their own responsibilities. She used the connection the way other people used mirrors: to reach out and speak to someone who wasn't immediately present.

That was how it had started with the cohort; had they not been exposed to the *regalia* in their childhood, that's probably how it would have remained, until and unless one of the twelve attempted to assert control over the others. Sedarias would have been her bet, for that.

But the attempt to exert control wasn't control.

Severn had tried it with Kaylin. Once. And then he hadn't spoken a word to her for weeks, as if the attempt—which she understood—destroyed any worth, value or self-respect he had. It had bothered her far less than it had bothered him, and in theory, she was the one who was affected by it.

And *maybe* this was like that: Sedarias had instinctively reached out to grab control, to force behaviors that she felt were in the cohort's best interests. It felt more wrong, to Kaylin.

Severn tensed; his arms tightened briefly. *Because it's "only" you, in your own mind. You don't ever think that should be done to someone else.*

Not true. I can think of a lot of people I'd love to have taken over by people I actually trust. But she knew what he meant, or how he meant it. And if she had been willing to both accept and forget, why shouldn't the cohort do the same?

Sedarias was part of them. Like...part of their thoughts, their way of thinking. Never separate. As prisoners in the Hallionne, they couldn't be said to have had their own lives; only Teela did, and that was because she'd had no other choice.

But they were free, now.

Serralyn and Valliant were part of the Academia. Teela was An'Teela and a corporal of the Hawks. Terrano was... Terrano. That left Mandoran, Annarion, Allaron, Fallessian, Torrisant and Karian, the three who almost never spoke or interacted with any of the cohort except each other. And Eddorian, who had elected to remain with his brother in the Hallionne, but who was nonetheless aware of what his chosen family were doing.

At least one of the banners had belonged to Reymar, Karian's family. Even if they interacted with no outsiders—except Helen—they had their own opinions and beliefs. And one had been Gennave's, which was Eddorian's; Eddorian, whose brother, like Nightshade, had searched for him. For him and power, and it was the latter that had gutted his mind.

What would she do if part of her mind rose against the rest of her?

How could she bring it back to normal? What was "normal" for the cohort and for Sedarias as part of it?

There, Hope said, an interruption she was almost grateful for. "Can you see it, unaided? There is a storm in the distance."

Kaylin squinted. She then elbowed Severn rather than saying no.

Severn was silent for a long beat, as Hope began to pick up speed. "It's Sedarias," he said, voice flat. "Sedarias and Mandoran."

16

What is the shape of Sedarias's fear? Hope asked as he tensed beneath her.

The answer seemed clear: the battlefield, and beneath it, the barren, rocky emptiness—through which water still flowed.

Yes. And?

But there was no necessary *and*. Kaylin understood, before Sedarias became visible to her eyes, what the shape of her fear was; she understood it because she had lived it and passed—mostly—through it. It wasn't the fear of isolation; it wasn't the fear of betrayal, although Ynpharion hadn't been wrong.

It was the certain sense that *this* was the only home of which she was worthy. This is what she deserved. The others? No. Even Terrano with his obsessions about the new and different had a spark of life or joy—ah, that word: *joy.*

Barren rock and the detritus of battle was what Sedarias had.

"Terrano!"

"I'm kind of busy," Terrano, disembodied, replied.

"How much control do you have over this space?"

"What? *Me?* I told you—it's Sedarias's space. It's her."

But Kaylin shook her head. "All of you are part of it. *All* of you. She's angry right now. I get that. But you're *part of her space*. You've got as much right to control it as—as she does."

"Dangerous and stupid at the same time. Well done."

"I mean it!"

"Obviously. It's not that simple. There are things Sedarias can do that we can all forgive because we've seen her and we know who she is. But there are things she'll never forgive."

"Does she hate Alsanis?"

"What?"

"Does she hate the Hallionne Alsanis?"

"I *know* who Alsanis is. I can't even make sense of the question. Maybe try it in Barrani?"

"I need you *all to do something*."

"To do *what*?" The skies, as they approached, were a vivid green-gray; the clouds had rolled across a clear, blue sky.

"To change the shape of this place. She's afraid—this is about one fear. We need to remind her—"

He laughed, the sound both reckless and wild. "What in the hells do you think we've been *doing*?"

Kaylin lifted her arms; the marks had lifted themselves off her skin, surrounded it in a moving nimbus of light. Terrano understood. Which was frustrating, because once again, Kaylin didn't.

"I like Sedarias," she said, and she felt the base of her throat swell, as if the words were song. "I want to smack her, but I want to smack Mandoran most days. And you," she added.

"I won't feel left out if you don't."

"I don't know all of you. But I've *liked* all of you. I think I envied what you've built, what you've made—because I saw the outside of it. Until yesterday. Until today. I didn't understand that it's work, right?" The light her marks shed was blue, not gold. "But I love Helen. She's my home. Sedarias *can't* keep doing this to Helen."

Terrano didn't argue.

Helen remained silent. But Helen was doing something incredibly important for both Sedarias and cohort, and Severn.

"Hope," she said, "drop me in the middle of the storm."

There is a danger, Hope said.

"You think?"

You don't understand the nature of the danger, Hope replied.

"Is this something you could do in my place without killing Severn?" Severn was the only thing here that might serve as a sacrifice—and Kaylin would die first.

I cannot do it at all, Chosen, he replied, with a great and almost distant dignity. *Get ready. I will drop you as you've requested, but I will need to be closer if you wish to survive it.*

"This isn't reality."

Is it not? For Sedarias at the moment it is the only reality. It is a reality that is not mine, Chosen. It is yours and hers. It is the province of the living.

"Wait—what do you mean?"

But Hope had reached the height of the storm. He turned over, and Kaylin fell. So did Severn.

The heart of the storm was, from Kaylin's vantage, a long way down.

"What are you *doing*?" Terrano practically screamed. His voice wasn't directly beside her ear, but she caught a lot of colorful Leontine regardless.

She reached instinctively for Severn as she fell—whether to anchor herself or to somehow save him, she couldn't say—but Severn was beyond her. Above her. And she could see Terrano's hands beneath her partner's arms. Severn was safe, for the moment.

Kaylin herself was victim to gravity. The marks on her arms provided no aerial buoyancy; she plunged toward the two people she could easily see: Sedarias and Mandoran. They both looked up as she approached at growing speed.

It was Sedarias who gestured, not Mandoran; Mandoran shouted in the same disgusted astonishment as Terrano. Kaylin's descent slowed as she approached Sedarias; she could see the color of the Barrani woman's eyes. They were obsidian with flecks of color, like black opals, a gem Kaylin had never liked: too hard, too much like the Shadows that threatened to destroy the city.

Sedarias's expression rippled as Kaylin continued to fall; her focus—which had been on Mandoran—shifted slowly, as if she were struggling to move the entirety of her enraged and bereaved attention to where it needed to be.

And where it needed to be, Kaylin thought, was where they all wanted it to be: on Kaylin, and on Kaylin's immediate survival. The rest of the conflict could wait the few seconds it would take to decide Kaylin's fate.

The leader of the cohort lifted her arms, opening them; Mandoran, facing her, did the same. Kaylin could not recall why she had thought this was a good idea; she had *intended* for Hope to *land*.

As it was, the landing was going to be hers. She prayed that Terrano had managed to prevent Severn's unintentional landing, but had no time to think anything else; she fell into Sedarias's outstretched arms.

And fell through them.

She didn't hit stone. Beneath Sedarias's feet—and beneath Mandoran's—there had been nothing but rock. There was no rock where Kaylin landed, if landing was even the right word. She looked down; there was nothing beneath her feet. But what she couldn't see was solid. Solid, dark, far less unforgiving than the rocks.

"You shouldn't be here, dear," Helen said, her voice disembodied.

"Where *is* here?"

Her home didn't answer.

"Are you an idiot?"

Kaylin turned in the direction of the voice. As she did she saw light: her marks. In the darkness they were the only thing she could see. "Often," she replied.

"It's no wonder Teela worries about you so much—you have a death wish. What were you *thinking?*"

Kaylin shrugged as the voice drew closer. "You really want to know?"

"I asked, didn't I?" Sedarias's voice was a rumble encased by sharp edges.

"I was thinking that Mandoran might need some help."

She could hear a second intake of breath, sharp but different from Sedarias's.

"Mandoran? You think *Mandoran* needs help?"

"She's really not as bright as she wants to be," Mandoran said. He coalesced in this darkness, shining faintly. Sedarias could still not be seen. To Kaylin, brow folded, he said, "Seriously, what were you thinking? You can't honestly imagine Sedarias would hurt me?"

"You're not a patch on Sedarias. She's powerful *and* martial. I wouldn't worry if it was Bellusdeo; Bellusdeo could hold her own."

"That's not what I meant, and you know it."

"I could," Sedarias snapped, appearing at last, as Mandoran did. She was about three feet taller, and she looked down—and down again—to see both her chosen brother and her landlord.

"Could what?"

"I could have handled the Dragon."

"*I* handled the Dragon."

If a storm cloud had dropped lightning bolts without warn-ing, Kaylin wouldn't have been surprised.

"Seriously," Terrano said, appearing—as they appeared—in the darkness. He glanced at Kaylin's arms, frowning. "None of us should have made any attempt to—as you put it—handle the Dragon."

"She needed help, though," Serralyn said. Serralyn, who was in the Academia with Valliant.

"If she can't pass the Tower's test, that's to *our* benefit." To Kaylin's surprise, it was Torrisant who spoke.

"It's only to our benefit if any of *us* can pass the test." Man-doran again. Kaylin wondered, then, why she'd come here at all, but the marks continued to glow, the blue depths of their heart giving way to gold.

"What did you do with Severn?"

"What you should have done in the first place," Terrano replied, although he didn't look away from Sedarias. "He's safe with Helen. Probably eating too, given the way she was fussing. You can't just drag him into everything—he's not suited to it."

"I didn't realize we were about to enter someplace danger-ous. It's Helen."

"Well, now you know."

"I'm kind of hoping this *never happens again*."

"And I was kind of hoping that Allasarre was dead, buried and forgotten. We don't always get what we want."

"We can get that," Sedarias snapped. Her eyes, still opal-like, were flashing, her translucent hands becoming fists. She was shaking, and the shaking seemed to make her body far less solid, less well-defined.

Terrano cursed. "Hold on," he told Kaylin. "It's about to get bumpy again."

"Hold on to what?"

"Yourself."

★ ★ ★

She understood the moment Sedarias began to speak; she could hear the syllables of a language that was both unknown and viscerally familiar.

Gods, she thought, does Sedarias *always* do this?

"She is speaking the names, dear. She hasn't tried to use them yet. Even if she did, I wouldn't allow the attempt to go uncontested."

"Meaning you don't think you could stop her."

"Not permanently, no. But she means to be heard; she is shouting their names to get their attention."

"She's shouting them where anyone can hear them?"

"No, dear. I have always heard them. The only difference is that she's shouting them where *you* can hear them. I'd suggest you cover your ears, but that's not the way you're hearing them. And that's not what I think you should be doing, regardless."

"What should I be doing?"

"Speaking to Sedarias."

Kaylin was dubious.

"Don't be, dear. Does her interest in the Tower threaten you?"

"No."

"Does it make her your enemy?"

"No."

"Bellusdeo's enemy?"

"Maybe—at the outside—her rival, but enemy? No. Bellusdeo wouldn't kill for the Tower. Well, she might try to kill the Avatar of the Tower, but no one else."

"Yes. Speak to Sedarias."

"The cohort—"

"It is too much a part of her at the moment; she cannot separate her concerns from theirs. It is why she is here, and why they are trying to reach her."

"And I'm the outsider."

"Inasmuch as an outsider has *ever* gotten this close to Sedarias, yes."

"But you're here!"

"Ah, no. No, I am not here in the way you are. She can usually hear my voice; she can certainly see the consequences of actions in my response. But she is not in a place I can now reach. You are."

"And I'm in a place that can reach her, too."

"Yes. You know what you have to do. You started it when you asked Hope to drop you into Sedarias's storm. This is its eye."

Kaylin didn't ask how long they had. And she didn't ask what she should, or shouldn't, say. She understood that Helen didn't know. She thought Helen was wrong. Helen understood people because she had to; she knew how to make them feel at home, and feel safe there. Kaylin had none of that ability. She couldn't read minds. She couldn't, unless someone communicated it, know what they wanted, what they needed, or worse, what would make them snap like dry kindling.

She had had to learn it the hard way. By observing—when observation was safe, or even possible. Or by making mistakes.

Even here, in the heart of Sedarias's mind—and she had no other word for it, but hoped to hells that no one ever walked into her mind-space like this—she had no better sense of who Sedarias was, of what she wanted.

She probably didn't want broken standards and crushed grass and an endless vista of stone; the only thing that implied life had been that grass. And the water, maybe. Kaylin had been following the rush of water to its eventual destination, and had found Sedarias before river met ocean.

Now she wondered where the water was going. Maybe it was headed to another cliff, and would become a waterfall.

Ugh. Water was easier to think about than Sedarias, here. If the cohort, who knew her and loved her and lived with her, didn't know what to do, how could anyone assume she would?

But the marks on her arm were spinning like concentric, magical bracelets. So maybe it was time to really think instead of feeling hard done by. She turned to look in this eye of the storm; she had seen Mandoran and Sedarias; Terrano had been a disembodied voice.

As she looked, as the light cast by the raised runes on her arms brightened the stillness and alleviated the darkness, the two remained: Sedarias, Mandoran. Mandoran wasn't obviously trapped—there was no cage, he wasn't bound—but his feet touched nothing; Sedarias's rested firmly on stone.

They were speaking. She couldn't hear them. She could see Sedarias's expression. And the back of Mandoran's head.

"You really shouldn't be here," Mandoran said.

"Kind of getting that impression. Not sure you should be, either."

"I can't leave."

"I know. Where are the rest of you?"

"You saw Terrano. Or heard him. The rest of us are here, as well."

"But I can only see you—"

"Sedarias is very focused at the moment. Very."

"And she can't hear you."

"Whatever gave you that idea?" She could almost hear the eye roll.

"She hasn't tried to cut you in two?"

He laughed; the laughter was wild and bitter. "Is that what you honestly believe?"

"She's in control of the space. If she wanted you gone—"

"She never wants us gone." His voice, stripped of sarcasm, sounded exhausted.

Kaylin found stone beneath her feet; the stone that didn't

seem to be supporting this iteration of Mandoran. Of the cohort, with the exception of Terrano, he seemed most comfortable off the ground—but not here.

She said, quietly, "Can you go away?"

Mandoran didn't answer as Kaylin came to stand in front of him, facing Sedarias. Sedarias didn't seem to see her.

"Not sure how this is going to go," Kaylin said quietly.

"What are you going to do?"

"So just be prepared if Sedarias loses it."

He laughed, the laughter wild. "You are insane. That's the right word?"

"It's the word you wanted, but I'd quibble *right*. Later." She lifted her left hand, as if Sedarias were a very dangerous door ward and she didn't want to risk the loss of the dominant one.

"I really think that's a bad idea. Teela is now screaming her lungs out, metaphorically speaking."

"Probably literally, too. Sorry." She touched Sedarias's shoulder.

The attention she wanted, she got. The stone beneath her feet shuddered; Kaylin thought it might break, and reminded herself that this space remained within Helen, and Helen was unlikely to let her die here.

She had Sedarias's attention.

"What in the hells are you doing?" she demanded.

Sedarias stared at her, her eyes black opal, growing larger and wider in her face. She opened her mouth. No words came out. She tried again, as if she had forgotten how to speak, but understood the theory of it. The third time, she said, "Why are you here?"

"You're hurting Helen. I want you to stop."

"I am *not* hurting Helen. I am having a *private* discussion with my friends."

"All eleven of them, yes. If this is your idea of discussion,

I'm here to suggest that you try a different method." Light pulsed around Kaylin's lifted arm; the marks were glowing. No, Kaylin thought, they were *speaking*. She couldn't understand what she heard as words. She wasn't certain, but thought Sedarias could. At least some of it.

The ground cracked. The stone broke. But it broke beneath both of their feet.

Kaylin fell. So did Sedarias.

What lay beneath the crust of lifeless stone was not the darkness Kaylin had imagined—if she had truly imagined anything. There was light here—sunlight—and trees; there was birdsong and insect rustle and the movement of small feet, the lifted voices of…children.

Mandoran was no longer present. Or if he was, he was, like Terrano, invisible.

"Be careful," Terrano said quietly. "Be very careful, here."

Sedarias was staring at Kaylin. "Come," she said, in a voice that almost defined the word *hostile*. Terrano sucked in a sharp breath, but said no more as Sedarias turned her back on Kaylin and started to walk away.

If this had been the world into which the door had led, Kaylin wouldn't have had to be here at all; here, with a table, two chairs, and a large umbrella protecting the people who might occupy those chairs from an excess of sunlight in a clear sky. The only shadows here were cast by the branches of trees.

Sedarias sat.

Kaylin took the empty chair opposite her.

"Why are you here?"

"You destroyed the rock I was standing on?"

Sedarias's eyes—still opal, but occupying the normal fraction of her face—narrowed. "I have not yet strangled Mandoran for his sense of 'humor,' and it is not entirely for lack of trying."

Right. "Helen was worried."

"I have not attempted to hurt Helen."

"No. But the thing is, you don't have to *try* to hurt her. Sometimes you can hurt people without even being aware they're there. We call that collateral damage. But intent doesn't cut it. What's damaged is damaged. *I didn't mean to* doesn't count as a legal defense."

"And you are here as a representative of Imperial Law?"

Kaylin exhaled. "No. No, and you know it."

"You brought up law."

She had. "Why didn't you build this place instead?"

"Instead? It's always here." Sedarias looked away for the first time. "It's always here but I cannot always reach it."

Kaylin closed her eyes.

"You don't have spaces like this one. You could; Helen would allow it. But you don't. You let Helen be Helen. This space, Helen also allowed me to create. She likes it," Sedarias added, voice soft. "I wish I had met her in my childhood."

"She wouldn't be the Helen you know now."

Silence.

"What were you trying to do?"

"I wasn't consciously trying to do anything. I was...angry. With Mandoran." Before Kaylin could speak in his defense, she added, "And I suppose with Serralyn and Valliant as well. With Eddorian. With Teela." She bowed her head again. "Terrano says I am always angry."

"You're not going to deny that, are you?"

"This was not created, this place, from anger."

Kaylin opened her eyes. She looked at the trees, at the sky, at the surroundings. "No. But it's not real, either. This, and the rock desert, neither are real."

"You don't understand Helen's power, a Hallionne's power, if you believe that. You could—were you any other mortal— die here. How much more real must something be?"

"Helen wouldn't allow any of my guests to be killed anywhere within her boundaries."

"No, perhaps not. No more would Alsanis, when we were his to jail." Sedarias rose. "What would you rather see?"

"You," Kaylin replied. "Your friends. My normal house."

"Nothing about your house is normal. What Helen does to create your *normal* house is akin to what has been done here. You've seen our rooms."

But it wasn't the same. Kaylin couldn't tell if Sedarias was lying or deflecting, or if she believed what she had said.

She can't hear us.

She could, however, hear Kaylin. "Why don't you trust them?"

Sedarias said nothing.

"I understand why you didn't trust your family. I always wanted siblings. I never had any. Not really. But your family has convinced me that I might have been extremely lucky not to."

This pulled a cold smile from Sedarias.

"But your brother is dead. Your sister is dead. You might have a whole host of cousins who inevitably join them, if your entire family culture is the same. I don't know. I'm not Barrani and I can't judge."

"But you do judge."

Kaylin shrugged. "I think it sucks, yes. I think the world is a better place without your relatives in it, yes. But I understand why *you* didn't trust them. They would have killed you if you'd left them any openings. They tried when you didn't.

"But they're not the cohort. You gave each other your names."

"That seems so significant to you," Sedarias replied. "The True Names. The core of our identities."

Kaylin nodded.

"Do you think that I offered mine because I immediately trusted them?" Clouds moved in across what had been clear sky.

"You were willing to take the risk."

"I'd *met them*. I did not consider it a risk. Or perhaps I considered it a calculated risk. Do you think they gave me their names because they liked or trusted *me*?"

Since that's exactly what she'd thought, Kaylin nodded.

"Honestly, it's no wonder Mandoran is so fond of you—you're beyond naive."

"But you don't understand why Teela also likes me."

Sedarias's jaw tightened, as if she was fighting to contain words, to keep them hidden. "They knew Mellarionne. They knew Teela's family—the family whose very name she destroyed in her endless grief and rage. We are a people built on grief and rage. Those of weaker families gave me their names because they felt they had no hope of surviving if they did not.

"Do you understand? I demanded and offered a facade of vulnerability I *never* felt. Not one of them could control *me*. They offered me their names because they were *afraid* of me."

Kaylin understood the heart of Sedarias's fear, then. Fear—to Sedarias—had been the cause of the original bond. Mellarionne had been powerful and known, and Sedarias was of Mellarionne. She had come to the green because she had fought—and bested—those in her family whose goal was, and had always been, power.

"And they're not afraid of you now."

Sedarias looked down at the table. She did not answer.

Kaylin exhaled. "You're wrong."

"You think they're afraid of me?"

"No, not about that." Kaylin held up one hand. Words. She had to find the right words. Terrano had said Sedarias wasn't good with words; neither was Kaylin. That just made it harder, because people who weren't good with words required very specific words.

"I think you're right—they were afraid of you. Or afraid

of Mellarionne. Given what I've seen of your family, I'd be afraid too."

"So you understand."

"No, I don't. That was centuries ago. I don't know what they saw in you—honestly, I don't. You're mostly terrifying."

"Only mostly?" Her voice was soft.

"You're not safe to be around, not normally. Mandoran *is*. And so is Terrano, when he's not trying to kill me."

"Hey!"

Sedarias's brows rose higher, and remained that way for a time; when they lowered, they lowered on very narrow eyes.

"You are such an idiot," Kaylin whispered.

Terrano appeared fully for the first time since Kaylin had entered this space.

Sedarias was armored now, literally. Kaylin understood this, too. She could have cheerfully strangled Terrano. "You interrupted me."

"He always does." Sedarias glared at Terrano.

"I can leave if you let me?" Terrano's attempt at puppy dog eyes was actually good.

"No, please, take a seat."

"There's no chair."

"I know."

Terrano rolled his eyes.

"I wasn't planning on having an audience."

"I don't count!" He spoke Elantran. Kaylin realized he'd been speaking Elantran all along.

"I'm trying to remember that," Sedarias snapped. "I could honestly kill you right now."

Terrano nodded as if she were talking about the weather.

"If you were going to kill him, he'd've been dead a long time ago."

"We needed him."

"And now?"

"Why don't you finish what you were saying before he interrupted you?"

Kaylin nodded. "I was saying—"

"That I'm unsafe. I'm frightening."

"I was saying that it's not always safe to be around you. Given today, you can't argue with that."

"I didn't try." Sedarias was also speaking Elantran.

"But...if I were one of your cohort—and I'm not, and I can't be—"

"Do *not* say it," Sedarias snapped at Terrano.

Terrano shrugged, but kept quiet.

"I would trust you with my life."

Sedarias stared at her in silence.

"I mean: you're not safe to be around, but you would always *keep me* safe. They don't stay with you because they had no choice. Terrano *did* have a choice. He didn't have to come back. He did."

"It wasn't necessarily for me—"

"Bullshit."

Both Terrano and Sedarias stared at her again, for entirely different reasons. Kaylin reddened. It was, not surprisingly, Sedarias who spoke first.

"There were twelve of us. It's not because of me—we fought all the time. We still do."

Kaylin turned to Terrano. "You tell her," she said.

"Well, but, she has a point. It's not just Sedarias I missed. All of us are part of the same whole—all except Teela. She doesn't quite know how to fit in."

"She probably doesn't appreciate the attempts to make her fit in, either," Kaylin said, thinking about the various cohort arguments—all removed, when they could be, to the training rooms as people disincorporated in their emotional distress. "But she went to the green with me *for you*. For all of you. You were, besides her mother, her biggest loss, her biggest regret.

"And he has you back. It's difficult—but it's always been difficult to fit eleven different people into one space.

"They're not afraid of you, Sedarias. They haven't been afraid of you for a long time. Afraid *for* you isn't the same. Yes, I agree, they probably traded names because they thought you were a threat. And I know that one: you give the dangerous people what they want so they don't notice you and you don't die. But you're always waiting for the moment you can flee.

"Not fight: flee. And you know this. You can't avoid knowing it. That's what you're afraid of: the flight. You're afraid that they'll leave because they're not afraid anymore and they don't need you.

"You're afraid that's already what's happening. Serralyn and Valliant. Mandoran."

17

As she spoke the names, the members of the cohort who owned them appeared, just as Terrano had done. It was a calculated risk on her part; she knew, intellectually, that they weren't physically here.

Ah.

That's why Helen had had difficulty preserving Severn.

"Yes, dear. You are here the way the cohort is here. You just don't realize it. You are not part of them; you could not be here at all if you weren't part of me."

Serralyn said, "I'd prefer not to sit on the ground, if it's all the same to you."

Sedarias said nothing. Loudly.

Serralyn exhaled and sat practically on top of Terrano. Valliant said nothing, but joined her; they'd sat this way in the dining room, admittedly with more pillows and a rug.

Kaylin was surprised to see Teela, and by her expression, so was Sedarias. She was warier, but that made sense: Teela had killed her father, had taken her family line, and had obliterated its name. She wielded one of The Three. She had fought in the wars that had been the sole reason for their exile in the

West March, wars the rest of the cohort hadn't seen. She was a power. She was recognized as a power, even by the former An'Mellarionne. No one messed with An'Teela unless they had a death wish.

She was what Sedarias saw herself as.

Was there envy? Probably some. And that was the thing with the cohort: they saw and heard it all. There was no privacy, and they'd grown up together in such a way that privacy was almost foreign.

Except for Teela.

Sedarias met her gaze, held it, and did not tell her to sit on the floor. Kaylin scurried out of the chair she occupied because she wasn't certain that Sedarias making a chair specifically for Teela wouldn't cause problems for the rest of the cohort.

Teela took the chair Kaylin had just vacated.

"I did not mean to endanger Kaylin," Sedarias said.

"No. I know. So does Kaylin. If Kaylin weren't so compulsive, there would have been no danger." She spared Kaylin a side glare, but most of her attention remained focused on Sedarias. "I apologize for my absence; it took me a while to find a way in, and I had to have Helen's aid—aid she was not immediately free to give me."

Kaylin said nothing much more quietly.

"She was taking care of Severn, because *someone* brought him in here," Terrano said.

Kaylin was pretty certain Teela already knew this. She really wanted to kick him, though.

"Please do," Sedarias said. "It will save me the trouble."

"We'd welcome being kicked," Terrano shot back, "compared to what's been happening for the last several hours."

Mandoran had taken a seat beside Terrano, and he nodded, but said very little. If Terrano accepted this as business as usual, Mandoran didn't.

Neither did Teela.

"This is where you need to be," Teela said softly. "Not the rock and the remnants of a battlefield. You must see that."

Sedarias said nothing.

"I didn't grow up with you," Teela continued. "Perhaps that's why I can see it more clearly. I did not give you my name out of fear. I was not afraid of you, then. I am not afraid of you now. You might believe it's because of what I've achieved in the interim, when you all went on without me and I could no longer hear your voices, even if I knew you were still alive.

"You would be wrong. I did not have Mellarionne. I had my mother's family, considered irrelevant and insignificant in the High Court of the time. They were not my father's family; they were not Mellarionne. My father would have approved of—did approve of—Mellarionne. He was wary, of course, but he considered them powerful and therefore worthy of respect.

"I did not believe that you could control *me*. I did not give you my name because of that fear. I did not believe you could kill me—although we must be grateful that was never put to the test.

"I cannot speak for the others."

"You can."

"I can't. You know what they remember. You know what they felt. But what I have discovered about memory is this: it is selective. If we truly look, we *can* see the truth, but we revisit the memories that we choose to visit.

"You remember the fear. But you remember it in a slanted fashion. I was not afraid of you."

"Then *why*?"

"Because I wanted hope," Teela replied. "I wanted to believe it was possible to trust others of my kind. I wanted to choose a future that my father would never have chosen for me. It was a pathetic act of defiance." She looked around the table, met Terrano's gaze and nodded.

All of the cohort materialized. Annarion. Allaron. Torrisant, Fallessian, Karian. Last came the physically distant Eddorian.

"I was afraid," Serralyn admitted, although her expression was far too sunny to contain fear now. "I haven't been afraid of you for centuries. I admit I'm a bit afraid of *this*, but that's because I'm sane."

Sedarias turned toward her, and then, at last, toward Mandoran.

Kaylin realized they had all spoken out loud. All of them. "Teela came back for you," she said quietly. "She had everything she was supposed to want—everything you've said you wanted—but she came back."

"You've never tried to use our names against us," Serralyn continued, when Sedarias remained silent. "Until now."

Kaylin closed her eyes. Closed them, and then forced them open again. It was wrong. It was wrong on every level. But Sedarias wasn't trying to do that now. She offered no defense. She offered nothing.

No, Kaylin thought, they were still in this odd garden and not on the plane of stone and rock.

"It must be hard," Kaylin finally said. All of the cohort turned toward her. "There are days when I hate my job. Days when I want to strangle my coworkers or scream at Marcus. There are days when I want the midwives' guild to just leave me alone and let me sleep."

Sedarias raised a brow.

"I can keep all of that to myself. I don't have to *act* on any of it. What defines me isn't how I *feel* on those days. It's what I choose *to do*. Emotions aren't a choice. They're emotion. They're a response. Maybe I'm hungry. Maybe I'm exhausted. Maybe I'm angry at myself because I made a stupid mistake and other people are going to suffer for it.

"I have *privacy*. None of you do. You're more like the Tha'alani in that regard. But the Tha'alani were raised—from birth—to seek the Tha'alaan. To trust it, to find comfort from it, and to seek knowledge in it. Not to own it. There is no chance that they'll leave it. No chance that it will leave them."

"They don't have any choice," Sedarias said, but her voice was a whisper.

"Neither do any of you. There's no way to let go of a name. If there was, I'd've done it. I asked. If I can't kill the person in question, we're bound for life."

"Do you think they'd all be here—" they, not we "—if they had any choice? You've seen what I'm like. You know what I'm like. You know—she just told you—what I tried to do."

Kaylin exhaled again. It felt like all she did was exhale here. "Severn tried to take control of me."

The silence that fell in response to those words was almost the entire reason she had never, ever mentioned it to anyone but Helen—Helen, who wouldn't judge Severn by anything but Severn himself.

Teela's eyes were blue, but they hadn't descended into midnight. "Why?" The word was a demand, a command.

"He wanted to stop me from doing something he was certain would kill me."

"Was he right?"

"I don't know. I understand a bit more about myself and my marks and the way I move through the world now. It was instinctive—it was like grabbing my shoulder or arm to pull me back or keep me still."

"They aren't the same thing at all—as you well know."

"He couldn't reach my arm or shoulder—he wasn't there." She looked down a moment, remembering. When she lifted her chin she said, "He was angry at himself for weeks. He avoided me for weeks after. Because he'd thought to manipulate me. It wasn't me he was angry at. He didn't try to justify it.

"I knew why he'd tried. I think I'd have done the same thing, if our positions were reversed and he wasn't listening."

"I don't," Mandoran said.

"Yeah, me either." That was Terrano.

"I think she might have," Serralyn chimed in.

"Don't look at me." This was Eddorian. "I'll just say that I'm *really* appreciating Alsanis at the moment."

Sedarias looked to Teela.

"Kaylin is just idealistic enough, just determined enough, that if she were panicking she might. But I doubt it. You said Severn tried."

Kaylin nodded.

"Did he succeed?"

"No, he stopped. He stopped himself. But...we both knew."

"And you were not angry." Teela had chosen to speak in Barrani, unlike the rest of her cohort.

"No—why would I be? I understood why he did it. He was angrier—at himself—than I was."

Teela then turned to Sedarias, and as one, they all did. "You are afraid of many things. Becoming your monstrous brother was—no, *is*—one of them. He would not have hesitated. Had he been in your position, either you or Mandoran would now be enslaved. Mandoran would likely otherwise be dead. You fear many things.

"So did I. But—we were taught to fear, in the end. We were taught that there was only *one way* to be fearless. Power. And even that was defined very, very narrowly. My father killed my mother."

They knew.

"I will not become my father, but I am afraid to become my mother, as well. It is why I will never have either spouse or children."

Kaylin had never heard this before. "There's no way you could become either your father or your mother, now."

Teela lifted a hand, palm flat, in Kaylin's direction. "I think it is past time for you to leave."

"I vote against," Mandoran said.

Both Sedarias and Teela turned to glare at him.

"...but she could try harder to stay on topic."

Terrano snickered, and Kaylin understood that the storm that had been Sedarias had passed. It had quieted.

"It is not *quiet* enough, dear, but yes, you are right."

"It's never going to be enough, though," Kaylin told Helen. "I didn't really think about it, but: this is all inside all of them. What happens here—it can be unpleasant or terrifying—but..." She stopped, because in answering Helen she had drawn the attention of the cohort. She reddened.

"You accept things from each other that I would never accept from other people. If someone tried to kill me on a battlefield, I'd assume that person hated me. Or wanted me dead. I'd assume *one thing*, one motivation. But if *I* daydream about strangling Marcus, I accept it because everyone does that on his bad hair days. I mean, *everyone*. No one *says* it. No one has to say it.

"But—you *have to* accept it. Because you're on the inside of each other's thoughts all the time." She turned to Terrano. "It's why you weren't surprised, just exhausted."

He winced but nodded.

"Look," she said, to Sedarias, "I understand your fears. All of them. I've had them. I get it. But: they know you. You can't tell yourself *if they knew what I was really like, they'd hate me*, because they do know what you're really like. They've known it for centuries. For practically ever.

"They're not trying to escape you."

"Serralyn and Valliant—"

"Serralyn was *born* for the Academia. You can't not know that. Valliant isn't as obvious, but my guess is he wants what the Academia offers as well. You didn't rage at Eddorian when he chose to remain with Alsanis and his brother."

"Oh, she did," Eddorian said.

"Fine. You raged at Eddorian. But you didn't try to force him to come to Elantra."

"No. She didn't try to force Annarion and Mandoran to wait, either."

"I wanted information," Sedarias snapped. "They were coming to Elantra. They'd be in reach of the High Halls."

Allaron said, gently, "You accepted that as the silver lining. But you didn't want them to leave until we were all ready, either. Not really."

The wind began to move.

Terrano rolled his eyes, but his jaw tightened.

"I was right," Sedarias said, voice low. "I was *right*."

The wind increased in strength; the trees above their heads began to lose leaves. Without thought, Kaylin stepped forward and caught Sedarias by the arm, her own arms glowing a brilliant blue. "Cut it out. Cut it out right now.

"You were *wrong*. I mean, I wish you'd succeeded—I lost friends and compatriots to the Barrani Ancestors when they attacked the High Halls. Even Bellusdeo was badly injured. But you were wrong. They don't love you less because Annarion came for Nightshade. You *knew* he would because you know Annarion as well as he knows you. Mandoran only came to keep an eye on Annarion and to back him up if it was necessary.

"You don't want the Tower because the Tower protects the rest of the world; you want it because it's another place you think you can build safety in. You want it because all of you would live there, not here. And there'd be no Bellusdeo there, no me, no Helen—no outsiders, nothing to disturb the family you've built."

"It's not family."

"To me, in every way that matters, it is. But you don't need the Tower for that. I don't know what your argument with Mandoran was. I can guess but I don't know for certain."

"He tried to commit suicide by Dragon," Terrano then said.

"He did not. He tried to protect the Dragon from herself. It's something we all need from time to time—ask Teela about me. No, ask her when I'm not here. Someone like you *really* needs it. When you can't completely control the impulse or the anger, having people who love you who can remind you of the truth is a gift. It's a gift most of us don't have, or never had."

"It's only a gift if she listens," Terrano muttered.

Sedarias stood. "I have had almost enough of you."

His grin would have melted ice. He walked straight to where she was shaking, her eyes midnight blue. Ah. Blue. They were blue again. Before she could say anything else, he wrapped his arms around her. "I missed you," he said, voice soft but still audible. "I missed this. I missed all of it. But I came back because I was worried."

"That I would harm everyone else."

"That you'd do everything you possibly could to isolate yourself."

"I'm not—"

"You are. You think you're holding on—but you drive people away by holding on too tightly. We know it. And we know you'd die for us."

"I would not be so ineffectual as to die. Dying is for our enemies."

"We are never going to be your enemies."

Mandoran's shoulders relaxed, but he gritted his teeth as he gazed at the sky. "None of us are afraid you're going to abandon us for Mellarionne."

Sedarias's head whipped around to glare. "No one sane would abandon *anyone* for Mellarionne!"

"But...you want it. You know it's a risk, and you're willing to risk everything to take it. To prove something to dead people."

Kaylin exhaled. There went peace.

"Yes, dear," Helen said softly. "But that is the nature of the cohort. I think it is time you left. Why do you think Mandoran understood the true danger to Bellusdeo? He is an independent person who is nonetheless part of Sedarias. The cost to Bellusdeo would be the same as the price Sedarias, unleashed and enraged, would later pay.

"Come."

"That was well done," she said, as she led Kaylin to the door that had disappeared when she'd entered it. "I am sorry I could not speak; I did not have time to warn you not to take Severn with you."

Severn would have listened.

"Yes. You are not happy."

"I just—" Kaylin exhaled. "I remember when I was afraid of how the existence of, the freedom of, the cohort would affect *me*. I mean—would affect Teela. She's an important friend. One of my first friends here. I *understand* Sedarias's fear. And...I don't really like it when I look at it from the outside."

"No. But you don't feel like that now."

Kaylin snorted. "No. Now I'm just worried about what the cohort will do, period. I was afraid Teela would have less time to—to think about me." She shook her head. "Sedarias is afraid of the same thing. But I had my mother. I don't know what Sedarias's mother was like. I don't know if she survived, or if her father killed her—or, given her brothers and sisters, someone else in her family did.

"And I don't really *want* to know. But Mandoran likes Bellusdeo—and Bellusdeo has had a really hard life."

"It's not a competition."

"No, I know. But I think Mandoran's been important to Bellusdeo. I mean, she'd never *say* that; she'd probably die first. But..."

"Yes. But that is now for the cohort to resolve. Thank you."

"Why couldn't they have done that in the first place?"

Helen was silent for an uncomfortable beat. "I try not to interfere, dear. I try not to ask intrusive questions. I know much of your life and your day—and I do strongly agree with Lord Nightshade—Karriamis is extremely dangerous, and I would vastly prefer you avoided his Tower. But you must make your own decisions, and I accept that."

"We weren't talking about me," was the uncomfortable reply.

Helen continued as if Kaylin hadn't spoken. "However, I have lived with you—with your words, your thoughts, your dreams and your nightmares. Let me ask you just one question. Do you remember what you did on the day you discovered the people who were kidnapping and selling children?"

Kaylin blinked.

"You used the power of your marks. Do you remember what you did? No, do not answer. It is not necessary. You do. Do you think that Teela or Tain could have stopped you?"

"They didn't care."

"No. Do you believe they could have stopped you?"

Kaylin looked down at her feet.

"You have very little in common with Sedarias," Helen continued, her voice much softer. "But not nothing. This is the danger, always, of power; if you lose control—and we all lose control some of the time—the damage done is far, far harder to recover from. What you did for Sedarias, you believe I could do. I could not.

"To Sedarias, I am a building. She would hear the words, but she would not listen, would not absorb them."

"But she lived with Alsanis for centuries!"

Helen nodded. "Alsanis was, in some fashion, the strict and severe parent that she had never had before. You think that her parents were both strict and severe. They were not. Alsanis was parental; he was old. He interfered. He decided what was best for the children in his care.

"In her own fashion, and as she is capable of it, she cares deeply for Alsanis—but she wants him at a distance while she finds her own feet. I am…a building. I am not Alsanis; she knows that. She trusts me to keep the people I choose to offer shelter safe. But she cannot listen to me; she could not listen to Alsanis.

"She could only barely listen to you—but she could and did. You are part of her family, even if she's afraid that in remaining here she will lose that family.

"I think it is good that she stays here and makes peace with the fact that they are all conjoined and they are also all separate. They are not Sedarias. The fact that they are not, and that they are still and will always be part of the cohort, is something she must face and accept.

"But as you have noted, it is not easy. You were afraid that you would personally lose Teela. But you also understood that these long-ago friends were a source of grief and pain, and you wanted Teela to be happy. Both of these feelings were true; they were both yours. You chose. Sometimes it is hard to make the right choice—but life without such conflicts does not exist.

"Sedarias is very strong, but she is also—as you have seen—fragile. Fragile in ways that you no longer are. Yes, she has had much longer—but not in *this* world. I will not call it the real world; her time in Alsanis was real. But there, no strangers intruded, no responsibilities to others had to be borne; they couldn't be.

"They thought of Teela as lost. They focused on trying to reconnect with her. But even that was not thinking of other people; Teela was a part of them.

"Now, they have left the nest. They are interacting with other people. They are taking on other responsibilities, or exploring possibilities that did not exist for them for almost the entirety of their lives. They are looking outward, not inward, because they can.

"Your fear of losing Teela was small, compared to Sedarias's fear. The cohort are the first people Sedarias dared to openly care for. She is afraid that now that they have choice, the only thing she has to offer is power. The power of Mellarionne, if she can hold it. It's what she was raised to believe and to value. She is of course wrong. But she is not good at listening, at hearing."

"She has to know they're not lying—they're talking, all of them, through the bond of their True Names."

"What she knows, what she feels, these are not the same. She could listen to you because you are an outsider. But not so much of an outsider that you have a vested interest in placating her, in pleasing her."

"So...if she liked me more, she'd listen less?"

Helen chuckled, but her mouth, when it came to rest, was drawn down in the corners. "Yes. But if you really think about it, you'll probably understand it."

"Will it make me any happier?"

"Probably not. You've often wondered why Teela cares about you. And sometimes you tell yourself it's only because you have the marks of the Chosen. Not often," she added softly, "but sometimes. You do not think as compulsively as Sedarias is wont to do, and you don't dwell often on the fears. But if you did, you would be far more like her.

"But what you said is true: she would die for them. They are her family in any way you define family. They will stand with or beside her against any enemies. But not against each other, not that way. She did not take control of Mandoran. She did try."

"But Severn—"

"It was not quite the same. But it's the same impulse, writ large. You weren't horrified at what Severn attempted."

Kaylin had already said this, but nodded.

"He was. It is Sedarias's own guilt and self-loathing she must work through. But this is a start: she has stopped making any attempt to justify the actions to herself. Severn never made the attempt—but his action was instinctive, primal. Sedarias has a singular ability to make the instinctive and the primal work for her, rather than against her—but there are snarls and pitfalls.

"I believe they will be talking for some time. You wanted to ask me something, and we began that discussion before it was so perilously interrupted."

Kaylin was exhausted. And hungry. She could barely remember what she'd wanted to talk about; it seemed like she'd been flying above rocks for a week. But Helen led her out of the basement, and back up the stairs to the long hall which led, at its end, to an open-air patio. Severn was seated. And eating.

He looked up as the two approached, setting fork aside.

"Sedarias is fine, for now. I used to envy what she built— but another day like this anytime soon would probably kill me."

Helen nodded. "Now, what did you want to discuss?"

It was Severn who answered. "Karriamis."

"Ah. I know very little about Karriamis's history. I understand what he now is—inasmuch as it is possible to understand a person one has never met. He is the core and the heart of the Tower he became to stand against *Ravellon*."

Kaylin nodded. "He wouldn't tell us why he chose Candallar. He wouldn't discuss that at all—he implied that you wouldn't either, but...that you might if I asked persistently."

"*Pestered* is an unfortunate word," Helen replied.

"It's probably deserved. I know better than to interfere in an argument between angry Dragons—but I did it anyway."

"You are young. It might be hard to believe, but ten years from now, twenty, you will find it much easier to do what seems pragmatic. You react emotionally. I trust your reactions. But you do not always see all of the context for any given set of emotions that others experience.

"You are mortal. You know that I choose mortal tenants."

Kaylin nodded.

"Some small part of you believes it's because you will die of old age, and if I have somehow made the wrong choice, I won't have to suffer with it for long."

Did she? Maybe. Maybe she did believe that. But...she didn't. She didn't, not most of the time.

"Exactly. But you wonder, don't you?"

Kaylin nodded.

"What is your answer, right now?"

"You wanted me because what I wanted from a home, you wanted to give." It was a practiced answer; she had said it to herself many times.

"But?"

"I don't give you anything."

"This is not true, but I understand the concern. You feel it often: you have taken so much, you have been given so much, and you have given so little in return."

"It's true."

"You fail to understand what it is you can give; you think of giving as work, as something that takes effort and will. You think of it as transactional, but only in relation to yourself. You can tell me, clearly, what Teela has given you. You can tell me, just as clearly, what I have given you. But you feel on some level you have done nothing to deserve it. You believe that you belong with the Hawks in the Halls of Law—and you can point to the many things you've done because on some level, those are *worthy* work.

"I like your openness. Teela could not give it. Bellusdeo could not give it. Severn?"

He shook his head.

"No. You are not a child, Kaylin—but you are not yet fully adult. You retain some of the impulsiveness of youth, some of the joy—and the despair and the anger, because nothing is unalloyed. When you are tired, when you are trying your hardest, we feel that we can give something of value to you. Perhaps what you give us is intangible: you appreciate us.

"You love us."

"But..."

"Love means different things to different people, yes. But even Sedarias understands why you are my tenant, and why she could not be. What she needs is so complex I cannot give it to her. She is not jealous of this. She understood, and understands, why Annarion and Mandoran are fond of you. It is Bellusdeo's interaction with Mandoran she finds difficult."

"Because our association will pass in a few decades."

"Yes, dear. She can be patient. She knows how to wait. Bellusdeo, however, is a Dragon, and if Sedarias accepts this—and she does—it goes against the brief childhood she spent in the real world." Helen exhaled; breeze came. Dishes vanished.

"She is angry because Mandoran and Annarion, in her view, have thrown away the entirety of their life experience in order to befriend her. Even Terrano has grown to like her—but he is similar in many ways to Mandoran. She is afraid. It is a fear you understand. Do you think Karriamis would accept her?"

"I don't know."

"No?"

"He accepted Candallar."

"Yes."

"Would you?"

"No."

"Why?"

"Because I could not ever give Candallar the home he wanted. I would always be a resting place while he looked toward and yearned for his real home. But you are not, I think, wrong in that one regard. He had nothing when he arrived in Karriamis. Candallar was made outcaste—and you must be aware of what that means to Dragonkind. You cannot imagine what Candallar was, when he first arrived."

"Why can you?"

"I have had experience with many, many people during the entirety of my existence. You think you are Kaylin, and you are. And you will remain Kaylin—but experience, for better or worse, will change you. Things that you feared once, you no longer fear. You do not fear starvation; you do not fear the Ferals. You know what you've done in a desperate, terrified attempt to survive. You know the moment you decided that survival was not worth the cost you had paid.

"You are not, now, the child you were seven or eight years ago. You will not be the person you are now in a decade. Some parts of you will remain, and perhaps you will think you have not changed much—but I will know. I will know *this* Kaylin, and I will know the Kaylin you will become. And perhaps what you will become in the future will not be the person who wanted what I have to give."

"That's never going to happen."

Helen smiled. "I will not discuss all the details, but will say it has happened before. What I offered was not, in the end, what the person I sheltered grew into wanting. Ah, no, perhaps *needing* is a better word."

"They left you?"

Helen nodded. "With my blessing," she added. "Sometimes a person needs a nest, but they may not remain wingless; as they gain strength and confidence, they need to fly."

"But…but…what about you?"

"I cannot be a prison. Ah, no. I *can* be a prison, but a prison is not a home. It is not the same with a Tower."

"Why?"

"Because the Towers understood that they would be under

attack—and they could not anticipate all of the forms of attack; as Bellusdeo said, Shadow is subtle and subversive. The captains *can* command the Towers."

"Not according to Karriamis."

Helen said nothing.

"You think he *can* be commanded."

"I do. And perhaps that is the other reason he chose Candallar. Candallar, Barrani and alone, would instinctively avoid offering commands to a Dragon."

"Bellusdeo won't have that problem."

"No? Perhaps not. But Karriamis chose to test her, to destabilize her, in order to claim the opposite. She is uncertain," Helen added, a rare intrusion into Bellusdeo's privacy. "The reason she is driven to consider the Tower is her personal war—and its loss. As if captaining a Tower will allow her to redeem herself from her failure."

"That wasn't her failure!"

Helen smiled gently. "Karriamis, I'm certain, does not agree. But failure defines and shapes us—and not solely because we did fail. How we deal with failure, how we deal with what it means about ourselves and our own capabilities, says more about us than almost anything else could. He does not know who Bellusdeo is, in the wake of catastrophic failure. But dear, neither does she.

"And while they may have similar goals in regard to Shadow, he is not meant to be a tool of vengeance. If that is all she has to offer, I do not believe she can take the Tower."

18

It took two days for the household to recover. Emmerian and Bellusdeo had finished their discussion by the time Sedarias and the cohort could even begin theirs. Bellusdeo didn't closet herself in her room, but she was orange-eyed and almost silent when she joined Kaylin in the dining room for meals. Mandoran was likewise mostly silent; he did dredge a smile out of Bellusdeo.

Although Helen said she wasn't worried about the cohort now, she was tense; Kaylin could tell because when tense, Helen forgot little details in her appearance—especially her eyes. They had been obsidian for two days.

Bellusdeo came to breakfast on the third day. She wore a dress, not the familiar Dragon armor; her hair was pulled back and up, but it was the only concession she made to possibly martial action. Mandoran was at the table when she entered the room, as was Kaylin. Terrano and Annarion had joined them. The rest of the cohort—or those who were present—did not.

"How is she?" Bellusdeo asked Mandoran.

Mandoran grimaced. "She'd be a lot happier if I left off accompanying you."

"Then stay."

"*I'd* be a lot happier if I believed it wasn't necessary."

To Kaylin's surprise, Bellusdeo didn't argue. She seemed subdued. Subdued but not beaten. "I will not argue. I owe you a debt."

Mandoran winced. "I would vastly prefer no talk of debt between us."

"Believe that I would prefer it as well. But it is simple fact. I would leave Kaylin at home, but that would cause arguments with the Emperor, and I am not up to those arguments at present."

"And Lord Emmerian?"

"He will meet us in the fief of Tiamaris; I believe he had questions to ask of Tara, and she agreed to answer what she could."

"Tara's worried about you?"

"He was kind enough not to mention it, but—you know Tara. What do you think?"

Tara was definitely worried. But that was fair. Kaylin had spent two days worrying while trying to look cheerful.

"You don't have to go back," Terrano told the gold Dragon.

"I don't want to go back," Bellusdeo replied. "But I could not live with myself if I did not choose to face Karriamis again. I will not descend into cowardice."

"Do you still want the Tower?"

"That is the question, isn't it? If you had asked me four days ago, I would have said yes. Now?" She exhaled a bit of smoke. "Now I am uncertain. I admit that although I've known Tara since my arrival, it did not occur to me that I would have to compromise with another individual—and at that, a Dragon. I assumed that the Tower would conform to the conflict that has defined both of our lives—mine and Karriamis's. That we would be compatriots.

"I am uncertain of anything now. And I am uncertain that I could prevent Karriamis from taking risks I would never, ever take. We could fight—if he confronted me in combat, I think I would almost enjoy that—but I could not *win* that fight in the only sense that matters. He is the Tower. Agree with him or no, he gave the remainder of his eternity to become sentinel against *Ravellon*.

"What we want, the war that we each perceive, is not the same. What I must decide is whether or not there is enough overlap that we might work together."

She did not add that Karriamis had to decide whether or not he wanted her to be the Tower's captain. Kaylin thought he couldn't do better—but no encounter with Candallar had been pleasant or helpful, and in the end, the fieflord had tried to kill Robin, a crime from which he couldn't recover in Kaylin's view.

It had killed him.

The Arkon—the former Arkon—had hoped to spare him for Karriamis's sake. Candallar had not allowed him that grace. Kaylin felt no grief at his passing, but wondered if Karriamis did. She was almost certain, if the circumstances had caused Kaylin to be like Candallar, Helen would still grieve.

"I would," Helen said softly. "And perhaps that is true for Karriamis, as well. Tara grieved the slow withdrawal of her previous captain."

"She's never going to have to deal with that again. To Tiamaris, Tara *is* his hoard."

"Yes. I believe she will be happier than she has been in her long existence as the heart of a Tower. I am less certain about Karriamis, but Dragons are not famous for their ability to be transformed by joy. It is time," she added, voice gentling.

Bellusdeo stood. "Past time. His choice is only one half of what is necessary. Today I wish to know if he is worthy of *me*."

Mandoran smiled.

★ ★ ★

Emmerian was waiting, as promised, in the fief of Tiamaris. He was not alone; Tiamaris was also waiting, his expression folded into familiar impatience.

"Don't look at me like that," Kaylin told him. "I was ready to leave on time. I wasn't even informed there was an 'on time.'" Hope was draped across her shoulder; he lifted his head and squawked at Tiamaris.

Tiamaris grimaced. "I have been *asked* to make sure that your travel through my fief is pleasant and without incident," he told them, still looking at Kaylin. "And I will check the border while I am there. Tara is worried."

"Tara's fief was without a fieflord for a long time. It's been weeks and Karriamis is not Tara. I get the sense that he's enjoying the peace and quiet. He really doesn't seem to be in much of a hurry."

"That is your impression, yes. Tara, however, is concerned." And Tara's concerns took precedence over anyone else's. Always. Kaylin suspected they were more important than Imperial concern—but was also uneasily certain that Imperial concern did exist.

Bellusdeo immediately turned toward the fief of Candallar and began to walk. Tiamaris joined her, and Emmerian pulled up the other flank. Kaylin and Severn took the rear; Mandoran and Terrano were neatly bracketed between the two groups.

Bellusdeo therefore raised her voice so that it carried to the back ranks. "Why is Tara concerned? Kaylin's observation is materially true."

"While she concurs with Karriamis—that the freeing of Spike was in some ways essential to the future of the High Halls—she considers the outcome almost random; it is not a risk that she would take unless pressured to do so."

"By you?"

"By me."

The gold dragon snorted. "Which means never."

"It is not a risk that you would take, either."

"No. But I have been reminded that risks were taken that I would not have countenanced either, and my people—and I—directly benefited from them. I would not have allowed it. The cost of failure was too high. I am here because I was not asked to make that decision. I am grateful for the outcome. I believe the High Halls, while unsettled, is grateful, in the end, for Spike.

"And Lannagaros is beyond grateful for the existence of, the emergence of, the Academia." She exhaled a steady stream of smoke. "I feel old," she said. "And young. And callow with youth. It is unpleasant."

Mandoran missed a step. Terrano caught him. Neither of the two Barrani spoke a word out loud—but that made sense. They were walking behind three Dragons, and they considered only one of them a friend.

That is not why he stumbled, Hope squawked.

"Why, then?"

She is openly calling attention to her failings, and in a louder than usual voice. It is…not like her.

"So…worried?"

I am uncertain. I have far more knowledge about many, many things than you will likely ever possess. He spoke without pride. *But what you did for Sedarias, I could not do. Nor could Helen.*

"She could have."

No, Kaylin, she could not. What bridged the gap between you and Sedarias was your personal experience and your willingness to expose it. The living, as Helen knows, change. Mortals change very quickly; immortals less so. But as you have seen with Tara, change can and does happen.

"Are you worried?" She spoke as quietly as she possibly

could, but suffered no hopeful illusion; she was certain Bellusdeo could hear her.

No. Not yet. But we have not yet arrived.

The Tower of Candallar no longer looked like a standing column of rock. It had lost the impressive majesty of height, although it was taller than any of the surrounding buildings. It hadn't lost the look of an entirely natural outcropping of rock, but where before it had been a craggy, rising column, it now resembled a cave.

Kaylin tried not to complain; it was clear that the cave entrance—girded with flickering torches—was the only possible entrance, and it waited like an invitation. Then again, so did plants that trapped and devoured insects.

Bellusdeo approached the cave entrance and then turned back toward Kaylin. "It is, as you suspect, a portal."

Kaylin closed her eyes and thought of the Emperor. "I'm not staying behind."

Bellusdeo did not insist, and Kaylin didn't point out that she was by the gold Dragon's side at Imperial command. They both knew it, and Bellusdeo didn't need to be annoyed or irritated by the Emperor right at this moment. "If you will not be sensible, come. Take my arm."

This was not how it was supposed to go. But sentient buildings didn't particularly care about hierarchical manners and customs. Kaylin, mindful of the fact that she could traverse Nightshade's portal without ill affects if he personally escorted her—by arm—into his castle, had some hope that this entrance wouldn't be as unpleasant as portal entrances generally were.

Sadly, Karriamis was not Castle Nightshade. She was grateful for the anchor of Bellusdeo's arm because she had to close her eyes to move, and the Dragon's grip was strong enough that she could allow herself to be dragged in the right direction. Portals weren't always particular about their connections from one place to the next.

It took Kaylin ten minutes to recover enough to stand on her own two feet, but Severn quietly replaced Bellusdeo, offering Kaylin the brace of an arm at her back and beneath her own arms until she could breathe without almost throwing up.

Sorry.

Don't apologize.

Can I apologize if I throw up on your shoes?

He appeared to think about this. *Maybe.*

She laughed. She felt the strength of his arm, envied his ability to ignore the disorienting shift of a portal's passage, and found her own feet again.

Karriamis was waiting in person when Kaylin emerged from her unpleasant fog. He stood in front of a large arch that had no doors. Emmerian stood by Bellusdeo's side, but one step behind, as if he intended to leave no doubt who was in command here. Mandoran, however, stayed beside Kaylin, his hands behind his back, his expression neutral. His eyes were a very dark blue.

Bellusdeo's were orange with flecks of red; Emmerian's were orange, with flecks of gold.

Karriamis's were black; there were no white bits. He surprised them, or at least surprised Kaylin; he bowed to them all. "My apologies if the color of my eyes discomfits you, Corporal. It is not what you are accustomed to unless there are difficulties at home."

She couldn't hear Nightshade, but could imagine what he'd say. She didn't think he would ever consent to enter Karriamis, even if he trusted its captain.

"No, he would not. But I would not extend that invitation. He is captain of perhaps the most difficult person it has been my displeasure to meet; I cannot imagine being confined in one place has done anything to improve Durandel's extremely regrettable disposition. If Lord Nightshade is naturally suspicious, it is no wonder; I consider it a minor miracle that he has held the Tower for so long."

"Durandel saved his life," Kaylin said quietly.

"I am astonished." If the Dragon Avatar didn't look astonished, he did look surprised. "I would not have thought he could show even that much care."

"I believe they have a partnership, and if Durandel is as difficult as you believe, he might not wish to train another suitable candidate."

"Most would not survive the training. It says much about Lord Nightshade that he did." None of it, by his expression, good.

"I don't think many people would necessarily survive yours either," Kaylin said.

"That was not training," Karriamis replied, his voice more pleasant than his expression. "It was a simple test. Ah, no, it was a complicated test. Many tests among your kind are pass or fail. This was not entirely that. You experienced something similar when you first entered the Tower of Tiamaris."

"I didn't *want* to be fieflord."

"No. And I did not test you. Such a test would be irrelevant, you are so completely open. But Maria was not Durandel. I liked her but I did not think her suitable for the position she occupied. She was fragile, and isolation increased her fragility. You were necessary," he added, "even if the Tower was not to be yours. And I believe she will be happier now than she has been since her ascension." His smile was gentle. It seemed genuine.

"It is. If I would not have chosen her, I found her warm and almost charming; I wanted happiness or safety for her. I see I have surprised you."

He certainly had.

"Anyone who wanted happiness for a person would never wish the fate and responsibility of a Tower upon them. It was almost our undoing."

"That wasn't her fault. It was the fault of the captain who abandoned her."

"Indeed. And I would not suffer the same fate, but perhaps, with my experience, I have more of a sense of how to avoid it." He turned to Bellusdeo, or perhaps to Emmerian.

"You have been thinking. I expected you to return the day after your departure. I am pleased you did not."

Bellusdeo didn't look pleased.

"Come, if you will. I have shown you very little in the way of hospitality. Let me now be host."

Kaylin had an admittedly academic knowledge of hospitality. Helen understood the general rules far better, and she was chagrined to admit that she relied on Helen to prevent the career-limiting gaffes that would otherwise have been guaranteed.

But even enduring Diarmat's harsh lessons did not prepare her for Karriamis's version of hospitality. He led them, not to a parlor of the kind Helen created for important guests, but on what appeared to be a tour of the interior of the cave.

The interior was not a cave. Not to start. It looked very much like the interior of a Barrani hall—but not the halls of stone that informed most of the High Halls. If the exterior of the Tower had been an entrance, the cave was a tunnel; when one emerged, one emerged into carefully cultivated forest. The trees made Kaylin think of the West March.

"I much preferred that decor," Karriamis said. "But there is stone here—good stone, and warm. It is not appropriate for guests at this time."

Probably meaning mortal guests, if Kaylin had to guess.

"Indeed. And two of my current guests are mortal, but I assume you are aware of this."

"We are," Bellusdeo said, glancing briefly and pointedly in Kaylin's direction. "But I admit I have seldom seen interiors with this style of decoration."

"You have not visited the rooms the cohort occupy," he replied.

Mandoran winced; Kaylin sympathized. He was about as good at hiding thought as she was. But he had Sedarias to drive home the necessity; Nightshade, today, was absent, no doubt by Karriamis's choice.

"We are said to be creatures of air and fire, and the latter is not conducive to preserve trees such as this. It is true," he added, "but it is not the whole of the truth. I was born in stone and warmth and darkness, but it was only when I could take wing as an adult that I encountered trees such as this. They were a marvel to me, something that existed in attenuated songs, in old stories meant only for the young.

"It was the start of my interest in studying the world and the mysteries it contained, and when left to my own devices, I prefer it. It is not like Castle Nightshade."

It certainly wasn't.

"I am not Arkon. I was once considered for that position, but I would have had to surrender too much of my academic work, and I was reluctant. I envy your Lannagaros; he accepted the weight of responsibility himself. I was younger than he when I was considered."

"Would you do it now?" Kaylin asked.

"Now? In a theoretical universe in which the heart of the Tower could be changed? I do not know. I have not asked myself that question; it is irrelevant, a daydream. There is no practical use for any answer I might offer."

"That's a no," Mandoran whispered.

Karriamis raised a brow in the Barrani's direction. He chose to otherwise ignore the comment.

"You will find rooms to the left and the right, but there are no doors to enclose them. For now, I will take you to one of the most important rooms within the Tower. It is a room that has never lost cohesion, and it has never been replaced; nor will it be in future. It is the heart, not of the Tower, but of the Tower's heart."

Kaylin was surprised to see a library. She shouldn't have been. It was as large as the Imperial library on first sight, but not as large as the library whose only entrance or exit existed on the grounds of the Academia.

She wasn't surprised to find books she could read, but they were perhaps a third of the collection. The rest, language made opaque. They might have been about cutting fingernails.

Karriamis coughed. His orange-eyed glare reminded Kaylin very much of the Arkon. She touched *nothing* but wondered why these two Dragons were so powerfully attached to words, even dead words—languages that no living person spoke in daily life.

"You cannot know that," the Avatar said. "There are worlds that are hidden, even from the wise, and it is possible that that language, or variants and descendants of it, survive. Once, we might have discovered it. But the ways are—with some exceptions—closed."

"Do you want them to be opened again?" It wasn't the question Kaylin had intended to ask.

Karriamis turned to her, orange-eyed. "You did not see *Ravellon* in my youth. You do not know what was lost when it fell. Could I have that city again absent the danger? Yes. Yes, I would like it, even if it is no longer something I could visit. We all have desires that are considered impossible. An end to war is one of them."

Emmerian lifted his head. "And what would you do were there an end to this war?"

"An unkind question," Karriamis replied, although his eyes didn't darken.

"It was not meant to be unkind," Emmerian replied, bowing.

"No. It was not, which is why you are still here." Before Kaylin could speak, he added, "It is my home, and my rules apply only to visitors."

"My home would never, ever do this."

"Your home has done worse to intruders; you do not consider intruders guests. When I have no captain, you are all intruders. Today," he added, "is different. Today, I have invited you in; you are guests. There will be no tests, no testing."

"We were intruders when we first visited Helen, by your definition."

"Yes. And in this, Helen and I have something in common. But if we are searching for a tenant or a captain, their role of necessity will be different. Helen can exist without a tenant."

"Towers can exist without a captain."

"You witnessed, in person, what almost happened to the Tower of Tiamaris. That did not, and would not, happen to Helen."

"And to you?"

Karriamis said nothing for a long beat. He turned toward the highest of the shelves. "I am arrogant enough to believe that I would not be subject to that fate. But young Emmerian's question is a relevant question.

"Lack of war will not immediately dissolve the boundaries of the responsibility I voluntarily accepted. There is no freedom in that, for me. Perhaps the Ancients will return to release us."

It sounded like death.

"That is my supposition, yes. And perhaps we, like Helen

and other abandoned, sentient buildings, will dwindle in significance and import. I am not Helen. Had Candallar not lost himself, he and I would have continued into the eternity that is our birthright.

"If Bellusdeo were to become the captain of this Tower, the same could be said." He turned, then. "I would, however, have you answer Emmerian's question. In the absence of war, what do you plan to do?"

Bellusdeo did not answer.

"We cannot eradicate war. In some corner of the land, war will be fought, by different people, for different reasons. If our war with Shadow ends, do you intend to leave this place in search of a war you can fight? Will you continue until you can find a war that can finally kill you?"

Emmerian stiffened, but remained silent. Kaylin couldn't see the color of his eyes, because he closed them. His hands by his sides were completely still. Unnaturally still.

Bellusdeo smiled. With teeth in. "I may appear impulsive in your eyes; I cannot deny that I have earned that. But I have no desire to throw my life away on some distant battle that will be swallowed by history and leave no trace."

"As your war was?"

"No. I remember. My people remember. My people's children will remember."

"They are mortal."

She said nothing. It was true.

Karriamis nodded, as if in approval. "I would have you answer my question."

"I cannot conceive of an end to this war. What I do when there is peace has not been my driving concern, it seems so impractical—a daydream, surely. The dream of—"

"A tired parent, perhaps, who desires their child to know peace and happiness for the brief duration of their life."

She said nothing.

"Consider the question, then. Consider the answer. You are living, you are breathing, and you dream. You have daydreams. None involve peace in the context of war. Come to me, return to me, when you have an answer. I will accept any answer you wish to offer.

"I will accept any lie you wish to offer. I will not believe it, of course; I am far too old for that. But I will accept it. I had hoped that we might dine, but I do not believe you will offer what I require today. Therefore retreat—in honor—and return."

He gestured, and the cave's mouth reasserted itself, a thing of rock and darkness, punctuated by torchlight.

"Honestly, Lannagaros, I cannot remember why I ever thought this was a good idea."

"You will regret it far more if you continue to damage my desk," the chancellor replied, although his eyes remained predominantly gold. Kaylin suspected the orange flecks denoted worry or concern for the Dragon who sat in the chair so close to his desk's edge she could damage it simply by holding on.

"I don't understand why you chose such a fragile desk," Bellusdeo snapped back. She sounded almost petulant.

The chancellor rose and came around the desk to stand beside Bellusdeo. After a moment, he reached for the hand that was gripping the desk's edge. "If you cannot remember why, will you change your mind?"

"You never wanted me to approach that Tower."

"Candallar was its lord."

"His."

The chancellor shrugged off the correction. He really didn't like Karriamis.

"He is annoyed, greatly annoyed, by Karriamis at the moment," Killian helpfully said. He coalesced—slowly—in the air beside Kaylin; she had taken up a guard position near the wall in a vain attempt to give Bellusdeo some privacy. Bellusdeo didn't care.

Emmerian, however, had wisely chosen to vacate the chancellor's office; Mandoran followed immediately on his heels. Bellusdeo was not in need of protection here, in the heart of the former Arkon's territory; of all of the living Dragons, it was Lannagaros who understood Bellusdeo best, and who held her in the greatest affection.

"You're not?" Kaylin whispered.

"It is a matter for Karriamis and Bellusdeo. I owe Karriamis a great debt, and when this moment has passed, Lannagaros will remember that he, too, owes Karriamis a great debt."

"I don't think he's forgotten," Kaylin replied. "But…gratitude isn't the same as love." She flushed at her use of the word.

Killian didn't appear to understand her embarrassment, or at least not to feel it. "I do not. Is it the wrong word? Did you wish for a different one?"

"It makes me sound naive. Like a child."

"Because only children love?" Right. Building. Kaylin didn't understand the odd alchemy that transformed person into building—but it seemed to leach experience from them, or understanding; Tara had once been *human* or at least mortal, but mortal subtleties caused her the same confusion they seemed to be causing Killian.

"No, of course not."

"I fail to understand why you feel the word inappropriate. Lannagaros loves Bellusdeo and the ghosts of her many sisters. She was a gift to him; when you brought her back to Elantra, he felt a hope and an affection from his long-buried youth. She was proof that the home the Barrani destroyed in the wars still survived in some fashion.

"It would grieve him to lose her now; it grieves him almost as much to see her in such pain."

To Kaylin, Bellusdeo looked annoyed. Clearly she couldn't see what the chancellor—or Killian—could.

"No, but that is for the best. I do not think it is something she wishes to share. She is strong, but she is fragile, and fragility is weakness. She cannot afford to become someone so easily broken."

The chancellor ignored Killian's words, if he even heard them at all. He spoke to Bellusdeo, and only Bellusdeo. "What will you do? You cannot reduce the Tower to rubble, as you well know. Even could you, I very much doubt you would make the attempt; you understand why the Towers are essential."

"I would not attempt to destroy someone for asking a question I could not answer. If I had simply chosen not to answer, I would not be here. I *could not* answer."

"No," the chancellor said softly, laying a hand on the back of her head with infinite gentleness. "And he knew it. It is not a question that anyone has asked of you since your return. We know what you lost."

"He will not allow me to enter if I have no answer."

"No."

"And if I have an answer and he doesn't like it, he will…"

"He will choose a different captain. That will not change your import to me, or to us; that will not change or invalidate your life." Very gently, he said, "It seems to me that he is telling you, in however unkind a fashion, that he cannot fill the void of purpose in your life. He cannot be your Tara."

"I do not want Tara. It would be suffocating."

Kaylin said nothing. The chancellor said nothing.

"He has told me what he cannot be," Bellusdeo continued, when it was clear interruption wouldn't save or at least distract her. "He has not told me what he *can* be."

"No. But Bellusdeo, neither have you. You are not mortal; what he builds with you will last for some time, and even its dissolution—should it happen—will be a long, long unwinding. He is asking you, very indirectly, that question as well. Decide what you need; it is clear that he believes he now knows what he does."

"You're growling."

"I admit a certain displeasure, yes."

"With me?"

"With Karriamis, as you are well aware. And you are in a delicate state if you can ask that."

She was silent. "War shaped my life."

"Loss has shaped it far more strongly. War shaped my life. What I wanted, I could not have. I was considered a competent soldier." At Kaylin's cough, he emitted a thin stream of flame—in the direction of Kaylin's feet. "I accepted the responsibility I was given. I accepted the responsibility of Arkon in the wake of the cessation of hostilities between the Barrani and our kind. It was not what I had dreamed of. It was not what I wanted.

"This," he said, "unlooked for, was everything I once dreamed of having, but there is a weight to it, a responsibility to it, as well. Perhaps I needed all of the early responsibility to be able to bear the one I would have chosen without thought in my distant youth.

"Were I to visit your Karriamis—and I will not until I am less angry—I would have an answer almost immediately. If my life was shaped by war, and by the responsibilities that followed because those more suitable to be Arkon had perished in the wars, it was never the whole of what I wanted for myself.

"If you define your life by the things you do not want, you cannot answer the question. I thought the Academia lost," he added, his voice softening. "And in time, a miracle such as this might be offered you—but you will not see or understand it clearly, and perhaps you will fail to grasp it with both hands.

"Think, Bellusdeo. Think of what you dreamed of, think of what your sisters dreamed of, when your life was confined in the Aerie. And if your answer is vengeance, so be it—but after vengeance, what will you seek? What will you do? If you desire the Tower, there must be an answer."

19

The dining table was empty when Kaylin went downstairs for dinner. She had changed out of work clothing automatically; Helen pointed out that she had somehow miscounted buttons.

Hope had been silent for the remainder of the day, but he sat on her shoulder, his snout against her cheek.

"I don't know if I agree with the Arkon."

"The chancellor, dear."

"Yes, him."

"Why?"

"Where's everyone else?"

"The cohort is somewhat exhausted, and Sedarias does not feel like eating in company."

Meaning the company of outsiders, Kaylin thought glumly. She didn't expect Bellusdeo to come down for dinner either. Emmerian had escorted them to the edge of the property, but had not passed through the gates that marked the actual boundary of Helen.

He had been silent—but orange-eyed—throughout the walk home. Since Bellusdeo was likewise silent, it had been an almost funereal walk, because Mandoran didn't poke or tease, either.

Helen's Avatar joined Kaylin at the table itself. "Yes, it's difficult," she said quietly. "But it is not a question you can answer for her."

"It's not a question I can answer for anyone," Kaylin replied. "When I was younger, I used to think that everyone should want to be a Hawk. Everyone would find what they needed or what they were looking for there."

Helen nodded.

"Because I did, and I deserved nothing. If I could find a life—a life I could be proud of—anyone could do it."

"That is not true."

Kaylin nodded. "I know. I know that now; I'm not a kid anymore." At Helen's very maternal smile, Kaylin grimaced. "I'm not as much of a kid. But sometimes I think I'll never really grow up. The chancellor was right, I think. But—I wouldn't have known how to answer, either."

"You would."

"I wouldn't. I'm a Hawk. I'm *proud* of being a Hawk. If I lost the Hawks somehow, I have no idea what I'd want to do."

"But that's not what you're thinking about."

"I'm thinking about an answer for Bellusdeo—and I know it's not going to do her any good. I just—she could do or be anything if she wanted to."

"She is not unlike you once were," was Helen's soft reply. "Karriamis was unkind but correct: she does not feel she deserves any sort of life because she failed her people. It's guilt that drives her; the rage is a product of that guilt. If she destroys *Ravellon*, it might appease guilt. It might appease the dead."

"The dead don't care."

"No, I don't believe they do. It is a metaphor. But unexamined metaphors are dangerous narratives. It is easy for either of us—for all of us—to believe that it was not her fault. What we think does not matter; it is what she feels that does. This is hers to untangle."

"You don't think she can."

"I am uncertain. I am very fond of her, but she is a cry of muted pain. Constant pain. The difference is that you have seen it. Karriamis heard it immediately—but Kaylin, so did I. What I wanted for Bellusdeo was a bit of peace.

"But she is my guest, not my tenant. I understand the chancellor's anger, but I do not agree; he wishes to spare her pain. He wishes to keep her from the Tower. I believe—although I was not there and did not hear him—that he is considering an inadvisable visit to that Tower. But he is not the only one."

Kaylin rose from the table. "Bellusdeo's leaving?"

"Ah, no. It was not to Bellusdeo I referred. She is drowning in broken dreams and broken hopes, and she attempts now to examine them for something that might resonate enough she can build an answer from them. She will not leave until she has something to offer."

"Then who? The cohort?"

"No. I believe Bellusdeo's experiences have…impacted Sedarias, because I do not believe Sedarias could answer the question Karriamis insisted must be answered."

"Helen…"

"Emmerian, dear. I am not entirely certain—but he is angry and he did not wish me to be aware of his intent; it is why he did not walk Bellusdeo to my door. He knows I would hear."

"Emmerian's going to Karriamis."

"I believe so. Sit, dear. You are not running out after him; he is a Dragon, and you are a hungry, tired Hawk."

"I'm also the Chosen." Kaylin set her napkin aside.

"Do not make me tell Bellusdeo."

"You wouldn't."

"I think you need sleep. She will, of course, worry—and

she will embrace worry because it's far easier than what she is now facing. I do not believe Karriamis will hurt Lord Emmerian; Karriamis is in no danger, and lethal force is generally reserved for actual danger."

"She'll be mad."

"She will possibly be angry, yes—but she has been angry for so long I'm not sure you would notice the difference."

"She's not always angry."

"It is always part of her; it is the other side of guilt. Eat, and sleep."

"You really should listen to Helen," Mandoran said as he entered the dining room. "Sorry I'm late." He glanced at Helen, who nodded.

"Were you guys fighting again?"

"No. Her anger burns out. It's just surviving until it does that's an issue. She would never have pulled you in deliberately."

"She didn't, dear," Helen said quietly. "I do not blame her or hold any of you responsible for Kaylin's involvement."

Mandoran exhaled. "Even at her worst, she understands that you're not like us. She doesn't really want to kill us, either. Mostly."

"Mostly?"

"Well, I think there are three occasions in which she would have cheerfully strangled Terrano—but we've all felt like that. But you know, I couldn't answer Karriamis's question, either."

"You don't care about the war."

"Not really." He grinned. "But I have no real plans, no real goals. I'd like to survive, and I'd like to be with people who care about me, and who I care about, without any of them trying to kill me in a black rage. I just… I don't have any big goals, you know?"

"You don't care."

"Not really, no. Sedarias's goals are big enough for a hundred people. I'm willing to help her with hers. Most of the time. You're worried about Emmerian."

"Do you eavesdrop on *everything*?"

"Only if it seems interesting."

"Dear," Helen said, in her disapproving voice.

Mandoran grinned. "You have to admit it's not boring."

"I have developed a taste for peace," Helen replied.

"Given how little of it you've had recently, I guess peace isn't boring either." He looked at the plate Helen placed in front of him. "But the question Karriamis asked has almost all of us introspecting. Serralyn could answer it. Valliant. They're living their answers, now. Neither of them want the Tower, though. What they want, they've been offered."

"Allaron?"

"He's a bit like me, but actually, he wants his family line."

"And you don't?"

"They abandoned me. I don't feel much guilt at abandoning them, and to be frank, I hated them. I hated growing up while having to watch my back. I hated that my friends had to do the same—because some of them were bad at it, and they died. This was before I was sent to the West March.

"I meant what I said. I'm not ambitious—but I'm okay with that. I'm okay with making the family I chose, the family who *chose me*, my life."

"Bellusdeo's not part of that, though."

Mandoran winced. "Don't ask."

"Ask what?"

"Never mind—I was talking out loud to someone who's not in the room. I like who I like. I like the Dragon. She risked her life to get half of us to safety when Sedarias's sister came to Alsanis. I feel like we owe her. Sedarias does, too."

"But she doesn't want to trade your life for hers."

"She didn't think Bellusdeo's *life* was in danger. If I hated my family, none of them actively tried to murder me. I hated the rules. I hated the coldness of that life. I don't want it back. Sedarias's family was…special. But you know that. As long as Bellusdeo wasn't in danger, what I was doing was beyond stupid."

"She's not wrong."

He smiled.

"But I'm grateful."

"Everyone has something that's important to them. In the Dragon's case it's not something she can hold on to the same way Sedarias can hold on to us. Sedarias doesn't feel guilt. She would—if all of us died and she couldn't prevent it, she absolutely would. Which in turn gives her different nightmares— it's a good damn thing we don't *need* sleep."

She was already overprotective enough, Kaylin thought.

"Yes, dear. It is very difficult to protect what you love when what you love is sentient and separate. I, for instance, can only guarantee your safety when you are here. Were I to prioritize your safety above all else, I would have to forbid you to leave."

Kaylin stared at her house.

"That would be the best chance of keeping you safe. Of protecting what is important *to me*. But confining you would not be protecting what is important to you. You have responsibilities that define you, just as I have. Love is always a compromise between fear and the desire that you be true to yourself."

"Sedarias is coming to understand that. Were it not for the cohort, she would not make the effort—her upbringing has formed so much of her automatic, visceral reactions."

"And she's not a thinker?"

"Ah, but she is. She is ferocious with thought—but that thought has always been turned outward. She is watching for her enemies, for assassins, for obstacles on her path to finally claim what should have been hers. She never stops thinking."

"You can say that again."

Kaylin rose.

"You are not going to the Halls of Law today; Bellusdeo is here."

"No; we're both still seconded to Bellusdeo. But—Severn is almost here."

"Has he eaten?"

"I think so."

Kaylin met Severn as he was walking up the path.

"Emmerian is not our job," he told her.

"I know. I know it. But—Bellusdeo is here, and Helen can keep her safe."

"And when she leaves—without us—we're in dereliction of duty. Helen has no way of letting us know if we're not on Helen's property."

"No, but—Mandoran can."

"Mandoran can what?" It was, of course, Mandoran.

"You can come with us, and the cohort can let us know when Bellusdeo leaves."

"And if you're halfway across the fiefs, how are you going to get back here in time to meet her?"

"We won't be halfway across the fiefs—we'll be in Candallar. It's not like we're going to be exploring anywhere else. You know exactly where we're going."

"Severn's right. Emmerian isn't your duty or responsibility. He's way, way more self-controlled than you have any hope of being, and he's also—in case it escaped your attention—a Dragon."

"Fine. You don't have to come."

"I'll tell Bellusdeo."

"You wouldn't dare."

"Why not?"

"Because you'll be stuck in front of angry Bellusdeo."

"Yes, but she won't stick around."

"I don't want her to be angry at Emmerian."

"Emmerian, the Dragon, who has the best chance of surviving the full force of Dragon rage. Got it. You're making as much sense as you usually do. Do you think Karriamis will hurt him?"

"I don't know. I would have bet against it—but..."

"Emmerian lost his temper."

She nodded. "Helen contained it. I'm not sure Bellusdeo was happy about it, but, well—she was angry in her own way, so she might not have noticed it. He was angry at Karriamis. Even I noticed it. Karriamis almost certainly did. And if Emmerian *does* lose his temper, Karriamis *can* hurt—or kill—him."

"Helen?" Mandoran said, although the Avatar was not standing on the lawn.

"Karriamis can hurt or kill him," Helen said.

Mandoran lifted his face to the sky as if pleading for some absent god to grant him patience. "You know, he always struck me as sane, rational and self-controlled. Like Severn. Fine. *Fine.*"

"Sedarias is okay with you coming?"

"Of course not. But she's okay enough that she's not storming out here to have words with Karriamis in person, and that's about the best we can hope for. I think this is a waste of time."

"Betting?"

"Fine."

"Stakes?"

"I get to choose dinners for the next week, and Helen has to make them *and* you have to eat them."

"You'll be eating the same thing?"

"Of course."

"Fine. Done."

"The thing I don't understand," Kaylin said, looking at the Tower of Karriamis—which was, for once, an actual Tower, not a cliff face or a cave, "is why he'd even come back here."

"You're not sure he's here?"

"No, I'm sure he's here—but only because Helen was relatively certain."

"He's here for Bellusdeo's sake," Mandoran said. "That was Sedarias, by the way. I personally think it's stupid." He winced at what was likely Sedarias's reply, but didn't share it. "Don't look smug—she thinks you're stupid as well."

"So, like usual."

"No, she thinks you're more oblivious than usual. Do you understand what Emmerian wants?"

"I think he wants Bellusdeo to be happy. Or happier."

"Well, I for one agree with Sedarias. You're clueless. Oblivious. Look—you were *even there* when Karriamis's Avatar asked Emmerian whether or not he felt he could be the guardian of his people."

"And?"

Mandoran turned to Severn. "You explain it."

Severn's smile was a pleasant, very polite wall. "I believe there are doors just beyond this hedge wall; you can see the peak rising above them. Shall we knock?"

"He knows we're here," Kaylin muttered.

"Manners have very little to do with knowledge. He knows we're here. He knows why; we are standing on land his Tower occupies and controls. Manners are rituals."

"We didn't have to knock at the cave."

"No."

"So why now?"

"Because there are doors."

They bounced a glance between each other, and Kaylin grimaced and nodded. She walked up to the door. Before she reached it, she felt the ground move under her feet. She looked down, and then back at the door with growing dread. Or resentment. "It's not a door," she said. "It's a portal. And I think we activate it by knocking."

Severn moved to join her, but glanced at Mandoran.

The Barrani shrugged. "A portal's a door. It's more complicated than your normal doors, but—it's a door. Karriamis has to open it if you're going to enter. I have no idea why portals make you sick. Sedarias says there are rumors that it affected some of our people—or our Ancestors—the same way, but none of us have any personal experience with people who react like you do."

"I'd love to know as well. Maybe it's the marks of the Chosen?"

"None of us have ever met anyone who's Chosen before. Maybe. Does it matter? I don't really care, except I don't want you to throw up on my shoes. So—I'll go last. Or first."

"I wish to point out," Karriamis said, as Kaylin found her feet, "that there are possible reasons for your allergy, as you incorrectly style it, to portals."

"Can I do anything about it?" she asked, still staring at the floor, although there were now feet in her limited view.

"Some experimentation would have to be done, and I believe you also consider yourself allergic to some variants of magic?"

A hand appeared. She hesitated, because she didn't immediately recognize whose, which meant it was Karriamis.

"Indeed. Unless you wish to remain huddled on the floor. In general, I would be considered a poor host if I did not attempt to alleviate your discomfort."

Given Bellusdeo's first introduction, Kaylin was pretty certain that being seen as a poor host was not a huge concern for the Tower, but she accepted the hand he offered.

The lights went out. She lost sight of the floor, of the stairs that rose from it, of Mandoran—and Severn. She didn't lose sight of Karriamis because she was attached by the hand.

"Your hospitality sucks."

"So I've been told."

"Recently?"

"Yes. But it has been a lamentably constant theme through-out my existence. I did not become a Tower to make random strangers feel at home. And I feel that my hospitality is not lacking when compared to Durandel's."

"Where are we?"

"We are in the Tower."

"Where are Severn and Mandoran?"

"I have left them in the front hall for the moment."

"They're not going to be happy, and Mandoran isn't going to remain there."

"He has incentive."

Kaylin froze. "Please do not tell me you threatened him with me."

"Not so bluntly, no. I am not completely oblivious. But I wish to speak to you without interference."

"Why?"

He smiled. "You have perhaps come here in search of Lord Emmerian. No, do not let go of my hand. I do not consider it safe for you."

"And you're worried about my safety." She rolled her eyes.

"In spite of your cynicism—and I will admit that there is possible reason for it—yes."

"Where are you taking me?"

"I am taking you to where Lord Emmerian is currently contained."

Contained.

"You will understand why when we arrive."

Kaylin—

Don't panic. You'll just set me off.

I won't—you're worried about Emmerian. I'm worried about you. If he meant to kill or hurt me, I'd be dead. We both know that.

Mandoran's not as sure.

Tell him to stay where he is. Add "please" if it looks like he's wavering.

She felt Severn's amusement. Beneath it, she felt his worry. He wasn't angry yet.

"I am afraid that at this moment I am not capable of reaching Emmerian; I believe you can."

Bellusdeo could.

"Ah, no. At this moment I do not believe that would be in his best interests."

"His? Or hers?"

"Either. You understand what her duties are."

Kaylin stiffened.

"Perhaps you are too young to understand and accept them. But she does. And so does Emmerian. Tell me, do you think he would make a good partner for Bellusdeo?"

"It's not up to me." *Why is he asking me this?*

She felt Severn's reluctance. Clearly, this was both personal and emotional—and it wasn't his to talk about.

I really think I need to know, given where he's said we're going.

Bellusdeo needs to have babies if the Dragon race is to survive. Sooner is better than later, because if she dies the possibility is lost.

Yes, I know *that.*

She therefore needs to choose a partner with whom to have those children.

Duh.

Kaylin—

Wait, you think it's Emmerian? Like, Emmerian, who's mostly almost invisible?

I believe, he said, with care, *that it is something that Emmerian desires, yes. Even if I am mistaken, it's something Karriamis believes he desires.*

Emmerian doesn't want to be captain of his stupid Tower!

No. But Karriamis was a Dragon, and possibly still considers himself one.

"I do."

He understands he has very few Dragons to work with, but... I think he's attempting to ascertain if Emmerian is the right father for the children on which the race depends.

But—but—that's not up to him!

Severn said nothing.

It's not. She tightened her grip on the Avatar's hand. "It doesn't matter what you think is best—the decision is Bellusdeo's."

"I can remove him from consideration."

"Not even you would be that stupidly arrogant."

She could hear Severn inhale; could almost feel it.

"Is that what you believe, Chosen?"

He had stopped moving, or rather, stopped leading; he did not let go of her hand. But the marks on her arms failed to light up, failed to move; there were no clues to be gleaned from their behavior. "If you think it's your decision, yes. That's exactly what I believe."

"They are young."

"Emmerian's not young. And Bellusdeo is almost as old as the chancellor. If by young, you mean, they don't agree with how you think they should be living their lives, then yes. But so am I."

"She wants something from me that you do not want."

"After this? I'm pretty damn sure I'll never want anything from you."

"Be that as it may. And I have something to offer her."

"You screw around with Emmerian and nothing on earth is going to persuade her to take it."

A slow, soft light began to lessen the darkness. "You are certain?"

Something in his tone caused Kaylin to shut her mouth. She knew he could hear what she was thinking—and she knew most of it would possibly get her fired; it would certainly get her busted back down to permanent private, because in theory she was working, and the office had standards of behavior that personal life didn't.

Was she certain?

Probably not. Part of Bellusdeo would never be separate from the war that had destroyed the life she'd built. "If you hurt him in any way," she finally said, "she won't negotiate. She has other ways of fighting this war. She doesn't need you."

"And if I told you that my primary concern is not, in fact, this war—as you call it—at all?"

Kaylin folded her arms. "I'm not the person who's going to be making any decisions here. This is between you and Bellusdeo."

"And you would advise her?"

To run screaming, but there was no chance that the gold Dragon would do any such thing. Kaylin was angry, and trying very hard not to be. "I wouldn't dare unless she asked my opinion. She is never going to ask my opinion about this. Where is Emmerian?"

"Here," the Tower replied. "Can you not hear him?"

She couldn't. She couldn't see him either. The light that had grown wasn't so much light as…glowing fog; it rose steadily, but fog wasn't generally great at revealing anything.

"What do you want from her?" Kaylin asked.

"Did you not just say that was none of your business?"

"Yes."

He chuckled. "We will be family, she and I, should we reach an understanding. But I am not Helen, and in the end, more than she and I would dwell here. I am sentinel against *Ravellon*; there is no stronger protection. She is likely, given her proclivities, to require that protection.

"But she cannot live here in an attempt to avoid or put off the responsibility she has to our people—the few that remain. If she is to live here, *I* will protect her offspring, may they be many."

"And decide who they're the offspring of?"

"Your grammar is atrocious. I will not argue with the conclusions you have drawn. I believe, however, you are impulsive and less observant than would be ideal. Perhaps you will grow into it in your short, mortal life."

Can I hit him?

I don't think he'd notice, but at this point, given everything else you've said, it can't do more harm.

You're not worried.

I'm less worried.

Why?

Severn didn't answer.

"Very well, Chosen. It appears Lord Emmerian does not wish to be seen. I will have to leave you to find him."

Mandoran says Bellusdeo's coming. Sedarias tried to stop her.

Kaylin groaned. *Did Mandoran say the rest of the cohort is* staying at home?

Severn didn't answer.

"I consider that a very positive sign," Karriamis said. "I understand that you consider it a disaster. It will be interesting to see which of us is proven correct."

He wouldn't be hurt in either case.

"Ah, Chosen. You are young. And you are wrong. But I must leave you now." He turned back. "That boy missed his calling in life."

It took her a moment—well, several—to realize that *that boy* referred not to Severn but to Emmerian himself.

"You are all young to me, but perhaps that is a product of my age; I see clearly if I focus, but I often fail to examine things that are neither of concern nor interest until it is perhaps too late."

★ ★ ★

They're all coming, aren't they?

Mandoran said Teela told them all to mind their own damn business, but with more colorful phrasing.

So… Teela's not coming.

He didn't say that. Have you found Emmerian?

She shook her head. *Still looking. Is Mandoran still with you?*

Yes. His tone implied worry. Kaylin was fine with this; it would keep Karriamis occupied. Not that that was necessarily a good thing; she remembered angry Emmerian wading into an argument in her own home. It had been the first time she'd had any hint that the Dragon lord had a temper.

But everything Dragons did was larger than life. She reminded herself of this as she stared into fog. The marks on her arms remained flat and lightless.

She turned up the sleeve that covered her lower left arm. Closed her eyes. In theory, that should have made visibility worse, but the marks had never relied on sensible theory or she wouldn't even have them. With her eyes closed she could see the faint luminescence of the runic shapes. They were a glowing gray, similar in some fashion to the light emitted by the fog.

Ugh. She could see the fog clearly with her eyes closed. She wondered if this fog was similar to the fog that comprised the unrestricted outlands.

It's likely, Severn said. *Also: Terrano's already here. None of the rest of the cohort have arrived yet—I think he probably trailed after us when Mandoran left.*

I wonder if Tara will let them pass through.

Mandoran seems to think they're all avoiding Tiamaris. He didn't because he was with us.

Never mind. I don't want to know. What I need to know now, she added, grimacing as she touched one rune and attempted to pull it off her skin—which was a lot less metaphorical than she'd've liked, *is where the hell Emmerian is.*

If he were angry the way he was the other night, you wouldn't have to ask.

She nodded. This should have been a good sign. It certainly didn't feel like it. If she found Emmerian and made it out of here, she was going to punch Karriamis.

I wouldn't advise it.

No one would—but he said Emmerian is stuck here. And he can't find him or at least can't get him out. I don't understand why. Helen could. I'm certain Helen could—she deals with enraged cohort members all the time.

It's pretty clear Karriamis doesn't.

Yes—but he was built to deal with Shadow. That's worse, isn't it?

No. I don't think he has to care whether or not Shadow, in whatever form the incursion takes, survives. Helen does.

This didn't make Kaylin any happier as the words sank roots. The implications made the situation far more dire. It wasn't that the Emperor would blame her if Emmerian failed to survive; he wouldn't. Nor would he blame Bellusdeo.

She was almost certain Bellusdeo would blame herself. The gold Dragon wouldn't blame Kaylin; Emmerian was a Dragon, so far above a corporal Kaylin was irrelevant. There was nothing she could face that he couldn't.

The rune rose from her arm, shedding gray as its light brightened; it became blue, and the light cast, harsh. It reminded Kaylin of the morgue. This was not a comfortable thought. She could heal, yes; it was the only truly unalloyed blessing the marks had given her.

But Kaylin couldn't heal a corpse. No one could. Karriamis, damn him, had once been a Dragon—he'd probably know for certain if Emmerian was dead. But if he was injured? If he was dying?

Surely he would have said something.

Damn it, what *had* he said? She'd been kind of angry at a lot of it and had probably overfocused on the parts she considered garbage. *Emmerian doesn't want to be seen.*

She exhaled. "Emmerian, I don't know if you can hear me—it's Kaylin."

Silence.

"I would like to get you out of here—preferably through the nearest back door—before Bellusdeo arrives."

She felt a tremor beneath her feet, and looked down. The ground on which she was standing was ice—or ice-like; it was what was shedding this odd fog.

Beneath the ice she could now see the open—and red—eye of a blue Dragon.

20

"Karriamis!"

The Tower didn't answer. One red eye flickered, as if, trapped beneath the frozen floor, Emmerian was trying to close his eyelids, with about as much success as one would expect of someone stuck in an ice block.

He's with us now, Severn said. *Karriamis is here.*

Tell him— She cut off words that would have been considered too foul for Marcus, her sergeant. *Tell him to let Emmerian go.*

He says he has not imprisoned Emmerian.

He didn't put himself into a freaking giant block of ice on his own!

Severn understood her anger. *He is saying that's exactly what happened. He apologizes for allowing it, but points out that he did not invite Emmerian to visit; Emmerian came on his own—and if Karriamis is a Dragon, he, too, is wary of enraged Dragons.*

How does that mean Karriamis didn't do this?

The Tower has defenses, he says.

And you believe him? You believe that any part of this Tower isn't under his control?

Severn didn't answer. Which meant no. *I believe he believes Emmerian can free himself if he so chooses.*

Then what does he expect me to do?

Convince him to choose. Those weren't the words the Tower had used.

She looked down.

Emmerian wasn't her favorite Dragon, but he was, aside from the old Arkon, Bellusdeo's. He was so diffident and apologetic on those occasions when he had been commanded to interfere that neither the gold Dragon nor Kaylin could take him personally.

And he truly seemed to appreciate who Bellusdeo was. What she had once been. He seemed to understand some part of the loss that the Arkon didn't. No, she thought, that wasn't true.

"Emmerian, listen. The Arkon—ugh, the chancellor—knew her when she was young. And there were eight more that were almost exactly like her. He understood what she'd lost when she lost the Aerie. He didn't know her when she was a queen. He knows she *ruled a world.*

"But...I don't think the chancellor can see that in her. Not even now." Kaylin was coming to some sort of conclusion, but without any sense that it was important enough to move Emmerian. And while she didn't believe Karriamis—he couldn't have put *himself* in here—she believed, reluctantly, that he could pull himself out.

She believed it because Severn believed it.

"The entire Dragon Court knows what she was. They believe it. But they see her as a *Dragon* first. She loves the Arkon, because he knew her. He indulges her because she was a child the last time he saw her—I mean, before she was freed and came to Elantra. She knows it. He's home—or what's left of that childhood home, and we all want that some of the time.

"He knows what she lost. But he can't see it clearly as part of who she is now. To the Arkon," she continued, giving up on the changed name, "what she *was* is important. He doesn't care about future babies. Not really. He thinks Bellusdeo will come around eventually because she *was* a queen. She understands responsibility and sacrifice better than anyone."

The eye moved. Emmerian was watching her. She could feel the ground beneath her feet rumble in a way that implied breath or breathing. It was almost as if she was standing on Emmerian himself, and not the barrier that separated them.

On good days, this would have been a terrible idea. But whatever she was saying, he heard. He listened.

"I've been told by almost everyone in my house that I'm oblivious. I miss things that other people don't miss. I didn't understand the significance of the words Karriamis said the last time we visited." But she thought, as she stared at the giant eye, which was still crimson, that she might, now.

Helen had said something about Emmerian weeks ago.

Something about Emmerian and Bellusdeo.

Karriamis must have picked up on that somehow, from someone—but she doubted it was Emmerian. What was it? What had it been?

But surely your ability to stand by while Bellusdeo is in danger makes you ineligible to be guardian of your race?

Guardian had many meanings in Kaylin's life. Marrin of the foundling halls was guardian of all of the foundlings beneath her large roof. Guardian of the Imperial Law was just another word for the Hawks and the Swords. But both Bellusdeo and Emmerian had been angry at Karriamis's dismissive question.

Oh.

He didn't mean *guardian* as Kaylin used the word; he meant *father.* As in, father to Bellusdeo's children—the children who were the future of Dragonkind. Emmerian did not step in when Bellusdeo fought. He had done it only once, and he had been embarrassed.

He understood that Bellusdeo chose—for better or worse—her own battles. She had never commanded Emmerian. He had fought in the wars that divided Bellusdeo from her people; he had been, or become, a warrior. He had—he said—looked up to the Arkon as the pinnacle of the height a warrior could achieve in his distant youth.

But the Arkon had never wanted war. He had fought it, yes. He had abandoned the one thing he *did* want. And he had returned to it. She didn't know what Emmerian had abandoned, if he'd abandoned anything at all. She had the sense that he was young when he joined the war flights, young when he fought—but not as young as she had been when she had unofficially joined the Hawks.

In the Hawks, she had found what she wanted; she had found the thing she could dedicate her life to.

Emmerian hadn't found that in war. Like Tiamaris, youngest of the Dragons, he seemed to be content to wait, to watch. He served the Emperor.

But Bellusdeo *had* found what she needed or wanted in war—and she'd lost it. And she'd returned to Elantra, a world that had been visited only in subtle ways by the damage that had destroyed her adoptive home. Her war wasn't over. She was not the Arkon, to set aside the mantle of battle.

Karriamis was right—she hated to think it, but did. The Tower could not be the instrument of, the tool of, vengeance. What Bellusdeo wanted she could not have, but captaining the Tower made her part of the front line. And Bellusdeo knew, now, that it wasn't as simple as that. Karriamis had asked her a question.

She had retreated because she couldn't answer it.

Sedarias wouldn't have been able to answer it had it been asked of her, either.

Emmerian never seemed to *want* anything with the visceral rage or desire that characterized either Bellusdeo or Sedarias.

He didn't seem to want with the visceral desperation that had caused Kaylin to attach herself to the Halls of Law and hold on as tightly as she could with both hands.

Oblivious, she thought. She folded her knees and sat on the ice while mist rolled up above her head. She closed her eyes. She could see the marks on her arms come to life, but they remained level with her skin. She understood, though; it wasn't the marks that were needed here.

If Emmerian was not Sedarias—and he was nothing like the leader of the cohort—he was trapped by some of the same things. They were things Kaylin understood—how could she not?

She had wanted the Hawks desperately.

She had been certain she had not deserved them. She had done things that would prevent her from ever joining their ranks—but she'd done them outside of the remit of Imperial Law. As if that made a difference. And it did—a bureaucratic difference. She could stay.

Teela had fought for it. Marcus—growly and terrifying—had fought for it. She hadn't understood why, but it didn't matter. What mattered was that they *win*. That she be allowed to stay in this life that she so desperately wanted to be worthy of *when she wasn't*.

She opened her eyes.

Emmerian stood opposite her, his back toward her, his hands loosely clasped behind him.

"Bellusdeo will not be happy that you are here," he said.

"You don't care about that."

"I do, actually. It is her relationship with—and her dependence on—you that has caused some difficulty at court. But," he exhaled. "I don't fear it in the same way, no."

"Is Karriamis right?" she asked.

He met her gaze in silence.

"Was it you? Or was it Bellusdeo? He must have taken that thought from someone." She stopped. "Oh."

He said nothing.

"But I don't understand—if it wasn't you…" She tried again. "You admire her. You respect her. You see her, not as a necessary mother, but as…Bellusdeo. If somehow it was her…"

"I am not the youngest of the court; that would be Tiamaris. And he has achieved something singular; he has found his hoard. He has claimed his territory. You know the chancellor. You have encountered the Emperor and Lord Diarmat. And you have personal experience with the current Arkon. You have seen them all fight."

"I saw you fight as well."

He shook his head. "I have never been considered exceptional among my kin. I was content not to be. I understood my duties. I performed them to the best of my abilities." His hands tightened. "Has Bellusdeo spoken to you about the phenomenon of draconic hoards?"

"A little?"

"Has Lord Sanabalis? The chancellor?"

"Also a little. I think Bellusdeo said that sometimes the Dragon involved would go insane."

"Yes. I have seen much of it, in my distant youth, before the wars that almost destroyed our ancient people."

"But the Empire is the Emperor's hoard."

"Yes. And Tara is Tiamaris's. Insanity is not always guaranteed, and in its absence, what is left is focus, responsibility, dedication. It is not considered a sign of adulthood; I am adult. But it is always considered significant. We do not dream of a specific hoard; it remains amorphous. To what, in the end, can we give the whole of our thought, our dedication, our love? What is broad enough to bear the focus of the Dragons?"

"The Academia is the chancellor's hoard," she said, frowning.

Emmerian nodded. "And, as you must suspect, it is not.

It is what he hoped for, yearned for, dreamed of in his own youth—but he is not as Tiamaris is; for Tiamaris it was instant—the yearning, the force of it, the commitment. For Lannagaros, it was different. The Barrani cannot see the difference, and will not question it. It is his hoard."

"You think Bellusdeo could?"

"Of course she could. But Kaylin, he does not have to be in the grip of that fate, that destiny, to commit everything he has or will ever be to the Academia. He has accepted the chancellorship. Nothing will move him from it. But he risks no insanity; the force of commitment does not skirt the edge of the long fall into darkness. He is flexible, and he will not feel easily threatened by things that are not a threat."

"You think Tiamaris would?"

"I cannot say. As part of a military flight, I have acted against those whose hoard has chipped away at all sanity; they are a danger that you cannot, from your position, understand."

"I think I can."

"Yes, because you are not a Dragon and you have not experienced that madness. Tiamaris is protective. You understand that. You would not raise hand against Tara, regardless. Tiamaris understands that Tara is a living person, and he values her happiness. He has allowed her to make questionable decisions—the lack of portal being one—because that is her desire. And I believe she is happy."

Kaylin nodded.

"I do not believe he will—or can—fall prey to madness. He could have reasonably denied her the request to dispense with portals. He could have denied the one, localized mirror he has allowed at her request. There are many things he could justify for reasons of security.

"He could deny her her gardens, so unusual even in the fiefs. He could deny her contact with any of the many citizens of the fief who have come to aid in those gardens, to work there. He could, in the end, command that she imprison herself—because again, it would keep her safe."

Kaylin stared at him. "It would destroy her."

"Would it?"

"There was a reason Barren almost fell. She could not live like that."

"Ah." He turned to her, a hint of a smile on his face, although his eyes carried no trace of amusement. "No. But for those who fall prey to the fear, Tara would cease to be a person. She would be an object of fear and possession."

"Do any of the others start out sane and reasonable and then...fall?"

"It has happened," he replied.

"You've seen this."

"Yes. Twice. No, more than twice, but twice it became more personal. These two were my friends, my comrades in arms, people with whom I had shared the rash idealism and optimism of youth. They trained hard. They worked hard— as did I. We were almost inseparable."

Kaylin waited.

"We are, in general, a far more solitary people than you are. We are more solitary than even the Barrani, who oft appear to live on and for suspicion and murder."

"That's a bit harsh."

"Yes. I assume that you have no desire to hear me be more harsh, and I apologize for the digression. We do not suffer if we are isolated for stretches of time; it gives us room to breathe."

Kaylin nodded.

"Therefore, our friendship—forged in youth and war—was considered odd. Unusual. One of the elders in that youth—he is long dead—took me aside and offered me advice."

"Only you?"

"I do not know. If he offered similar advice to my two

friends, they did not share—but I did not choose to share, either."

"The advice was about hoards?"

"It was. It was about the effect that the compulsion can have on the young. Tiamaris is sometimes called 'young Tiamaris' by Lord Sanabalis and the chancellor, but he is not young by my reckoning. Younger than I, yes. But old enough that he has had experience and interests that offer grounding.

"Our interest was the war, and our experiences in it. We did not know how to return gracefully from it; we felt diminished. It was a shock to us to see the Arkon—Lannagaros as he was, then—become a...scholar. A Dragon who preferred a desk and books to arts military, arts arcane."

"He knows a fair bit about the arcane, if I'm any judge."

"Yes. He does. Much of it subtle, and not meant for war."

"His was the defining spell in the battle for the High Halls."

Emmerian's smile was genuine; he shook his head. "I told you—we were young. Young and ignorant. I did not understand how he could have been the pinnacle of achievement—in our eyes—and settle for what he became.

"But my belief in him was strong enough that I began to look at what consumed his time, his attention."

"Your friends didn't."

"No. They were bitter, but people oft are when the object of their worship is shown to be less than perfect. They did not understand my attempts, either, and we grew distant."

"You're not like him, though."

"No. His academic desires remained a mystery to me. The only overlap we shared was curiosity about languages—living or dead. The Empire has not existed for as long as the wars between the Barrani and my kin, but when the Emperor chose—was driven *to* choose—there was work to be done. It was a stretching of wings, for me; a return to my youth.

"It was not so, for them. They were my age, and if we were

not born in the same clutch, we were born at the same time. The Empire did not yet exist when the first of my friends, restless and drifting without a solid sense of purpose, found his hoard."

"Can I ask what it was?"

"You may—obviously—ask."

"You won't answer."

"It is not relevant, and it is still oddly painful. He was…not the Dragon I had known. His sense of responsibility, his sense of *duty* had been deepened and warped; he could not even see us. But he had destroyed mortal settlements, and killed a handful of Barrani, and we had no desire to rekindle the wars; they served neither Barrani nor Dragonkind well. My friend and I traveled to him.

"He could not hear us. He could not identify our voices. I remember that clearly. What he heard when we spoke, I do not know. I could hear his voice from miles away."

Given his expression, Kaylin didn't ask what had happened to the friend. She was certain she didn't want to know.

"We made vows on that day, my remaining friend and I, that we would not fall into the same terrible trap. We didn't understand what had happened, and the elders merely said it was hoard-madness, hoard-sickness. I think…they had memories similar to the ones I share with you now. I was no longer a whelpling; I could not press for answers.

"But…I had access to Lannagaros, and he was, if not patient…" and at this memory, he smiled again, rueful. Happier. "…he was informative. The subject itself—hoard-sickness—had been studied by both Dragonkind and other races; the Dragons are not famously good record keepers in general. It is what made Lannagaros's postwar choice so strange. But he was not the first to be so strange, and in the absence of the responsibility of war, it was the life he chose. He was not happy," he added. "It took me many decades to understand that his melancholy was not due to the lack of war, the lack of position. But he was so dedicated to the preservation of knowledge, I understood it, at the time, as his hoard. It was not a hoard that I, as a young Dragon, would ever have accepted."

"And now?"

He shook his head. "Even now. But that knowledge, that preservation, came with a willingness to share—if one was careful about approaching him when he was not absorbed in either study or cataloging. I am not certain you would consider all Dragons who have chosen their hoard entirely rational or sane. There was a reason you were told to touch nothing in Lannagaros's library.

"He said that some had reached the conclusion that maturity was required. I pointed out examples of mature Dragons who had also...been destroyed. By their madness, and in the end by us."

"You killed them?"

His lack of answer was an answer. She winced. "Sorry."

He appeared to hear neither the question nor the apology she offered in its wake. "I digress, perhaps because I wish to speak or think of any other subject."

"You don't have to talk. I mean, you don't have to tell me anything you don't want to."

"You don't understand," he replied, his voice soft, his eyes closed.

"I get told that a lot."

"Yes." His smile was slender. "My second friend was older than the first when he found his hoard."

She waited, almost holding her breath.

"You understand that the Empire is the Emperor's hoard; you understand that he is unusual. It is...an amorphous concept, this Empire, and it requires a flexibility that most would not possess. Whatever else you think of Dariandaros, this much is true: he is exceptional, singular, and his decisions are never made without an understanding of the consequences. Not one of us would have imagined the caste courts and their laws of exemption; not one of us *could*.

"Most, however, have less...philosophical hoards. The desire to possess and protect coexist, but you understand why that is always a difficult balance. Tiamaris holds *Tara* dear, not her fief. But he understands that the people of the fief are important to Tara. What brings her happiness—without risking her existence—he will give her.

"And she has shown...remarkable flexibility. I like her. I could not love her as Tiamaris does. I have never loved anything or anyone that way."

"Your second friend was...insane? Hoard-sickness?"

"No, not in the manner of the first friend. Both he and I understood, because of Lannagaros and the loss of our mutual friend, that our lives—the whole of our beings—must be formed, must be rooted and grounded in ourselves, before we could safely bear the weight and demands of a hoard. It is...not dissimilar to how mortals interact with their families and their work. The family might be, on one day, the driving concern; on another, it might be the work itself. You are a Hawk, and you consider the work you do to be your calling, your vocation."

Kaylin nodded.

"But the import of your friends is not lessened. You cannot always prioritize them over the duties you've undertaken, but they are also essential to you."

She nodded again.

"That is...not the drive of the hoard. It *can* be, but it takes effort. Lannagaros felt that because the Empire is so large, the Emperor is choosing between different consequences, different outcomes. There is balance because of his hoard, not in spite of it. But again, he is unusual. My friend did not choose something as ambitious as an Empire.

"He understood the risks—as did Tiamaris—and he accepted them." The silence that followed these words was longer, as if Emmerian had decided to break it but couldn't find the words.

"Did he lose his hoard?"

Emmerian nodded. "What the hoard itself could not do to him, loss and grief did. His single drive in the absence of the hoard to which he had dedicated his life was vengeance and death; in the grip of the madness of grief he lost the ability to care about either his welfare or the welfare of any of the rest of us.

"I went with the flight that was sent to stop him; we were not numerous and we were not a war flight. I asked," he added. "I asked to be included. I had known him, if not for the longest period of time, then for all of the formative ones.

"But I knew. When I saw him, I knew. He recognized me," he added, voice soft. "He recognized me. But he understood why the flight was there; what its purpose was. I think he intended to die—but he could not do so on his own. He was not...himself. My presence to him signaled betrayal. Only betrayal. The loss had taken every element of our history from him; he was overwhelmed.

"He attacked me. I tried—as perhaps Mandoran tried, with Bellusdeo—to avoid him, to avoid hurting him." His eyes closed. "In the end, that was not possible. The decision was not mine to make. And I have asked myself times beyond number if, had I gone alone, I might have been able to pull him back, to pull him out of that moment, that pain.

"Lannagaros was not kind; he said it was possible. But we have no easy way of going back, and even had we, I would not have been allowed to make the attempt. He was not the only Dragon to die that day."

Kaylin nodded. She understood exactly how he felt beneath his carefully chosen, almost neutral words. She had lived in the same place for years. The reasons were different—of course they were—but the guilt and the pain were the same. She was certain of that.

Had Emmerian been part of the cohort, had he been Bellusdeo, had he been Severn, she would have reached out for him physically. She had no words of comfort to offer, because those words had never helped her when she was in this place.

Maybe this was why Karriamis had sent her to speak with Emmerian. Maybe not. Buildings—even Tara—just didn't think like normal people.

She waited, but Emmerian offered no further words.

Kaylin didn't consider this a comfortable silence. "You can't leave?"

"I cannot leave. I have tried. And I fear that you will now be trapped here as well. I cannot say I approve of Karriamis."

"Karriamis clearly has mixed feelings about you if you can be stuck here. And about me, as well, I guess." She exhaled. "He said, when we first met, that you were good at masking your thoughts. Do you think that's true while you're trapped here?"

"Yes."

"The comment he made that angered both you and Bellusdeo, the comment about being guardian of your race, did he kind of mean father?"

Emmerian nodded, and once again looked away.

"But—he didn't get that from you."

"No." His hands were by his side; they were in loose fists, but the fists began to tighten.

"I can't see your eyes," she said.

"I know."

"Are they red?"

"Probably."

"Bellusdeo is only good at hiding her thoughts when she's calm and deliberate. Which she...wasn't."

"Indeed. I do not believe, if she wishes to captain this Tower, she can keep those thoughts hidden. Karriamis is thorough and invasive in his testing. You said she was coming here."

Kaylin nodded. "She's *not* going to be happy."

"It has been a long time since Bellusdeo has expected happiness, or even desired it. I will not call the world that was destroyed her hoard. But it was, to her, what the Imperial library was to Lannagaros. If his situation was not easily remedied, there was remedy for it. Bellusdeo, however, cannot be Emperor. She cannot be queen to this world as she was to the one on which she was trapped."

Kaylin nodded. "So...the guardian comment came from her. From her thoughts."

He said nothing.

"Helen didn't tell me what the two of you talked about when we returned home."

"And you wish to know?"

"I don't need to hear the whole thing, no. But...did you discuss the... I mean, did you talk about Dragon babies?"

"Yes and no."

"I think it's kind of important, given Karriamis."

"It is deeply, deeply important to Karriamis. But he is...old. Old-fashioned. If the immortals change slowly, they nonetheless change. What a Dragon was in Karriamis's time, and what a Dragon is in the Emperor's reign, are not the same. He wishes to know what I want, and I wish not to tell him. We may discuss it in the hells."

"Why? Why not just tell him?"

"Because it is not up to me, Corporal. It...did not occur to me that Bellusdeo had extended even that much thought to the question of...more Dragons. She has never professed even the slightest interest in such a discussion. Only Lannagaros was unconcerned about this; he wishes her to be happy. He wishes her to be herself, because he is aware that he does not know her; he knows only what she once was.

"That has been a comfort to Bellusdeo. It has provided an anchor, a sense of the home she once had on our world—and lost. But she cannot retreat to childhood, in this. As a child, she would never have been forced to make this choice. She knows this. She has always understood why it is important.

"Diarmat assumes, because she has not thrown herself into the logistics, that she does not. He thinks her feckless, reckless, ultimately selfish."

Kaylin tried not to bristle. She tried hard. "That's easy for him to say. It's not Diarmat who has to have the babies. Or the clutch. Whatever."

"As you say."

"Wait, Diarmat has talked about this?"

"Kaylin, we have *all* talked about this. Lannagaros as well. The only person who has reserved opinion is Tiamaris—and Diarmat assumes that is because Tiamaris is young."

"You don't."

He smiled. "No, I don't. We are all agreed that this is important enough that it must happen, and until it does, Bellusdeo is not to risk her life needlessly."

"But she's here."

"But she is here. The Emperor would vastly prefer that she remain in the palace, but Lannagaros argued forcefully against that. His prior experience with Bellusdeo led him to believe that this would not work well; the Dragon Court has existed for centuries and it functions well. Adding Bellusdeo to—"

"To any gathering that also includes Diarmat? That's going to be a disaster."

"Yes. Lannagaros was perhaps not as blunt, but it was not required. He believed—and believes—that she cannot be caged, and she will see all protection offered as a cage. It is too small to contain her.

"Helen was the compromise. But she would not be with Helen—and with you—if Karriamis chooses to accept her." He inhaled; he exhaled smoke with a heart of red flame. None of this was pointed at Kaylin, and as there wasn't a lot of architecture here that Dragon breath could destroy, Kaylin didn't mind it. It made Emmerian seem more human.

"When Karriamis spoke," he said, after the smoke had drifted further away, "I was...surprised." His smile deepened, but it was rueful. "No, I was shocked. Bellusdeo has refused to discuss this element of her future with anyone; Lannagaros has not asked. Nor would he. I thought that she would bear the Emperor's children, in the end."

Kaylin's eyebrows were still attached to her face, which was a small miracle. "Are you *insane?*"

21

Emmerian turned fully toward her; his eyes were orange-red.

Kaylin made no attempt to claw back what was only charitably a question. "He's *exactly* the wrong person for Bellusdeo. And if she were somehow his Empress, she'd be part of his hoard. She'd be part of the Empire. If you can't see how much of a disaster that would be, I don't know what to say to you."

"For someone who doesn't know what to say, you speak a lot."

"Fine. I don't know what to say in a tongue that isn't Leontine. You've already talked about how dangerous it is to have a hoard. How difficult."

Emmerian nodded at the understatement.

"She can't be part of his hoard. She's his *equal*. She can't be husbanded and protected as if she were a precious and loved child. That would kill her."

"There are two elements to a clutch," he replied, his voice much more neutral. His hands, however, were fists. "The first, the most important, is Bellusdeo. There are no elders who would not have approved of her, even had there been others who might serve the purpose of continuing our race. She is strong. She is healthy.

"But the father is of equal import. And of the court—the waking court, the active court—who would be better than the Emperor?"

"Literally anybody breathing. Anyone else would be better." Kaylin hesitated. "Diarmat would be a disaster. Can you at least agree with that?"

Emmerian nodded.

"Lannagaros is right out—it'd be like sleeping with your father or your uncle."

He winced but nodded again.

"Sanabalis doesn't want it. I think you *could* pressure him into it if Bellusdeo chose him, but—she won't. He's like a mini-Arkon. Well, no, I guess he *is* the Arkon now. He doesn't have the former Arkon's affection for her, but I think he could develop it. Over centuries.

"That doesn't really leave many people. You don't agree about the Emperor. It doesn't matter. Helen agrees with me. The Emperor and Bellusdeo would destroy each other—and that's long before there are babies."

"This is not about friendship. This is not about preference. This is about the *future of our people.*"

"Yes, and? Do you think you're somehow too weak and too insignificant?"

Oh.

"You do."

He turned away.

"You feel you're the least important of the Dragons. The least significant."

He did not turn back.

But Kaylin knew this one. She knew it so well it was painful. He was a Dragon. He was immortal. He was part of the Imperial Court. Her own doubts about her suitability to be a

Hawk had plagued her for the early years; sometimes, when she looked at a criminal and saw herself—entirely herself—in their actions, it hit her hard. She was a *hypocrite.* She had no *right* to enforce laws she'd *broken herself.*

And yet, this was the life she wanted. She told herself that *because* she'd been there, because she'd broken those laws, she understood the why of it; it made her a better Hawk because she could see the humanity in the criminal.

But she didn't always believe it. Couldn't always believe it. The doubt was still there, and she could poke at it, pull it out. On bad days she couldn't put it aside. But the bad days were fewer now. She accepted what she couldn't change. She had changed what she could, when given opportunity and a semblance of safety.

Emmerian had no reason to doubt himself. He'd done everything, and he'd done it right. Yes, he wasn't the Emperor—but Kaylin was hugely thankful for that. He was the only one of the Dragons that Bellusdeo almost accepted, and she accepted him because he didn't press her, didn't pressure her, didn't *judge* her.

No, Kaylin thought, it was more than that. He *saw* her. He admired what she was: Warrior Queen. She could hold her own against any of them. He accepted her sense of humor, her temper, even her rage.

Bellusdeo knew it.

It was Bellusdeo's thoughts Karriamis had read. But it was Emmerian's reaction that had provided the damn Tower with an in, a hint of weakness, a way of reaching Lord Emmerian.

"You...you want this, right?" Kaylin asked.

Emmerian nodded; he did not turn to face her.

"Am I the person you would have chosen to *be* the Chosen?" He turned his head, his brows folding.

"You don't have to answer that. The answer is no. The answer would be no if I asked it of any of my friends. Any of them. They'd say no for different reasons. Some because they think I'm incompetent, some because they think I won't survive the situations I'll get into because of the marks. If I surveyed people who aren't my friends, most would think I don't deserve them. I can't even use them. I'm lazy, I'm not interested in magic. I'm a waste of the marks."

He nodded.

"And you know what? It doesn't matter. Did I want the marks?"

"No."

"Exactly. But I have them. I can't peel them off my own skin. My ignorance, my weakness, my mortality, didn't make a damn difference. I have *no idea* why I was Chosen when Nightshade was standing right there—but I was.

"And I can heal with them. I've done good with them. I've done things that maybe people who understood them better wouldn't have done—but I don't consider those things a waste.

"I didn't choose. I was chosen. And guess what? You've said—and I think you've always meant it—that Bellusdeo *gets to choose.*"

"She has never said—"

"No, but she wouldn't. You know that. You could ask her. She wouldn't answer."

He said nothing.

"Unless your life was on the line, and even then, she'd find it embarrassing. But if Karriamis is actually right—and I think he might be—you're her choice."

"I'm her choice because I am the least offensive choice she might make?"

Kaylin stepped back, because that's exactly what she'd been saying, and she realized that in his position, she'd feel what he was feeling. Being chosen because you were the least offensive, the least undesirable, was not the same as actually being wanted. The lack of negatives wasn't a positive. "I didn't say she was madly in love with you, no. But you've all been saying this is a necessity. You all agree."

"And you?"

"Since when have you cared about my opinion?"

"Very recently." His smile was wry. "I am not certain you will be able to leave this place; I cannot." The smile dimmed. "Do you understand anything I've told you?"

This was annoying. She understood it all.

"I do want this, as you called it."

"And you're afraid to want it."

"It is difficult to give one's life to someone—to something—that does not want it in the same way. To know, when making any decision, that were there others, I would not even be considered. She asked permission to wake those who chose the long sleep—it is not death, as you perceive death, but it is not exactly life—and it was denied her.

"I have considered doing what she asked, but I swore oaths to the Imperial Flight; I could not easily break them, not even for the sake of a choice she does not want to make. There is a reason that the long sleep was chosen; the disruption to the Empire would be significant."

"She understands that, as well. But you haven't answered my question."

"Which question?"

"That was a poor attempt at avoidance, even for you."

Kaylin, we have an angry Dragon here.

Karriamis let her in? Did she actually come up with an answer to his question?

Not the time for that.

Do we also have angry Sedarias?

We do. Her anger is nothing to Bellusdeo's. Things here could get... interesting.

Tell her that Emmerian is fine. I've found him. He's fine.

You want me to tell her that you're trapped with Emmerian? And you think that will make her less angry?

Fair point. Kaylin exhaled. "Bellusdeo is here."

Emmerian's eyes widened.

"She heard the cohort making a ruckus and she's not stupid. She didn't intend to return—Karriamis told her not to—until she could answer his question. Now, she probably doesn't care about the question."

"Understand," Emmerian said, as he looked up at what passed for ceiling in this space, "that what *I* want, is not what Bellusdeo wants; she wants to *get things over with*. She just wants it done. She'll take the least offensive option available to her in order to do her duty. But I don't consider her to be the least offensive option; I don't consider the Dragon race to be a simple weight to carry, a thing that must be seen to so that she can *move on*.

"I understand duty. I understand responsibility. But Kaylin, I understand *hoard*. And...I am not certain that I can do this duty in this paradigm and remain sane. The Emperor could. Diarmat could. I am less certain about Sanabalis, and as we've discussed, Lannagaros could not.

"I could begin," he continued, his voice dropping, his eyes reddening. "I am considering it. We would still have children. We would still have the promise of the continuation of our race.

"But how promising will that beginning be if I can see a day coming in which those children—and the court and Bellusdeo—will have to destroy me?"

"I don't understand hoard," Kaylin finally said. "I just don't. I understand it better because of what you've told me—but I don't get it. You speak as if it's not a choice. And I accept that. I'm not a Dragon. I'm not immortal. But...I don't understand what you want. I understood, sort of, what the former Arkon wanted. I understood what he'd devoted his life to. Wouldn't work for me, but I'm not him.

"And I understand some part of what Tiamaris wanted—but only because I've seen him with Tara. And that—that makes sense to me. She's his wife. I mean, she's a Tower and she's a building and they're not going to have children and raise happy families—but it doesn't matter. That's what I see, as a mortal.

"What do you *want*? What does Bellusdeo mean to you? What do you want her to mean to you, and…what do you want to mean to her?" When he failed to answer, she said, "I'm sorry. I've been thinking of Bellusdeo, and only of Bellusdeo. I've been thinking of the possible disasters around this decision because you're right—this *isn't* what she wants. She wants the war. She wants to be on the front lines until there's no more Shadow, ever.

"But she understands the need for young. She gets that. It just isn't what she wants. I understand what she wants. I understand why. I'd want it, too, if I were her. If every person I had ever loved had died or been corrupted and enslaved by Shadow, I'd want it dead.

"But I don't understand what you want. I assumed—I'm sorry—that the 'more Dragons' part of the equation was something the entire Dragon court agreed on. I didn't really think beyond that, and obviously, that was stupid.

"So: tell me what you want. Tell me what would drive you insane."

At his expression, she quickly added, "Or not." She stepped back instinctively, and realized as she did that she hadn't taken enough steps back. Emmerian, in this enclosed space, was going full Dragon.

But if what he wanted was to be Bellusdeo's hoard—if female Dragons even had any—it wasn't going to happen. Not now. Probably not ever.

"Tara is Tiamaris's hoard—and with her, the whole of the

fief, because that's what her duties are. But he's not *her* hoard; she's a Tower, she's not a Dragon. He's not insane. He's not in danger of going insane. And they're both happy. They're both fine. I don't understand."

You should probably keep that to yourself, Severn said, his voice heavy with a concern that had not yet become fear but hovered on its edge.

I can't. I don't think he's going to be able to leave this place if he doesn't know.

Yes. But it doesn't mean you have to know what that answer is.

I don't think he has one.

Bellusdeo has entered the Tower.

Karriamis let her in?

Karriamis didn't continue his attempts to keep her out.

Ugh.

Mandoran and Sedarias were helping.

The mystical equivalent of picking locks?

He nodded.

Great. So we're going to have three angry Dragons.

I don't think Karriamis is actually angry.

Not yet.

"I want to be part of her flight," Emmerian said, the words elongated and rumbling with the depth of the much larger Dragon throat. "I want to fight by her side, as I fought—long ago—by the side of my closest companions. If she is to war against *Ravellon*, I want to be beside her. I want to—how do you put it?—have her back. Always.

"You do not *see* her. You see her as *a* Dragon. But Kaylin— had I been born to, or brought to, her world, I would have seen her as my queen; I would have had no other."

She stared at him. None of this—none of the regard he had just put into words—had ever leaked out. He served the Emperor; he was like a...a minder. A guard. She had only seen him leap to her defense once—and he had been humiliated by it, by the lack of control, the lack of trust.

No, she thought; he trusted Bellusdeo; it was Helen, the cohort, Kaylin that he didn't trust.

He had stepped back—he had had to step back—because some necessary layer of protective armor had been stripped back completely, and what it had revealed was too raw, too *wrong*. It went against every word he had just spoken—and she thought it went against every word he had once believed.

She swallowed. "And that's all?"

"It is not. I want her to bear a clutch of my eggs. I want the children to be of both of us: the Dragon I admire and would have sworn my life to, and…me. I'm not worthy of her. I know I am not. I will not be, no matter how I strive—and the ability to strive in war or battle is gone; only the battle against Shadow is left us in which I might—*might*—prove myself."

"Don't," she surprised herself by saying. "You'll never believe it. If you compare yourself to her, you'll never, ever believe it. No matter what you do. No matter how well you do it.

"Look—do you think she likes people because they deserve it? Because they're worthy of it? If she did, she'd have reduced Mandoran to a pile of ash on day two. She'd never have moved in with me. If you're not worthy of her now, how am I? Because I'm Chosen?" Kaylin inserted a single Leontine word.

"I am not talking about *like*."

"Then what? Love? Aren't they the same?"

"I begin to understand the corporal's difficulties far more clearly. What I want is not the same. Were I to serve her, were she to be the leader of my flight, I would be hers."

Kaylin nodded.

Emmerian exhaled a stream of fire. It wasn't aimed at Kaylin, but it was hot. "I do not want—I am not certain I could survive—*temporary*."

★ ★ ★

Kaylin waited for the fire to die down.

"After we visited the first time," she said, meeting giant dragon eyes as she carefully chose words, given how very red they were. "You two went off to talk. Did you discuss *any* of this?"

Silence.

"You were talking for hours. What did you talk *about*?"

"The Tower. The Tower, the Tower's question, the necessity of the Towers, *Ravellon*."

"You didn't talk about what Karriamis said about being guardian of your race at all?"

"No."

"You know you're allowed to bring things up, right? That's why it's called a discussion?"

"She is allowed privacy. Had she wished to discuss it, she would have mentioned it herself."

Kaylin was frustrated.

Don't be. If you're angry at Emmerian for not opening discussions about extremely personal, difficult subjects...

Yes?

It's what I do. Severn's internal voice was soft.

But doesn't that put the pressure and onus entirely on Bellusdeo?

Do you feel that the pressure of any discussion we have is entirely on you?

It's not the same thing.

You understand that I want to be helpful to you, don't you?

She nodded.

I understand why Emmerian chose not to open this particular discussion. It's the source of most of her conflict with the Dragon Court. The former Arkon never discussed it; he didn't allow it to be discussed in his presence at all. If Bellusdeo had opened that discussion, Emmerian would have accepted it. She didn't. It's far, far too personal.

Kaylin muttered a quiet Leontine curse. *If he's going to be the actual father of her children, they're going to need to discuss things.*

They have time. And even if they didn't, even if they were both somehow mortal, time is necessary. Time. Space. Look, he cares about her. He clearly cares about her. But those feelings are his problem; they are his to untangle. If he opens that discussion, they become her problem.

But it is her problem.

Not by choice. In my opinion, he sees her clearly. Prior to Karriamis's intervention, they could have continued to interact as they have. Given time, they might have been able to build a stronger connection.

But they could still do that.

Look at him. I'd tell you to look at Bellusdeo but she's vanished, which is probably for the best. They no longer have the time to pretend none of this exists, and even if they had, Karriamis wouldn't allow it.

I don't like him.

This amused Severn.

I mean it.

I know.

He's done nothing but cause pain to people who don't deserve it. I don't even understand why this is necessary.

It's not necessary for you. But Karriamis is like Helen. He's not disinterested. His involvement will be personal should he offer Bellusdeo the Tower.

At this point, I'm not sure she'd touch it.

Severn was. *I think this is a question or a decision that Emmerian himself has to make, and Karriamis knows it. Bellusdeo is angry because, if she's willing to talk about far more than Emmerian, she, like Emmerian, doesn't step across unspoken boundaries. She knows what it would cost her; she doesn't intend others to pay a price she won't.*

I'd like to punch Karriamis in the face.

So would both Dragons.

Emmerian was not a small Dragon, if Dragons could ever be said to be small. In the muted, gray light, the blue of his scales had shifted to a color that was almost purple—not as

dark as the Imperial indigo, and not as red as Tiamaris often
was in draconic form. His wings were gathered, but not folded,
and his front legs left the ground as he extended his neck, lifting his jaw until the under-scales of chest and neck formed a
single straight line.

I think he's leaving.

He roared.

Kaylin lifted her hands to her ears as that roar echoed.

That's not an echo.

No, she thought, as the sound enlarged and the ground
beneath her feet began to truly rumble. She thought it was
Bellusdeo.

But no, the third voice that joined the two was the familiar
one. The first reply—if it was a reply—had been Karriamis.

The three draconic voices clashed and rumbled; it was like
being caught in a thunderstorm—from inside the clouds.
There was no place to which she could retreat, and no polite
way to muffle the sound.

It might have helped if she could understand what the three
were saying, but if she'd shown aptitude for learning unfamiliar languages, she doubted that extended to the draconic. They
weren't even supposed to be speaking it in the open streets or
public areas because…it sounded like a disaster. Even if people could get used to it, it would cause nothing but hideous
traffic jams when horses panicked, horses not being stupid.

She wasn't surprised to see a gold dragon crash through
the sky—and shatter it. The shards dissipated before Kaylin
could move her hands from her ears to her face, and a tunnel appeared to form above what had been sky, as if they had
been stranded at the bottom of a dry, empty well and could
only now see the walls.

The walls, that is, that weren't gold and orange and red;
Bellusdeo's roar contained fire. Kaylin couldn't see the color

of her eyes immediately, but didn't really want to; she knew they'd be blood red.

What she hadn't expected was the presence of the third Dragon.

He was not gold, not red, not indigo or blue or purple; he was not green—which was often the color of Dragons in art and storybooks. He reminded her of Kavallac, the Arbiter librarian, although she couldn't say why; he was...white or silver or something in between—like a Dragon ghost, and not an actual Dragon.

Bellusdeo's fire hit him.

So did Emmerian's.

She would have been surprised had either injured him, and she remained unsurprised, but the fire didn't pass through him; he wasn't insubstantial; both streams struck him and pierced him, and he seemed to absorb the white and orange and yellow, his scales shifting in color as he did.

It was almost disturbing.

Had he chosen to return fire, she might have moved. His mouth was open, but his words weren't accompanied by flame, or even streams of speckled cloud.

The marks on her arms were glowing a bright, bright gold.

She wasn't surprised to see them rise, leaving her skin as if they were concentric, moving bracers; she lowered her hands.

"I think," a familiar voice said into the ears she had just exposed, "it's time to leave."

"Past time," she told Mandoran. "Is it safe?"

"About as safe as any place that features enraged Dragons trying to destroy something, yes." That was Terrano.

"Is Sedarias here?"

"Sedarias was with Bellusdeo—I don't think she joined her in the descent."

"She didn't," Terrano confirmed.

She felt two hands on either of her arms.

"You might want to close your eyes," Mandoran said. "We're not moving through normal space here."

"Portal space?"

"You said it was okay inside the Hallionne. This should be like that."

She closed her eyes.

The Dragons could still be heard when the trio landed, if *landing* was even the right word. Kaylin, between them, opened her eyes; she didn't feel queasy and didn't immediately drop to her knees—which would have been difficult in any case, as her arms were still attached to Terrano and Mandoran, and they weren't kneeling.

They stood in a long, stone hall, the ceilings high enough to allow Dragons some flight; they were certainly wide enough and empty enough.

Sedarias was standing there, arms folded, expression pinched. She opened her mouth, but her words were lost to the sound of Dragon rage. If Kaylin couldn't understand the words, she couldn't ignore the tone.

You are an idiot. Sedarias chose to mouth the words, lips moving emphatically over very familiar syllables. *Teela is worried.*

"She's not allowed to worry about me," Kaylin shouted. Dragons clearly had humongous lungs; there was almost no break into which normal words could be wedged.

"You tell her that," Sedarias shouted back.

She's not here, Severn added.

You're sure?

She felt his nod.

"We should leave," Sedarias said.

"But—"

"He is unlikely to kill her. Or Lord Emmerian. Not when they're like this."

The roaring grew in volume; some of the pillars to either side seemed suddenly remarkably fragile. One cracked. Sedarias was right.

Leaving was easier said than done. The stone hall was longer than city blocks; Karriamis could have easily housed all of Elani in it. And while she hated much of Elani street, she wouldn't really want to see it buried under tons of falling rock.

The entire hall shuddered, emphasizing the end fate of anything that remained in it. Kaylin had no doubt that the cohort could avoid falling rock; she was far less sure of herself.

Hope squawked loudly in her ear. *The rock will not kill you.* His tone implied, "if I haven't, and I'm reconsidering."

She had entirely forgotten his presence in Emmerian's prison. He had not made a single sound.

I did make the attempt. Given the presence of Lord Emmerian, I decided against forcing the issue, but I am not pleased.

"Can you please remember that I'm not the one who trapped us there?"

Hope snorted. *You wish to turn left here.*

Since left more or less looked like the same configuration of shaking pillars and stone floor, Kaylin grimaced. Whatever it was Hope saw, she didn't.

Clearly the cohort didn't see it either.

"Sedarias!"

Sedarias came to a halt and turned toward Kaylin, her eyes blue, her expression annoyed.

"Hope says turn left here!"

The addition of the familiar's name made a clear difference. "Does he say what's to the left?"

She shook her head.

Sedarias gave Hope a very pointed glare. But she nodded to Terrano and Mandoran, and the entire small group headed toward the left. Beyond the closest pillar, Kaylin saw more wall; there was no door, no arch, to indicate that anything but wall existed.

Hope squawked loudly. The volume wasn't necessary; Hope's voice was either close enough to her ear Dragons shouting didn't swamp it, or magical in nature. Or both.

Kaylin didn't understand the squawking, which meant his words weren't aimed at her. She no longer required him. It wasn't a branching hallway they were looking for. It was the pillar itself. She closed her eyes as she approached it, collided—gently—with its curved, engraved surface—and then passed through it.

The roar of Dragons "conversing" vanished, which caused her to open her eyes and pivot. She saw Sedarias, Terrano, Mandoran. There was no pillar, and no obvious door, but absent either, this was a room that reminded Kaylin very much of Helen's parlor when they had significant guests. There were chairs here, and the walls were adorned with shelves that held both books and the assorted detritus of various tenants. There was even a window that took up half of one wall; sunlight fell to the carpeted floor, without so much as a dust mote to break its beams.

"It's only the three of you?" Kaylin asked.

"Here, yes."

"Only three of you came to Karriamis?"

Sedarias shrugged, but behind her, Mandoran rolled his eyes. "Karriamis didn't appear to be open to visitors."

"So you just walked in without an invitation?"

"Bellusdeo insisted. Look—I've never seen her eyes that color before, and even if the rest of the fief is composed of flimsy, mortal buildings, from what you've said, the ones that are still standing are full of actual people. We didn't think—"

"You didn't," Sedarias corrected him.

"—that the immediate buildings would survive. She was

looking for a fight. There aren't a lot of Dragons in this fief at best guess; people were probably huddling under tables. Point is, they weren't fleeing their homes to get as far from the fire-blast radius as possible.

"So Terrano offered to let her in."

"Me?"

"Fine. Terrano *and* I offered to let her in."

"Who else did you let in?"

"Sedarias."

Food appeared on the largest of the tables. Kaylin wasn't hungry, but it didn't occur to her that the food itself was poisoned; Karriamis had many, many ways of killing them all. Or at least killing Kaylin, Emmerian, and Bellusdeo; the rest of the cohort were accustomed to getting around the rules and laws of a Hallionne. Towers were created to stand against the incursions of Shadow; they hadn't been built to take the cohort into account.

She once again communicated with her partner. *We're out. Emmerian and Bellusdeo aren't. Who else is here?*

Annarion entered behind Sedarias. *Allaron and Karian are with me; I think the rest of the cohort remained with Helen.*

I doubt it. They're probably in the fief somewhere.

According to Sedarias, Helen disapproved of their intent. She didn't try to keep them locked up; she argued. Nothing she said could reach Bellusdeo—again, according to Sedarias—but the cohort chose to split up. Helen made clear that there was a risk; she considered Annarion far enough along in his lessons that he could head to the fiefs.

Karian as well. She strongly urged Sedarias to leave Torrisant and Fallessian behind, and given they intended to enter the fiefs...

She nodded. A large, destructive battle—a battle that had cost the Hawks and the Swords dearly—had occurred in Elantra because of the cohort, or more particularly, Annarion. Something about their presence could be felt and heard by creatures that lived in *Ravellon*, and Candallar was closer to *Ravellon*.

Where are you guys, anyway?

We haven't left the foyer. I think Annarion is probably scouting and relaying that information back to Sedarias. Karriamis has made no attempt to throw you all out?

Not yet.

Has he spoken to you at all?

No. He's clearly willing to speak to the Dragons. Kaylin winced. *I think he'll have time to speak if Bellusdeo and Emmerian don't somehow manage to reduce his Avatar to ashes. They were trying when I left.*

I don't think they have any chance of succeeding.

Kaylin was less certain. *It's an Avatar, so no. It's only if they're really determined to take the Tower out that they'll do anything intelligent. Right now they're both...angry.*

She felt something different from Severn then: confusion.

What is it? What's happened?

A different voice—a familiar voice—said, *We are knocking on the door, and I believe the corporal can hear us.*

It was Nightshade.

22

Wait, who is "we"?

An' Teela and I.

Why? To Severn, she said, I thought you said Teela wasn't coming. It's Teela and Nightshade at the door. Possibly Tain as well, although Nightshade hasn't mentioned him by name.

Severn came to a decision; he answered the knock. Teela, without Tain, was standing beside Nightshade in the large frame.

"Where is Karriamis?" Teela asked.

"He's apparently occupied at the moment—he has two angry Dragons on his hands." He stopped as he looked more closely at the weapons Teela and Nightshade now bore. Because he did, Kaylin saw them as well.

"We have a problem," Teela told him, speaking Elantran.

Severn, not stupid, added one and one together. "The outcaste is on the move?"

"The outcaste is on the move."

"Alone?"

"What do you think?"

Why now? He'd been holed up in *Ravellon* since his failed attempt to somehow corrupt the Aerians. Or so she'd assumed. But he'd been in the Aerie *as* an Aerian. He could take Aerian form; he could probably take any form he damn well wanted. Which meant he could have been causing trouble anywhere.

But she was certain, given the weapons Teela and Nightshade now carried, that he hadn't bothered with that subterfuge. He was draconic.

Sedarias was clearly receiving the same information Kaylin had, albeit from a different source.

"Do you think the outcaste wants the Tower?" Kaylin asked. The question filled the room, and Severn heard it as well.

"The Tower would not take him," Sedarias replied, which wasn't entirely a no. "I think he's here for Bellusdeo."

"Why?"

"Why do you think? She's the only female Dragon. We've all been concerned—don't make that face, you already know this—about Imperial Dragon babies. That would, however, be entirely preferable to outcaste Dragon babies."

"You think he wants children?"

"If he has any dynastic ambitions, yes. In the end, we all require them if our lines are to continue."

"Wait, do you want them?"

"*All* dynastic ambitions, Kaylin."

The idea of Sedarias as a mother caused a mental cramp. She shook her head to clear it. "Bellusdeo would kill him first. If she knows he's here, and her mood hasn't gotten any better, that's the first thing she's going to try."

"She is not a fool." Sedarias's tone implied that Kaylin certainly was. "Annarion is going to join his brother."

"Are you sure that's a good idea?"

"I'm sure it's a terrible idea," Sedarias replied, eyes a darker blue than they had been. "But I'll be there as well."

"There's no door here."

"And?"

"I don't think you have a reliable way to join them."

Even Mandoran rolled his eyes. "Look, we can't do anything with the two raging Dragons. I don't think they need us. We might be able to do something about the outcaste, especially if we have two of The Three here. And if he starts to attack here, those rickety buildings surrounding the Tower are going to get flattened without any effort on his part. Preserving them would be harder."

Kaylin turned to Hope.

Hope, however, shook his head. *It is the same,* he told her. *You must be willing to sacrifice something of value if you wish me to intercede to save the fieflings. It is not something you could do on your own; it is not something you could do with your marks. Not as you are.*

She grimaced. On days like these, she was grateful that she wasn't the Emperor, wasn't a fieflord, wasn't, in fact, a ruler of anything. The choices she could make without consequence were far more varied than the choices the Emperor could make. She thought it would be exhausting.

Fine. We'll figure it out ourselves.

Hope nodded.

Kaylin turned to the three members of the cohort in time to see them become transparent, losing solidity as they did.

"Hey!"

Mandoran rematerialized.

"Don't leave me here—take me with you."

"We will," Sedarias said, although she could no longer be seen, "if you promise that we won't have to endure your endless whining afterward."

"No good," Terrano added. He, too, could no longer be seen. "Teela wants us to leave you here."

"There's nothing I can do here!"

"Teela asks, 'And your point is?'"

Kaylin replied in Leontine. Nightshade was amused.

"I can get people to leave their homes."

"You've already said that being homeless in the fiefs is almost a death sentence."

"Even fieflings won't stay in a burning building—but they'll get trapped in one that's crushed."

"Teela says she'd like you to use your head for a change."

"What's that supposed to mean?"

"Karriamis, this close to the outcaste, has actual power. You have both Bellusdeo and Emmerian, and if you can get them to stop arguing, the outcaste will be far, far less of a threat."

"She wants me—*me*—to interrupt *three Dragons* while they're fighting?"

"She wants you to get their attention, and she believes you can."

Severn didn't like it, but didn't disagree. Sedarias, Terrano, and Mandoran fell silent, which probably meant they'd left to join their cohort.

Nightshade probably wasn't going to be happy to see Annarion. She'd always wanted a sibling, but had come to understand that sibling relationships weren't always all they were cut out to be. Or at least not Barrani siblings.

She stood in a hall that could accommodate flying Dragons and began to look for a door. At least she wouldn't have to keep screaming just to be heard.

Hope bit her ear. She reached up and inserted her hand between his small jaws and the rest of her ear when he let go. "What?"

He huffed. The breath was visible, a small cloud of hanging gray and colored particles. Although all of the Barrani of her acquaintance turned practically green when he breathed anywhere near them, she was more worried about Dragons and fieflings than a cloud of strange smoke.

This, he said, annoyed, *I can help with. Unless you'd prefer to spend hours pounding doorless walls and pillars.*

"Can you keep me alive while I try to get the attention of at least two enraged Dragons?"

Yes. If Karriamis chooses to intervene—against you—I am less certain of my answer; the range of weapons at his disposal in this place is much less predictable.

Kaylin nodded. Hope lifted himself off her shoulder and flew, and she followed.

The ground shook, and the cracks in the pillars that had caused her to abandon this hall in the first place were wider. But she knew, if it felt like stone, it wasn't; it was part of the Tower. Karriamis could kill her easily if he wanted her dead. He could preserve her if he wanted her alive. If he was aware of her at all.

She came to a stop, skidding on smooth stone, when she saw the fissure that bisected the hall. Red and orange light radiated upward; it looked like a vision of the hells. She didn't ask Hope if this was where she needed to go; she knew.

The Dragons no longer encased their roaring with syllables; the cries were raw, but this close she could almost hear the differing textures, and she wondered then if anger had always, always been mixed with so much *pain.*

She kind of wanted to strangle Karriamis right now; her anger didn't have a lot of pain in it. But that wouldn't help Bellusdeo or Emmerian, and it wouldn't help Teela, the cohort, or Nightshade.

Shouting her lungs out wouldn't help, either. Closing her eyes, she looked at her arms, and the marks—which were glowing blue—left her skin. She could see them clearly—but could also see the marks imprinted on parts of her body her eyes couldn't normally reach.

Today, she felt their weight. They'd become so heavy she was forced to her knees; this wasn't what the marks normally did.

But she couldn't wait, couldn't sit here and let the marks themselves decide what it was she was supposed to do. She *knew* what she had to accomplish.

She didn't know *how*.

Words were tools—but they had to be understood, right? She had to understand them, to put them together, to make sense of things. That was the point of language.

Why the Ancients had thought it was a good idea to have so damn *many* different languages was a constant irritation. But she didn't want to give up her mother tongue; she couldn't reasonably expect others to want to give up theirs. She'd learned how to speak Leontine, Aerian, Barrani. She needed to learn how to speak...

True Words.

What, then, did she need these words to do? What could she ask of them? "Make my voice louder"? "Make my words clearer"? But if she said the wrong thing, if she couldn't break the cycle of anger and rage and pain, volume didn't matter.

Yes, she needed to communicate.

But they had to be willing—or able—to listen. Kaylin in a rage didn't think clearly; Bellusdeo in a rage didn't either.

She had no idea what Emmerian did with rage; whether it ruled him or he ruled it. At the moment, she was pretty certain it was the former. He'd immediately turned on Karriamis when the Avatar had appeared. Bellusdeo hadn't been far behind.

Hells, if normal daggers could injure the Tower, Kaylin might have been tempted to join in. But only briefly.

What she *really* needed was a giant bucket of extremely cold water that she could just upend over the damn crevice. Something entirely different from what the three Dragons were doing now—which probably involved claws, teeth, wings, and fire. Things that caused a different type of pain, maybe in an attempt to avoid the deeper one.

Kaylin understood this.

She hadn't expected it of Emmerian or Karriamis, the latter of whom was ancient, which meant old enough to Know Better.

But no. Old or not, ancient or not, they were people, and people who'd had more than enough time to amass a world of pain. Kaylin had had two and a bit decades, and mortal memory being what it was, she probably didn't remember a lot of it clearly anymore.

She was pretty certain that the marks themselves wouldn't turn into a giant bucket full of ice-cold water. They probably couldn't be used as a bracing slap in the face either. She needed something...something...

Silence.

Silence. Quiet. The peace that existed when the silence wasn't a product of conflict. The whole of the congregation of moving, circling marks stilled. They began to recede, to once again occupy her skin—all save one.

It would have taken hundreds of words—she'd've spent them gladly if she were good with them—to describe what she now felt, to define it, to speak it clearly in any of the languages she knew. And even then, she thought she'd fail to fully explain, to fully capture, what this particular silence was.

She might have expected that it would be a simple rune, not a complicated one; she'd've been wrong. It was dense with lines and squiggles, and three dots were set in an almost triangular pattern contained by the rest of the structure. But if she thought more about it, this made sense: silence had many textures, and peace had many textures.

She caught the rune in the palm of her hand and quickly brought her second hand to bear, because the mark grew, maintaining the pattern, but...enlarging it. Here, lines that resembled delicate brush strokes became solid enough to carry the weight of an entire department's worth of coats. They became substantially heavier; she was glad that she'd already dropped to her knees to brace herself, because it was necessary.

"I could use a little help here," she grunted.

Hope sighed. He could hear her clearly, and she could hear him, although the Dragons hadn't become significantly quieter. Not yet.

I do not believe it is wise to send Bellusdeo out of the Tower at this precise moment.

"We don't know what else is attacking—no, shut up." The mark wavered, becoming momentarily transparent. She lost the thread of the thought that had allowed her to even find the damn thing, and struggled to bring it back.

Hope snorted. *This, I can do. You are a very odd master. I am not displeased with you, but cannot decide if you are kind or cowardly.*

She knew the moment he began to transform. He became equal in size to most of the Dragons.

The size was helpful, and the wings—in other circumstances—allowed flight when he was willing to carry her. She thought the mark was heavier than she was, or was becoming heavier.

It has not changed, Hope said. *It is your perception of it that has, no more. You could do this without my interference, but you rely on the paradigms with which you are familiar. You are very odd,* he repeated. He set a clawed paw beneath the weight of the mark. *You are certain?*

She was.

He walked it to the edge of the crevice that split the ground, and dropped it in.

Kaylin was certain the Dragons still shouted, but a silence fell across the great hall, and it seemed to spread—as if it were ice to their fire, calm to their fury. She rose, her legs tingling as blood flow returned to the parts below her knees.

The red and orange of fire and melted stone faded until the color in the hall was once again gray. She listened—but she wasn't certain for what; she had wanted silence, and she'd been given it. Very carefully, she peered down the crevice. She could see glints of gold and glints of blue, although the blue was dark and less immediately visible.

"Move," Bellusdeo shouted up at Kaylin.

Kaylin backed up, and then backed up again for good measure. Both Dragons remained in their draconic forms, but they'd have to. The bottom of the crevice was a long way down, and even in mortal form, they were heavy enough that they couldn't leap up to the ground on which Kaylin stood.

"Okay," she said to her familiar—who had immediately shed the larger size. "What were you saying before?"

It is not necessarily wise to send Bellusdeo out. If what your friends feel is true, she is most at risk. You have seen her lose her temper—as you put it—twice in a very short period of time; she is unsettled. This is not likely to make her more settled.

"Yeah, but if she finds out we didn't tell her, she's going to be pissed off for decades, and I have to live with her."

If Karriamis accepts her—and I cannot, frankly, see how, given the events of today—she will not be living with you.

"Helen would never keep her out."

Hope snorted. *Because you wouldn't. She will still have permission to visit the Halls of Law and to accompany you on your regular duties.*

Bellusdeo cut the conversation short by landing. Emmerian followed. She thought the blue Dragon was injured, but couldn't tell at this distance; he didn't transform, and she thought injuries would be more obvious if he had.

Bellusdeo's eyes were orange. Emmerian's eyes were orange. Peace, such as it was, had returned them not to a happy

place, but to a cautious one. She didn't see Karriamis. As if
the thought were an invocation, the last of the Dragons flew
up, to the height of the ceiling. He did not land.

In this light he seemed copper, or perhaps orange with a
silver cast to the color. She knew Dragon color could shift—
as their eyes did—with emotion, but Bellusdeo had always
remained gold.

"Chosen," Karriamis said, in full draconic rumble.

Kaylin ignored him. She headed toward Bellusdeo, but
stopped short as her housemate lifted her head in warning.
She glanced at Emmerian, who had turned his head to look
up at Karriamis's draconic Avatar.

"Before the three of you start up again, we have a small
emergency."

Karriamis said nothing. Bellusdeo, however, turned immediately to Kaylin. "What's happened?"

"Well, half of the cohort decided to follow you here. Or
get here before you."

"That's not generally considered an emergency."

"No. Teela was minding her own business, but she's here.
Nightshade is here."

"Lord Nightshade is in *my* fief?" Karriamis's voice was
thunder.

"Yes. He has eyes and he watches his border, and something
rose out of *Ravellon* and flew here."

Bellusdeo growled, "Climb," to Kaylin. Kaylin struggled
up her back and took a seat as the Dragon began to run. The
hall elongated; it was a trick Kaylin had seen before.

"Karriamis—we don't have time."

Karriamis roared. If he had been affected by the mark of
the Chosen at all, it wasn't obvious. Emmerian pushed off
the ground, his wings snapping out and moving as he gained
speed.

The Tower's Avatar flew. He could cover far more ground

than the normal Dragons could, and did; he landed in front of them and spread his wings. It was not a gesture of peace. He roared again.

Bellusdeo stopped, skidding across stone.

Emmerian, however, did not. He turned to the gold Dragon. "I'll go."

"I'll be right there."

Kaylin started to dismount, and Bellusdeo growled. Clearly Emmerian was considered independent enough to make his own decision, and Kaylin was not.

To Severn, she said, *Emmerian's coming.*

I heard. Tell Nightshade.

He's not with you?

No. He and Teela headed into the street.

"That is unwise," Karriamis said. "This is not the fief of Nightshade; he is far more vulnerable to attack here than he would be should he stand his ground in his own fief."

"He also has a personal score to settle with the outcaste; the outcaste interfered with his fief. He's not stupid enough to go *into Ravellon* to reach him, but if he comes out..."

"Perhaps you did not hear me."

"Nightshade wields one of The Three. And Teela wields one as well. Look—they've fought Dragons before. They've survived."

"Outcaste Dragons are not Dragons," Karriamis snapped.

"No. Not entirely. But—Teela isn't entirely Barrani either, and never say that where she can hear it. Her companions are here, and they're definitely not normal Barrani. You met one. Mandoran. And Terrano. The swords were made to fight Dragons, and I've seen them in use."

"The outcaste did not come here alone."

Bellusdeo exhaled smoke. No fire, not yet. "Show us— please show us—what's happening in the fief."

"I cannot divert the power to do so," Karriamis replied.

His eyes were no longer Dragon eyes; they were shadow eyes, obsidian and flecked with moving color. "This is very poorly timed."

"For you," Kaylin replied. "It's not poorly timed for the outcaste—he must know you have no captain. We need to join our friends."

"No, you do not. Your Sedarias understands why the outcaste has come. It is not to take the Tower; he would not survive his entry should he be bold enough or foolish enough to make the attempt. It is entirely about Bellusdeo."

The Dragon tensed beneath Kaylin.

"He can *try*." Kaylin didn't need to see the color of the Dragon's eyes. She knew.

"Bellusdeo—" Before she could speak, Hope did. In his angry squawking voice, which happened to be beside Kaylin's left ear.

This didn't make Bellusdeo any less tense.

"He is right," Karriamis said. He began to dwindle into a more familiar, mortal form. "If you follow me, you may see the state of the streets and the skies. You may make your decision at that time. I admit I am curious; I did not see The Three in active use."

"But you knew of them."

"Of course. We all did."

Bellusdeo exhaled again, told Kaylin to get off of her back, and then resumed the much more familiar "mortal" form. "Lead," she told the Avatar.

He raised a brow at her tone but nodded and turned.

Lead in this case had a slightly different meaning than it would in another building. The hall contracted without narrowing, and they reached the end of it between the first step and the second. The end led to stairs, and the stairs led up. They were wide—too wide, in Kaylin's opinion; they were also tall, but the width made the height seem shorter than it actually was. They were constructed around a central pillar, very much like the stairs that occupied Helen's training room, but at least these had rails, and the drop over the rails was well lit and ended in floor.

"They are constructed for your use, of course," Karriamis said. "Stop dawdling."

Kaylin would have resented this more, but Bellusdeo was jogging up the stairs. She was taller than Kaylin in this form but not by *that* much. Kaylin therefore sped up, allowing Bellusdeo to set the pace.

The stairs ended on a wide landing, and the landing became a large, wooden floor that extended without obvious doors or arches separating it from the stairs.

"I find them too fussy," Karriamis said.

Bellusdeo didn't hear him. She followed the floor until it reached wall—although *wall* was the wrong word for it, as it was mostly window, and appeared to be open to the air. They had reached the Tower's height; beneath them, the fief of Candallar spread out. The Dragon wasn't looking at the fief.

She was looking at the skies, and what the skies contained. Shadows flew—but no, Kaylin thought, they couldn't be Shadow. The Towers had control of the space. But they could be like the outcaste: not one thing, not the other. She didn't understand—couldn't understand—how the outcaste could get past all of the Tower barriers that kept *Ravellon* and its occupants caged.

At the heart of a cloud of wings was the outcaste; he was ebon, and wing-tip to wing-tip the size of Bellusdeo. As he approached with what seemed either escort or soldiers, she recognized the forms and the wings: Aerian. These were Aerian. But their wings? They were as black as the outcaste Dragon.

Kaylin turned to Karriamis, who stood at a distance. "Well?"

He met her eyes, his obsidian. "Well?"

"Did you *allow* Candallar's friend to take a Shadow you knew was there? Or was the Shadow masked somehow by its carrier?"

"I would not have sensed it," he finally replied. Bellusdeo wheeled.

"But you said—"

"I said I had hope, Lord Kaylin. I said that the outcome, in the end, was fortuitous. I said that I was aware of the plan."

"You're lying."

"Yes." He was watching the skies. "The outcaste, as the Barrani Lord, masters; he is not mastered by. I am aware of him; were he to land in my streets, I would know. But I would not know that he was of Shadow, or that he had consumed it; I would know because he is outcaste, and I am now aware of his existence.

"He entered the fief of Nightshade, I believe."

Kaylin nodded.

"I think members of your cohort have taken to the air."

Kaylin couldn't see them. Neither could Bellusdeo—but at the moment, Bellusdeo had eyes for only one creature: the outcaste. Everything else was irrelevant detritus. Kaylin could see her face in profile, but didn't need to look to know the color of her eyes.

"Look," Karriamis said quietly, his voice much closer to her ear than the rest of him.

She did.

Bellusdeo's eyes were orange with deep, deep flecks of crimson. Rage had not fully transformed their color. "How permeable is this window?" she asked, the question almost casual.

Karriamis wasn't fooled. "As you suspect, the window can serve as a portal."

The gold Dragon slid her hands behind her back as she watched.

Emmerian had reached the street; he had joined Teela and Nightshade, dwarfing them in his draconic form. Kaylin couldn't hear what they were saying.

No, wait. She *could*.

Nightshade. She didn't have to ask. He let her in as she closed her own eyes and looked through his. Emmerian and Teela were speaking; Nightshade, sword unsheathed, observed the skies while he listened.

"We have never attempted to fight a war as a cohesive unit," the blue Dragon rumbled. "I do not feel that today is the correct time to make the attempt."

"It won't be the first time I've ridden on a Dragon's back. *Kariannos* is capable of ranged attack, as you should *well* know."

"I know that the sword was effective against Dragons when you did not have the simple option of flight," the Dragon snapped.

How long have they been going at it?

Subjectively?

Objectively, Kaylin snapped, as annoyed as Teela sounded.

Since Lord Emmerian emerged from the Tower. I confess I do not understand the outcaste's target, here. Karriamis will not accept the outcaste as its lord. There is a small possibility that other Towers might, but Karriamis is a Dragon at heart.

Kaylin was appalled. *The other Towers are occupied.*

Yes. Clearly the outcaste understands that if damage is to be done in any significant fashion, it is to be done before the Tower takes a captain.

Kaylin turned to Karriamis. "How limited are your powers if you have no captain?"

"Against Shadows I can perceive, I have no limits."

"And these?"

"Are not Shadow as it was once perceived. I am *old*, Lord Kaylin. And I fail to understand why you, as Chosen, remain within the Tower."

"Bullshit." Bellusdeo reached out and place a very heavy palm on Kaylin's shoulder—which was not her mouth. She took the unspoken warning.

Karriamis smiled. "It is not a lie. I fail to understand how you—with your paltry decades of probable life should you learn to be cautious—do not *understand* how to invoke the power of the marks of the Chosen. In other worlds and at other times, the weapons of the Barrani would be irrelevant in comparison. As would Lord Emmerian, and even Bellusdeo."

Kaylin turned toward the stairs, or tried; Bellusdeo's grip tightened. "I need that shoulder," she snapped.

"It's a collarbone, and yes, you do. Do not let him goad you."

"Why not? You did!"

Emmerian took to the sky. He was carrying Teela.

Yes, Nightshade said. *Annarion and Sedarias offered to...show her how to take advantage of very specific weight reduction to...climb, I believe. It is not something An'Teela has done before, and Lord Emmerian, given the nature of the cohort, wished to avoid any other unpredictable catastrophes.*

Where are the rest of the cohort?

I believe they are attempting to convince the occupants of the buildings that directly surround the Tower to leave. He thought it a waste of time. This predictably annoyed Kaylin.

It is a waste because they will not be heeded. They themselves are not in any danger yet, but the mortals who shelter here will not be moved except by force—and force takes far more time. Will Bellusdeo join us?

No. But I'm pretty sure we're going to see Tiamaris soon.

Indeed.

Kaylin fell silent for a long beat. *You don't think it's going to be enough.*

I think the Aerians have been in Ravellon, and while they are not of Shadow, they have been transformed. Ah, no, he added, *the words are not precise. Ask Karriamis what happens when those who are infected by Shadow are overcome by it.*

"The living are not all of one thing, they are not all of another. Especially mortals. While they are bound by simple truths—birth, death—everything in between can be radically different. They have mortal forms, of course—but those might take damage, they might lose arms, legs, eyes or hearing; they have different proclivities, and in a matter of a simple decade they can transform so much they might not be recognizable as the same individuals without prior experience.

"They are already shifting, mutable existences; they age. Tests for purity could not be performed on mortals. Not even your animals." He glanced at Kaylin. "There is a reason your Ferals exist; a reason they can leave *Ravellon* and return to it. The Towers were not created to prevent their escape; they were not created to take note of each rodent that crosses the border."

Bellusdeo pulled a piece of rock from the window frame as the outcaste drew closer.

"Therefore Shadow of a certain type can enter a mortal; it can make changes. You yourself have experienced this; you bear Shadow now as an intrinsic part of your hand. It is not, however, sentient. Such a power is a tool, just as sword or bow might be."

Bellusdeo growled. Her hand, however, remained on Kaylin's shoulder.

"The danger with Shadow as a power—a summoned power—is the sentience. Summon fire, water, earth, air, and you are aware of the danger of that sentience, such as it is; it is a battle of, a contest of, will. Shadow is not, and has never been, the same. It is far less elemental, and it does not require the exercise of will in the same fashion; it is far more subtle.

"However, I feel you are not asking the correct question, and Bellusdeo grows impatient. The outcaste is powerful enough that he can carry that Shadow; it will not overwhelm him. He is intelligent enough to understand, however, the limits of those who fly at his side now.

"They could pass the barrier we created when they first left *Ravellon* by air. They would not, however, pass it so easily now. In an hour, perhaps two, they will be hollowed out, dead, and yet ambulatory."

"Can't you do something about them?"

"Soon, Chosen."

23

Tiamaris did fly in; Kaylin could see him as a glint of red that hurtled toward the fief—and its attackers—as if he were a ball of fire. He was, to her knowledge, the only other fieflord who could take immediately to the sky to deal with threats to his fief.

Or to Candallar's, apparently.

Bellusdeo's hand twitched. "Tell him to turn back," she said.

Karriamis did not reply.

Bellusdeo turned. The Avatar was no longer in the room. Kaylin had enough warning to clap her hands over her ears as the gold Dragon roared.

There was no answering roar. But the stairs had apparently vanished with the Tower's Avatar. Kaylin kept her hands firmly in place while Bellusdeo roared in outrage; she thought she could hear Leontine roll over her shaking hands.

The problem with angry Dragons was their size. While size didn't necessarily imply strength, in the case of Dragons, it didn't matter; the subtleties of stronger or weaker were only relevant to other Dragons. Kaylin had no physical way of restraining Bellusdeo if she chose to go full Dragon.

There was enough room in the Tower that she *could*, and Kaylin suffered no illusion; she moved away as Bellusdeo's physical form began to shiver in place.

She had words. "Don't! It's *you* he wants! It's *always* been you he wants!"

Bellusdeo's roar was caught between a mortal throat and the expanding depth of a Dragon's. Kaylin lost voice for a moment as Emmerian's breath lit the sky with a cone of fire. Most of the Aerians were flexible enough—fast enough—to drop or rise to avoid the flame's heat; the heart of the fire was met with...fire. The outcaste's fire.

It was red and purple, to red and orange, but the core of both cones was almost white.

A glint of sword could be seen, but Teela hadn't summoned the power of the blade, not yet.

From the ground, however, Nightshade did. Lightning leaped up, and up again, clipping the outcaste's wing before he could withdraw it; he was pinned in place by Emmerian's fire and his own. Four of the Aerians peeled off instantly.

Kaylin had watched Aerian maneuvers at every opportunity during her tenure at the Halls of Law. She was impressed. They moved as one; even the fold of wings as they dived was synchronized. They were armed, although the Aerians could do a great deal of damage with their wings.

Nightshade's experience with flying enemies was largely draconic. He backed into an alley made of the buildings the cohort had not yet emptied. She saw a glint of flying blades; Severn had unhooked his weapons and set the chain spinning. Never a good sign.

She turned; the single advantage of Bellusdeo's almost transition was that she'd been forced to let Kaylin's shoulder go.

Kaylin went immediately in search of the damn stairs. "Karriamis, you son of a—"

"I would not say that, were I you," the disembodied Dragon said. "I understand that you are not responsible for your thoughts, and I therefore tolerate a certain lack of necessary respect."

"Respect is *earned*."

"Respect is a necessary element of survival."

"What are you even doing? Where did the damn stairs go?"

"I am waiting," he replied, in a tone that the Arkon—the former Arkon—might have used.

"For *what*?"

"She was Empress. Queen, if you will. She ruled. It is hard, watching her reactions, to understand this, or even to believe it; I believe it because I have seen some of her memories."

If Karriamis were in front of her now, Kaylin wasn't certain she wouldn't have tried to stab him.

"Yes. You might. I would not, however, kill you in response. You fail to understand what she was—you see what she is, what's left in the wake of loss. I wish to see some proof that what she was has not been utterly destroyed by loss."

"Why?"

"Because she is, regardless, the future of her race. She has just commanded Tiamaris to withdraw."

As if she could hear Karriamis, Bellusdeo once again resumed her human form; the lines of transformation that blurred body and allowed for the change had once again hardened. Her back was to Kaylin, her gaze on the sky itself.

Tiamaris, however, was now hovering.

"Why does she want him to go away? The outcaste is a danger to all of you."

"*You* refers to the Towers?"

Kaylin nodded.

"She understands that his power is in part dependent on

the power of his Tower—and he will not have that, here. She is not wrong, in my opinion."

"She didn't tell Nightshade to go away."

"No. Nightshade, however, has been fieflord for centuries; Tiamaris for less than a year. Lord Nightshade understands the limitations of the Tower's power and his own. And he wields one of The Three. To Bellusdeo—perhaps incorrectly—the weight of The Three is almost mythic; it dwarfs the weight of the Tower.

"She also understands that Lord Nightshade will simply fail to hear her; Tiamaris will not."

Probably why she hadn't told the cohort to get lost, as well.

"Ah, no. That is different. She acknowledges Sedarias as the leader of their flight. The analogy is not perfect, but it is surprisingly solid. Sedarias is ally, here, but allies control their own forces; they do not obey. She has not joined her friends," he added.

"Is that why you kept me here?"

"No. Had you chosen to depart with Emmerian, I would not have stopped you. But I told Bellusdeo—you were there, and mortal memory is not *that* inefficient—that she had chosen her friends well. You are one of them. But the cohort in concert is another."

"And Emmerian?"

"He is too young," Karriamis said, in a familiar—and annoying—tone of voice. "He would not be my choice, were I to be given one—but it is not my choice. It is not, as you discovered, entirely hers, either. The weight he commits to carry, however, he *will* carry; he sees her clearly."

"And Bellusdeo?"

"She has made no choices," he replied. "Since her arrival, she has made no choices. Yes, yes," he said, as Kaylin opened her mouth. "She chose to come here. But she was drifting, Lord Kaylin. It made sense to her that she become captain of this Tower, her hatred of Shadow is so strong. She was look-ing for a… I do not have the word for it. She felt that our pur-pose would match exactly, and there would be no conflict."

Kaylin snorted.

"Respect, remember. Even coming here was not a *choice*; she drifted on currents of events. But now? Now, Chosen, she makes a choice."

She was just standing in the window.

"Yes. She can leave at any moment she desires to leave."

"Does she fail, if she leaves?"

"Fail?"

"Your stupid test."

"Mortals are clearly cut from different cloth than they once were. And the answer is, it depends. I can feel her rage and fury from anywhere in the Tower, it is so visceral, so loud. The outcaste betrayed her," he added, the words softer. "She trusted him, in a long-ago world; that world is gone, and she will never trust again.

"Nor should she. But she ruled. And a ruler cannot be ruled by hatred; it is almost as bad as fear."

"You've said she's not in command of the cohort. She's *certainly* not in command of the Dragons, and if she had any ability to tell you what to do…"

"Yes?"

Respect, she thought. "She's *not* the ruler here. She doesn't exactly have an army; she doesn't have a squadron. She's—"

"Tiamaris has withdrawn, at her command. You do not understand our tongue, and that is fair—but it was a com-mand, not a request."

Bellusdeo roared again. This time, there was less rage in the voice, but more volume. Emmerian veered instantly to the left as spears of shadow skittered off his flank. The outcaste's fire wouldn't hurt him.

"You are wrong," Karriamis said, in an entirely different tone. "And now, you will stop speaking."

He was gone.

Bellusdeo once again began to shimmer in place, but this time, she was silent.

Emmerian was not; the outcaste's fire clipped his right wing, and the wing burned; the fire seemed to cling to it. The blue Dragon shifted, mobility now impaired; Kaylin could see the flash of light, of blade, of something that might have been lightning if lightning moved in circles.

From the right, the Aerians—the shadows—moved. Teela's lightning struck all but one from the air; the one did not skitter off Emmerian's side, but pierced it.

"Kaylin," Bellusdeo said, voice a rumble of sound, a distant thunder to Teela's lightning, "climb."

Outside was where Kaylin wanted to be; she instantly climbed up the gold Dragon's back. She didn't know what kind of test Karriamis intended this to be; she had no idea if, by making this decision, Bellusdeo was failing, or had failed. She didn't much care, because Bellusdeo didn't.

But as she settled on a back that wasn't really meant for riding—not that Kaylin had mastered horses, either, although her initial attempts had amused the hell out of the Swords— she heard a very familiar voice. It was raised in a cry of pain or warning, and it guttered in the middle like a doused candle's flame.

She tightened her legs, head bent to break the wind, and shouted a name as Bellusdeo leaped through a window that served as portal.

"Mandoran!"

He's alive, Severn said, before the bulk of the gold Dragon had cleared the window. *Sedarias says he's alive.*

What the hell hit him? I didn't even see him!

The Aerians. Sedarias says they're phased—what we see isn't all that's there. The parts we can't see are growing. I don't think they could have left Ravellon had they been what they are now. But now is what we're facing.

If she'd remained in the Tower, she was certain she would strangle the damn Avatar, she was so angry. *"Hope!"*

Her familiar came instantly to her shoulder and lifted a wing to cover both of her eyes.

With Hope's wing in place, she saw what Sedarias meant. For one, the Shadow that rode them was larger—taller, certainly, but also longer; it extended past the natural length of their wings, and it lengthened in tendrils from all four of their limbs.

The spears that she'd seen thrown were…still attached to their bearers, even after they'd unleashed them. Nor did they seem to have only one—the spears seemed to grow and solidify from the shadows that surrounded the Aerians, like a slow refill.

She turned in the direction Mandoran's voice had come from—but it was harder to see past Bellusdeo's head and neck, as Bellusdeo had immediately leaped toward the cutoff scream.

"Move over," Terrano said.

She could see him clearly with the aid of Hope's wing. "What are you doing?"

"I'm going to help the idiot before he gets cut in half." He raised his voice. "Bellusdeo—when I ask, give me five seconds of cover. I need you stay in one spot when I shout 'stop.'"

She didn't ask him why.

What Bellusdeo could see was clearly not what Terrano—or Kaylin, vision augmented by translucent wing—could see. What she couldn't see at all, even with Hope's wing, was Mandoran. She couldn't hear him, either.

"Relax," Terrano shouted in her ear. "He's still alive."

"Where?"

"We're about to find out. *Stop!*"

Terrano jumped off the Dragon's back.

"He better know what he's doing," Kaylin said—before she, too, came off the Dragon's back. Bellusdeo hadn't moved. Terrano had.

This time, Kaylin did shriek—but in Leontine.

"I need my ears—bad enough all the Dragons are shouting in their native tongue. Pay attention; I don't think we're going to have long."

"To do what?"

"Grab the idiot."

"I can't even see the idiot!"

"That's harsh," a familiar voice said. Mandoran. Free of Bellusdeo's back—or the large parts of her body that weren't transparent—Kaylin could finally see Mandoran.

Terrano had wrapped both arms around her midriff; he was holding her tightly enough it was almost difficult to breathe. On the other hand, down was a long way away. Her arms were free; she could see Mandoran, but only barely, even with Hope's wing plastered to her face. He was almost the storybook definition of a ghost, and she could only see his upper body. The rest was enmeshed in the overlapping strands of Aerian-carried Shadow.

"Why is it always me?" Mandoran asked, the words almost, but not quite, a whine.

"It's not always you," Kaylin snapped.

"It was in the Aerie."

"True." She reached out for his arm. Her hand passed through it. She cursed.

"Impressive," Mandoran said, grimacing. This close, she could see that he was in pain. "Sedarias is starting to tilt."

"Tilt?"

"Over the edge—I don't want to rush you, but can we get me out of here before she falls off it?"

Shadow spears flew toward where Kaylin and Terrano now hovered. Toward, Kaylin realized, Bellusdeo, who remained in position just as Terrano had asked. She spared one quick glance, saw the body of the outcaste grow larger as he approached, and turned all of her attention back to Mandoran.

And then she closed her eyes.

She could see her marks clearly, as she'd always done with closed eyes. They were glowing with a gray, steady light; none had risen. None would rise.

Her skin was the same luminous gray as the marks, as if they were all of a thing. She could see her skin. Mandoran had said that this was her way of phasing; this was her paradigm. She accepted that, although she had a few questions about seeing her own skin when her eyes were closed.

She let that go, because one of her hands was not gray—or not entirely gray. It was covered in what looked like a badly made lace glove. This was Shadow, as Karriamis had divined, but it was like...dead Shadow? Shadow separated from whatever force controlled Shadows from *Ravellon*.

And it was what she needed. She reached out for Mandoran with the gloved hand. His hand, beneath the glove, was solid. When she reached out with her right hand, it wasn't.

"We're running out of time," Terrano said. His voice was audible; the rest of him was invisible. She didn't open her eyes. If Terrano wasn't precisely where Mandoran—and Kaylin herself—were, so much the better.

"I'm *trying*."

"What exactly are you trying?"

"Can you see him?"

"Yes."

"Can you touch him?"

"No, duh. Look—we need to pull him out of there before—"

She almost lost Mandoran. She'd gripped his hand, his fingers interlocked with hers. If Terrano hadn't been holding on to her so tightly, she would have fallen; Mandoran suddenly gained weight. She met his eyes; they were entirely black, and the flecks of livid color they contained were both familiar and almost terrifying.

She tightened her grip as she lost feeling in the one hand that Mandoran could actually grasp; she was surprised she hadn't dislocated her arm. She opened her eyes.

Kaylin was grateful that Mandoran was holding on so tightly. What she held with her left hand, she could now see. None of it looked like Mandoran. Not even through Hope's wing.

"Tell the rest of the cohort what's happening here—they mustn't close in combat!"

"We didn't—"

"Let the others handle it!"

"Kaylin?" Bellusdeo said, voice a rumble.

"It's all Shadow," she snapped. "Something's grabbed Mandoran and I'm trying to—to pull him out."

"What? What's grabbed him?"

"I *don't know.* I'm not sure if he caught a spear—"

"I'm not deaf," Mandoran said. His voice was slurred, difficult to hear; there was an odd echo to the words.

"Fine—you tell us. Just don't let go." She closed her eyes again. Eyes closed, she could see Mandoran, or at least the top half of him; the rest was enveloped in something. To Kaylin's eyes, that something didn't have the visual characteristics of Shadow, not here; eyes opened, it was Mandoran himself who looked like he was slowly transforming, or slowly being transformed.

She prayed as loudly as possible that Bellusdeo couldn't

see him. Mandoran in this state might be able to survive Dragon breath; she was almost certain it would pass harmlessly through him.

Kaylin was more certain that that wasn't going to be true of either her or Terrano.

Free me. Kaylin blinked. *Kill me.*

The voice sounded like Mandoran's; the words overlapped each other. She could pick apart overlapping sentences when she was in the middle of a crowd that might, at any moment, transform into a mob, and she applied that training now.

"Say that again," she told Mandoran.

"Say what?" Terrano shouted in her ear.

"Not you—Mandoran, say that again."

"Say what?"

She wanted to shriek. The pressure of time was becoming an almost unbearable weight—worse, by far, than Mandoran. Her hand was numb. Mandoran's voice, wrapped around the same two words Terrano had spoken, was once again an odd, echoing sound, filled with words that he *hadn't* spoken.

Words.

Language.

She understood them. She understood them because both Terrano and Mandoran were speaking her mother tongue. But the overlapping words, the eddies, the echoes...weren't Elantran.

Free me.

Kill me.

The words were clearer. The texture was clearer. They weren't Elantran. She couldn't identify the language—but she understood it. Understood, in the end, what it must be. She wasn't surprised when the skin on her arms, her legs, her back, began to tingle.

No, she *was* surprised, because the "allergy to magic" problem rarely occurred when Shadow was involved. This tingle became pain, as it usually did—but pain implied magic in the here and now, magic cast with intent, by people nearby.

"Hope!"

I have you.

"Someone's casting something—"

An'Teela. And Sedarias. It will not hit you.

"No—it's different!" she shouted.

Hope did not reply. No one did.

She opened her eyes. Hope wasn't with her. Neither was Terrano; she could no longer feel his arms around her. But she didn't need them to prevent a very messy fall; she was standing on firm ground. The ground itself was stone, not dirt; there was no grass here, although she could see the hint of weeds that implied dirt beneath the stone.

The weeds, however, were purple.

To the side were buildings—or what might have been buildings; there seemed to be an organized structure to them but they certainly didn't look like the streets of Elantra, high or low. She was certain magic must have been involved in the building—and the maintenance, if any was still being done—because normal buildings would have collapsed in all kinds of disastrous ways otherwise.

But the weeds were strange, too. Almost everything was; it was like reality but slightly off. And as she gazed down the street, it was much more than slightly off.

She clenched her fist, and felt—although she couldn't see him—Mandoran's hand. She couldn't feel Terrano's arms, couldn't hear Bellusdeo or Emmerian's roars. Wherever she was now was not the same place that she had been. But Mandoran was here.

Mandoran was *almost* here.

She shifted her stance, bent into her knees, and *pulled*. There was no resistance: Mandoran immediately fell into the street. So did Kaylin. She didn't let go of his hand.

"I don't think we should be here," Mandoran said as he looked at his surroundings.

"Tell me what you see and *don't let go of my hand*."

"Why not?"

"Just tell me what you see."

"We're standing in a...street. There's something like stone beneath our feet and most of the buildings look like they're about to collapse on our heads."

She nodded. "Okay, so we're mostly seeing the same thing."

"Weren't you supposed to get me out?"

"Shut up. Can you hear the cohort?"

He nodded, but hesitantly.

"Is that a yes or a no?"

"It's a yes but...their voices are less distinct."

"Blurry? Fuzzy?"

"Not clear. Or not as clear as they normally are. Why exactly are we here? Where is this?"

Kaylin had a guess. She didn't want to say it out loud because she wanted it to be wrong in every conceivable way.

Mandoran grimaced. "How are we going to get out?"

That was the question, wasn't it?

"How did *you* get here in the first place?" the Barrani cohort member demanded.

"I don't know—I was trying to listen to your voice."

Both brows rose in the center.

Kaylin tried again. "I could hear you—but you were fuzzy. It's like...like your words were caught in some kind of tiny space and the echoes made it hard to distinguish individual syllables."

"And now?"

"Now I can hear you easily."

"Which...doesn't tell me how you wound up here."

"Because some of the blurry words I heard, some of the echoes, weren't actually from you. They weren't your words. You weren't speaking them. I needed to hear them more clearly than I could hear you."

"And?"

"So I closed my eyes and listened. And when I opened my eyes, I was here."

"Fine. What *exactly* did you hear?"

She hesitated again, and then she said, *"Free me. Kill me."*

"What?"

"You didn't understand that?"

"No. What language is it?"

"Mine."

"I think I understand yours pretty well, I hear so much of it." He frowned. "I'm saying the wrong thing, aren't I?"

"It's fine. I'm used to it. Can you hear anything?"

He listened. Barrani ears were better than mortal ears in the city streets; she had no idea whether actual ears were involved in this, because she had no idea where their physical bodies were. Admittedly, hitting the ground had probably bruised her left shoulder—but she'd have to check that when they got out of here.

If they ever did.

"Yes."

"Good, because I can't." She lifted their joined hands. "Lead on."

"Where's Hope?"

"Not here. I notice Terrano didn't come through, either. Is he still holding on to me?"

"He says no. Bellusdeo is not happy. But to be fair, Teela is *really* unhappy."

"It's not Terrano's fault."

"Like that's going to make any difference."

"Tell her it's your fault."

"Uhhh, I'll give it a pass." He began to walk down the street, avoiding the overhanging buildings, inasmuch as that was possible. Kaylin noticed they cast no shadows; if there was light here—and there must have been, as she could see—it wasn't the type of light that cast shadow.

But there were shadows here, against the ground; they didn't follow the formation of the buildings or the weeds, but she could see them. She looked at her arms; tingle had become pain. Her attempt to roll up a sleeve with one hand attached to Mandoran took time; it was clumsy enough that he chose to help. In this case, two hands were better than one—but not, honestly, by much.

However, sleeve rolled up, she could see the marks; they were, and remained, flat against her skin, but they were glowing.

The glow was a livid purple, very similar to the color of the weeds. Similar, she thought, to the purple fire that some of the Mellarionne-aligned arcanists had cast.

Kaylin. Two voices. Nightshade's. Severn's.

It was Severn she answered. *Still here. I have Mandoran, but we seem to be stuck someplace else. Does Terrano still have my body?*

No. Not that I can see. Annarion says—

Annarion's with you?

He is. He says that Terrano is holding on to something. He's not entirely sure it's you. Hope is here, he added.

Well, he's not with me. Where is he?

Beside Bellusdeo. He's not small.

What's Bellusdeo doing?

Fighting. Sorry; I can't look up for any length of time, because some of the Aerians chose to land.

Why?

Because they're trying to kill the fieflings who are close to the Tower.

Got it. Shutting up now.

She did shut up. She turned to Nightshade, metaphorically speaking. He could, and did, look up; the view on the ground was blurred by the light of *Meliannos*. He was aware of the mortals who had entered the street in a panic, but they were not his concern.

What she wanted to see was not what he wanted to see. He spoke Severn's name, and leaped, sword in hand, to the Aerians.

Be careful of the spears—they're Shadow.

I know. The reply was terse; he was irritated. Kaylin understood this was not the time to tell him something he already knew. But it wasn't clear that he did know; certainly Mandoran hadn't. She glanced at Mandoran.

"I'm not speaking to the cohort," he surprised her by saying.

"Why not?"

He shook his head. "Are you talking to Nightshade or Severn?"

"Both."

"Normally?"

She nodded.

"There's...interference when I try. And I'm not sure that the interference isn't somehow attached to the attempt. I don't think it's safe for them to talk to me the normal way."

Since *the normal way* had an entirely different meaning for Kaylin, she nodded, but she was now disturbed, and as the street didn't seem to be ending anytime soon and there were no obvious enemies lying in wait, she said, "Why do you feel it's unsafe?"

Mandoran hesitated for one long beat, and Kaylin tightened her grip on his hand, as if hesitation might cause him to vanish. "I don't know. It just... You heard something else. You heard a different voice, different words, when I used my own voice."

Kaylin nodded.

"I could almost hear it as well. I don't want to share it. I don't know what it means."

"This," she said quietly, raising her free arm. "This is what it means."

"Do you know where we are?"

She'd been avoiding it. Avoiding saying it. Avoiding thinking it. She hesitated, and then punted. "Do you?"

"I wouldn't ask if I knew, but…"

She nodded. "Don't say it. I don't think it's safe to say the word."

"So you're thinking what I'm thinking."

"I'm trying hard not to."

"Is it working?" He hesitated again. "I think something injured me and entered me—and if I were Severn or Nightshade, I would have become like the weird Aerians. But… it's not physical."

"It is physical."

"It's not."

She started to argue and stopped. Mandoran was *here*. She could grip his hand tightly. She reached out and punched his shoulder with her free hand, and this time, it didn't pass through him.

"Does that mean you can let go of my hand now?"

"Absolutely not."

He didn't seem to resent this but reached out to pat her on the head. His free hand was also solid. "So…where are we going?"

"How should I know? I wouldn't be here if I hadn't tried to reach you!"

But was that even true? She wouldn't be here if she hadn't tried very hard to hear the secondary voice that had caused Mandoran to fall silent with his cohort. She was right; something was attached to him—in the best case, because attachment implied removal—and it was that something she had followed.

Because she had understood the words.

Because they were True Words.

The marks on the one arm she exposed continued to lie dormant across her skin, but the pale, livid purple was distracting. "Do these look purple to you?"

"Yes. I've never seen them that color."

"Great. Me neither. Are the weeds here the same color?"

"Weeds?"

"Those things that are growing up from the ground?"

"I don't see weeds there."

"What do you see?"

"I don't know. I'd almost call them rips or tears in the air. You want to investigate?"

She nodded. Hope wasn't here. There was no wing to look through, no way of seeing things that were otherwise hidden or, as Mandoran had once said, out of phase. Whatever she could see here would have to do. Mandoran said the weeds looked like holes—but in what, exactly?

She knelt awkwardly; having a hand as an anchor made normal movement surprisingly difficult. If she'd had a better way of tying their hands together, she'd have taken it— but she didn't trust the cuffs that came as part of her kit to do the same job.

As she knelt to examine what she'd seen as weeds—in a landscape that made no sense, although it looked almost familiar enough everything was disturbing—she saw what Mandoran meant. What she'd assumed were stems or stalks were tendrils of Shadow that seemed to surround the tear.

She readied herself to leap back, to leap away, as she inched closer to it.

The marks on her arms—which had been painful—seemed

to rear up; the purple of the marks and the purple of the what she had assumed were awkward blossoms were the exact same color.

Severn, in the distance, was worried. Nightshade was worried, but as he was in combat, he had less thought to spare for it.

Mandoran shouted; Kaylin was yanked back from the weed. Whatever he saw, she couldn't see. But the light from this rip intensified and the shadow that framed it shuddered, darkening as well.

Light erupted—purple light—as if in attempt to escape the confinement of Shadow. Kaylin, pulled to her feet, didn't avoid all of it; it hit her stomach, her legs, and her free hand.

It was the hand that was going to be a problem. Although she was accustomed to the pain that random magic seemed to cause, this was different, and she knew it; her palms weren't marked in the same way her forearms were, but it was her exposed palm that felt the blast of light as searing heat, as if she'd shoved her palm into the center of a white fire.

The pain of burning remained as the light vanished.

24

She held her arm away from the rest of her body; the light that had hit clothing didn't seem to penetrate it. Mandoran said nothing while she waved her hand around as if it were on fire and movement would put the fire out.

But she stopped waving and put more of her reactive energy into Leontine. As far as she could tell, her hand was fine, but she was squinting as she examined it.

"Does it look normal to you?"

"About as normal as you ever do."

"It felt like fire."

He nodded. "It's gone, though."

"What's gone?"

"The tear."

He was right. The non-weed she had been examining was gone; what was left was a small tendril of upright Shadow. She had an answer, of a sort: it was a tear in the fabric of Shadow. But she had no idea what the collapse of that tear meant, and given it was her own hand—her *right* hand—she had to struggle not to panic.

Panic was useless here. Caution was good. But being here

at all defied every possible definition of *cautious* she could think of.

Heal, Severn said. *Panic later.*

She nodded. This was her own body. These were the marks of the Chosen. She could—and did—use the power to heal; she could use it to see if there were any changes in her body, any attempts to change it.

She remembered healing injured Barrani, near the West March. She remembered that the Shadow or chaos that had been left in the wake of injuries done by forest Ferals had *not* felt foreign, although it was. The injury or the damage done by that Shadow was transforming the body into which it had been injected, attempting to establish a new "normal" that didn't match Barrani normal.

She really didn't want to have to cut off her own hand.

But her hand seemed…normal. In pain, yes, but normal. The muscles, the tendons, the bones, even the skin—normal. Except for the pain. She cursed more viscerally as she opened her eyes and examined the palm of her hand.

A new mark now resided across the mound of her palm. A new word.

"I don't understand," she whispered.

"Don't look at me. I've never met a Chosen who wasn't you, and I know even less than you do."

The mark was complicated; it reminded her, in some ways, of the outcaste Dragon's name—a name she could see because he'd exposed it to her, probably hoping she'd be stupid enough to *try* to say it, try to use it to control him. She could barely manage simpler runes; she knew she couldn't manage his.

And if she couldn't, the attempt would mean that the person enslaved would be Kaylin, not the outcaste. The mark on her palm—her *right* palm—was purple; its delicate edges resembled glass or glass shards. It did hurt—but all of her skin did.

"Maybe we don't try to examine the tears," Mandoran

said. He looked up, and then added, "On account of there being none left."

She rose, very carefully not making a fist of her right hand, and looked down the street. Mandoran was right. There were no more non-weeds. They had, she thought uneasily, served their purpose. The buildings that overhung the street began to retract, as if their odd shapes were overlapping carapaces.

"This is...not good," Mandoran said.

"You think?" She tightened her grip on his hand, and turned back; the street continued for as far as the eye—or her eyes—could see. But it widened; what passed for light here both brightened and darkened as the hue of that light changed.

Kaylin decided she really didn't like the color green—not when it was blended with a livid purple. It hurt to look at. Especially when it was captured perfectly in Mandoran's eyes; they didn't look like Barrani eyes in any way, except the base shape—and even that was too large, as if the light was emanating from Mandoran himself and it was struggling to fully escape.

No.

She drew on the power of the marks of the Chosen to reach into Mandoran a second time. She knew what he should feel like.

No, that wasn't true. Barrani normal, she knew—because Barrani normal, Barrani bodies knew. It was the same with mortal bodies, Aerian bodies and Leontine bodies. She was certain she could heal the Tha'alani as well, if it came to that. But the cohort were not Barrani. They could mimic it convincingly—and did—but when they lost control of their emotions, they lost control of the mimicry. There were things the cohort could do that most of their kin couldn't.

She didn't *know* what normal, for Mandoran, was.

And to be fair, she didn't know if normal for Mandoran was normal for any of the rest of his cohort. She couldn't tell if what she was now touching was Mandoran as he was supposed to be, or Mandoran, contaminated.

But she was certain that whatever it was he'd been hit with had somehow led them here, and here was not where either of them wanted to be.

She'd come here because she had listened to the voices that appeared to overlap Mandoran's; she'd come because the words spoken were not the words that Mandoran was simultaneously speaking. If those words were Shadow's words, things made no sense—because she now carried a new mark on her palm, and it was, to her eye, a True Word.

As were the words that she had heard.

Free me.

Kill me.

She had completely sympathy with the former, and a bitter kind of empathy for the latter.

"Kaylin."

But Mandoran didn't feel like Shadow to her, and she wondered if that were, in part, because the hand attached to him was the hand that she had gloved in strands of Shadow—inert Shadow, as her hand had never tried to speak with her or control her.

The idea of inert Shadow didn't exist for Bellusdeo. But Kaylin had come to understand that Shadow was a single word that was meant to cover a plethora of living, sentient beings. It meant—had meant—death. Until Gilbert. Until Spike.

She didn't know what normal for Mandoran was. She knew, however, that he wasn't being transformed into a thing of Shadow. "You're not in pain?"

"No. I really, really think we should leave."

"No problem. You lead."

"How did you even *get here*? I'm only here because you dragged me in!"

"I got here *through you*."

Kaylin—not the time for this.

Right. Right. She exhaled. She missed Hope. She missed someone who had some sense of what was happening. Even Terrano would be better than Mandoran.

"Can we reverse it?" she asked, when she was certain she wasn't going to be pointing figurative fingers. "Because I think you were already almost here when I grabbed you. Terrano meant for me to pull you out and drop you on Bellusdeo's back."

"I was almost cut in half," Mandoran replied, more edge in his tone, but less blame.

"Healer here," she replied.

"No one is going to care if I'm almost cut in half on the way out. Everyone's going to be pissed off at me if you are."

"Look—if you've got better ideas—"

The rest of Kaylin's words were lost to a roar; the ground beneath their feet buckled. Kaylin fell because Mandoran lost his footing. She was afraid to let go of him—the last thing she wanted at this very moment was to lose him to...this place.

She banged her knee; Mandoran landed on his free elbow. Pushing themselves to their feet was an act of coordination that the ground only barely allowed. The buildings were now entirely retracted, as if they were hunkering defensively beneath thick shells. Kaylin tightened her grip on Mandoran's hand.

"Where are we—" The words were lost, again, to thunderous roaring; the whole of the road buckled, as if attempting to shake the sound off. Kaylin was better prepared for this, and managed to retain her footing; Mandoran, however, had ceased to rely on the solidity of the ground beneath his feet. His arm remained solid, and he remained visible, but the roar of the Dragon—and it was draconic—no longer caused him to stumble.

Kaylin's weight, when she did, didn't pull him down.

Mandoran didn't bother to ask her another question; mixed

in with the roaring that caused the ground to buckle was other roaring: Bellusdeo, she thought. Emmerian. The fiefs weren't Elantra—but they were close enough that Dragons in aerial combat would be seen across the city the Emperor did rule.

The first roar, the roar that caused the breaking of this Shadowed ground, was no doubt the outcaste's.

She kept running, stumbling, righting herself, and running, because she could see one building that had not withdrawn, like a turtle or snail, into its shell. That building, unlike the streets, wasn't cracking and fissuring as the cadence of the outcaste's voice grew louder and louder, and it appeared to have a door.

Well no, it appeared to have something that might have been a door. It might have been a mouth. Mandoran's grip tightened and he yanked Kaylin off her feet as the stone beneath her soles cracked; the crack spread, like dark lightning in a sky of stone, and the rock surrounding the crack began to tumble and fall.

Door.

Mouth.

Kaylin cursed in Leontine and followed Mandoran's lead as he dragged her toward the only solid stretch of ground: inside.

In between one step—outside and inside—the roaring died. She couldn't hear it, couldn't feel the aftershocks beneath her feet. She checked her hand—the one attached to Mandoran—and exhaled. This was a door, not a mouth; no Shadow saliva or breath greeted their entrance. Mandoran came to stand upon something shiny and hard that nonetheless carried both of their weights.

"I really hope you know what you're doing," he said.

She failed to kick him.

It was dark. Thinking this, Kaylin raised her arm—the free arm—and opened her hand; the hall lit up. She hadn't summoned light, hadn't dragged a mark off her skin, suspending its considerable weight in order to be able to see. She'd lifted her arm in order to do just that.

But light had appeared. It was purple-white, a color that wasn't nearly as uncomfortable as green to the eyes. It was uncomfortable in other ways; it appeared to match—exactly—the colors of her marks. The color of her new mark. She wondered if there was a place to leave this word here; she really didn't want to carry it back with her.

If back was even a possibility.

"Was that your stomach?"

"Shut up."

This hall—and it seemed to be hall, of a kind—continued, but seemed to end in a wall. All of the walls were oddly shaped; they weren't completely flat, but seemed to bulge outward, as if something was straining to get through them to the two people within. Not a comforting thought.

"See any doors?"

Kaylin shook her head. "Do the walls feel solid to you?"

"They look solid."

"Not what I asked."

"Why don't you touch one and find out?"

"Because I'd either have to let go of your hand—and that's not happening unless someone cuts my hand off—or I touch it with this." She lifted her palm and waved it in front of his face.

He looked at the mark. "Your skin looks burned."

Which is what it felt like as well.

"Did any of the other marks cause that?"

"No. Not even the ones I picked up later." She hesitated, and then said, "But…it's the same color as the rest of the marks, currently. I think we need to get out of here."

Mandoran exhaled, lifted his free—and unmarked—hand and pushed against one of the walls.

Kaylin was not terribly comforted when he practically fell through it; her grip tightened to numbness as she tried to yank him back.

"Sorry—something's attached itself to my hand."

"What—again?" She grimaced and pulled. She wanted Hope, here; the sense that he could instantly protect her from malevolent magic had become so much part of the way she walked in the world she felt almost naked without him.

But she'd spent almost all of her life without him. What she had right now were the marks of the Chosen—in a livid white and purple—and the hand that gripped Mandoran tightly. She added her free hand to gain more leverage—and found that here, at least, the grip was solid in a way it hadn't been when they'd been suspended in mid-sky in an aerial battlefield.

"Mandoran?" He was stiff, tense, rigid. Kaylin went from worried to terrified in the time it took to see his profile clearly. "Are you still in there?"

"Yes—but I think things are going to get difficult." His voice was strained.

Kaylin was holding on with both hands. She reached out for him as if he were injured—and she found what she'd feared to find in the open streets. Shadow. She remembered that the right hand bore an entirely new mark. She could hear a voice she recognized—a voice she was now certain wasn't Mandoran's.

Kill me.

Free me.

Killing was not what she wanted, now. What she wanted was to pull Mandoran out of the wall and find some way of leaving this place as soon as humanly possible. The strongest voice she could now hear wasn't Mandoran's. It was the other. And her own fear. She could lose him here. He was in her hands—and it wouldn't matter.

Kaylin!

Don't talk to me—don't listen. I don't think it's safe. Mandoran is alive, tell the cohort—but he's trying not to communicate with them until we're out of here. So—don't talk and don't listen.

Silence. Severn withdrew, and only when he did did she realize he'd been in the background all along, so much a part of the way she viewed the universe that only in absence was she aware of it. But Mandoran was afraid *for* the cohort, and he wasn't an idiot. Well, no, he was an idiot some of the time— but so was she. And he had a better sense of the risks. What he wasn't willing to risk, she shouldn't be.

She wanted to ask Severn where Hope was or what he was doing. She didn't.

She had found Mandoran.

Given that she was physically attached to him, this shouldn't have made sense, even to Kaylin. But she could now feel the strands of Mandoran as distinct and separate from strands of Shadow. The Shadow felt more solid than it had the first time she touched him, and she began to pull at it, to attempt to rip it out.

Mandoran snarled, his fingers tightening around hers as he uttered a string of Leontine. She stopped, and he uttered a different string.

"You're not cutting out anything important," he snapped. "Just keep going."

"You're stuck in a wall—"

"I'm almost unstuck. Whatever you're doing—keep doing it."

She—like most sane people—didn't like causing pain. She could do it, was doing it now, but her hands and teeth were clenched, almost locked, with the effort. Even if she felt it was necessary, she hated it.

"We don't always get to do the things we like. Unless we're Terrano." More cursing.

The Shadow entwined with Mandoran was not inert. It fought her, and the battleground was Mandoran himself. But she'd done something like this before, in the Aerie that seemed farther away at the moment than the West March. She couldn't physically mime the motion of wrapping, of spooling; her hands were locked in place.

No, she thought. One hand was locked in place. She had always given preference to her left hand when it came to door wards or Shadow—the consequences of which were unpredictable. But she had a suspicion that the clarity of Shadow came from the new mark she'd gained.

Her right hand was dominant; she didn't want to risk it. Didn't see that she had a choice. She pulled on Mandoran with both hands; he didn't budge. But he didn't seem to be moving forward, either. She could risk weakening the brace her weight provided.

She lifted the right hand, pulling it slowly back; she could see it rise, a nimbus of dark light enfolding it. Shadow? It looked wrong for that, but the light here wasn't normal light.

"Keep going," Mandoran said.

"Can you even—" she grunted, her feet moving against what she hoped and assumed was stone "—see where you are?"

"I can, now."

"Good. Can you leave it?"

"I...don't think that's what we want."

She used perfectly functional Elantran cursing. He laughed. The sound was weak and shaky, but the amusement in it was genuine. "What are you looking at?"

"A library." Mandoran's tone implied he'd seen enough libraries for this lifetime.

"You're going to make me hate books."

"What can you see?"

"Shadow. A hall of sorts—the one we were walking down before you touched the wall."

"No doors?"

"No doors."

"There's a door here, farther in. I can see it." His words were interrupted by grunts and the occasional single-syllable curse.

"You are really, really making me hate libraries." She bit her lip. "Fine. You're sure?"

"Here? I can't be sure of anything. But...I don't think it's an illusion."

"Could you see it before?"

"Before you started torturing me, you mean?" Before she could answer, he said, "No."

She exhaled. "Let me finish what I'm doing."

"Is there *any* end in sight?"

She nodded, and then said, "Yes."

The Shadow didn't leave Mandoran in threads, as it had the last time. She could feel and see it as strands, layered between the more physical elements that she could identify as Barrani, but as she detached them, those strands seemed to coalesce into the fog that now shrouded her right hand, her right forearm. It seemed to hover above her skin, but didn't sink beneath it to do whatever it had been trying to do with Mandoran.

"Can you see your feet?"

"Yes."

"Can you see my hand?"

"Yes—it looks disembodied, which is disturbing."

She shifted position, then. "Step forward. I'll follow." She made it most of the way through what she saw as wall. She was only a little surprised when her right hand got stuck. There was no wall on Mandoran's side; no hint of rounded tunnel, no hint of darkness.

Her arm appeared to be stuck or caught on nothing. But that nothing was better than Shadow. Mandoran, however, felt like Mandoran. And when she looked at him, he no longer looked like a nightmare configuration of himself.

"Are you just going to stand there?"

"Having a bit of difficulty extricating my hand from the stuff I pulled out of *you*, yes."

"I'll wait. Quietly."

She snorted. Working her hand free wasn't painful, but it reminded Kaylin of watching Caitlin remove an old ring—the ring itself too small to easily fit over a knuckle, but small enough that it fit the finger beneath that knuckle. The analogy helped. What had Caitlin done in the end?

Oh, right. Soap. Water.

"Your language is really foul."

"Quietly, remember?" She cursed again. This time, Mandoran lent her his weight as she pulled.

She landed on him when her arm finally came free. The hand was no longer ringed with a cloud of Shadow. She then exhaled and turned to look at the room.

Mandoran had been right: they were in a library. It reminded Kaylin very much of the library space within the Academia: the height of the shelves, the ceiling, and the intimidating number of books it contained. If she could read them all—and her guess was she couldn't—she wouldn't finish before she'd perished of old age.

She began walking, dragging Mandoran with her. Even if he looked normal, she didn't want to let go of his hand. Not yet. She was willing to hand him over to the cohort, but none of the cohort were here. At eye level, she could see a third of the shelves; she could crane her neck up, could reach maybe the half point if she stood on her toes.

"I wouldn't touch anything here if I were you," Mandoran helpfully said.

"I just want to see if they're actually books."

"I *really* wouldn't touch anything."

"We're already touching the floor. We're going to have to touch the door. I just want to see if this is actually what it looks like it is."

"I am so glad I'm not in contact with everyone else."

"Terrano would check."

"Terrano knows what he can survive."

"And I don't?"

"Just don't, all right?"

She turned a glare on him, and then reached out and grabbed a book—fingers on the top of the spine, not the edge of the binding. It felt like a book, albeit ragged at the top of the pages, and she pulled it off the shelf.

Mandoran looked unimpressed, not worried or concerned. He stopped breathing when she tried to open it—which was difficult to do with one free hand; he wasn't offering help.

"The Arkon—the chancellor," he corrected himself, "would reduce you to ash for the way you're handling that book. You *do not* open a book by holding on to one of its covers and letting the rest dangle."

"Yeah, well he's not here. You're going to report me?"

"It is entirely unnecessary," a new voice said.

She fumbled to close the book—without dropping it—as she turned in the direction of the voice.

Mandoran, being as mature as ever, said, "I told you."

In the bright light of this library was a spider. It was a giant spider, eyes evenly spaced across the large, central—and hairy—body from which legs or arms extended. The librarian was one of the Wevaran.

"Starrante?" she said, without much hope. All of the Wevaran she had met—and she had met very few—looked the same, to her.

The spider clicked. A lot. Kaylin tensed, readying herself

to leap out of the way of the webbing that the Wevaran used as both weapon and escape.

The clicking, however, stopped. "Did you say Starrante?" the Wevaran said—in Barrani.

Kaylin, book now closed and carefully clutched to her chest—because librarians were unlikely to kill someone if their attack would also damage the books—nodded.

"Do I *look* like Starrante?"

She decided honesty was not the best policy. "There are similarities," she finally said, "and I haven't met many of your people."

"I have met very few of yours—especially not *here*. In fact, now that I look at you both, I do not believe you have permission to be here."

"Who would we get permission from?"

"That is the question," the unnamed Wevaran replied.

"I'm Kaylin, and this is Mandoran. We didn't mean to come here, but my friend kind of fell through the wall."

"Wall?"

"Wall," she replied firmly.

"I am Bakkon," the Wevaran said. "You are both unusual. You should not be here," he added, as he slowly approached. "But the book should be returned to its shelf. You will give it to me," he added. "Your handling of something so precious is appalling." His tone implied a growl of disapproval.

He approached; Kaylin forced herself to stand still, rather than to retreat. Every story she had ever told herself about spiders and poison reared its terrified head. But Starrante had saved Robin, and he was gentler in interaction than either the Dragon or the Ancestor who formed the other two points of the librarian triangle. She held the book out, trying to stop her arm from shaking.

It wasn't that he could kill her—most of her friends could. But none of those friends invoked that visceral response. To part of her brain, the Wevaran were death; everything else about those friends was part of normal life.

Bakkon reached out with two limbs to take what she held out. His arms froze inches from the book. "What are the marks you bear?"

Since the marks were mostly hidden, Kaylin hesitated.

Mandoran, however, said, "She is Chosen. She bears the marks of the Chosen."

"Impossible. She is mortal. Even I can taste that."

"She is not—in this world—the only mortal to have borne those marks."

"What has happened to the world while I've been sleeping?"

It was Kaylin who answered. "It depends. Where did you go to sleep? In this library?"

"Is that what you call this space? It is not an accurate description."

"We've seen the library in the Academia, and it seems similar."

"You have seen Starrante's space. Once, we might have been able to meet—but not now. I am concerned," he continued, his body rising as his legs lengthened. "You should not be here. We have taken precautions—but even precautions must age and wither. Time is kind to none of us. If we do not feel it as the continual wound that you experience, we feel it nonetheless." Bakkon exhaled. "It has been too long. I should have destroyed you when I first sensed you."

"Why didn't you?"

Kaylin stepped, hard, on Mandoran's foot.

"Time," was the soft reply. "Our kin—my kin—leave the nest having devoured most of our clutch; it is a fight for both dominance and survival. It is only once we leave that we truly open all of our eyes; only once we interact with adults—and with outsiders—that we understand that there is more, must be more, than hunger and survival.

"You are not my kin. You are not young in the way we are young. And here, in this empty space, I have perhaps desired a reminder: I am not a youngling. Not a child. You remind me. It has been so long." He did not take the book. Instead, he turned away, his legs stretching. "It is not safe for you to walk in this place. You, because you are mortal; you, because you are unstable."

"We're trying to leave."

"If you are Chosen, you might be able to do so. I do not give much for the chances of your friend."

"Can you get us out of here? With the web portals?"

"The portals are anchored," he replied. "There is no external area into which you might safely walk. Do you not understand where you are?"

"*Ravellon.*"

25

The ground beneath their feet rumbled.

The Wevaran clicked and screeched. Kaylin wondered if the latter was the Wevaran version of cursing. It was an oddly comforting thought.

"Chosen," Bakkon said, "why have you come?"

"I didn't intend to come here. Where we live, this place is death. Worse than death. It's surrounded by six Towers, and Shadow is trapped within it. We *can* walk into it, and we can leave. But the Shadow—"

"That is not the way it works," was the soft reply. "I have preserved this space for far longer than you have been alive, hoping. Why did you come?" he asked again, as if aware that she hadn't really answered his question.

Problem was, she wasn't sure she *had* an acceptable answer. "I'm not sure how I arrived here. But—outside of the barrier, we were under attack and my friend—the unstable one—got hit with…Shadow spears."

Kaylin couldn't tell if Bakkon's gaze had moved to Mandoran, he had so many eyes.

"He is not afflicted now."

"No—but I couldn't heal him in midair, which is where most of the fight was taking place."

"You were outside."

"Yes."

"And now you are inside."

"Yes."

"You did not deliberately attempt to enter."

"No—that's what I've been saying. I was trying to heal him—to remove the Shadow the injury had introduced to his body."

He said nothing.

"But...I could hear the Shadow. No—not exactly that, but I could hear something that wasn't my friend, and it was speaking. It wasn't loud, but it was steady. I focused on that."

"Why?"

"I don't know—I thought that maybe if I could separate the two voices, I could more easily separate the invasive Shadow from the healthy body. I could separate the voices, but...we ended up here, and not where we were. We ended up in the streets of...wherever this place is."

Bakkon hissed.

She lifted her hand. "And I picked this up, there." Her palm was open. She could see the purple-white light reflected in all of the eyes that were turned toward her. Or visible.

The eyes widened. "You picked this up *how*?"

"I stopped to examine what I thought was a weed."

To Mandoran, he said, "What is this *weed*?"

Clearly the Wevaran was not much of a gardener. Which was fair; neither was Kaylin.

"It's a term that refers to plants in a garden or road that grow where they're not meant to grow."

"Are you a weed?" he asked of Kaylin.

Mandoran coughed back obvious laughter.

"I've been called worse. I don't have roots in the ground, but I don't always fit comfortably in most places."

"And you are Chosen."

"And I'm Chosen. Most of my kind ignore that."

She could sense that Bakkon was appalled. "And you allow this?"

"I can't force people to pay attention to me if they don't want to."

"You are Chosen; I am certain you have means of gaining their attention."

"I don't want their attention. And we're kind of losing track of what we were talking about."

"I have not lost track of any of it," Bakkon replied. "I am not as easily distracted as the younger races often are, and can see multiple possibilities from each slender line; it is how we weave, after all. But that mark was not given to you by the Ancients."

Kaylin's brows rose. "You can read it?"

The Wevaran missed a beat. His response was decidedly chillier. "You cannot?"

"No." She still hated it when people thought she was stupid. And she knew there was no way to avoid it here, other than lie. She almost did.

"How is that even possible?"

"No one asked before *putting marks all over my body*, maybe?" Having confessed ignorance, if resentfully, Kaylin said, "What does it mean?"

He appeared to be staring at her. A chittering sound escaped a very large mouth before he shuddered in place. When he spoke, he spoke a word Kaylin didn't recognize, in a language she didn't know. But she knew that it was a single word, broken into syllables with pause for breath.

A True Word.

The Wevaran repeated the word as she closed her eyes. Eyes

closed, she could see the marks—even the new one—glowing brightly; purple gave way to gold, the light she was most familiar with. Even the new mark on her hand adopted that color, its edges burning.

He said the word a third time; she could feel every spoken syllable as a beat against the palm that currently contained the mark, as if the mark itself were alive, its heart exposed. This wasn't a particularly comforting metaphor.

"You know I don't understand that, right?" When Bakkon failed to respond, she spoke in High Barrani, the words far more formal.

To Mandoran, the Wevaran said, "Did you understand what you heard?"

"No. I'm sorry. It's not a language that my people are now taught."

"It was never a language that was taught," the Wevaran replied. "You are—both of you—younger races."

"You always understood it?"

"How could we not? It is the heart of all language. It is what lies beneath the skein of the language we speak now; it is the drive to communicate without prevarication. There was always risk in that; we hide. We seek the shadows—there is safety in being unseen.

"But unseen, we cannot speak truth. And to speak this tongue at all is to refuse to hide. Perhaps you cannot understand that."

It was Mandoran who answered. "We understand the need to be unseen."

"Yes. When I was young, I learned to hide. I hid my strength. I hid my weakness. I made a web of both; I was hungry. We were hungry. I did not speak these words. None of us dared to speak them; they could be heard. They could be felt. They could be seen.

"We are many at birth and few when we leave the birthing ground; it is our nature. Those who die, die; those who are strong, live. I see, from your expression, that you do not approve."

Kaylin shrugged. She didn't—but human birth wasn't Wevaran birth.

Mandoran seemed to have no difficulties, however. "The strong live. The weak die. We don't…consume each other the way you do, and we have far fewer young."

"Don't you ever think about what those others might have become if they survived?" Kaylin demanded.

"No."

"Why not?"

"Because they did not survive." The last word tailed up, as if the Wevaran didn't understand the question. "Regardless, when we heard the words, we understood them."

"Wait, if you didn't speak them, where did you hear them? Did your mother speak them?"

"Our parent? Yes. Our parent spoke the words. They would have to be spoken or we would not emerge."

"Do you have True Names?"

Silence stretched around the question, as if the Wevaran were examining it carefully. Or as if he didn't understand it. Maybe both. Kaylin was reminded, again, that language arose from cultural experience, something she had never considered as a child in the fiefs. Words were words, then.

Even learning Barrani hadn't changed that feeling; the learning had been entirely in service to translating one set of words—those she naturally spoke—to another.

But True Words had meanings, and those meanings did not shift with the speaking or with the experience of the speaker. She'd been told this, and she believed it. True Names were True Words—but words that were owned, words that were lived.

To reveal a True Name was the ultimate risk, the ultimate vulnerability.

"I do not understand your question," Bakkon finally said.

"The Barrani—Mandoran is Barrani—have a word at their core. They do not wake without the word itself. The Dragons have words in a similar fashion—"

"It's not similar at all," Mandoran interjected.

"—and in both cases, if one knows the word, which we call the True Name, of the Barrani or the Dragon, we can communicate with them without speech. And we can—if we are strong enough—force the Barrani or the Dragon to do what we command them to do."

"I see. And you wish to know if I have such a word?"

"I wish to know if your people have such words, yes."

"Your people do not?"

"No. My people do not. It is why the Barrani sometimes consider the mortal races to be little better than animals."

"And these animals?"

"Do not speak."

"I see." The Wevaran chittered again. "No. We do not have words as your friend has words. We do not have words as your skin now does. But the words themselves, like the words on your hand, we speak. We speak them among our own kin— or we did, before the fall.

"It is the language we hear at birth; it is the language we speak—must speak—at death. We speak to each other in this fashion where it is required. But it takes effort, Chosen. It takes will."

"Why?"

"Because truth carries inherent risks."

"So do lies."

"Not in the same fashion. We are responsible for our truths."

Kaylin felt that people were responsible for their lies as well, but failed to say this.

"But the words themselves are part of our weaving. The words are the reason we can open doors into other worlds, other states; the words are the reason we can survive our explorations. It is not wise to speak often, but in our thoughts, it is those words we utilize in order to understand what we are seeing. It is those words for which we reach."

"And this word?" she said, coming back to what she felt was the point.

"It is an ending. An ending, a finality." Chittering. "I find the Barrani tongue so slight I must struggle to find words that might somehow trace the entirety of this meaning. But you said you picked it up on the streets?"

She nodded.

The clicking became more frenetic, and the Wevaran began to move in a circle, counterclockwise.

"Is this a good idea?" Mandoran whispered, in Elantran.

"Where we are?" she replied, in the same fashion. "There are no good ideas here. If we relied on good ideas, we'd be at home."

The Wevaran trembled and finished with a keening that almost sounded like a distant scream.

The scream echoed in the library; the ground and the shelves began to shake. Kaylin couldn't speak Wevaran. She couldn't speak True Words without effort and a lot of serious coaching, none of which she had now. But she needed neither. She knew grief when she heard it.

Mandoran stiffened, retreating in place, as people did when confronted with unexpected grief; he didn't know what to do; didn't know what it was safe to do. He did nothing.

Kaylin took her biggest risk. She released Mandoran's hand and reached out with her left hand, stepping beneath the Wevaran's raised legs and attempting to avoid what she assumed was his mouth.

She touched him. Beneath her hand she felt hair and chitin and an unexpected warmth. Life, she thought, was warm. Bakkon was alive. He wasn't Starrante, but Starrante had had to deal with students at the Academia. Kaylin suspected that Bakkon had dealt with no one for a long damn time.

Bakkon froze instantly. All noise—chittering, clicking, even breathing—stopped. Before Kaylin could withdraw her hand, before she could even consider it, two of his arms snapped out and folded around her; it looked, given the angle, as if they should have broken.

Mandoran moved, then; the Wevaran lifted two more of its limbs to block the Barrani. She lifted her right hand and placed it beside the left. She wished that Wevaran bodies were soft and furry; they weren't. They felt very much like they looked: large, hairy, chitinous insects. With too many eyes, too many legs, and a mouth that seemed much larger when viewed at this distance.

She fought instinctive terror. If she'd intended to give in to visceral fear, she would never have approached him.

Even as she thought it, the marks began to glow—to glow and to rise from her skin. The only mark that remained where it lay was the one on the palm that was now pressed against Wevaran flesh.

"What happened?" she asked, voice soft. She might have been speaking to a foundling.

Bakkon shook. "I do not want to kill you," he said. Which was promising, in a fashion.

She felt no Shadow in him, which she hadn't expected. But she hadn't touched Starrante; she trusted the Arbiter because he had saved Robin, and Robin had not been afraid. Robin, a child, had not been afraid.

Kaylin wished she could be that child. She had to fight fear, here, but she fought it. "I would prefer that you didn't try to kill me, too." She had no doubt, given the lack of her familiar, that she'd be dead if he wanted her dead. "Why do you think you might have to?"

Mandoran coughed and Kaylin turned to look, briefly, in his direction. His back was against one of the shelves and his feet were no longer touching the ground; she could see a delicate skein of webbing around his legs and arms. "Possibly not the *smartest* question to ask *right now*."

She shrugged, watching the marks as they rose. So did Bakkon.

The marks didn't rise evenly; some hovered above her arm, and some rose to the level of her eyes. She didn't recognize most of them; they looked different in three dimensions than they did when they were flat against her skin, as if her skin were parchment.

But Bakkon did. She didn't speak the words; she couldn't. She didn't fully understand their meaning, either; she could sometimes choose words that had meanings solely by the feel they invoked—but it took a long time. She therefore hadn't consciously or deliberately chosen the floating words.

The Wevaran's eyes were glowing the same color as the marks, as if they absorbed the whole of his attention, his focus. He didn't answer the question, but as they stood—one human, one Wevaran, and the marks of the Chosen—he once again began to keen.

"They spoke," he finally whispered, his Barrani shaky. "We heard their voices. We always heard their voices."

"Whose? Whose voice?"

"Ravellon." The word that she heard and the word that he spoke were not the same. She tried to catch the syllables, to impress them in memory, but failed; her own understanding overlapped his voice.

The ground shook, and shook again.

"You should not have come here, Chosen."

At any other time, she would have reminded him that she

hadn't arrived deliberately; now, she simply listened, her hands relaxing.

"You should not have come."

"No. If it's possible to safely leave this place, we're going to leave. But…Mandoran was being pulled here."

"It's not my fault," Mandoran said.

"I didn't say it was."

Bakkon coughed. It was much louder than Mandoran's prior cough but had the same meaning.

"Can you help us leave?"

"No. If I leave, this space will collapse and everything in it will be lost. I have been asleep here, waiting, since the madness began."

"Will you be safe if we leave?"

This was not the question he had been expecting. It was clearly not the question Mandoran had expected either. "I do not understand the question."

"We fell into your space. Into the library, I mean. And we need to leave it. I assume the doors lead out. But if we open the doors, will your library be at risk?"

"The doors lead out of the library; they do not lead out of this space. I no longer know what you will find if you open the doors; they have not been opened since the fall."

"Why can't you leave your space and come back to it? Starrante could."

"It is too complicated a question to answer; I would have to teach you much about my kin in order for you to understand it. And I do not wish to risk the whole of the collection. It is not mine—but it is my duty to preserve the knowledge here."

"What is the knowledge here?" Mandoran asked.

The Wevaran lifted a leg and Mandoran fell off the wall, landing easily and gracefully on two feet.

"Our history," was the soft reply.

"The history of the Wevaran?"

"No—our history. You will not understand it. You will never live it. You will never see its like again." Each word wavered. Kaylin had heard this before, as well, and it hit her far more strongly than the fear of spiders could.

"We have to leave. Our allies are fighting the Shadows that have flown out of *Ravellon.*" This wasn't strictly true, but she too felt she would have to explain far more for it to make sense. "We can't stay here. You could come with us."

Mandoran grimaced but said nothing.

"You could come with us, and you could visit Starrante."

"I cannot leave this place." He disengaged his limbs, allowing Kaylin free motion once again. She was loath to remove her palms; the marks that now floated in front of her face—three in all—were still glowing. Something should be done here; she wasn't certain what.

Lifting a hand, she touched one of the three marks; felt its immediate weight as it lost buoyancy. The new mark on her palm became instantly heavy as well, as if the two words—old and new—were now interacting or merging to form a single whole.

She didn't know what either meant, but she could guess, given the Wevaran's reaction to the new one. Somehow, the new mark encapsulated what she had heard—what she had tried to hear clearly. Her attempt to do so had brought her to this place.

Kill me. Free me.

As if death and freedom were the same thing. And she knew that one too well. On the day she had first entered the Hawklord's Tower, they had had the exact same meaning to her: death was the only freedom she was allowed. There was no other way to escape from...herself.

From the truth of what she had done and been. From the future that stretched out, endless, before her: more of the same. More killing. More failure. More death. If she had died as she had intended, she would have rid the world of one more ugly thing it didn't need.

And yet, death wasn't what had awaited her there. Death wasn't what she'd been offered. The horror that she had turned her life into was not the only life she could live; it was perhaps the first time she had truly seen that since she'd fled Nightshade.

Her life had become more than pain and self-loathing. She had done everything she could—everything, no matter how resentfully—to walk a different path. To seek a different end. To live a life that had never seemed possible. It was a life she had wanted. A life she still didn't believe—on the bad days—she deserved. She was arresting people who had done far less than she'd done in Barren.

But she was grateful to the Hawklord. To the Hawks. To the life they had offered someone who didn't deserve it. She was grateful to see the foundling hall, the midwives' guild, the Leontine quarter. Even the Tha'alani.

She knew that death was not the only freedom she was allowed.

And she knew that death was the freedom that voice—thrumming through Mandoran's body—wanted. Had she followed it, had she desperately listened for it, because of her personal experience? She wanted to tell whatever was whispering or shouting those words that there was another way. A better way. A different way.

Harder, she thought, but better.

As if he could hear what she did not put into words—and given her experience with people who built and owned the spaces they occupied, she thought he might—he said, "You are not the same. You are mortal, child. There is an end to you. There is an end to your words, your voice. There is an end to the words that you might speak with any truth or strength."

"And there's no end for you."

"Not that way. Time itself is not an enemy. It is not a friend." But speaking, he looked at the word she now carried in her hand.

"Do you see it?" she asked, because she was now aware that others didn't see what she saw when she looked at her marks.

"I hear it," was his quiet reply. "I hear what you are saying, even if you do not. I wish you had fallen through a different wall—and that is unlike me."

"What will you do?"

"Is that really the question you should be asking?"

Kaylin shrugged. "Probably not." Most of the training she had received when it came to asking questions involved crimes, possible criminals, and general interrogation. "But I'm not sure how long this space will last."

"The instability is unusual," Bakkon replied. "It will not last." The entirety of the Wevaran's body shook, as if he were a wet cat who had come in out of the rain. All of the many eyes closed as Kaylin withdrew.

The mark, however, remained suspended in the air between them; the rest once again came to lie flat against her skin, their light dimming. She opened her hand to see that the new mark was also flattened against her right palm.

"How important are these books to you?"

"They are not more important than my life."

She thought of Starrante. And then of the Wevaran who comprised Liatt's Tower. And last, of the baby spiders devouring each other. This time, it was Kaylin who shook, as if to clear her head.

"Your life won't be in danger if you stay?"

"I do not think it matters," was the thin reply. "Mandoran, I must ask you to refrain from touching the books."

"I wasn't *touching* them. I was brushing off webs. Are you ready to go?" he added, in Elantran.

"I don't think we should leave him behind," Kaylin replied in the same language.

"If he's like any other librarian you've ever met, I don't see how you have a choice."

The Wevaran headed toward the books that Mandoran had been dusting, for want of a better word.

"I think—if we can leave here at all—we can take him with us."

"I think that's about as good an idea as enraging a Dragon." Mandoran grimaced. "You're worried because he was crying."

She nodded.

"You don't even know why he was crying. And no, I'm not asking him. Or her. And I'm not sure we *can* leave."

"I'm sure we can—the outcaste and his deformed Aerians did."

"You can't fly."

This was true. "Candallar's Tower let the Barrani carrying Spike pass through the border. He wasn't flying, either."

"And that doesn't make you more suspicious?"

She exhaled. "It makes me worried, yes. But the Towers didn't stop us from reaching the streets. I think, if we can return to those streets safely, we can make it out. I'm worried," she added.

"Which would be smart if you were worried about yourself. Or us, even."

"What if someone else gets hit by one of those spears?"

"None of the cohort will. Not now."

"They're not the only people there."

Bakkon cleared his throat. The sound was very loud. "Perhaps," he said, in the Barrani neither Kaylin nor Mandoran were using, "you might have the rest of this discussion when someone who cannot understand it is not present. In my day— which clearly far precedes yours—it was considered rude to speak a language that all people present could not understand." The ground shook beneath their feet, but Bakkon didn't sound angry.

Kaylin could see the mark that had detached itself from her body; it floated—very slowly—toward Bakkon.

"I hope you know what you're doing," Mandoran said—in Elantran.

"As much as I ever do."

"That's bad."

"Apologies for my terrible manners," she then said, to the Wevaran, and in Barrani. "We were discussing the chance that we make it out of here alive. Ummm, what are you doing?"

"I am gathering volumes of particular interest." Which is what it looked like he was doing. He paused to spit a glob of webbing. From here, it looked almost opalescent. "There are books here that you will find nowhere else—not even in the vaunted library girded by the Academia."

Her heart, such as it was, sank. If he had simply pulled a couple of books off the shelves, she would have been fine—but if he intended Kaylin and Mandoran to carry these, they'd be staggering down streets heavily overburdened. Running would be out of the question. She opened her mouth. Closed it.

"He doesn't mean for us to carry those, does he?" Mandoran asked, in Elantran.

"You could ask him," she replied—in Barrani.

The Wevaran began to move more quickly, scuttling up the sides of shelves to pluck a single book or two from the heights; he vanished around the corner without bothering to come back down to floor level.

"What's happening now?" Mandoran whispered.

"I have no idea." She glanced, once, at the word that had separated itself from her skin; it was growing in size. This, too, she had seen before—but not usually in someplace as physically solid, as real, as this.

"There is no reason to shout," Bakkon said, his voice carrying from wherever it was he had scuttled toward.

"I was not shouting," Kaylin said, raising her voice. "Bakkon—what are you doing?"

"I am, as I said, collecting those books that are unique, now. I will not be long."

The ground shook again. This time, Kaylin could hear a steady, slow *thump*, as if the stone of the floor had been situated above a giant who intended to physically join them. She almost said, *Can you hurry?* but stopped the words from leaving her mouth. "Can we help?" she asked instead.

"I highly doubt you can help with the collecting. You do not strike me as a scholar, and it is highly unlikely that you have spent enough time in libraries that you might immediately recognize those books that are singular. There is history in the knowledge, but I do not imagine you would, in the time you are allotted, gain enough knowledge to be of use in an emergency."

"Never mind. Can Mandoran help?"

"I would rather he not touch the books. Some are delicate and some are…not books as you would understand them. He is, to my eyes, unstable; he could be injured, or the books might be damaged." It was clear which of the two was the primary concern.

Mandoran rolled his eyes but said nothing.

This continued for what felt like hours.

But she was more concerned with the floor than the books or the librarian. The tremors had become much stronger, the floor buckling and cracking beneath her feet. Mandoran was no longer on the ground; Kaylin, impeded by gravity, had to struggle to remain standing. She eventually crouched.

"Are you sure that's wise?" Mandoran asked, as she pressed her hand—her left hand—against the stone.

"Probably not. The stone is warm."

"I highly doubt it's stone."

"Bakkon—we can't carry half your library out the door, never mind down the streets."

"Of course not."

The words she said next were lost to the sudden sound of things hitting the floor. Many things. Kaylin rose and sprinted immediately in the direction of the sound. Mandoran followed, drifting above the stone she had said was warm.

Bakkon didn't appear to be injured. Kaylin had assumed a book, stuck between too many other books, had caused the Wevaran to pull the contents of a shelf down.

She was wrong.

One book remained curled in the folds of a limb; the Wevaran threw it to Kaylin—or Mandoran, as they were both approaching from the same general direction. The volume flew over Kaylin's head—she'd ducked instinctively; Mandoran caught it and staggered back, coming to ground to gain traction.

She drew her knives.

Standing on the other side of the Wevaran, between two very tall shelves that seemed to be bowing inward, was a Shadow.

26

The creature was not like the Ferals of Kaylin's childhood. Ferals—like Barrani and apparently Aerians—could leave *Ravellon* to hunt in the streets of the fiefs that surrounded it and return.

This creature was what Kaylin thought of as a one-off: it couldn't breach the barriers erected by the Towers unless something was badly, badly wrong with the Tower itself.

She was aware that a year ago—maybe less—she would have assumed that Bakkon and Starrante were pure Shadow. But even entities that couldn't leave *Ravellon* on their own had surprised her: Gilbert. Spike.

She tightened her grip on the daggers, moving toward Bakkon. Bakkon flicked a limb in her direction, holding it up so that it was almost in front of her face. She knew this was probably the same gesture, in a spider's body, that she might make if she wanted people to stop moving—but she stiffened as the small claws that comprised fingers flexed in front of her face.

Looking past those claws, she studied the Shadow from what she hoped was a safe distance. It wasn't—but Bakkon was a living wall.

Without thinking too much, Kaylin reached up and grasped those claws, surrendering the dagger in her left hand to do so. She wanted to tell the Wevaran to be careful, but didn't. The advice was ludicrous on its surface; she had no idea what the Wevaran could do in battle, and the Wevaran's knowledge of the creatures of Shadow was like an ocean compared to her puddle.

"Do not get involved in this," the Wevaran now said.

She looked at the Shadow. She couldn't see Gilbert in him. Couldn't see Spike. What she saw was a large mass of darkness, Shadow roiling beneath invisible skin. Its feet were smoke and dark mist, colors sparkling within its moving folds.

It had three eyes roughly positioned where a face might have been; in some ways it was less disturbing than the Wevaran. It had no discernible limbs, but even thinking that, she could see blobs extend from its middle. They appeared almost jelly-like.

Bakkon lifted a second leg in Kaylin's direction. In its claws, he held a small, pale bag. Kaylin blanched as it reached her; it was the color of his webbing. The Wevaran coughed; Kaylin thought it was an unsubtle nag. It wasn't; he was spitting web in the forward direction.

The jelly-limbs...burst.

Dark liquid fanned out in a spray. Bakkon's webbing caught it, preventing it from reaching his face or body. The fluid flew in a circular arc, hitting the shelves to either side of the Wevaran's webbing.

The books began to dissolve. Kaylin grabbed the small sack from Bakkon's back leg.

"You must leave," the Wevaran said.

"What are you going to do?"

"I am not your concern."

Mandoran reached out and grabbed Kaylin by the shoulder. "This is not the time to argue."

"He wants us to leave him—"

"We stand no chance against that creature, and he knows it."

As books melted to the left and right of the Wevaran, she looked at the web he'd constructed. It was uneven, but the substance that had melted through books—and the shelves on which they sat—hadn't hit Bakkon. Regardless, she wasn't certain Bakkon could survive this either.

Wasn't certain that he wanted to survive.

She had touched him with both hands; she had studied—briefly—the shape of his body, the composition of organs, had felt the beat of a heart, or hearts, and the movement of something that might be lungs. The Shadow had not apparently touched the Wevaran himself.

You won't survive this, she told him—because she could. She was connected to him by touch. It was the reason the Barrani considered healing an act of hostility.

Bakkon clicked, spitting web as he did. The web was pale, a white-gray color. Starrante's, by the end, had been pink.

Do not worry about my survival, the Wevaran said, as the creature he faced elongated, and a new round of jelly-like limbs began to protrude from the column of its otherwise featureless body. Bakkon's front legs moved so quickly they were a blur; it was the shape of the web that made clear that his limbs were moving.

Come with us.

I cannot leave this library. I cannot leave this space.

It'll destroy the books.

Yes. If I cannot stop it. And I regret that. But I cannot leave the library—not with you.

Why?

Because I will become what they have become. I will become grief and rage and pain, absent will. I am not what they are—but I re-

member what they were, in ages past. This has been my sanctuary.
It has been my cage. I should not have allowed you to enter.

Is the space weaker because we're in it?

Yes. Bakkon was lying. She could feel and hear a clamor beneath the surface of the words, a disharmony, even if there was only one voice speaking. *It is a wonder to me that you have survived.*

Survived what?

Anything.

Why—look out!

I understand the nature of the attacks I may face here. I am capable of defending myself. I have given you anything of value left here. I trust you will take it, in the end, to Starrante. Starrante will understand.

She didn't want to leave him to die.

"Kaylin," Mandoran said, lips almost attached to her ear. "The Shadow is eating away at the stability of this place. It won't hold for long."

"He'll die," she replied.

"Kaylin—"

"No, you *don't understand*," she snapped, one hand becoming a fist around the neck of the bag she'd been handed. "He's staying because he *wants* to die."

"He's an adult. He's allowed to make choices. But we shouldn't be staying because we *don't* want to die." His grip tightened. "Look, Teela will kill me if I lose you here."

"Then leave. Take the books."

He is right.

I don't care. You don't have to die here.

Did you not understand? I cannot leave. Here—here is the only place I do not hear Ravellon's voice. That voice has driven all who can hear it to madness. It is here I must stand if I wish to die as myself.

She should have accepted that. She knew it. But she could hear what lay beneath perfectly reasonable words, none of which were lies. Bakkon did not want to leave. He fought now because survival was so instinctive it had governed the entirety of his life, from birth.

No, he wanted to die.

Just as she had wanted to die when she had first entered the Hawklord's Tower. Not for the same reasons—his reasons were murky and he didn't put them into thoughts she could touch and hear—but the emotion, the despair, were almost identical.

Mandoran was right; Bakkon was not the child she had been. But that child had lost the life that had given her any meaning, any hope. Absent that life, she had struggled to survive in the fief of Barren, and she had done things in the name of survival that she would *never* do again while she lived.

But she was grateful that the Hawklord hadn't killed her. Hadn't even tried. She was grateful for the life she now led, and she tried—in all the ways available—to balance the harm she had done with help. She couldn't erase the damage to other people. She could stop herself from doing that damage to anyone else.

She was certain that the Wevaran who had survived the fall of *Ravellon* and the rise of the Towers would be beyond grateful that Bakkon had survived—but only if he did.

Your friend is correct. I do not want to escape. More web rose; Bakkon began to build a translucent dome in front of and above himself. The Shadow attacking them could be seen through it.

Did you know that Shadow? Did you know what it used to be?

Yes.

You don't want to kill it.

No. What they do now they would not have done had they not become prey to the madness of the fallen.

Can you wrap them *in your web?*

If I have no other choice. You must *leave.*

Wait—what madness?

Bakkon didn't answer. Maybe Bakkon couldn't answer. But

Spike probably could. He had been captive to Shadow, and had been freed from it.

She felt an eddy of confusion, and realized the Wevaran had caught that thought drift, or had been caught by it. She could feel the sudden turn of his thought, the dangerous edge of hope. *Can you—can you free them?*

"Mandoran—do you understand what Terrano did when he freed Spike?"

Mandoran said nothing.

"This—whatever it is, the moving blob over there—is caught the same way Spike was. It was Terrano who freed Spike, mostly. Can you do what he did?"

"You freed the thing in the basement of the High Halls."

She wasn't certain she had. "Spike did that."

"What did Spike do?"

"I *don't know*. It's why I'm asking you. What did Terrano do?"

"I don't, you might recall, want to *ask them* right now. Whatever you did to drag us both here, Shadow was involved. I don't want to take the risk of opening them up to the same thing."

"Don't try that with me. You were watching us at the time. You know what Terrano saw."

"Fine." The hand on her shoulder tightened. "I'll look—but I can't guarantee anything. Whatever Bakkon is fighting, it's not like Spike."

"Are you sure?"

"Does it *look* like Spike to you?"

"Spike was a historian—this would be the right place for him." But no, he looked nothing like Spike did, at least not in the normal world. "What does he look like to you?"

"I'm trying to see him," was the snappish reply.

Bakkon was holding his breath, and not for the same reason Kaylin was. *The High Halls—the creature at its center—what happened to them?*

They're more or less what they were before Ravellon *fell. I think.*

The Shadow we face is not like your Spike, if I understand your thoughts. But they were once a friend.

"No," Mandoran said, his voice much softer. "What Terrano did, I can't do. Not here. Not with that." He hesitated.

"What would you need, to be able to do it?"

"I'd need to be able to catch it in my hands. I'd need to be able to cut it off entirely from the source. While not dying and not being absorbed by it."

Or not being transformed by it. Kaylin bit her lip and made a decision. Yes, if it were in her power she wanted to save everyone; that was her *job*. But Mandoran was a friend; the blob was a stranger who would probably kill Mandoran if Mandoran made the attempt. "Bakkon—come with us," she said again.

She could feel his hesitation. Could feel something that was almost hope—and she knew this one well. Hope was bitter. Having hope—and she had had none when she had finally crossed the bridge over the Ablayne the first time—led to nothing but pain. Because hope was for fools. Hope was for the naive. Hope didn't change reality, didn't alter truth.

She swallowed. She had been afraid, in the early days, of hope. Of speaking of a future that was different from the past. She'd been afraid to crawl out of the darkness of herself, and into something that might have been light.

And maybe, for Bakkon, there would be no light. She didn't know. She only knew that she didn't want to leave him to die. She was certain that the bag she carried contained the books that were unique. Copies of the others were probably contained in the library Starrante served.

I am tired, Chosen, Bakkon said. *I am tired. Do you understand why I have remained here? My kin do not feel isolation as keenly as the other races. There is safety in isolation. But I did not remain here merely to be safe. Nor did I remain here to preserve what I built. I have been waiting. I have been* waiting. *And you have brought me word that all waiting is in vain.*

He spit out webbing, and it remained in the air, as if it had a will or a life of its own. *This was my life. This was the life I built. The life I wanted. But it is* here *and not elsewhere because this was the heart of* Ravellon. *There is nothing for me if that heart is ash.*

I'm not leaving without you.

Then you will die.

So will the books.

She felt a glimmer of something that might be annoyance; it was different from grief, from despair.

Black fire launched itself from the core of the blob on the other side of Bakkon's defense.

You don't have to kill them.

They are difficult to kill or they would not have survived our first encounter. And here, a glimmer of amusement, if dark. *I was not lying. I cannot leave this space. I will fall into the same madness, and I will become a mindless part of it. I will kill you.*

Kaylin shook her head. She drew a long, steadying breath, and began to speak.

The light in the library slowly changed as she did. She started to lower the hand that was pressed into the Wevaran's side, but changed her mind; it was her last deliberate thought as she gave herself over to the very slight sound she could hear. It was different from the voice she had followed in her desperate attempt to separate Mandoran from the contagion of Shadow; clearer, for one. Clear enough that it was entirely foreign to her.

But it was the sound of the word itself—the sound Bakkon could hear when the word had fully separated itself from her skin. A word, a True Word. It had grown larger at her back, but as she turned toward it, she could see that it was drifting to where she stood.

She repeated, slowly, what she could hear, syllables merging to form one long, complicated word.

The tint of golden light changed the color of Bakkon's webbing—both the slender strands he had built into a dome, and the glob that remained, ready to use, between his forelimbs. It also changed the color of the Shadow attacking Bakkon. It changed the shape of the creature as well.

"I don't think it was trying to kill Bakkon," Mandoran said.

She shook her head, concentrating on the spoken word as she repeated it, her voice stronger and more certain. The word grew larger and brighter as she spoke; had she not been physically attached to Bakkon with her free hand and Mandoran by one of his, she would have been able to walk around it, and walk beneath its tallest stroke, which formed an arch, like a keystone, above them all.

Bakkon was shivering; she could feel the tremors beneath her palm; could see the shaking of his raised limbs. Beyond him, she could see the quivering, giant blob; it lost height as it listened, the protrusions from which Shadow exploded sinking back into the trunk of its form. It reflected the light of the True Word, becoming a thing of gold, on the surface.

And it finally opened its eyes—or pushed its eyes to the surface of what passed for skin—as it looked past webbing and Wevaran to where Kaylin stood. The marks on her arms were glowing the same gold that the True Word did. It opened a mouth. No, two, or three that she could easily see.

It spoke.

It spoke the same word that Kaylin herself was speaking; she almost lost the syllables in surprise. The voice was deep and resonant. It was almost singing, and when she continued to speak, she did so quietly, because she couldn't sing, couldn't bring anything to its voice but a dissonant harmony.

Bakkon's legs lowered, the webbing he'd ejected unused. He began to back away from the Shadow; the Shadow did not follow. Kaylin saw that the word that would never again fit on her skin was moving—but it moved through her, through Bakkon, and toward the Shadow that was singing its syllables, combat, for the moment, forgotten.

This time, when Mandoran tugged on her shoulder, she backed up. The Shadow continued to sing. Kaylin stopped speaking the word. "You're sure you can't save him?"

"Not safely. I don't know what you've done, but I think we should take advantage of it."

"It's a word," she said quietly. "It's a word that the Shadow can see—and speak."

Bakkon seemed to lose height and size, although he never reached the diminutive shape of Spike as he'd been when they first encountered him. "I will try, Chosen," he said, his voice wobbly. "I cannot promise anything but that."

"We'll take it."

There was one door that could be easily seen from where they were standing. Kaylin, when she was certain Bakkon was following, turned toward it. It was an internal door, although it was wider and taller than the doors in either the Hawks' office or her home.

"I will ask you both," the Wevaran said as they approached it, "to climb on my back."

Mandoran said, "It's not necessary. I can travel without touching the ground." He looked pointedly at Kaylin. "You should ride."

She'd seen Liatt and her daughter ride Wevaran, but had had zero desire to ever try it herself. Grimacing, she nodded. It was very, very hard to override the visceral impulse to get as far away from the Wevaran's mouth as possible. But one of the things she'd learned with the Hawks was how to override visceral impulse.

She'd also learned when to trust it. Ugh. Bakkon bent his limbs until his body was almost flush with the stone beneath their feet. She closed her eyes as she clambered up his back. She settled the bag—made of webbing—with the books he had intended Kaylin to preserve in her lap, where it...stuck.

The Wevaran helped, readjusting her seat as she tried to make herself at least partly comfortable.

"Stand away from the door," Bakkon told Mandoran. Mandoran moved instantly, casting a backward glance at the Shadow, whose voice could still be heard. It seemed to be growing louder; the ground shook in time with the syllables.

Bakkon had eyes everywhere and didn't need to reorient his body to look back; Kaylin didn't. She turned her head. It seemed to her, as the doors flew off their hinges, that the Shadow was weeping.

Kaylin understood why the Wevaran had asked them both to mount the moment he started through the empty space left by doors that had been blown off their hinges; he *moved*. She tensed her legs and knees, and placed both hands flat in front of her, against his body. From there, she began to reach out as a healer. He had said he couldn't leave the library safely, and she believed him—or believed that he believed it; he hadn't lied.

But she didn't know what or how he might be enslaved—that was Spike's word—or corrupted; she assumed that it would be similar to what had happened to Mandoran. Mandoran, however, was mostly himself; she cursed and wished she'd insisted that he join her. If he were here, she could physically reach out to touch him, to keep the strands of Shadow separate from the rest of him.

He wasn't in reach now—but he proved that he could easily pace the Wevaran. The door didn't open onto the same street

that she and Mandoran had walked—and that was a pity, because the street it did open onto wasn't empty. The buildings
were similar—they looked in places like normal buildings but
melted or tilted into shapes she found instantly *wrong*.

It wasn't the buildings that were a problem—it was the
Shadows in the street; the streets were beginning to fill. Kaylin
had some experience with crowds, and some experience with
the way crowd could become mob with very little warning.
This felt like the latter.

Bakkon scuttled up the side of a building, above the heads
of the shorter or smaller Shadows. He spit webbing, tossed it
behind them—Kaylin had to duck—and sped up.

"Mandoran!"

Mandoran, however, had seen the wisdom of Bakkon's suggestion; he pushed himself off the ground in a trajectory that
ended roughly on top of Kaylin, who reached up with her
right arm—her stronger arm—and pulled him down in front
of her. She then wrapped one arm around his waist and leaned
to place a hand against Bakkon, keeping her mouth shut so
that she didn't bite her tongue when the Wevaran's trajectory
changed. He wasn't flying, but he was spitting out webbing
as he slowed, and that webbing seemed to be strong enough
to bear both his weight and theirs.

The air was heavy with fog. She missed Hope badly; she
wanted to examine that fog beneath the veil of wing. "What
does the fog look like to you?" she shouted, in Mandoran's ear.

"Fog?" Bakkon shouted back, spitting web between the
start of the syllable, and repeating the uncomfortable action
at the end. All of his eyes were open; the lids seemed to have
retracted fully into his body. They moved, darting in all directions; Kaylin wanted to move her legs—or jump off his
back—because she found it disturbing.

She had never liked spiders. The part of her that screamed
he's not a spider was almost too quiet. But spiders didn't have

eyes all over their bodies either. She spun sideways as Bakkon leaped above the fog, too preoccupied with staying seated to look down. The marks on her arms were glowing, the gold giving way to the brilliance of white.

Bakkon grunted as he leaped again, as if the marks had a weight that he could feel, even if Kaylin couldn't. Mandoran let loose a volley of Leontine, and that pulled Kaylin back to reality.

Shadow tendrils burst out of the fog, thin and dark and faintly opalescent; they caught the web Bakkon was barely spinning, and began to burn. Mouthless, they screamed. The web ignited; Kaylin could see purple fire race up the strands the tendrils had grasped. She focused on staying on the Wevaran's back and keeping one hand on each of her two companions.

"Chosen!" Bakkon shouted. "Speak!"

Words—not that there were many available—would have failed her completely. "Speak about what?"

Bakkon growled; the growl extended into a roar.

Chosen. She looked at her arms; the marks were glowing. *Speak.* The marks remained flat against her skin; there was only one mark that had fully risen, and she had left it in the library, if any of the library remained.

But it had done *something* to the blob-Shadow, which had bought them just enough time to get through the doors and out. She looked over her shoulder as Bakkon leaped; cursed in Leontine because it was better than screaming, and tried to think. Hard, when her stomach was trying to find an entirely different place in her body to sit.

"Mandoran—can you fly? Can you carry us?"

"I could carry you," he shouted back. "I don't think I could carry the spider!" He spoke in Elantran.

Praying that Mandoran wouldn't get hit with another Shadow spear, Kaylin lifted a hand; it was the hand gloved in

Shadow. In the light of these particular streets, she could see the strands as a dense web of lines. Those lines were moving, crawling in place as if struggling to escape. It was not a comforting thought.

But the Shadow on her hand didn't speak; it didn't try to take control; it sat there, above her skin, the same way the marks of the Chosen did. Even here, in the heart of the fiefs: *Ravellon*.

She touched Bakkon with the gloved hand; she touched him with the marked hand. He had heard the mark that had risen from her skin—and he'd wept. She had seen the Dragons speak these words. She had seen the words themselves when the former Arkon made the attempt. She had seen the marks on her arms grow in size—but she'd attributed that, until today, to the quasi-dream state that she'd been in.

Bakkon had heard the words she couldn't say because she didn't have syllables. Bakkon spoke them. Bakkon was something that had been trapped in *Ravellon*. She wasn't certain he could leave it—and that probably should have been her first thought.

But there were Wevaran in the actual Tower of Liatt. And if the Tower accepted them, it meant they weren't like Spike; they weren't physically Shadow in the way that Gilbert had been. Bakkon *should* be able to join the few kin that remained, hidden, from the rest of Elantra.

If, that is, they could even reach the border. Kaylin wasn't particular about which border at this point, and her geographic sense of the fief boundaries was completely flattened by the warped streets and buildings across which Bakkon leaped.

"Chosen!"

Trying not to panic, she glared at her arms. The marks remained stubbornly flat; she couldn't hear them. None rose. And she couldn't just choose one that meant "die" or "freeze." But...but if she could get *Bakkon* out of here, he might be willing to teach her. The only other possible teacher was the former Arkon, the current chancellor of an institution that he must both build and protect.

Bakkon, she thought. At the moment, he no longer had a job.

She exhaled, closing her eyes, her hands now anchored only to the Wevaran. Eyes closed, she could see the one rune she had left in Bakkon's library—even if it was theoretically behind her.

She listened, trying to separate the sounds of escape, of climbing, of spitting, from the sound of the word itself. The syllables fell into place and she began to speak them, almost to chant them. She'd never been any good at singing, but she'd been trained to shout—and to shout in a way that projected voice without sounding as if she was panicked or on the verge of screaming.

She did that now. She pitched those syllables into the growing noise of a mob, her voice rising above it. As she spoke, the mob stilled. Tendrils of shadow still strained upward in a cluster as they attempted to catch Bakkon, but they moved more slowly.

The mark had eclipsed the building they'd fled; it rose above the twisted, melting heights, and continued to spread past what would in a normal city be its walls, its boundaries. She could see what she'd identified as fog begin to darken— perhaps in response to the light the word shed.

She spoke more emphatically, repeating the word, and as she did, the gray seemed to settle into the core of her. She thought of Bakkon's reaction—but Bakkon was himself. The Shadows who had gathered in the streets to stop Bakkon were not. But the blob had stopped as the word had made itself clear to him—and the Shadows were slowing and turning toward what she saw as a word. Not to Kaylin—who was speaking it—but to the word itself.

The light of the rune dimmed, thinning as the fog began to gather around it; she could see tendrils of shadow curl up the lines and swallow the smaller dots. Shadow could influence the shape of True Words—she'd seen that in the Tower of Tiamaris.

But this word was not the very heart of a Tower. It wasn't the heart of anything; it was a word. A word that she thought the Shadows might understand, even if she didn't. She could see the lines of it thin, elongate; could almost hear the sound of it change, as if there were now two voices speaking its syllables—hers and the bending rune itself.

It was like an argument, and Kaylin felt sweat bead and trickle down her forehead, almost as if she carried the weight of the larger-than-building rune just by speaking the syllables that comprised it. Mandoran's grip on her arm shifted, as if he understood that Kaylin, at his back, was beginning to flag—while trying to stay seated on the back of a giant spider who was making a run for the border of *Ravellon*.

She couldn't see it; couldn't see anything but the words and the Shadows. And that made no sense, if she stopped to think about it; she had always been able to see the marks, when they glowed, with closed eyes; she had never been able to see *Shadow* the same way.

Here, she could. And she had no more time to think about it, about what that meant, because thinking broke the rhythm of the syllables, and the syllables had caught the attention of the Shadows, diminishing pursuit.

Mandoran loosed a volley of Leontine; Bakkon barked an order in a clicking screech that neither she nor the Barrani cohort member could understand. Kaylin's eyes flew open as a cone of distinctly purple fire attempted to incinerate the Wevaran—and the passengers he carried.

The Dragon outcaste had arrived.

27

The cone of flame, anchored as it was by the very wide jaws of an enormous black dragon, hit the ground. Kaylin shifted her grip on Bakkon, placing a hand, once again, on Mandoran as the spider clambered up the side of a building. Purple fire with a heart of white turned the ground into a molten mess; out of the steam that arose, she could once again see what she had called *fog*.

It was difficult to reorient herself, but the presence of a Dragon made it easier: he took up a third of the skyscape from any vantage. They were close to the border. They had to be close; she could see street, and could see buildings that looked normal—if run-down—which implied a border was close.

That way! she shouted at Bakkon. He leaped down the street, and then up the side of a building and over a roof as the outcaste inhaled. Kaylin was willing to bet money that she could hear the sound of his drawn breath from where she sat, wind whistling in perpetual loose strands of hair.

Some of that hair was singed; the blast was close, the Dragon closer. She could feel the fire strike Bakkon's back legs, which had been closer to the splash. She had some idea of what *healthy* meant for a Wevaran now, because it felt like she'd been in physical contact with one for hours. She immediately started to heal the damage the fire had caused.

To no one's surprise, it was far easier thought than done; the purple fire was not like the regular kind, and the damage it caused seemed more persistent, as if the flame itself were like a worm or invasive insect that sought to spread beneath the flesh it had hit.

Thank you. Please continue to do that. You are certain about our direction?

Yes—but so's the Dragon.

Dragon? Is that what you call it?

I call it a lot of things, but Dragon will do. Outcaste Dragon, she added, in case it mattered. To Kaylin at this very moment, it didn't. The shadow of the outcaste loomed above them, more dangerous than the Shadow that the fiery breath had dislodged beneath.

Bakkon was attempting to reach the barrier of the border, but it was clear what his destination was, and it made targeting the Wevaran far simpler. The fire could strike in front of the next location, the next leap. Bakkon's version of a straight line wasn't the usual version, but it didn't matter. If they wanted to survive to get out, no straight lines could be run.

Kaylin shifted her hold on Mandoran—more to keep herself on the Wevaran's back than make sure the Barrani didn't fall—trying to find the cadence of the syllables she'd been projecting; she lost them instantly as fire once again clipped Bakkon.

She fell silent as she healed the damage the fire was doing; concentrated as she uprooted tendrils of flame, ejecting them. Bakkon said nothing; she wasn't certain he was even aware of the fire, he was moving so quickly.

Fire once again singed strands of Kaylin's hair as it hit Bakkon; for the first time, flames licked up the back end of his body. All thought of True Words fled. She could heal the damage done, but it was work to remove the threads of flame that still bound themselves to Bakkon's flesh.

She was aware of the moment that the Shadows surged again—tentacles burst from the sides of buildings, from the roofs, all places that Bakkon momentarily touched as he landed and leaped. He spit webbing, but none of that webbing formed the shield that it had formed in the library.

No, Chosen. I cannot weave that and run—and here, it is not enough defense.

She wished, briefly, that she hadn't all but demanded that he come with them.

If I had not, you would be dead or lost. And the loss of the Chosen to the fallen is far more dangerous than the loss of one Wevaran.

Why?

Hush.

Fire. She could hear the roar of the outcaste, and she could see him clearly now, his great wingspan and the aerial advantage becoming more and more clear.

I'm sorry, she told the Wevaran. *I don't think we're going to make it.*

Continue with what you are doing. You might tell the boy to leap; I believe he has ways of escaping that are not available to you.

You can't do the weird portal thing?

Not from here, no. I can create a portal, but it will not take us anywhere you wish to go. She felt a wave of pain pass through him, and caught it, hoping that the body's sense of "right" or "healthy" conformed in some way to the healing she was attempting to do on the fly.

"Mandoran—Bakkon wants you to jump off. He thinks you can escape on your own."

Mandoran shook his head. "One, I might accidentally dislodge you. Two, Teela would kill me."

"She's not here."

"Look right," he shouted back.

Kaylin immediately turned to her right. She saw a blur of melting building tops—"roofs" didn't quite describe them—and a small burst of black dots that emerged from one of them.

"No, look up and right!"

Bakkon almost unseated them both as he leaped, his only attachment to anything solid a glistening thread of webbing; she lost any sense of direction as he spun. Mandoran didn't have that problem. Bakkon didn't either; he leaped, and leaped again. Kaylin briefly closed her eyes to avoid the dizziness the constant shift of visible landscape was causing, and managed to keep one hand on the Wevaran in case he got clipped—or worse—by fire again.

It didn't happen. She realized that his frenetic hopping traced a large circle, from building top to side to street and back up, and when he'd finished, there was a literal web in the space transcribed by his leaping. He screeched and clicked what sounded like three distinct words, and then the web suddenly snapped shut—loudly—detaching its various threads from their moorings.

The black mass of what looked, at a distance, like an insect swarm was swallowed by the shuttered trap.

She looked up.

A gold Dragon was in the air, her breath a plume of constant flame aimed in its entirety at the Dragon outcaste. Bellusdeo had arrived. As lightning flew in a forked streak of light from the Dragon's back, Kaylin understood why Mandoran had said Teela was here.

Kaylin cursed.

"Tell Teela to get Bellusdeo *out of here!* What in the hells is she *thinking?*"

Mandoran, however, said, "Bakkon, run *now*. And I'm not talking to Teela—to anyone—until we clear this place. I won't take that risk!"

Kaylin was willing to bet any money that the rest of the co-

hort didn't share this prohibition; they were probably screaming in his figurative ear by now.

Bakkon's path was clear. He skittered and jumped from roof
to roof, almost falling when one building collapsed, melting
into the streets far beneath his feet. A spit glob of webbing
prevented the fall as it attached itself to a building that wasn't
dissolving, or at least prevented their subsequent landing. The
Wevaran *moved*.

Kaylin could see past the barrier; she could see the run-
down and very mundane streets.

Just as she had when she was a child, she looked at those
run-down buildings as salvation—they only had to *reach* them,
and they would be safe.

But reaching them was going to be more of a problem, because the two Dragons were no longer the only thing in the
sky above the one fief that had no Tower.

The Aerians—the shadow-melded Aerians with spears they
seemed to extrude from their own bodies—had arrived. The
cacophony of sound—the Dragons roaring, among others—
was almost welcome. The Aerians were not.

"Incoming!" she shouted, as the much smaller flying enemies began to circle the streets and buildings across which
Bakkon ran. She could see the spears; could hear their sibi-
lant hiss as they were launched. She hadn't heard that the first
time. It was almost as if there were words in it.

They were words, she thought, that had somehow dragged
both her and Mandoran here. She had no idea what would
happen if those spears struck them while they were already in
Ravellon. None of her best guesses were good.

No, Bakkon said, as she was still attached to him, still healing the small injuries that he'd taken. *Nothing good will happen.*

Can you stop them from hitting you?

Yes.

Us?

I am less certain. The noise took a back seat to Wevaran eyes as they bulged their way out of the sockets that contained them, rising on slender stalks that looked...not much different than strands of Shadow.

Wevaran legs were flexible. Far more flexible than mortal legs or midsections. The spears did fly; they simply failed to connect. She wanted—needed—time. No, wait, that was Bakkon's thought. He wanted time. She had no way to give it to him.

Bellusdeo roared. This close, she could recognize the cadence of unintelligible draconic.

Another Dragon roared in response—not the outcaste, although his voice surged forward as if it were a shield against hers. A blue Dragon joined the fray, but it was an odd blue—metallic, almost shimmering, the color pale as clear sky. She caught a glimpse, no more; Bakkon was moving frenetically. But the glimpses—of gold, of black, and of blue—yielded a patchwork of information. The blue Dragon seemed to almost fade in the light of the sky above *Ravellon*. Lightning struck—this time, not the outcaste, but his small, flying squadron—and where it struck, screams followed. Screams of rage.

She saw the moment when the webbing spit from a thankfully obscured mouth came out pink, and understood what it meant; she'd seen it before. Bakkon had pushed past any reasonable, healthy limit that constrained the use of spider magic. He was continuing past those limits, and she gave up trying to catch a glimpse of the Dragons and concentrated on the healing.

Kaylin!

She thought she would never again be so grateful to hear Severn's voice. *We're here—there are three of us. One's like Starrante. We're not dead. Yet. Where are you?*

At the border. I cadged a ride with Emmerian. Could you not hear me until now?

No. Ummm, we're coming out of Ravellon.

I can see that.

Can you let the people who might flame us to ashes know?

I'll tell Terrano. He's…surprisingly mobile in the air.

A blast of lightning brightened the sky; it came from the ground. Nightshade, she thought. She made no attempt to bespeak him. Nor did she ask Severn whether or not they'd emptied enough of the fief's buildings before the outcaste had started his rain of fire.

Bellusdeo roared, and this time, Emmerian replied in kind.

Emmerian's coming down, Severn said.

He can't come into Ravellon!

Demonstrably he can. He hesitated and then said, *Bellusdeo asked.*

Is that what she just said?

According to Terrano, yes.

It didn't sound like any variant of "ask" Kaylin was familiar with. To be fair, no spoken Dragon ever sounded like anything other than rage and fury to her ears.

What did she tell him?

To take care of the Aerians—and not to turn you to ash when you leave the barrier. In that order.

Is it me, or is Emmerian almost silver?

He's silver.

She could see that now, because Emmerian began to descend.

Tell him not to do that, Bakkon said, voice urgent. It carried the undertone of both panic and exhaustion. Kaylin immediately passed the message to Severn and left it in his hands; hers were full.

Please, Bakkon said, *stop feeling guilty. The request was yours. The decision was mine.*

Since she hadn't said a word of apology—well, okay, not more than a few—she was surprised. But surprised or no, she knit fibers of his body back together, alarmed at how they seemed to almost be separating—as if they were threads in a tapestry.

Emmerian didn't land. Instead, he flew low, over them, his body a solid cloud; he breathed fire in front of Bakkon, and behind him, scorching what passed for stone until it screamed.

Stone screaming, buildings dodging, Bakkon leaping from unstable ground to unstable building over and over again beneath the shadow of a Dragon. The storm in the air above didn't drop rain; in one or two cases, it dropped bodies. Aerian bodies, the unnatural gray of their wings seeping, once again, into the ground or the air from which it had come.

She could see—through Severn's eyes, as hers were closed—some of the Aerians peel off in an attempt to land while their wings were burning.

And then, one last burst of costly speed, and Bakkon reached the barrier, slowing markedly at the last moment.

Get off, he told her. *I am not certain that the barrier will allow me safe passage.*

Then why did you come???

Because Ravellon *would not have allowed you safe passage to reach it.*

I am not getting off.

"Mandoran—get off. Go through the barrier."

"What about you?"

"I'll go through with Bakkon."

"Seriously?"

She lifted a hand and smacked the back of his head. "Get. Off. Right. Now."

Severn—

Terrano says they're arguing with Mandoran. Well, no, they're shouting at Mandoran and he's not answering. Terrano is offering to come help persuade him in person.

No!

No, indeed. Now they're arguing with Terrano—and he's arguing back. According to Terrano. I think this might have even been deliberate.

And you're not arguing with me.

No point. You're not going to leave the Wevaran until you know he can get through the barrier. Or until you know he can't.

She tried to push Mandoran off Bakkon's back, but there was only so much she could do with one hand, and she was unwilling to release the Wevaran. She didn't know what the barrier would do. She had seen Shadows stop at its edge before, but hadn't seen them take a run at it and bounce. And Bakkon was still moving, but with less frenetic, dizzying speed.

I asked you to stop feeling guilty, the Wevaran said.

I don't. Not yet.

You do understand that you cannot lie to me while we speak in this fashion, yes?

Fine. Whatever you're sensing now is nothing *compared to the* guilt *I'm going to carry for the* rest of my life *if you don't somehow survive this.*

For the first time, she felt genuine Wevaran amusement. Amusement and a kind of bright resignation. Bakkon approached the *Ravellon* barrier at what was, in comparison to the rest of their sprint, a jog.

Tell Terrano to tell people outside of the cohort that Bakkon is like Starrante in the Academia. He's not—

Not a Shadow?

He's not under anything else's control.

Severn nodded; she felt it. She started to speak and stopped, because even internally words and syllables were broken by the roaring of Dragons. This time, it wasn't the outcaste—it was Bellusdeo, whom she recognized, and Emmerian. She looked up, and then had to look down again; Bakkon's more straightforward approach wasn't exactly done on the ground.

Fire clipped him again, but the fire banked almost before

it had a chance to cling. Bakkon saw the barrier. Kaylin saw the effect of the barrier, but not the thing itself.

You cannot see it.

No—but don't try to show me, okay? You have way too many eyes, and I think I'll just get dizzy, or worse, if I try to look through all of them as you do.

Fire touched the ground, this fire orange-yellow; purple fire split as if to allow it passage. The ground screamed. That, she didn't need Wevaran ears to catch.

"Mandoran—"

"I'll teach you useful words when we leave if you *stop nagging me!*"

"Fine! What are you *doing?*" Mandoran was becoming transparent. He was still attached to Bakkon's back; she could touch him. But she could see through him now, as if he were made of glass.

He said nothing, and it was loud enough she couldn't hear him grinding his teeth, which she was pretty certain he was doing.

Emmerian roared; his shadow covered the zigzagging up-and-down path Bakkon was now following. Mandoran cursed—in Leontine—and said, "Fine, you win." He leaped up, off Bakkon's back. He didn't land on the ground. He didn't attempt to reach it; wind seemed to yank him off his perch, as if the only gravity he was now subject to had been dependent on the Wevaran's back.

"Duck!" That was definitely Mandoran. She ducked. Bakkon all but flattened himself. Emmerian, almost dragging enormous claws across the ground, passed them at speed, the underside of his wings visible. There wasn't a lot of dust to kick up on this side of the *Ravellon* border—the only positive Kaylin could think of.

"LEFT!" Mandoran shouted.

Bakkon veered instantly.

Emmerian did not.

Rising from the previously flat street just in front of the border itself was a giant pillar of Shadow.

Emmerian veered to the same left as Bakkon had; there were no longer any buildings to prevent this. The buildings across which the Wevaran had scuttled at speed had melted or transformed, an instant before Mandoran's shouting, into something that was taller than any of the visible buildings in *Ravellon*.

This, she thought, as it solidified, gaining width as well as height, was like a Tower in shape. Bakkon was utterly silent on the inside of his own head, the whole of his attention given to maneuvering. The street he'd been following, under the wings of a silver Dragon, was gone.

Emmerian ascended, moving more quickly than Bakkon— but not by much.

Terrano says Mandoran says there's no exit the way you were running.

Was it there before?

Unclear. Mandoran saw whatever defense was mounted a little bit before the rest of you did. He's with Emmerian now.

With?

I believe he's on Emmerian's back. What he can see, Emmerian can't see.

And without her familiar, neither could she. Not for the first time in her life, she wished that people could see the same things, could understand all languages, could communicate perfectly. That was the sole benefit of True Words as a language; the meaning of each word couldn't be mistaken or misunderstood.

Which was probably why no one could easily speak them.

Which way? Does Terrano have any other instructions?

Silence. She could sense Severn, but couldn't hear him ask

the question she'd asked. She was too afraid of falling off Bakkon's back to focus on the listening as Severn listened.

Mandoran says the Shadow that looks like a building to you—he's frustrated with that, by the way—extends both left and right. He also says the rest of the Shadows in Ravellon aren't standing still behind you. Terrano doesn't think it's safe for either Bellusdeo or Emmerian to land.

The outcaste does it!

He believes that proves his point.

She cursed. Bakkon was exhausted, and the exhaustion wasn't something she could simply heal or cure. He hadn't, and wouldn't, stop until he couldn't move on his own anymore. She was worried that that would be soon.

If they can't land and we can't even touch these...walls, what's his suggestion?

Not certain. Terrano says wall *is a good description—and the walls are spreading so that they overlap the barrier from the inside. He asks how you got in in the first place.*

She started to tell him that this wasn't the time for that, but stopped herself. It was a good question; it was a fair question. Maybe if she understood the actual answer beyond *I don't know*, they'd have a better chance of surviving this.

Terrano says your best chance of escape is to continue to the left; he thinks there might be some chance the wall there could be permeable.

Why?

It's Tiamaris, and Bellusdeo's presence in the sky has pulled all of the Norranir out of their homes. They're drumming.

They wouldn't make it. And more permeable was a gamble she was almost certain would end in death.

Enslavement, Bakkon said, correcting her.

Kaylin exhaled. *Tell Terrano—tell anyone who can move* fast—*to head to Liatt.*

For the Wevaran?

She nodded. *Get them to come to Candallar.*

Severn fell silent.

When Mandoran rejoined them, she almost fell off the Wevaran's back, he appeared so suddenly. He was the color of old—and bad—cheese, and his eyes were a little too large in the contours of his otherwise Barrani face; they were also the wrong color.

"I think I know what I'm doing," he told her. He wasn't shouting, but his voice could be clearly heard, and given the constant presence of roaring Dragons, this said something. "Terrano says Riaknon is on the way." He spoke in Elantran, but the very Barrani pronunciation of the name caused Bakkon to stumble.

Did he say Riaknon?

Yes. Riaknon is in the Tower of Liatt; he's been there since the Towers rose.

And he is on his way?

Ummm, on his way to someplace outside of the barrier. I don't think he intends to cross it.

"A little bit of attention, Kaylin."

"Sorry—Bakkon knows Riaknon."

"Fine. Does Bakkon think Riaknon can do anything?"

It is possible, if it's Riaknon. Starrante could do it—but Starrante is bound. He will not be able to join us.

"He says maybe. Who did you send to Liatt?"

"Nightshade."

She didn't swallow her tongue, but it took effort.

"Tiamaris is in the air from the edge of his fief, just in case you haven't been watching."

She considered pushing her housemate off Bakkon's back, but not for long. *Is there anything you could tell Riaknon—through us—that might help us?*

You could leave, Chosen. It would be better if you did.

Let's not go there again. Is there anything you want Riaknon to know?

His answer was a cascade of clicks and almost bell-like sounds. She was touching him, and in theory, she could understand him as clearly as he could understand her. None of this odd music, however, made sense to her.

"Nothing I think could be passed on."

"What did he say?"

She tried to repeat it.

"Oh."

Nightshade.

I am at the Tower of Liatt. She didn't ask him how he'd gone from Candallar to Liatt so quickly; she was *almost* certain she didn't want to know.

It would not be something you could easily repeat, no. He was amused, but there was enough of a grim, grim undercurrent to the amusement she felt none in return.

Where is the Wevaran?

A very good question. He left the Tower, returned to it in haste, returned to me and ordered me to wait. He then created a web with which you would be familiar and stepped through it, shutting it from behind.

You're waiting for Liatt?

That is my assumption, yes—and there she is. She is with another of the Wevaran; her daughter, however, is not present. I will leave you now; if there is more information—ah, no. Lord Liatt has just asked me if I believe the Wevaran you are currently riding is corrupted.

Tell her no!

I have indicated that I would not be here if I suspected that he was, yes. She is heading to the former fief of Candallar now.

"Pay attention. I need your help now," Mandoran was saying. Kaylin's head hurt. Her eyes hurt. Her stomach was more than queasy. Her ears were also ringing.

"What do you need me to do?"

"We need to shift a bit to avoid easy detection by the Shadows here."

Tell him that is impossible.

"Bakkon doesn't believe we can do that."

"I didn't say we'd be invisible—I said we'd be harder to detect. Does that pass muster?"

What does he intend? The depth of suspicion in the question was like screaming the word *no*, loudly, in her ears. It wasn't, however, a *No*.

"We're not like Shadow," Mandoran said—a fact that Kaylin knew well. She assumed he was speaking for Bakkon's sake as well as her own. Fire changed the temperature of the air at their back, but the fire was Dragon fire, not outcaste fire; it didn't cling. Or it didn't cling to Bakkon. "But we're no longer entirely like the rest of our kin, either. Terrano believes we can navigate—for a brief period—in *Ravellon* without falling prey to the corruption that lies at its heart."

"How in the hells does he know what lies at its heart? He said he's never been stupid enough to try to enter!"

"Not asking that question Right Now," Mandoran snapped back. "But Terrano thinks it's how *you* could get in here at all."

"I got in *through you!*"

"I wasn't *here* until you did whatever the hells it was you did!"

"You must have been partly here—that was the *whole point* of the Shadow spears!"

Bakkon cleared his throat. Loudly. "While it goes against my upbringing to stop the younglings from killing each other, there is a time and place for everything." He spoke in Barrani. "Chosen, if you are to have any chance of leaving this place, if you are to do the duty for which you were Chosen, you must come up with better answers. I am sorry to add to the pressure."

"I told you—I got here by listening. And I'm pretty damn

sure what I was listening to so intently won't get us to the *other damn side* of this wall!"

Fire. Shadow. Where they met, the Shadow screamed and withdrew—or at least most of it did. The parts that were visible to Kaylin. She was so accustomed to having Hope slap a wing across her face she felt as if she'd lost the ability to see at all.

What had she done? Truly, she'd just *listened*. She'd listened really, really intently. Why? Because she was almost certain that what she heard was part of not-Mandoran, even if she could hear it because she was touching his injured body.

"Here!" Mandoran shouted.

Bakkon came to a skittering stop. While the streets were smoking—literally—he looked to an ebon wall—a wall in which hints of all known colors swirled beneath a solid surface. She wasn't surprised when the wall sprouted eyes.

She *was* surprised when they opened and focused on Bakkon, leaving the wall on the slender stalks that Bakkon's eyes also possessed.

Emmerian, above, had come to a halt, and now circled in the air in almost a holding pattern. The Aerians—those few that remained in the sky—were engaged enough they couldn't immediately attempt to turn the Wevaran, and his passengers, into pincushions.

Bakkon froze for one long moment, and then began to speak. The sounds—chittering and clicking and the soft music of bells—continued for some time. During it, Mandoran dismounted to once again join Emmerian in the air. She could hear him giving directions; could see the fire Emmerian exhaled in plumes seconds later.

Emmerian, who had been so worried about the cohort's possible attack on Bellusdeo that he had practically broken into Helen to intervene, had chosen to trust the cohort. Not just Mandoran; Emmerian wasn't a fool. He knew that the cohort was, in many ways, one being that cast a lot of shadows when in the light.

The eyeballs withdrew only when Bakkon had finished speaking.

Do not speak to me for a moment, he said before she could ask him what he'd said. *I need to concentrate now. I need to listen—as you listened.*

"Kaylin, we *really* need to get moving. I don't want to panic you, but an *actual* Tower is growing in the center of *Ravellon*—and we do not want to be here when the doors of that Tower open!"

As they had never wanted to be here at all, Kaylin tried not to grind her teeth. Instead, she took a few steadying breaths, and then slid off Bakkon's back. Or tried. Bakkon caught her and pushed her back into her impromptu seat. *It is not safe for you to touch the ground here.*

Is it safer to touch the wall?

Silence.

But Kaylin had been thinking, in spite of the noise and the fear and the multiple different strands of worry that she'd been unconsciously weaving.

Bakkon was listening, he said, as she'd listened.

He spoke again, in what she assumed was his native tongue. She closed her eyes. Either she could hear an echo in the miasma of *Ravellon* air, or a different Wevaran was speaking across the divide of border and wall. As she listened, she saw the wall undulate.

She could see the wall with her eyes closed.

A brief glance at her arms confirmed that the marks of the Chosen were glowing—but they also seemed to be vibrating in place, as if they wanted to lift themselves off her skin as they so often did, but couldn't.

She could almost hear them, as if they, in concert, were

trying to speak—to join their voices to the voices of the two Wevaran.

"Bakkon," she said, "let me get down. I think I'll be safe."

The limb applying the pressure did not lift.

"Okay, yes, that's an exaggeration. But I think I need to be on the ground—or in arm's reach of the...wall. I think I can make a space here that we might be able to get through."

"What do you intend to do?"

"Listen to the wall," she said quietly.

"How will that help you?"

"I don't—I don't know. But I think I can make the wall *listen*."

He spoke his own tongue; the voice—the other voice—grew louder and less bell-like. His own voice remained almost frustratingly calm.

"Your friend on the other side does not think this is a good idea."

"He probably doesn't think it's a disaster," Kaylin replied, without much thought.

"Oh?"

"If he did, he'd make Mandoran come back down here right now."

"Funny you should mention that," a very familiar voice said. It was, predictably, Mandoran.

28

"Terrano is with the other Wevaran, right?"

"Yes. He's trying to be helpful, but he can't completely understand what they're saying. Our Wevaran has some ideas; their Wevaran is pretty sure it's either unsafe or impossible."

"I don't think we have time for this. Emmerian can only keep things clear for as long as no other winged Shadows take to the air, and Bellusdeo—"

"She moved. She's fighting in the airspace over Candallar, now. She told Emmerian to retreat," he added.

Kaylin winced, because Emmerian was still here.

Mandoran surprised her; he grinned. "Sedarias pretty much said the same thing to me that Bellusdeo said to Emmerian. I can't answer. But I've been listening really, really carefully. I'd like to go home," he added. "Maybe at home the screaming will stop."

"It's Sedarias. If you die—or worse—it'll break her."

"Funny, that's what Emmerian said, too. Except not about Sedarias. He doesn't think Bellusdeo can handle your death. You ready?"

She blinked, exhaled, and accepted that she was, in fact,

ready. She lifted both hands from the Wevaran's back; the palm of one was glowing white, the other, glowing black.

"Bakkon."

This time, when she attempted to slide off his back, he allowed it—possibly because he could see both of her hands. She was right beside the wall. Mandoran, standing just behind her—uncomfortably close—put his hands very firmly across either of her shoulders.

Kaylin placed both hands against the wall.

The wall appeared to part as she touched it—at least on one side. Where the new mark shone, the fiber of the wall retreated. Where the shadow-laced glove shimmered above her skin, the wall moved toward her; the shape of it therefore changed.

"What are you doing?" Mandoran asked.

Sarcasm died as Bakkon asked the same question. "Never mind what I'm doing," she told them both. "Concentrate on what you should be doing."

"What I should be doing, if I'm listening to everyone else screaming—"

"I am *not* screaming," Terrano's distant voice proclaimed.

"—is to pull you away from the wall and get you up to Emmerian. So...what are you doing?"

"Does it look like I know what I'm doing?"

"About as much as usual."

"Young man," Bakkon said, his voice hissing and crackling, "I'd advise you to step back."

Mandoran's hands tightened slightly on her shoulders. "I know I'm standing in possibly the worst place I could be for general safety or sanity purposes, but I am forced to ignore your request. And actually, it does look like you know what you're doing. To at least four of us."

She wanted to know which four, but decided now was not

the time to ask; if she remembered, she should ask later. "Is Sedarias one of them?"

"No."

She tried to empty her thoughts, to concentrate on what was now happening with the wall. The move to—and away—from her hands caused the type of undulations she associated with jelly, but bigger. "What can you see?" she asked the only available member of the cohort.

"Do you see a wall?"

She frowned. "Before I touched it, yes. It looked like a wall."

"Now?"

"Now I have no idea. It looks like...a barely cohesive jelly mold."

"That's definitely not what it looks like to me. I think there are strands of Shadow woven throughout this mass—but it's not like Spike was in the outlands; it's more like something grabbed whatever was in reach and dumped them into a mold. I don't think it will hold for long.

"Some of what I see is attempting to wrap itself around your hand, the way the strands of Shadow did in the Aerie. Almost as if they're trying to merge with it or join it."

"And the rest?"

"The rest are pushing the boundaries that define the physical shape of the whole they've been pressed into. I can almost see distinct forms—none of them large—emerge in the crush to get away from your hand. If you could figure out a way to ditch the Shadows that are trying to cling to you, you'd have a chance of clearing the wall on your own."

"Bakkon?"

"I can see what you see; I can see what your companion sees. Your base nature does not merge easily with Shadow; the Shadow can infiltrate and alter you—but it requires the right, hmmm, platform. You are fundamentally different. I am less fundamentally different; I believe I could withstand some form of attack, but if it were not brief, I could not deny the merging."

He began to speak loudly, and in what she assumed was his native tongue. On the other side of this wall, on the other side of this barrier, something replied.

Bakkon hissed. He spoke again, this time with less bells and more clicking.

Kaylin's arms and legs were glowing. She was certain the marks on her back were glowing as well.

She took a larger step forward. To her right, there was space. To her left, the thick, almost gelatinous wall seemed to harden. Gritting her teeth, she pulled at it, closing the gloved hand around the area in direct reach.

She could almost hear squeaking, as if she'd caught a very surprised mouse. "Is the miasma closing behind me?"

"It seems to be listening to you. Or to Bakkon; there's a definite loss of cohesion. But I think the parts that seem to be shying away are listening; they can't approach."

"Or they don't want to?"

"Or they don't want to."

Bakkon chittered.

"Can you see them as separate, Bakkon?" she said, over her shoulder. "Because this wall seems to go on forever."

"If you are not careful, it will. It is not unlike a portal in consistency, and I believe it is not unlike a portal in its eventual goal."

"Meaning whoever tries to breach the wall ends up somewhere else?"

"It is suspicion only. What can be done to me—to us— cannot as easily be done to you, if it can be done at all."

"And if you try to cross?"

"I have my own defenses, but they will not be enough. I believe you can make your way through."

Without him. If she were going to leave him here, she could just meet up with Emmerian and fly; the barrier was unlikely to prevent her departure.

She waved the arm with the new mark in front of her, creating eddies of movement. Fine. The hand in which she'd grabbed Shadow, the hand in which it almost seemed to be solidifying, couldn't move as freely. She brought the mark to the hand that was gripping Shadow.

The Shadow melted; she could almost feel it screaming. No, she thought, frowning, not screaming—weeping. Weeping and crying out in agony. She recognized the sound of pain. Of loss.

When she unclenched the fist with which she'd grabbed the smallest part of this conglomeration of Shadow, the Shadow fled. It made no attempt to return as she moved the hand on which the mark now burned.

And *burn* was the right word; it grew hotter as she held her arm out; her palm, callused over the years, started to tingle. She knew that pain would follow, as it often did—but there seemed to be no peak to it, no end. She could almost smell flesh burning, but her eyes couldn't see corresponding damage.

Not to herself.

Not to the Shadows in front. None of the rest of the marks on her body moved from their flattened place, but they shifted color until they were one with the exposed mark on her hand, as if her skin had windows in the exact shape of the marks themselves, and everything on the inside was a white, burning light.

"Bakkon!"

"Yes, yes, there's a window." He started to click and whir and, yes, peel. Before he had received an answer of any kind, he paused to spit out webbing. This was a pale pink; whatever recovery time he needed, this small period of stillness hadn't given him. If he was concerned, it didn't show; he lifted his front legs and began to work with the webbing, to move strands so slender she could barely see them.

"I am not certain this will work," he told her, sounding almost cheerful in his stilted Barrani.

"If it doesn't work, what happens to you?"

"I will be unable to leave. Nothing will change."

But she thought of the library and of the books—and what had Mandoran done with the damn books?—that he had preserved since the fall of *Ravellon*, and realized this wasn't true. Grimacing in pain, she held her palm out in front of herself, directly ahead, not to the side.

The light brightened. She could hear herself grunt, but could hear, as well, the edges of something that sounded like familiar speech. It was the word. The word was speaking. At its edges, as if pushing back against it, or denying it, the Shadow undulated and hissed and whispered.

And burned.

"Mandoran?"

"Be careful; the bulk of what was here has withdrawn, and some of it is overhead."

"Warn Bakkon?"

"I think he knows. Some of what he's building looks like an umbrella. With a lot of holes in it."

She walked forward more quickly; only once was she forced to reach out with the gloved hand to touch the Shadows, to catch them. The weapon she now carried, etched on her skin, was a word.

But the words on the rest of her body, words that had forced her to abandon childhood and all the dreams it had contained for too long, were also beginning to burn. The Shadow did not touch them. Even the tendrils that attempted to grab—or join, which was worse—her hair hissed and melted away.

She began to move more quickly. Experience whispered the truth: the pain was going to get worse if she couldn't clear this miasma and jelly that had once been a wall. She wanted to look back to see if Bakkon was somehow following, but couldn't, because her neck was on fire, and the touch of the collar of her shirt seemed to be peeling her skin off.

Mandoran's hands, however, didn't have the same effect. He began to offer single-syllable directions she could follow as she lost the ability to think through complicated strategies. She could put one foot in front of the other. She could hold her arm out. More than that, no—and had Mandoran not been there, she wasn't entirely certain where "forward" would have led her. But what he saw, she couldn't see as clearly.

Bakkon chittered loudly. That sound was echoed from somewhere in front of Kaylin, beyond the darkness. All she had to do was continue to walk through it, surrounded by weeping and wailing, the aural sounds of severe distress. Some of it might have been her own.

Mandoran's hands didn't burn. She couldn't feel them—the touch was far too light at this point—but she took comfort from the steady voice, the monosyllabic directions. It was less steady when he shouted back to Bakkon, and Bakkon's reply had an edge of screech to it that made her skin crawl. She didn't look back. She looked forward into darkness punctuated by captive, squirming color, and realized she was on the edge of nausea. The wrong edge. Her legs folded, but she didn't touch the ground; there was no ground here.

No, that wasn't right. Mandoran's hands were no longer on her shoulders; they were under her armpits.

"Someone needs to lose weight," he muttered.

She replied in very weak Leontine. The sound of laughter traveled the length of her spine; she bent with it, or would have if he hadn't prevented it. She missed Severn.

I'm here.

I meant—I miss having a partner by my side. Mandoran's fine, but he's not you. All of this was threaded with pauses as she moved. But she didn't lose Severn's voice or words.

Terrano says you're almost through. The wall can't be built across the actual border; there's a small amount of space between wall and border. It's not wide enough to stand in.

She nodded, wordless.

Riaknon has built...something. He's talking to your Wevaran. When you manage to get clear of the Shadow, Bakkon will have to move, and move quickly. Whatever it is they're trying to build or do, they can't do if there's no gap in the wall. Terrano is talking to Mandoran. Ah, no, sorry, he says he's talking at *Mandoran.*

She was in pain, and she was exhausted; she felt like she'd crawled twenty solid miles without sleep, food, or water. None of this was true. *I don't want to collapse again.*

He said nothing; he didn't even offer her odds, which meant he was worried.

Not worried, he said, his internal voice soft.

Liar.

I can't, remember? It's a bond built from your name. I can't lie to you here.

Nightshade can.

Successfully?

She couldn't answer. One step. One more step. Just—step and step and step. She closed her eyes to prevent the spinning whirls of color from causing more nausea than they already had.

"No," Mandoran shouted, above her head. "It doesn't burn me."

What didn't? Who was he talking to? Who was she talking to?

Severn? No. Nightshade? No. Ynpharion? He'd been mercifully silent for days. But she felt her lips moving, the steady hum of syllables broken by small grunts of wordless pain. Her arm trembled; it was heavy, possibly because she had to keep it lifted, had to keep it in motion. When the Shadows ahead got too dark, too bright, she grabbed at them for long enough she could bring the marked hand to bear; the Shadows instantly dispersed.

There seemed to be more of them, as if they understood that their sole purpose was to prevent Kaylin from leaving their home. Home? No, she thought. Their cage. As Spike had been, they were trapped here, their will suborned to some greater entity—one she could neither see nor hear.

The thought made her move faster—or try. She had to touch her feet several times, to prevent the Shadows from pooling around her boots, her ankles. Throughout this, Mandoran remained behind her, hauling her back to standing when she faltered or stopped, curling in on the pain and her grasp of the whispering, the almost-language. There was blood in her mouth; her lip hurt. Had she bitten it?

No.

She wanted to ask Mandoran if the wall behind her was closed. Couldn't manage the words, although she tried twice. Shook her head to clear it and focused, once again, on the almost inaudible voices of the Shadows who had momentarily lost their forms in an attempt to build this wall. She could hear despair. She could almost taste it. The pain felt like a bridge between creatures she did not know and herself.

Once, she might have stayed where she was. Seven, almost eight, years ago, when death had been the only thing she desired because it was the only thing she felt she deserved. She could feel the edges of that certainty press in on her, and she pushed it back as a new wave of pain hit her arms and legs.

She was never going to complain about magic again. Ever.

Almost here, Severn said. *You're almost through.*

She didn't ask him how he knew. She stumbled forward—*walk* would be too kind a word for the motion—until she felt actual breeze across her cheeks; they were cool with it. Ah. She'd been crying.

Yes.

She turned slowly, with Mandoran as a brace, and looked back at the tunnel she had carved with a hand and a word; she could see Bakkon as if through an arrow slit, the space too narrow to contain the bulk of his form. She could see the webbing that stood in front of him, a translucent door.

Could see the moment he exhaled, chittering and screeching, and stepped through that door.

Severn had stepped across the border. He looked past her to Mandoran; she had no idea what form the member of the cohort had adopted. But his hands, at least, were solid and real, and he was anchored to her, more for her sake than his.

For both, Severn said. He stepped forward as the wall shuddered, shouting in a cacophony of raised, desperate voices.

She was unprepared for Severn's desperate lunge; he pulled her—and possibly Mandoran—across the border, shouting Mandoran's name as the wall suddenly and completely collapsed, becoming, in an instant, a mob of smaller Shadows.

She was through the barrier; the mob crashed against it but could not follow. The pain dimmed; her skin was extremely sore, but no longer felt as if it were being flayed and burned off at the same time. "Mandoran?" Her voice was a croak.

"Here," Mandoran said, behind her. "And possibly regretting it."

Terrano laughed. His feet, Kaylin noted, were not touching the ground and he seemed to cast no shadow. But neither did Mandoran. "Sedarias is seriously pissed off."

"I didn't want to take the risk of talking *to* any of you. I didn't want any of you pulled in."

"Tell Sedarias, not me." He turned to Kaylin. "I think Riaknon might need your help."

She immediately reoriented herself toward the Wevaran

and understood what Terrano meant without need for further words; all of the Wevaran's eyes were bulging, although none had leaped out of their sockets yet.

She placed a hand across his body—between his open eyes—and, as she'd done for Bakkon, assessed the damage Riaknon had done to himself. The two bodies were surprisingly dissimilar, which she hadn't been expecting. But the webbing he was spitting out and cursing as he did was also pink; a darker pink than Bakkon's had been.

There were no obvious spinnerets, not that she'd really attempted to heal spiders before; it was harder to find the area of damage that was causing the bleeding.

We are not arachnids, Riaknon snapped. *Do you think we're spiders? Bakkon has clearly managed to retain some good humor if you are still standing. We are not spiders. Spiders are the echoes of us, diminished and lacking in sentience. Our webs are not simple physical extrusions; they are magical and they require speed and will.*

They obviously had very different personalities. But if their bodies were far less uniform than human bodies, they were still of living flesh, and she could heal the damage done by the use of this webbing, this magic, in the same fashion she could heal Bakkon. She did that now.

I do not mean to sound ungrateful, Riaknon then said. *But patience is often wasted on the young.*

Bakkon was not here.

She could see the shadows cast by large, flying Dragons; Emmerian had left the airspace above *Ravellon*. She could hear his bellow, similar to and different from Bellusdeo's; above them both, she could hear the fuller, richer sound of the out-caste Dragon.

This part is exceptionally difficult. I wish Starrante were here instead; he was the master of portals. I lack his confidence.

What are you trying to do?

I am trying to allow Bakkon to leave. I cannot create the portal from the other side of the barrier—only he can do that. But he is struggling as well.

What happens if it doesn't work? Is he just trapped there?

Riaknon didn't answer. He was Wevaran, not human, but the lack of answer had both weight and meaning.

Can I help?

You are helping now, perhaps more than you know. But I would ask that you stop nattering. Which probably meant *shut up.*

She opened her mouth and shut it again as a translucent projectile struck her shoulder. Her left ear became so full of random squawking she forgot that she could, with concentration, understand the words that left her familiar's mouth. At least she could when he was speaking to her.

He lifted one wing and smacked her face with it—harder than was necessary, in case she couldn't tell from the tone of his squawking that he was angry. She looked through the wing, her hands freezing in position against the Wevaran trunk.

She looked toward Bakkon.

If the Shadows had amassed, briefly, against a barrier that would not grant them exit, they had also turned, in smaller numbers, toward Bakkon. She had no doubt that if they reached him, he would become part of them. But he had built a shell, a web, around most of his body, and the webbing caught them, held them in place, preventing them from actually touching him.

She could see the strands of bright, bright silver grow taut as the weight of more Shadow joined the attempt. And she could see that even now, he was concentrating, weaving. Riaknon's voice was a physical sensation as he spoke his native tongue. At a distance, she could hear Bakkon doing the same.

And she could see the strands of webbing from this side of the border rise, extending like minute tendrils toward the border—and through it. Terrano spoke in Barrani, his voice low enough that she missed the words; Riaknon didn't. He grunted in response.

Mandoran shouted. Before he could interfere, Terrano touched the webbing, or rather, the loose strands that seemed to serve no purpose. She understood what he was doing only when he shifted his grip and began to disperse.

Through the eye that wasn't covered in Hope's wing, she saw Terrano vanish. But she could see something, an echo of his physical form, through the wing-covered eye. That echo, that odd impression, not quite mist but not at all physical, reminded her of sunspots, the things she got when she stared at the sun for too long; Terrano was more detailed but still out of place.

He crossed the boundary set by the Towers as if it didn't exist. And then he walked through the press of Shadow bodies, through the odd tunnel that Kaylin's walk had created. She could still see it, but only through Hope's wing.

He approached Bakkon without attempting to catch the Wevaran's attention—but Bakkon's eyes, or at least some of them, rose from their sockets; the Wevaran was aware that something, or someone, was approaching.

Kaylin shouted, "He's with us! He's trying to help!" And then had to repeat it in Barrani. She would have lost sight of Terrano, there was so much Shadow—but through Hope's blessed wing she could now see each Shadow element as a distinct shape, a distinct form. Terrano was not. But the thread he held—and it seemed to be one thread—was a bright, pale light; she knew where he was because she could see that thread clearly.

Shadows seemed to move through him as if nothing about him was solid; his movement across the ground didn't slow.

Mandoran wasn't happy, but if Terrano believed this was necessary, Mandoran was probably shouting into the void. When Terrano reached Bakkon, he lifted the single thread, and attached it to the webbing that protected the Wevaran from all the other attacks.

He then withdrew, fleeing across the border without touching the ground.

Kaylin moved from Riaknon to Terrano instantly.

"I'm fine," Terrano said, as he once again solidified. He was a shade of green that was in no way appropriate for Barrani, and his eyes were all of black.

Mandoran was there in an instant. "Sedarias is going to kill us," he said.

"She'll have to catch us first." Terrano turned and shouted a single word in Barrani: *Now.*

Bakkon stepped forward into his own webbing.

He appeared through Riaknon's. "That went better than I expected," he said, in Barrani.

"You owe the young...Barrani a debt," Riaknon replied. "And the fieflord."

"Fieflord?"

"I will endeavor to explain it all later." He looked up, and then down to the two members of the cohort. "I believe there is still some danger here." He began to spit more webbing; it was pink, but a lighter pink than it had been before Kaylin had attempted to heal him.

"I wish to remain here," Bakkon said.

"I am not certain it is wise." Riaknon raised one leg. "Can you see him? They call him outcaste."

Bakkon's eyes shifted; he didn't raise a leg. "I see him."

"He is a danger. I do not think they understand what they face. I did not understand it, either. I must speak with Lord Liatt, but if you remain here, I will return." He stepped through the portal he had created and vanished.

Bakkon didn't appear to notice. He was looking at the outcaste—and by extension, the two Dragons, gold and silver, who had engaged him. "They should not be there," he said.

Kaylin turned to Mandoran. "Go to Bellusdeo—try to get her to—" A roar cut the rest of the sentence. Mandoran glanced at Terrano before nodding. He then headed up, framed on two sides by lightning that traveled toward the very physical black cloud that hovered above them.

"He's not as good at this as I am—but he likes the Dragon, and the Dragon seems to mostly like him. Has to be him."

Hope squawked. *She will not hear him.*

"Would she hear you?"

Not apparently, Chosen. But...you were not here then. There was a note of accusation in his words.

"Can you try again?"

Hope pushed himself off her shoulder. He didn't follow Mandoran into the air; he moved down the street and began to transform, the tiny delicate familiar becoming the enormous, draconic familiar in the space of a few seconds.

Mount. He roared—at this size there was no squawking. Mandoran sprinted toward them as Hope pushed himself off worn cobbles and into the air, his wings snapping out to carry his greater weight. Mandoran joined her, sliding in behind, rather than in front, as Hope headed in a straight line for Bellusdeo.

No, she thought—not Bellusdeo.

The outcaste.

29

Kaylin didn't have a wing-eyed view of the conflict she was rapidly approaching; she was seated on the familiar who usually offered her that advantage. She did, however, have Mandoran.

It was Mandoran who shouted in her ear; Mandoran who made clear that the outcaste was not the only thing in the air. Most of the Aerians—all, to Kaylin's view—had been brought down one way or the other. Teela and Nightshade could fight aerial creatures with both feet on the ground.

She could see the three Dragons—Bellusdeo, Emmerian, and the outcaste. But Mandoran's tone made clear that he could see something she couldn't. Whatever it was, it wasn't aiming for Kaylin.

No, Hope said, his voice more a physical sensation than a sound. He then followed the word with a roar.

"Got it!" Mandoran shouted—not bothering to move his mouth away from the vicinity of Kaylin's ear.

Hope approached Bellusdeo, edging under the cone of the flame she unleashed against the outcaste's fire—a fire that had always looked purple to Kaylin from a distance. This was not enough of a distance; here, she could clearly see the sparks of other colors, limned in gold and silver and orange, as if each were alive and struggling for dominance. Green collapsed into blue; blue gave way to red; red was destroyed by yellow and green. The colors didn't merge; it was as if they couldn't coexist, couldn't transform.

The flame, however, was *hot*.

Emmerian approached the outcaste from the flank. Mandoran cursed under his breath. "Don't fall off!" he shouted, as he failed to follow his own advice. He ejected himself—she could feel the bunching of muscles at her back—and rode towards the silver Dragon, alighting on his back.

This is a bad idea, Hope said.

"Why?"

Neither Lord Emmerian nor Mandoran has native resistance to the outcaste's power. Mandoran can see. I do not believe he has enough influence on Emmerian.

If Kaylin had been less tense, she would have wilted in place. She didn't think she had much influence on Bellusdeo, either. Bellusdeo's fire pushed the outcaste's fire back—but not all of it.

Not all of it. Strands of purple, eerily reminiscent of the tentacles that rose from the ground in *Ravellon*, appeared to be slowly threading their way across the outside of Bellusdeo's flame cone, and inching up, and up again.

"Hope, do something!"

Silence. She knew what the silence meant; knew that this was not something she could do herself, and not something he would do for free.

It is our nature, he said, agreeing, his tone leavened with something that might have been regret.

"Can you drop me on Bellusdeo's back?"

Not safely.

"I don't care about safely—can you *do it*?"

In reply, he flew in a wide arc around the current—and moving—combat. She glanced once at Emmerian; the silver Dragon had allowed Mandoran to mount. If they spoke at all, she couldn't hear a word. Hope was a far more stable mount than Bellusdeo had been; she could pull her legs up, tuck them beneath her, and still maintain her balance.

That went out the window when she pushed herself off in Bellusdeo's direction. From this distance, she could see that the gold Dragon's eyes were crimson; the color was reflected off the scales closest to those eyes. She fell short of a perfect landing. Sadly, she fell short of any landing.

She trusted Hope to catch her on the way down, but it wasn't Hope's claws that caught her by the shoulders. Bellusdeo couldn't breathe fire and speak at the same time—and she couldn't stop breathing fire under the outcaste's assault. While Dragons were immune to the effects of Dragon fire, the outcaste was not a normal Dragon. Kaylin was absolutely certain that his fire wouldn't burn Bellusdeo.

No, it would do worse.

Bellusdeo knew it as well—better than Kaylin, in the end. This was her war, a continuation of the conflict that had destroyed her adoptive world and had enslaved her Ascendant. There was probably nothing new Kaylin could tell her about the consequences. Bellusdeo didn't shift her grip; Kaylin couldn't climb the Dragon's claw or leg to reach her back.

But she could reach out and grip those claws; she'd healed Bellusdeo before. Bellusdeo stiffened as she began to focus on the injuries the gold Dragon had taken; to her surprise, they were both minor and physical.

The only disadvantage to the healing attempt was that Bellusdeo could talk to her while also ejecting a lot of fire.

What are you doing? Are you suicidal? Tell your familiar to get you out of here right now!

I can't—no one could hear me over this ruckus.

I'll drop you.

You can drop me after I make sure— What the hells was she doing? *You need to avoid the outcaste's fire—some of it, some shadow part, is winding its way up your fire.*

Bellusdeo fell silent, assessing the warning. Because she was Bellusdeo, she didn't ignore or dismiss it; her expertise in her own failed war had taught her that Shadow was flexible, devious, the attacks evolving with time. And she had never fought the outcaste like this before. He pressed the attack.

Severn spoke, his voice overlapping Nightshade's. *You'll need to get her out of there. Emmerian is going to attack the flank, according to Terrano. Nightshade and Teela are going to combine their lightning attacking from the same side. Get Bellusdeo down while the outcaste isn't breathing fire.*

When?

Terrano gives you a three count. He also says there are people near the Tower that need your help.

I don't think that's going to work, she told him, internal voice more urgent. *I think if the fire collapses—on her part—she's going to get hit with Shadow.*

Your job is to make sure that it doesn't overtake her.

She had no more time to argue. Emmerian swooped in front the outcaste's right and as he did, the sky changed color as lightning leaped from the ground. She couldn't see Nightshade or Teela, because she wasn't looking—but she could follow the lightning as it split the sky. Both bolts hit the outcaste as Emmerian did, claws extended, jaws wide.

She almost screamed at him *not to bite*, but she wouldn't have been heard anyway. She didn't have to tell Bellusdeo what the plan was; Bellusdeo had ceased the exhalation, ducked her head, and changed the placement of wings so that she plummeted instantly out of the range of the outcaste's breath.

Out of the range of fire, but not of danger. The outcaste's fire stopped seconds after the joint attack; the threads and filaments continued to travel, without the resistance of natural Dragon fire to keep them in place. They sped toward Bellusdeo.

"Hope!" Kaylin shouted. "Breathe!"

The familiar didn't move. Kaylin cursed—cursed loudly—as the filaments sped through sky. Her hands gripped Bellusdeo's feet as her stomach reasserted its natural position; she braced herself for the Shadow impact.

It didn't happen.

A silver form, as large as Bellusdeo's, flew between the Dragon and the Shadow tendrils. The outcaste roared in fury, undercurrents of pain shifting the texture of the roar.

Kaylin was frozen as she watched the slender threads strike Emmerian. "Emmerian!"

Terrano says there's going to be trouble.

No kidding. "Bellusdeo—take me to Emmerian right now!"

The gold Dragon hesitated, eyes too red, a few yards above the ground. Kaylin was extremely surprised to see Teela leap—from either ground or rooftop—toward the outcaste, great sword in hand. The outcaste turned toward her, jaws open; they snapped on air and steel.

Teela held the sword, dangling from it without apparent concern; the outcaste didn't release the blade until Nightshade joined her in the air. There were no wings; neither of the two appeared to be capable of actual flight—but the arc of the leap from ground to air could be seen as *Meliannos* carried Nightshade to just above the outcaste's closed jaws.

Kaylin!

The outcaste roared; Teela fell. She didn't hit the ground.

Kaylin, however, found her vantage shifting as Bellusdeo dragged her over to Emmerian and dropped her on his back. The gold Dragon spoke in her native tongue, but there was no sign Emmerian had actually heard what Kaylin was certain was a command.

Mandoran caught her, stabilizing her landing; she turned and shouted to Bellusdeo, "You have to retreat—he's done here, he knows it!"

Bellusdeo roared.

Kaylin reached out for Emmerian.

"I told you," Mandoran murmured. "She's going to be pissed off for days, if you're lucky."

Emmerian did not reply.

The moment Kaylin reached out to heal him—and she knew he'd be angry about it later, because the only immortal who willingly let her touch and heal was Bellusdeo—she knew no reply would be forthcoming.

She had touched this Shadow before, when Mandoran had been pierced and almost bisected by the weapons the altered Aerians bore. Then, she had had to listen hard to hear what it whispered—and that had landed them both in *Ravellon*.

She didn't have to try at all, now. The attenuated voices she could barely hear in Mandoran felt as if they had taken control of a Dragon's vocal chords; they were a roar of sound, and given she was physically attached to the Dragon, they were a sensation, each syllable wracking the body in which it was contained.

She didn't recognize the language the Shadows spoke at first. It didn't feel familiar to her in the way spoken True Words did. She wasn't certain it mattered. What mattered here was Emmerian.

She is going to be so pissed at you, she told the silver Dragon. The Dragon who, until this particular transformation, had been blue. She knew, in a vague and inexact way that would never pass muster as knowledge, that Dragons didn't always maintain the same color when they adopted their draconic form. She had no idea what caused the shift in color—Bellusdeo had always been gold—but assumed that it, like eye color, varied depending on the mood of the Dragon in question. *Emmerian*.

She is likely to be angry, yes. But the Dragon Court will be angrier, and it will not be at me.

Wait—me?

You should not be attempting to heal me. This voice buckled, thinning; she pulled it back almost unconsciously. *Let go and get Bellusdeo out of here.*

You're obviously delirious with pain if you think I can tell Bellusdeo what to do.

If he wasn't delirious, he was definitely in pain. She could see why. In the roar of non-Emmerian syllables, she could feel his flesh contracting, reshaping; she cursed in very voluble Leontine because she had seen something similar before.

I'm sorry, she told the Dragon.

He said nothing; he understood what she wanted to do: excise infected flesh completely in an attempt to prevent the body from adapting to a new normal that had little to do with Emmerian himself. In the background, she could hear and feel a second roar of sound—this one outside of Emmerian's body, and therefore not a threat.

Except it was Bellusdeo, and Bellusdeo was *angry.*

No. No, she couldn't think about that, couldn't act on it now, or she would lose Emmerian. They would lose him.

Stop moving! she shouted, although she didn't open her mouth.

She is hurt—

She's pissed off. She's angry. And she doesn't have to be hurt for that. We have two of The Three here, on the field. If the outcaste can get through them so quickly, we never stood a chance. Stop moving.

I am attempting not to move, he replied, just a hint of anger and frustration underpinning the words.

She inhaled. What had happened to Mandoran had happened slowly. What had happened in the West March—the only other experience that was in any way similar to this— had happened quickly. Had these Shadows been the point of attack in the West March, she would not have been able to save the Barrani who'd been injured; she had time only because Emmerian was many, many times the size of a single Barrani warrior.

She almost despaired—but had she, Emmerian would have noticed instantly.

No. She had gone to *Ravellon* for a very brief visit *because* of Shadows like this. She had emerged with Mandoran and Bakkon. How?

Ah. The word. The word on her palm, the new mark. The word and the glove of Shadow. The Shadow was not the only spoken voice she could "hear." The mark on her palm, much quieter, was in its own way a continuous march of syllables. It was the quieter part she needed to work on.

She began to speak the syllables of the new mark. She began to speak them out loud, to put all of the mechanisms of throat and lung and jaw into the pronunciation, the flow of syllables. The Shadows within Emmerian slowed, the words they spoke coming to a halt as if words were motion. She could see the mark on her palm clearly, although she couldn't see her palm, pressed as it was against Emmerian's silver scales.

As she focused on the word, the Shadow tendrils slowed, coming to an uneven stop in various parts of the Dragon's flesh. They did not retreat; they spoke, the uniformity of their foreign language giving lie to the idea that they were separate entities.

She heard Emmerian's labored breath as if it, too, were just one component of that aforementioned crowd—the member that she had come here to save. She spoke more clearly. The Shadows hissed; she saw them begin, once again, to move. She couldn't physically reach into Emmerian's body to touch them, as she had with the wall. She had to force them out.

Had to excise the small trails of flesh that were no longer

entirely Dragon. Was this what had happened to the outcaste? Was the outcaste enslaved, just as Bellusdeo had been?

Did it matter?

No. Not right now. She forced syllables of her own out, trying to maintain the strength of her voice while simultaneously ripping out parts of Emmerian's body—the parts transformed, the parts where a new normal had been established. New normal meant the body would not consider itself damaged; she couldn't save him by healing alone.

Her voice faltered every time she encountered a mass of this transformed new version of healthy, and every time the syllables paused, the Shadow tendrils moved. She managed to force one out of the body; she didn't look to see where it went. She wasn't alone here; there were others present who could deal with Shadow if they knew it existed.

But the syllables lagged as she struggled, and the lag caused the damage to spread. It spread more slowly than it had before she'd begun, but she was almost certain that she was going to be overwhelmed—or that Emmerian would. This close to him, if he lost control over himself, she was unlikely to survive.

As she worked, as she switched focus between the necessary extraction and the word that seemed to halt the Shadows' spread, a voice joined hers. It was Bakkon—she was almost certain it was Bakkon; there was a bell-like inflection to the syllables, and he spoke them as if they were his native tongue.

Spoke them as if they were a dirge, a lamentation, an ending that he had not desired; his pain reminded her that bells were often sounded at funerals. But he spoke the syllables clearly, his voice so strong he might have been speaking into her ear. And she could follow his syllables, could mouth them and be pulled along by them while she focused on Emmerian.

She felt a hand on her shoulder; another voice joined Bakkon's. To her surprise, she recognized the voice: Sedarias. She had expected Mandoran or Terrano. But no, she was certain they were present, no matter where in the fief they were.

She swallowed air, and exhaled fear. She wasn't winning this fight. Although she forced strands of Shadow out of the Dragon, it wasn't fast enough. It wasn't *enough*.

She was going to lose him. She was going to lose him, and Bellusdeo would lose him; Sedarias could probably get away. Nightshade and Teela had two weapons that could kill Dragons if it became necessary. Bakkon continued to speak; she continued to work, her lips moving almost unconsciously across the syllables the Wevaran had well in hand.

"ENOUGH!"

Bellusdeo's voice. Bellusdeo was on the ground; the force of the roar—in very clear Barrani—caused tremors.

"When the war is over—when it is finally *over* and if I survive it—I will captain the Tower while the Tower stands. I will learn the names of the people who will become *my* people. I will build a better home, a better life, for anyone born here, past or present. I will raise my children in the Aerie of the Tower, and I will teach them to fly and to fight and to seek the freedom of the skies and the weight of the responsibility that comes with that freedom.

"I will claim no other home. I will surrender no territory while I live.

"I will *learn*, Karriamis. I will learn what you have to teach. I will offer you my name."

"And is this what you want?" a familiar voice replied. Karriamis, the Avatar of the Tower. And of course he was aware—they were in his fief.

Emmerian struggled to rise, moving beneath Kaylin's splayed palms. She heard the wet sound of webbing being spit and attempted to ignore it.

"This is what I want," Bellusdeo said.

"Child—"

"I didn't say I would tolerate condescension or disrespect."
Karriamis chuckled. "And why do you say this now?"

"Because you asked what I would do when the war was
done. You asked what I want to do when the war is over—
and it's an ending I don't and can't believe will happen. It's a
game of make-believe."

"No, it is not."

"It *is*. But I will play this game with you. I will play it with
myself. I will *let myself believe*—for just long enough—that I
can see an ending and that I'll survive it."

"And if you do, this is what you want?"

"I want a home of my own," she replied, voice far lower.
As if to say it was somehow disloyal. Kaylin didn't believe she
was lying, though. "I want a place in which I can stand and
be...myself."

"I see. And you did not want this on prior visits?"

Kaylin wanted to stand up, turn around, and punch Karriamis in the jaw—assuming he was in his human form.

Don't, Emmerian said. It was the first time she had heard
his voice so clearly.

You're just saying that because you want to hit him first.

Hit was not what I had in mind, no.

She was surprised at the clarity of his voice, surprised at
the sudden dwindling presence of Shadow within him. She
had struggled to contain it, to force it out—but she knew this
wasn't down to anything she'd personally done.

Bakkon surprised her. He started to chitter, an agitation of
sound broken by tiny bells.

It was Karriamis who replied. "Yes, old friend." He spoke
in Barrani. "I thought never to see you again. And I am heart-
ened by your appearance here; it is clear that you were allowed
your escape in the presence of the battle between the Dragons and the Shadows."

"I am not so easy to kill as all that," Bakkon replied.

The Shadows were gone, now. Kaylin looked up; she could see no outcaste in the air above the fief.

"He is no longer here. I admit that he is far more subtle—and more powerful—than the Shadows that have previously managed to infiltrate this fief. Come, Chosen—join us."

She hesitantly lifted her hand from Emmerian's flank. When she did, he dwindled in size, his shape changing, the entirety of his presence once again contained in—confined by—a mortal form. He wore silver plate armor; from a distance, he might have been an Imperial Guard.

Kaylin turned toward Karriamis, who had adopted a similar form; he wore clothing, not the scale armor forced on the Dragons who would otherwise be butt naked in the streets. Not that this would generally bother Bellusdeo.

Bellusdeo wasn't butt naked; she was draconic. Karriamis stood beneath her, tilting his head to meet her enormous eyes—which were, sadly, red.

"You're going to want to get in there quickly," Kaylin murmured to Emmerian.

"We can all hear you," Bellusdeo rumbled.

"We can," Karriamis agreed, although he didn't look away from the gold Dragon. Her eyes remained red. "My apologies, Lord Bellusdeo. You were correct in some fashion; this is not the time for testing. I have been watching the borders for the entirety of my existence—but that one, I had not seen."

"Which variant of *that one*?"

"The outcaste."

Kaylin, however, understood. She continued to watch the Dragons but spoke to Nightshade as she did. *Can you hear it? Can you hear the name of the fief?*

I can.

Is it Bellusdeo?

It is. I am not sure I approve of this Karriamis—but neither he nor the fief is my problem. She felt him wince and sought sight of him with her actual eyes; he was bleeding, but the wound didn't seem deep.

It is not deep, and no, I do not require healing. His tone suggested she'd be the one who required it if she tried.

"Lord Bellusdeo," Karriamis said. "We await you." He then turned to Bakkon. "Is it foolish to hope that you have not made a commitment to the Tower of Liatt?"

"To Aggarok? No. I believe some negotiations might be required, and Aggarok was always difficult. Unless they have changed markedly in the centuries since last we met."

"I cannot say. I am not permitted—by construction and design—to leave the fief over which I stand sentinel. But you returned without speaking to him?"

"I felt the young Chosen might require aid. And to be frank, Aggarok was unsettling before his ascension, and I don't have the stomach for him at the moment." He then turned to Kaylin. In a slightly more anxious voice, he said, "You did not lose the bag?"

"I gave it to Mandoran."

"I have it," Mandoran said, from a distance. "Are you sure you don't want to take the bag—and the books it contains—to the chancellor of the Academia?"

"I am certain of very little at the moment, your city seems so bleak and lifeless," the Wevaran replied.

Karriamis turned toward Bellusdeo; he lifted a brow in question.

Smoke jetted out of her nostrils before she lowered her head and began to transform. Her eyes remained red when she was no longer an obvious Dragon. "I can hear Kaylin's stomach from here. If any of you would care to join us, we're repairing to the Tower." She paused. "You *can* adequately feed everyone?"

It was Karriamis's turn to snort. "Of course. I must say it

has been quite a while since I last offered to entertain quite so many people—but if that is your desire, it will be my pleasure."

Bellusdeo snorted again. She glanced, once, at Emmerian; Emmerian met—and held—her gaze. When she didn't look away, he nodded. She offered him an arm, Imperial style; he grinned, because he had lifted his arm to do the same. He lowered his arm, accepting hers, and she led them all toward the Tower she had finally claimed as her home.

Sedarias stopped at the border of the Tower's strongest influence. Terrano, not paying attention, stopped at Sedarias and earned a glare.

Karriamis turned to the leader of the cohort. "You will not enter?"

"We are all exhausted," she said quietly. "And at the moment, I desire no further conflict."

"And you believe by entering, such conflict will be engaged?"

Sedarias exhaled. "I wanted to take the Tower."

"No, you did not."

One brow rose.

"You wanted the Tower to be taken. You would not have captained it yourself. While I grant that there is enough connection between all of you, you are nonetheless separate beings."

She said nothing, although she shifted her glare to Mandoran.

"Yes," Karriamis said, smiling. "But none of your kin—and I will call them kin, forsaking the more exact term—desired this responsibility for anything but the sake of the cohort."

"Like you'd care," muttered Terrano.

"What makes you think I would not?"

"Candallar."

The Dragon Avatar's smile sharpened. "You almost make

me regret my choice," he said, with no hint of regret in his tone at all. "I believe I would find association with you interesting and challenging."

"Candallar," Terrano repeated.

"Do not attempt to silence him; it is a wasted effort." These words were offered to Sedarias.

Bellusdeo stood on the periphery of the Tower but had turned to observe the Avatar and the cohort. Her eyes were an orange-red, but as Kaylin watched, they lightened into a purer orange.

"I could not accept what you offered," Karriamis said. "Not when the future of the race that birthed me is at stake. Candallar once showed promise; he did not live up to it because he chose fear. He believed on some level that he was not worthy because others did not value him as he desired to be valued.

"You are not Candallar, An'Mellarionne. But I am not your home. Nor could I be. Yes, there is safety for you and your chosen kin within my walls, but it is not safety you desire; no more do you desire to fight the war I was created to fight. Should you require safety beyond what the mortal can provide—ah, apologies, beyond what Lord Kaylin can provide—you have it."

Sedarias was silent for a beat. "You are not offering us that hospitality."

"No. It is not mine to offer. I believe Lord Bellusdeo would, should it become necessary—should nothing change. But life is change. I referred to the Hallionne."

It was Terrano who said, "Alsanis."

Karriamis nodded. "Should you desire safety, Alsanis would always offer you a home—all of you."

"We cannot fight our current battles from the West March," Sedarias told the Avatar.

"No. Not yet. But I hear his name, an echo of a different time. He was your home for centuries."

"He was our *prison*," she snapped.

"So, too, must the very young think, when they cannot yet walk or run independent of their parents."

Kaylin winced, but said nothing.

"He would not imprison you now—any of you. But he, as you, was trapped in his responsibility, and I believe that even a Hallionne can grow lonely. Should you require a fortress, it is the Hallionne who will provide it. Do you doubt me?"

It was Terrano who said, "No."

Bellusdeo came back down the stairs—for the Tower now looked like a Tower, not a cave or a cliff. Her eyes remained orange, but there were now visible flecks of gold in them. "I would take you all in," she said quietly. "And I offer that now. I will offer it as blood oath, if you require it as proof."

Silence descended on the cohort; Sedarias, whose eyes were not surprisingly a martial, Barrani blue, turned toward her. Sedarias wasn't Teela; she had never shown Bellusdeo the camaraderie that Teela had. She had never descended into teasing at the dining room table, as Mandoran had.

But they were connected to Sedarias, and she could not avoid feeling some of what they felt. "I didn't come here to aid you," she said, voice, like the rest of her, stiff.

Bellusdeo nodded, as if it were irrelevant.

"I came to the Tower," Sedarias continued.

Kaylin raised a brow in Mandoran's direction; he nodded.

"I meant to take the Tower while you were distracted."

"Did you try?"

Silence.

Bellusdeo turned to Karriamis, raising the same brow that Kaylin had at Mandoran.

Karriamis smiled. Unlike Mandoran, he neither confirmed nor denied.

Bellusdeo exhaled. There was smoke in the air, but it dissipated as she turned her gaze on Sedarias. "I don't believe you did try."

Sedarias said nothing. Mandoran and Terrano winced but remained silent.

"But I understand what you wanted," the Dragon continued, when Sedarias failed to speak. "I understand it, now. We have some things in common; war defined our lives in different ways when we did not have the power to decide for ourselves. But if we are not kin, if you do not consider me part of the family you have built, you are Kaylin's family. And she is, clearly, yours."

"She is *not* mine."

"I understand her mortality is a concern. She will age. She will die. When she does, Helen will seek a new tenant—a mortal tenant. If you have not consolidated your power enough by that point—"

"How could we in a scant few decades?"

"—come to me. I will offer the safety that Helen offered; I will offer you a home. I owe you that much."

This stopped Sedarias. "You owe *us*?"

Bellusdeo nodded.

"You came to the West March. You found us!"

"I came to the West March by accident—it was largely Kaylin's fault."

"And you helped her find us?"

"I was bored."

For the first time this evening, Sedarias cracked an actual smile. "Things are certainly never boring when Kaylin is around. It's a wonder she's survived."

"It takes deliberate effort on the part of the people who are unaccountably fond of her," Bellusdeo agreed. "But you must know I would have killed her when Karriamis first tested me."

Kaylin stopped breathing for one long beat.

"I know Mandoran feared it," Sedarias finally conceded.

"I'm fond of him. I didn't expect to be—half the time I have to struggle not to turn him to ash."

"Half the time, I agree with that impulse."

Mandoran rolled his eyes.

"The war *is* important to me. Your war is important to you. Where I can, I will aid you. And you—all of you—will have a home here if you need it. I can't offer more than that."

Sedarias exhaled slowly. She closed her eyes. Nodded.

"You don't have any say in this?" Mandoran asked Karriamis.

"Not apparently." He did not seem displeased.

"I would like to return to Helen," Sedarias said. "We should tell her that Kaylin has—yet again—survived. But we would all like to visit, even those of us who are currently resident in the Academia. Would that be acceptable?"

"More than acceptable. I will have to return to Helen myself—but not today."

Sedarias smiled, then. "I didn't ask," she said, in Elantran.

Bellusdeo matched her smile and her language. "I guessed."

EPILOGUE

It was dark by the time Kaylin made her way home. She didn't arrive alone; the cohort—those who still remained beneath Helen's roof—accompanied her, as did Severn and Emmerian.

The cohort was mostly silent. In fact, so were Severn and Emmerian; she could think of funereal marches that had been more lively. If the cohort didn't have their True Name bonds, she was certain the walk would have been louder, and decided, given their expressions, that silent had advantages.

Severn didn't return all the way to Helen; he peeled off toward his own apartment. Kaylin was almost tempted to follow—but if the conflict between the various members of the cohort got out of hand, she wanted to be with Helen. Hope, having intervened as much as he felt he was allowed, was now sprawling across her shoulders like a dishrag.

You're worried about Emmerian, Severn said.

Just a little. I don't understand why he didn't stay with Bellusdeo and Karriamis. Karriamis seemed to expect it.

Did Bellusdeo?

She didn't know. She could understand why the cohort felt no pressing desire—or even interest—in remaining beyond the time a celebratory meal demanded. And Karriamis had shown himself equal to Helen in hospitality—when he chose to offer it. But Bellusdeo was pale, Emmerian was pale, and Mandoran actually looked exhausted.

In fact, the only two people in that Tower who had seemed cheerful were Karriamis and Bakkon. They chittered and roared and spoke Barrani, switching seamlessly between the three languages depending on whom they were addressing, and Karriamis even left them all alone to take Bakkon on a tour of something or other. Since Towers could alter their interiors at will, Kaylin considered this symbolic. At best.

She thought Bellusdeo was the one who should be given a tour, but Bellusdeo was decidedly uninterested in doing so.

"I'll have to come back for Maggaron," the gold Dragon said. "I have one or two things I would like to bring with me—but very few."

"You've got the court dresses."

"Very funny."

"Are you sure you're okay with all this?"

"No matter how blighted my childhood, no matter how unnatural my coming of age, I am a Dragon. The moment I accepted the responsibility of the Tower—for whatever reasons—it became mine. I could not be here if I hadn't accepted it."

"That's not what she means and you know it," Mandoran said, his voice quiet, his expression almost forlorn.

"No?"

Mandoran snorted. "She wants to know if you're happy with the decision."

"Why don't you explain it to her on the way home?"

"Because she hasn't asked me if I'm happy with it?"

Bellusdeo snorted, with steam. "There was no other choice," she finally said. "I did not think Kaylin could preserve Emmerian. I've seen similar...attacks before. And this may sound strange, but I wasn't looking forward to killing him."

"That's why you did it—but..."

"Perhaps it is Karriamis to whom you should speak. Had he made his decision earlier, we would not have been in as dire a position. I was always willing to take command of the Tower; he was the one who hesitated." She glanced at the silent—and notably stiff—Emmerian, and Kaylin remembered just how much immortals of her acquaintance appreciated being in debt.

"Should we send Maggaron?"

"No. As I said, I'll come collect him. I would like to speak with Helen again, and I'm not sure that's possible from the Tower." She lowered her head briefly. When she lifted it, her eyes were copper-colored.

Emmerian stood when food faded from the table, the dishes slowly becoming transparent as they watched. His eyes were orange-gold, although when they met Bellusdeo's they also shaded toward copper. He offered her a perfect, Imperial bow—a bow reserved, to Kaylin's knowledge, for use in the presence of Emperors.

Bellusdeo said nothing.

When they were at the door, Karriamis appeared. "I would like to have further words with you, Chosen."

"I'm beat," she replied. "I need to go home and fall over."

"Ah, you misunderstand. I merely mean I hope you will visit again. Soon."

"That's up to Bellusdeo."

"No, Lord Kaylin, it is not." His voice was soft. "She was queen once; queens do not beg. She will, I am certain, accept a visit from you at any time you choose to do so—but she will not ask. It is not, yet, in her."

Kaylin exhaled.

"You are thinking I will not be much company."

She'd been thinking exactly that. "She gets bored and restless pretty easily."

"She will be far less bored, now. This is what she was meant to do. Ah, no, not the captaincy of a Tower, but rather, the war against Shadow. Against the outcaste. She will have less time to fret here, and less time to feel…helpless or without purpose. But even so, I believe you have been good for her. She was safe within your domicile; she will be safe within my borders. As will you. But return in a day or two."

Kaylin nodded. And left.

"You have had a very, very eventful day," Helen said, when Kaylin reached the front door of her house. This would be because Helen was standing in front of it.

Kaylin nodded and allowed Helen's arms to enfold her.

"Yes," Helen said softly, "you will miss her. She will miss you. I believe she will miss Mandoran as well."

"I knew she couldn't stay here," Kaylin said, into Helen's shoulder. "But I thought she'd leave later. Years from now."

"She is not dead, and she is not very far away."

"She probably won't come to work with me anymore."

"No, dear. I believe she will have duties of her own, now. And those, she has always required. Come. It's late." She drew Kaylin out of the door and the cohort filed in.

"You think they'll be fighting?" Kaylin asked, when they had disappeared.

"More than they are now?"

"Something like that."

"No. Not tonight. Not all of the cohort were attached to Bellusdeo, but some of them were, and they understand the sense of loss because they can all feel it, even if they don't agree.

"They don't like goodbyes."

Neither did Kaylin.

"I know. I know, dear." She looked up. "Lord Emmerian. Please come in. I assume you've also eaten?"

"He didn't eat much," Kaylin murmured, by which she meant, he hadn't eaten at all.

"I see. Will you join us?"

Emmerian nodded, and Helen disentangled herself. "Come in, dear."

Kaylin wasn't surprised to see Maggaron in the dining room, although he seldom joined them without Bellusdeo's express demand. He occupied the table, given his size, and looked up almost anxiously when they entered.

"We're not supposed to tell you anything," Kaylin said, when he turned his enormous—and worried—eyes toward her. "She wants to surprise you." The words shifted the worry from one spectrum to another; he winced. "Yes, she's fine. I'm not sure she's any less angry, but she's fine."

He rose, scuffing the legs of his necessarily heavy chair across the carpet.

Emmerian, however, cleared his throat. "Would you do me the favor of remaining?"

Maggaron resumed his seat with much more hesitance.

"I see," Helen said. "Do you think you'd like a drink if you aren't quite up to food?"

Emmerian nodded, unperturbed by Helen's ubiquitous ability to hear the quiet parts.

Kaylin looked at the Norranir and the Dragon and decided this was probably a more personal talk than she was ready for. She started to rise—a much less cumbersome and obvious motion than Maggaron's.

"No, dear," Helen said, before Kaylin could straighten her knees. "I think he'd like you to stay." She sat.

Both Kaylin and Maggaron looked toward Emmerian; he

had taken a chair and now seemed to be staring at his reflection on an otherwise empty table.

"I want to talk about Bellusdeo," he finally said, his expression heavily implying that the words were harder to push
out than the Shadows had been.

Maggaron didn't tense, to Kaylin's surprise. She did. Neither spoke, and eventually the Dragon took silence as assent.

"You have said that she wishes to surprise Maggaron, which
makes the discussion somewhat more difficult, but not, in the
end, impossible." To Maggaron, he said, "I would dedicate
my life—my personal life—to her if she allowed it. I have no
desire to harm her. I have no desire to cage her—and even
had I, it would now be rendered irrelevant for reasons you
will discover shortly."

Kaylin expected Maggaron to be confused; he wasn't. "I
have served her all my life," he said, his voice gravelly. "And
were she to allow it, were things in this tiny city to be more
hospitable to my kin, I would never leave her side. But this
city is…not what my city once was." He spoke slowly, and he
spoke Barrani. "I would only get in her way, here.

"You can blend in, Lord Emmerian. But…what you want
is not what I wanted. I was her Ascendant—I was chosen for
that role. I spent the entirety of my childhood focused only
on being worthy. She is…difficult. Her humor is…" He shook
his head, and Kaylin remembered the time Bellusdeo had
transformed from Dragon form into a decidedly naked mortal form—and insisted on staying that way because it embarrassed Maggaron.

"I have seldom seen her sense of humor; I have certainly
heard her sarcasm. I believe I could survive it."

"What is it you desire?" the Norranir asked. "I could tell
you stories of her humor."

Kaylin lifted a hand. "I think we can skip the humor, for
now."

They both looked at her; they both shrugged.

"I could tell you stories of her valor."

Emmerian shook his head. "I have seen that, more than once. And I believe I understand her anger quite well."

"I cannot tell you very much. I am mortal, as Kaylin is mortal. You are not. The earliest of stories about her life in the Aeries of this world I have only heard secondhand; she talks very little about them. If there are secrets you do not understand, they are not my secrets to tell." Maggaron hid nothing. He did not dissemble, ever. It was one of the things Bellusdeo liked best about him.

"No; I would never ask you to betray her confidence—even if I thought it possible."

Maggaron nodded as if he believed this—which made sense, because Kaylin did. She'd seen people in her office fall in love before; she understood that "fall" wasn't entirely a decision. Once or twice, she'd seen older and wiser people attempt to intervene; sometimes it worked and sometimes it failed spectacularly. From the outside, it had always looked like a type of fevered insanity that crossed boundaries and caused trouble.

Emmerian didn't resemble the Hawks. She doubted that he could. But even thinking that, she remembered that he had entered her house in something close to raging panic because he was worried about Bellusdeo. He *knew* that Helen was a sentient building; that Helen could keep Bellusdeo safe. But the knowledge hadn't prevented the panic.

And, to be fair, that was often Kaylin's impulse as well. Teela *hated* it, and Kaylin had learned the hard way to sit on that response. Emmerian didn't have Teela looming over his shoulder like a deadly older sister; the Emperor was decidedly unlike the Barrani Hawk.

"I think the war with Shadow has consumed some part of her," Maggaron finally said. "But I did not see her before the war."

"It consumes her," Emmerian said, his voice softer. "But it has defined her, as well. Karriamis was concerned about that. I believe he thinks her sense of failure is so profound she cannot look beyond it; if she were to succeed here, the lack of war would merely allow the sense of failure to envelop—and possibly destroy—her."

Kaylin was surprised.

Maggaron, however, was not. His nod was grave; it made him seem older and more certain of himself than Kaylin had ever seen him. "That has long been my fear—but it is a distant fear. I am not certain the war will ever end."

"Karriamis was also uncertain that the desire for vengeance would not cause harm."

One Norranir brow rose. "Does Karriamis speak for you as well in this?"

"Possibly. I see her when she fights; there has never been any hesitation in her transformation. You did not see the wars of old—the wars between the Dragons and the Barrani—but had you, you would understand that very, very few could hold a candle to her. She forged herself into a weapon, and she is perfect.

"But she did not lose sight of you. She did not lose sight of the people she fought *for*, or the people she needed to protect. Until the end, until she herself was almost irretrievably lost, she tried to keep her people safe. I do not know how she ruled—but I believe she was not unlike the Emperor." At Maggaron's wince, Emmerian smiled. "I have never said that to her."

"I think it unsafe. But she is not used to being ruled; she is used to ruling herself. And that control slips when she encounters the outcaste. He is the one thing that draws the two worlds—and the one war—together."

Emmerian nodded.

"What do you want from Bellusdeo, Lord Emmerian?"

"I want… I want her to be happy."

Maggaron's smile was soft; it was also sad. He did not reply.

"She doesn't see herself," the Dragon continued. "She doesn't see what I see. And no, this is not about the future of the race. At this particular moment, I do not give a damn about the future of the race."

"She understands that responsibility," Maggaron said after a long pause in which he seemed to be choosing his words more carefully.

"So do I—I *am* a Dragon."

"And you do not care?"

"No. At this juncture, it is entirely secondary. I think her children would be a wonder—and an agony. But I am not certain that it is the right thing for her."

To Kaylin's surprise, Maggaron smiled. She wondered, then, if she had seen him truly smile before.

"I have always thought," the Norranir said, "that she would be a good parent—but perhaps too protective. But it was never a possibility before. I will not be here forever," he added, the smile dimming. "And she will not have another Ascendant; I am a relic—is that the right word?—of a lost world. But you—you will live forever. If you are cautious," he added. "You will see what I will not.

"Do you intend to father her clutch?"

Emmerian's jaw snapped shut.

"Not yet, I see," the Norranir said, rising once again from his chair. "You are right. She does not see herself clearly; she sees and hears only the echoes of her failure." These words were spoken much more smoothly; Kaylin suspected that Helen was helping him translate. "She wishes to expatiate on that failure; it is what she wants, right now, more than anything else.

"I do not consider her a failure. None of my people did. She never surrendered. She never gave up. She never quit. It was because of her that we did not quit, either. Even when the world was lost. What remains of my people are here, on the borders, ever watchful."

"Waiting for her?"

"Perhaps. I have seldom returned to them. She has seldom returned. She understands that this world has an Emperor, not a queen. She does not despise him," he added, voice softer. "But they are two heads and there is one crown. What do you want for yourself?"

"Her."

"And the Emperor? You are sworn to serve him. You are a lord of the Dragon Court."

"I believe I can do my duties to the Emperor regardless; it is what most of humanity does."

Maggaron nodded. "See her, then. See her clearly. Hear what she cannot say, what she will not say. It was always, always best to allow her to come to you." He turned toward the door; Emmerian did not attempt to stop him. But at the door, he turned again. "I wish you well, Lord Emmerian. Of the Dragons, I believe you understand her best."

"Lannagaros understands her best."

"No. Lannagaros sees her as the child she was in the long-lost Aerie. He sees her past. And perhaps that is why she values him: he sees the potential he once saw; he sees her as the mischievous child she once was, with the world awaiting her maturity. He does not expect her to be what she expects of herself, does not see her failure as she sees it.

"He offers her the comfort he might have offered when she *was* a child. It is with him that she can be naturally more... joyfully difficult. And she desires that comfort, in a fashion—but she cannot be wed to it, cannot be bound by it. She will see *you*, Lord Emmerian. In time, she will see you as clearly as you see her; you see what she *is*, and it is what she is that the future will be built on."

Kaylin waited until Maggaron had left before turning to Emmerian. "Why did you want me here?"

"You have a tendency to interrupt when you feel people are going in the wrong direction." He laid his hands across the table and stared at the tops of them as if they were a very poorly drawn map. "Am I?"

She shook her head. "You're not trying to make decisions for her—you're not that stupid." She shrugged, uncomfortable now. "I'm not the person people come to for relationship advice. To me, it seems like you care about her. A lot. And you want as much information as you can get from people who also do."

"Is this what she wants?" The words were a whisper.

"You'll have to ask her." Seeing the color of his eyes, she relented. "Of the Dragons, I think you do see her—or try to see her—as she is. Look, I thought I knew Teela. I've known her for half my life. But I didn't. I knew her as a Hawk. She's been a lot more than that. Doesn't mean I don't care about her. What I thought I knew wasn't nothing. But knowing more doesn't change the fact that she's important to me.

"You see Bellusdeo in a way I don't. Doesn't mean either of us are wrong. We don't want the same things from her, and she probably doesn't want the same things from us. You need to figure out what you want, because she'll figure out what she wants."

"I don't want," he said, in Elantran, "to be a pressure or an obligation."

She nodded. In a quieter voice, she said, "Bellusdeo found an answer for Karriamis in the heat of the moment because she didn't want to lose you. Ummm, if you could avoid throwing your life away in order to protect her in the future, I'd *really* suggest it."

His smile lightened the odd color of his eyes. "So Bellusdeo has already informed me."

"Was she melting walls when she said it?"

"Only one."

Kaylin was awake in the morning before Helen added obnoxious morning light to her room. She was dressed, and occupied the edge of her bed, fidgeting. Hope was cranky, and shared.

"You awake?" Mandoran asked, through a closed door.

"More or less."

"You owe me a week of dinners."

"I don't remember that."

"Mortal memory isn't that bad. Also, Bellusdeo's here."

Kaylin exhaled. "I'll be right there." She slid off the bed and headed to the door.

"Did you sleep at all?" Mandoran asked. "You look terrible."

"You look lovely, too. How long has she been here?"

"She just arrived." He held her gaze for a beat before offering a very fief shrug. "I hate goodbyes, too."

Kaylin wanted to tell him that Bellusdeo wasn't going far—but he already knew that. So did she. Bellusdeo would be getting her life back—or at least a life she'd chosen, one that she *wanted*. She'd be happier. Much happier. That was a good thing, right?

It was. It was a *good* thing—for Bellusdeo. And there'd be a lot less conflict in Kaylin's life, because the Emperor couldn't blame her for anything that happened to Bellusdeo.

"I'll miss her, too," Mandoran offered. His life would be less complicated as well. Funny how neither of them seemed to prize it. As silver linings went, it was distinctly black and tarnished.

"I don't mean to rush you, dear," Helen's voice said, "but Bellusdeo is waiting."

She was. She stood—in plate armor—at the foot of the

stairs, tapping her foot impatiently. When Kaylin and Mandoran came into view, she frowned. "You look awful. Did the midwives call?"

"She had trouble sleeping," Helen replied. Her Avatar was in the hall beside the gold Dragon.

"Where's Maggaron?"

"He's gone ahead with my belongings. Are you just going to stand there?"

Mandoran gave Kaylin a nudge.

"I'm not just talking to her," Bellusdeo told him. "For some reason, I'm not as delighted to be rid of you as I expected I would be."

"I'm delighted," Mandoran said.

Her smile was genuine, softened by the gold of her eyes. "Come downstairs. Don't make me go up there."

Mandoran smiled and shook his head. He descended beside Kaylin—if there was going to be sentiment, he wasn't going to endure it alone.

Kaylin was grateful for his company. And surprised when Bellusdeo exited Helen before they'd reached her. Helen, however, was smiling, her eyes the warm brown that implied all was right with the world—or at least the parts for which she was responsible.

"Have a good time, dear."

"What?"

"Go."

"You realize," Kaylin told her almost former roommate, "that you're breaking the law, right?"

Bellusdeo, in full draconic form, stood on the front lawn.

"I'll apologize later."

Mandoran snorted. "I am not hugging you while you look like that. I have *some* Barrani pride."

"Stop dawdling."

"What are you doing?"

"Waiting for you to get on my back. If I recall, you always loved flight."

"Yes, but in my daydreams, I was doing it on my own."

The Dragon snorted. Kaylin climbed up on her back. "I hate goodbyes," Bellusdeo said, her voice a deep rumble.

"Me too."

"So I'm avoiding them." She pushed off the ground.

"Where are we going?"

"To the Tower," Bellusdeo roared back. Draconic voices weren't lost to simple things like too much wind. "I asked Helen, and Helen thought it was a good idea."

"What was a good idea?"

"You're going to spend a few days with me. You can prevent me from attempting to kill Karriamis. You, too," she told Mandoran, who appeared to be keeping pace with her. "I want guests. Karriamis isn't silent, but he's like Lannagaros when he's interrupted—he accepts it with obvious tolerance.

"Helen said this was a housewarming," she added. "I want to show you my house."

"I don't need to see any more of your house," Mandoran told her. But he didn't drop back.

"I need you to see more of my house," Bellusdeo replied.

"So much for quieter," Mandoran told Kaylin, his voice normal, the words completely audible. But his eyes were green.

Kaylin's eyes were brown, mortal eyes being what they were, but she felt as if they might be another color—one that matched pure gold and pure green.

★ ★ ★ ★ ★

ACKNOWLEDGMENTS

As of this writing, it's December 2020, and it has been…2020.

We've been at home since March, when my long-suffering husband's office shuttered and all of its employees were sent to work from home.

I am doing far better than many, in that I'm essentially the living version of Oscar the Grouch; I am not suffering from prolonged isolation, because I see people every day—the rest of my family, who are also shut in. Zoom call dinners have replaced the weekly dinners with my sons' godfather's family. My mother drops groceries and essentials at the back door. Our shopping is mostly done online, and when groceries are necessary, my husband goes out because he has a driver's license.

But our lives, though cramped and uncomfortable, are nonetheless decent.

And that would not be possible if it weren't for essential workers. If it weren't for grocery store clerks and courier and postal drivers and fulfilment warehouse workers—people who never got to shut down in safety because without them there would be panic and riots. (One of our delivery drivers said it's like Christmas rush *all the time*, since March.)

I know I'm missing people, here. But the point is this: the only reason many of us could stay home and stay relatively safe is because some people didn't. And I'm incredibly grateful.